LOVE IS ALL AROUND

THE RED HOT EARL, THE GIFT OF THE MARQUESS, JOY TO THE DUKE

DARCY BURKE

ZEALOUS QUILL PRESS

THE RED HOT EARL

THE RED HOT EARL

The Earl of Buckleigh was once an untitled misfit, tormented at Oxford. Now, he's overcome his challenges and is eager for the future, especially when his oldest and dearest friend, Bianca, needs help to save the annual holiday party. Ash has a plan to rescue the event, but when the bullies from his youth are up to their old tricks, he must risk everything to put the past behind him and find true love.

Furious when her brother refuses to host the St. Stephen's Day party, Lady Bianca Stafford is committed to giving the villagers their celebration. In Ash, she sees salvation for their local tradition, and perhaps a future she never expected. But her brother has other plans for her—a Season and marriage, and not to Ash. When disaster strikes, everything she cares about is threatened and it will take a miracle—or a hero—to save the day.

The Red Hot Earl is inspired by the song and story, Rudolph the Red-Nosed Reindeer. Be sure to check out the Red Hot Earl version of the song on my website at darcyburke.com!

Do you want to hear all the latest about me and my books? Sign up at Reader Club newsletter for members-only bonus content, advance notice of pre-orders, insider scoop, as well as contests and giveaways!

Care to share your love for my books with like-minded readers? Want to hang with me and see pictures of my cats (who doesn't!)? Then don't miss my exclusive Facebook groups!

Darcy's Duchesses for historical readers
Burke's Book Lovers for contemporary readers

For all the misfits

CHAPTER 1

County Durham, England
November 1811

"Come to Thornaby's house party with me. Please." Lady Bianca Stafford didn't want to beg her brother, but she was close to doing so.

Calder Stafford, the eighth Duke of Hartwell, pressed his lips into a thin white line, absolutely unmoved by her passionate pleas. "There is no reason for me to attend, nor do I have any desire."

Bianca walked around his desk, forcing him to turn his head to follow her movements. She stood next to his chair and gave him her most earnest stare. "There's every reason. This is the start of the holiday season. It's where the informal planning for the annual St. Stephen's Day party happens. You *must* come."

He pinched the bridge of his aquiline nose. "Bianca, I am not going to host a St. Stephen's Day party."

She couldn't keep herself from gasping. "You can't be serious. We always host the St. Stephen's Day party." It wasn't *a* party, it was *the* party. The entire town came, and it was the very center of the Christmas season.

He dropped his hand to the arm of his chair and stared up at her unblinking, his dark gray eyes as cold and unyielding as the nickname some still used for him: Chill. Because he'd been the Earl of Chilton his whole life. Until their father's death seven months ago.

Regret and sadness squeezed Bianca's heart, because of the loss of their father and because of the vast breach between him and Calder that had never been healed.

"*I* am not hosting it, and that is the end of it." His tone was soft but sharp.

She gaped at him, unable to find words for what seemed an eternity. "But, but—" she stuttered before snapping her lips closed at the distaste in her brother's eyes. How he'd become such a remote, unfeeling person was beyond her. But then she'd rarely seen him the past ten years while he'd lived in London. He'd never come home, not once.

Taking a deep breath, she sought to calm her racing heart and outraged mind. "Calder." She used the name their sister Poppy had always called him. The name their mother, who had died a few days after giving birth to Bianca, had used, or so Poppy had told her. "You have a duty as the duke."

"I have many duties, and none of them include hosting a St. Stephen's Day party." He turned his attention back to his desk and the papers upon it. "Now, run along to your house party."

His condescending tone grated. She would go as soon as Poppy, who was the Marchioness of Darlington, arrived to act as her chaperone. "Your tenants adore the St. Stephen's Day party. It is the highlight of their year. Surely that's important."

He didn't look up. "It is not."

Grumbling low in her throat, Bianca glared at her older brother's bent head. "Papa would be disappointed. He's likely spinning in his grave."

Silence was her answer, and so she turned and stalked from his study, not stopping until she nearly ran into Poppy in the entrance hall.

"Goodness, you look as if you want to commit murder," Poppy said, her gray-blue eyes wide. "Well, perhaps not murder. That's rather gruesome."

"In this case, however, it's accurate. I would cheerfully choke our brother if I could manage it."

Poppy exhaled. "Should I go and speak with him?"

"You don't even know why I wish to strangle him," Bianca said.

"I feel certain you will tell me."

"Yes, yes, I talk too much." Bianca waved her hand. "In this case, I could talk until my tongue fell out, and I'm afraid it wouldn't matter. Calder refuses to host the St. Stephen's Day party." Just saying it aloud deepened her anger.

Poppy's delicate dark brows arched high upon her forehead. "You found this surprising given his behavior the past six months since he returned?"

"Yes." But she shouldn't have. Still, she'd hoped. "How can he not care about the tenants and how important that day is to them?" The day after Christmas, it was a time for everyone in and around the village of Hartwell and the estate of Hartwood to come together and celebrate, to cast off their cares and responsibilities and rejoice in fellowship and love.

"The day can still be important. It will just be up to you to make it that way." Poppy gave her a supportive smile. "I would offer to help, but…" Her voice faltered, and a shadow dashed through her eyes.

Bianca reached for her sister's gloved hand and gave it a

squeeze. "I wouldn't ask." Poppy was going through a difficult time, and it was more than enough that she'd consented to accompany Bianca to this three-day party at Thornhill, the Viscount Thornaby's estate an hour away.

"Thank you, darling," Poppy said, squeezing her hand in return. "The footman is loading your luggage onto my coach. Are you ready?"

"I am." Bianca cast a sad look back toward their brother's study. She still had time to change his mind. But not much.

Her maid, Donnelly, entered the hall with Bianca's accessories. When she'd donned her hat, cape, and gloves, they departed the house. The Darlington coach awaited them outside, Poppy's maid ensconced within.

Once they were on their way, Bianca turned toward her sister, her mind churning. "We'll have to be careful not to reveal Calder's hesitance to host the party. I don't want anyone to know he was against it, even for a moment."

Poppy blinked at her, then pursed her lips. "Bianca, he *is* against it. And not just for a moment. He isn't going to change his decision. You must let it go, unfortunately."

"I refuse. It's tradition—the village of Hartwell will be devastated if it doesn't go on as it has for the past... I don't know how long."

"I've heard there has been a celebration of some kind since the first duke, even under Cromwell when it was forbidden to celebrate Christmas." Poppy glanced out the window, a dark curl bobbing against her temple beneath the brim of her smart pine-green bonnet. "However, Calder is the duke now. It is up to him to continue the tradition. Or not."

Frustrated at her sister's lack of outrage, Bianca stared at the passing landscape. The fields were hard and barren with the onset of winter, the hedges rich and green beneath the naked branches of the trees. Turning her head to look at her sister once more, she asked, "Aren't you the least bit disappointed?"

"Of course I am. But I am far more disappointed with other matters." She looked out the window and murmured, "Never mind."

Bianca tamped down her irritation. Poppy had other concerns. "I apologize. This isn't your worry. It's mine." And she'd ensure the party happened. She had to. Maybe Calder didn't care about tradition or about spreading goodwill amongst the people of Hartwell and the retainers and tenants of Hartwood, but Bianca did.

Several minutes passed before Poppy made a quiet observation. "I can see your mind working."

Bianca's mouth tilted into a half smile in spite of herself. "Can you?"

Poppy chuckled softly. "It never stops. And that is a compliment. Your ever-turning brain is what makes you Bianca."

It also made her unwed. Most gentlemen, it turned out, did not care for a wife with excessive opinions and a penchant for sharing them. Not that she'd spent much time concerning herself with finding a husband.

At twenty-two, she was a tad overdue on the Marriage Mart, owing to her father's illness the past few years. Beyond that, she had no desire to have a Season in London. She loved Hartwell and the surrounding area, and, if she *had* to marry —and she wasn't certain she did—would much prefer to marry a local gentleman. The problem was that there weren't very many of them who hadn't gone off to war. There would be several at the house party, however, including Viscount Thornaby himself.

She didn't want to marry Thornaby or anyone else at this

juncture, but perhaps he would be interested in taking up where Calder refused regarding the party. Thornhill was an hour by carriage, and even longer by foot, which made the location less than ideal, but if it was all she could find... Yes, she'd take the opportunity of this house party to devise a contingency plan. Just in case Calder proved exceptionally stubborn.

Or coldhearted.

She feared it was the latter. The brother who'd returned from London was not the brother she remembered from her youth. But then neither was her sister. She slid a look at Poppy. Faint lines pulled at her eyes and mouth as she gazed out the window, making her look slightly older than her twenty-four years. Bianca wished her sister would share more of her struggles, but she didn't.

Sometimes Bianca wondered if she wasn't really from the same family as her older brother and sister. Both Calder and Poppy held their emotions close, while Bianca displayed hers for everyone to see. Papa had said she was just like her mother. How Bianca wished she could have known that for herself.

Oh, this was turning into a melancholy day! Bianca straightened her shoulders and pressed her spine against the squab. It was nearly her favorite time of year—the time when people were more apt to share themselves and find joy. A time of peace and happiness.

And she wouldn't let Calder ruin it. The St. Stephen's Day party would happen at Hartwood. She refused to accept anything else.

∽

*S*tanding in the drawing room of Thornhill, the Viscount Thornaby's country home, Ashton Rutledge, Earl of Buckleigh, took a deep breath and counted to three. The exercise came easily after so many years, and he prayed it would work as well as it typically did. When he didn't cough or grunt or angle his head, he knew it had, and he thanked heaven for it.

He smiled blandly at his host, Thornaby. "Thank you for the invitation."

"Couldn't ignore the new earl!" Thornaby chuckled, but it wasn't jovial. Perhaps it was the way his gaze darted to his friends, Keldon and Moreley, or the underlying smirk teasing his thin lips.

Ash swallowed the response he wanted to give—*I'm sure you tried*—and worked to focus on the future rather than the past. Perhaps they'd all grown up—as he had.

"Must say you aren't at all what I remembered," Moreley said, sizing Ash up and seeming perplexed by what he saw.

Ash could well imagine what Moreley and the others were thinking, that Ash scarcely resembled the scrawny boy who'd finished Oxford ahead of them ten years ago. "I would say the same of you," Ash responded as he took in Moreley's receding hairline, Keldon's slight paunch, and Thornaby's... what? He looked much the same. Still tall and angular, his nose long, and his eyes small and hungry.

"Could you?" Keldon said, glancing at his friends. "We haven't changed at all." The others nodded and laughed amongst themselves as if they were sharing a jest that only the three of them were privy to.

Well, that was discouraging. Change, Ash had long ago decided, was an excellent thing.

Moreley sniffed. "Won't lie to you. We miss Lyndon terribly."

Ash kept from scowling, both to keep from insulting the trio before him and because it wasn't polite to think ill of the dead. But it was blessed hard not to think ill of the former earl, his morally bankrupt cousin. Ash heard his mother's voice, a constant refrain in his youth: *"We must pity poor Lyndon for he didn't have the love and support you did. To be raised without a mother and with a cold, dispassionate father is a tragedy in and of itself."*

It hadn't made Lyndon's abuse of Ash any easier to suffer.

But that was the past, and Ash meant to concentrate on the future. No matter how difficult, especially here and now, when the past was in his face.

"I'm sure Lyndon would rather he was here with you," Ash said evenly.

Thornaby snorted. "That's bloody obvious."

"We will shoot tomorrow in his honor," Moreley said, his voice lifting in tribute. He cast a pitying look toward Ash. "Too bad you can't join in."

That had been true once, and Ash supposed it still was, in a way. "I can, however I choose not to." He was new to the earldom, and hunting for sport was not something he'd ever done, nor was it something he particularly desired to learn. He could, contrary to their assumption, ride *and* shoot.

Moreley's dark gaze flickered with surprise, and he exchanged knowing glances with his friends before returning his attention to Ash. "You can remain here with the ladies. Perhaps they will allow you to play piquet."

Keldon snickered. "The perfect solution."

"Or you could arrange for me, and anyone else who prefers not to hunt, to ride," Ash suggested smoothly, looking toward his host.

Unfortunately, the butler interrupted the conversation before Thornaby could respond.

"Lady Darlington and Lady Bianca Stafford, my lord," the

butler said before stepping aside as the two women he'd announced moved into the drawing room.

Though it had been years since he'd seen both ladies, Ash recognized them immediately. Lady Darlington was slightly taller with gray-blue eyes that assessed her surroundings and a reserved demeanor evidenced in her stiff, compact stance with her hands clasped together at her waist.

Lady Bianca, on the other hand, seemed to brim with enthusiasm. She took a step toward them, her bright blue eyes sparkling with curiosity and verve. Though small, she seemed a mass of tightly controlled energy, her legs slightly parted, her hands at her sides as if she might sprint forward at any moment. Dark curls framed her heart-shaped face.

Thornaby bowed. "Welcome to Thornhill, Lady Darlington, Lady Bianca."

The other gentlemen bowed and murmured a welcome. Ash stepped toward the marchioness and offered his leg. "It's a pleasure to see you again, Lady Darlington." Then he turned and gave the same bow to her younger sister. "Lady Bianca."

"I'm afraid I don't—" Whatever Lady Darlington had been about to say was cut off by Keldon.

"This is the new Earl of Buckleigh," Keldon said. "He was Lyndon's cousin. Surely you remember the red hair."

Lady Darlington smiled as she shook her head in bemusement. "How silly of me. It's lovely to see you again, my lord."

"Ash?" Lady Bianca said, stepping toward him. "I didn't recognize you at all! We were so sorry to hear about Lyndon's passing. I'd heard you'd inherited and were now at Buck Manor."

She remembered him. And she called him Ash without reserve or remorse. It was right that she called him that, for in their youth, he'd been Ash and she'd been Bee.

"Yes, I'm there now. It feels a bit...odd." Perhaps he

shouldn't have admitted that out loud, but this was Bee, the girl who'd followed him around one summer collecting insects and climbing trees.

"Odd?" Thornaby said with more volume than was necessary. "I should think it would be lovely. An improvement, to be sure."

"Perhaps not," Bee said with a shrug. "Ash is entitled to feel as he ought." She gave him a warm smile that lit her eyes. "I imagine it would be odd—Buck Manor, the earldom, all of it. You cut a fine figure of an earl," she added, her gaze surveying him with approval.

Bloody hell, but she was direct and absolutely without guile. Ash hadn't been sure such people existed.

Then she turned abruptly to their host and subjected Thornaby to the same perusal. "We'd like to take a rest before dinner. What time shall we come down?" It was as if she were in charge. Ash suppressed a smile.

"Six," Thornaby said, glancing between Bee and her sister.

"Excellent. And may we expect dancing after?"

"For those who are able." Thornaby cast a disdainful stare toward Ash, whose shoulders twitched in response.

Ash gritted his teeth, and every muscle in his body tensed.

Bee's vivid blue eyes narrowed as she slanted a glance at Ash and then fixed on their host. "I can't imagine what you mean by that, but I shall presume there will be entertainment to amuse everyone. If not, I'll see that there is."

Thornaby bowed slightly. "I would be honored, Lady Bianca. I am without a hostess, and if you would like to claim that role—"

"You overstep," Lady Darlington said crisply. "Come, Bianca." She gave Thornaby a scolding glare before taking her sister's arm and retreating from the room.

"She's a lively one!" Keldon said on a laugh.

Thornaby smoothed the front of his coat. "I know for a

fact that Hartwell wants to be rid of her as soon as possible, preferably before he has to provide her with a Season. This party is an excellent opportunity."

Moreley flashed a smile displaying his horrendously crooked teeth. "Indeed, the timing is perfect. Do let us know how we can assist you in your pursuit."

Ahem, you are aware that I am standing right here? Ash didn't ask the question aloud, but it was a near thing. Instead, he took another deep breath, counted to three, and said, "You'll need a very solid plan to win the Lady Bianca. She told me once, years ago when I lived near Hartwell, that she would never wed." *Never, ever, ever* had been her precise pronouncement, followed by her making a nasty face that looked as if she'd eaten a slug.

Had that been the day she'd licked a slug? He couldn't quite recall.

Keldon peered at Ash as if he were a...slug. "You can't mean to reference something she said as a child. In any case, her guardian, and in this case, it's her brother, will dictate what she does."

"That's the right of it," Thornaby said smugly. "And based on that, I would say this courtship will proceed exactly as I expect."

Unable to stand another moment of their arrogance and self-absorption, Ash excused himself and went to the entry, where other guests were arriving. He waited patiently for the butler, who asked if he was ready to be shown to his room.

"Yes, please." As he ascended the stairs, he questioned why he'd come.

Because you're the earl, and earls attend house parties.

Ugh.

Because they are your neighbors—sort of—and you ought to get to know them.

Gah.

Because you have something to prove.

He tightened his hands into fists, a familiar reaction given how he'd spent the last ten years of his life in London. No, he had nothing to prove, especially to those "gentlemen" he'd left downstairs.

The butler led him into a large sitting room with several doors leading from it. "Here you are, my lord," the butler said, opening one of the doors. "Will there be anything else?"

Ash glanced inside and caught a glimpse of Harris, his valet. "No, thank you."

With a nod, the butler left, and Ash went into the bedchamber, closing the door behind him.

"All unpacked, my lord," Harris said with his usual ebullient efficiency. Just twenty-one, he was likely a poor choice for a valet, but Lyndon's had left after he'd died, necessitating the hiring of a new one. Since Ash had little experience with hiring valets, he'd simply promoted the most pleasant, eager footman he could find.

Attitude could not be taught. Everything else could.

"Thank you, Harris. We have some time until dinner. I suppose I shall read." And devise a plan to rescue Bee from Thornaby's pursuit. If she wanted to be rescued. Perhaps she'd changed her mind about marriage. Thornaby was right that she couldn't be held to something she'd said as a child.

Yet, the woman he'd seen downstairs seemed every bit the confident, outrageous young girl he remembered. The type of woman who listened to the rules and then promptly bent them to suit herself. The type of woman who could stir something deep inside him if he allowed himself to respond.

Ash began to remove his coat, and Harris darted toward him to help. Once Harris draped the coat over his arm, Ash tugged at his cravat and handed it to the valet as well. "That will suffice," Ash said, and Harris took himself into the small dressing chamber.

Turning toward the hearth, Ash noted that Harris had placed his book of poetry on a table beside a chair. Ash sat and plucked up the book, opening it, but then didn't read. Instead, he thought of Bee and how wonderful it was to see her again.

If I allow myself to respond…

He would *not*.

*D*inner dragged a course too long, but then Bianca often felt that was the case. She never wanted to eat as much as was offered or sit as long as was expected. By the time the ladies removed to the drawing room, she was more than ready for the entertainment to begin.

More importantly, she was eager to discuss St. Stephen's Day with Viscount Thornaby. She'd sat beside him at dinner, but every time she'd tried to broach the topic of the St. Stephen's Day party, he'd waved it off and said they'd discuss it later, then asked her some inane question. Did she paint? Did she like to ride? Did she enjoy the theatre? Was she looking forward to going to London?

No. Yes. She couldn't say—because she'd only been to the theatre once. And definitely *not*.

Poppy walked with her into the drawing room and went toward a settee.

"I can't sit just yet," Bianca said.

"Of course not. I forget you are typically wound full of energy after a long meal." She shook her head, smiling. "How I could forget that is a mystery."

Bianca touched her arm gently. "You have a great deal on your mind."

Poppy didn't respond, but her expression was grateful.

Mrs. Chamberlain and her daughter, who was a couple of years younger than Bianca, approached them. "We're sorry the duke didn't come with you," Mrs. Chamberlain said. "He must be terribly busy now that he's inherited."

She had the terrible part right. "Yes," Bianca responded. What else could she say? That he'd wanted to come but couldn't get away? She supposed that would suffice, but he didn't deserve excuses. Let people think what they wanted.

"Well, I imagine we'll see him at the assembly next month and on St. Stephen's Day after that." Mrs. Chamberlain looked proudly at her daughter. "I wonder if he'll remember my Marianne."

Bianca opened her mouth to tell the poor woman to forget about any hope of snagging Calder, but Poppy spoke first. "I imagine he will. If you'll excuse us?" She offered a benign smile, then roped her arm through Bianca's and ushered her away.

"You can't think Calder will actually attend the assembly, not with the way he's been acting."

"I don't, but neither is it our place to say so." Poppy frowned. "However, perhaps we should mention that the St. Stephen's Day party will not be happening."

"No!" Bianca kept her voice low but urgent. "I said we mustn't let anyone know."

Poppy took her hand. "And I told you that you aren't going to change his mind. The sooner you accept that the party isn't happening this year, the better off you will be. In fact, if Calder's manner doesn't improve, and honestly, I can't see it doing so, you should come spend Christmas with us."

Oh, that was precisely what Bianca wanted to do—insert herself into her and Gabriel's household when Poppy was suffocating in despair. "Thank you, but Hartwell is my home, and as such, I should have a say in what is done there, including whether there is a St. Stephen's Day party or not."

Staring at Bianca in disbelief, Poppy said, "You can't host it without Calder's permission. How would you even pay for it? And that's just the beginning. The staff won't go against him."

"But they will want to have the party!" Bianca's frustration grew even as she knew Poppy was right. She couldn't hold the party without Calder's support.

Bianca wasn't sure she was still in the mood for entertainment. Naturally, this was when the gentlemen entered the drawing room. Her gaze instantly found Ash, perhaps because of his magnificent red hair. She'd always found it fascinating. Her hair and that of her siblings was dark and still and boring. But Ash's was light and fire and energy.

"Lord Buckleigh appears quite different," Poppy murmured.

"Does he?" Bianca asked, her gaze still lingering on him.

"Don't you remember what he was like? He had trouble with words and he would…twitch."

Bianca tried to recall but couldn't. She shook her head. "That doesn't sound like the Ash I knew."

"It was later, just before he was sent off to school with his cousin," Poppy said. "Perhaps I was more aware because I am closer to his age. He was also rather small. Looking at him now, you would never know."

Had he been? Bianca didn't remember that either, but then *she'd* been small, so her perspective was likely different. Whether he'd been small or not, he certainly wasn't now. He was taller than every other man in the room, with broad shoulders and long, athletic legs.

He also didn't have freckles anymore, just bare sculpted cheekbones and a slightly square jaw. His gaze swept the room until it settled on her, and the hint of a smile tugged at the side of his mouth.

Thornaby moved to the pianoforte in the corner. "My sister will play for those who wish to dance." He gestured to an open area near the instrument, from which all the furniture had been cleared. Then he walked directly to Bianca. "May I have the pleasure of the first dance?"

She couldn't say no, and her mood *could* use improvement. "Yes, thank you." She gave him her hand, and they moved to the makeshift dance floor, where they formed a square with another couple.

As the music started, he said, "About the St. Stephen's Day party, how strange it will be not to have it this year."

Bianca fumbled her steps. "What?"

"The St. Stephen's party," Thornaby repeated, looking at her in slight confusion. "The duke sent me a letter indicating it would not be happening. I presumed that's what you kept trying to talk about at dinner."

So he had been changing the subject on purpose despite the fact that she'd clearly wanted to discuss it. She gritted her teeth. Her mood was *not* improved. There was also no hope for keeping Calder's decision quiet until she could change his mind. "I'm surprised he wrote to you. We've still been discussing whether to hold it."

"Ah, well, I will need to know soon because we make arrangements well in advance." His family provided food and ale for the celebration, as did a handful of other local families from the gentry.

"Did you say the St. Stephen's Day party isn't happening?" the other young woman in their square asked. She was Miss Keldon, and her partner was Mr. Lamphrey.

"That is correct," Thornaby said.

"It isn't quite," Bianca contradicted. "My brother is mulling whether to host it. He's a trifle overwhelmed by the dukedom, and I just need to convince him we can handle the event." She offered what she hoped was a serene smile, though her insides were a tumbling riot. Calder would not be pleased if he heard she'd said he was overwhelmed. He would say that once again her mouth had run faster than her brain.

She met Thornaby in the center of the square, and he touched his hands to hers before they retreated. "He sounded rather firm in his letter," Thornaby said. "It's not the end of the world. It's a massive event to undertake. My father always said he was glad he wasn't the Duke of Hartwell so he didn't have to do it!" He laughed, and Lamphrey joined in.

"Well, my father enjoyed it," Bianca said tersely. "As did I. And our retainers and tenants. And the entire town."

"I liked it too," Miss Keldon said in solidarity.

"Alas, all good things must come to an end." Thornaby's tone held a superior note. He looked toward Lamphrey. "Who said that?"

"Shakespeare," Lamphrey said with confidence.

"Actually, it originated with Chaucer," Bianca said with some disgust. She suffered the rest of the dance and quickly made her way back to her sister. Who was talking with Ash.

He smiled warmly as Bianca approached, and some of her agitation washed away. Not all of it, though. She looked to Poppy. "Calder sent a note to everyone about not hosting the party."

Poppy exhaled softly and gave her a look of sympathy. "I suppose that's that, then."

"You can't think I'll stop trying?"

With a light chuckle, Poppy lifted her hands. "I should know better."

"What party?" Ash asked, appearing confused.

"The annual St. Stephen's Day party," Poppy answered.

Ash nodded. "I remember that. Huge affair out at Hartwood. Food, games, revelry regardless of the weather. I missed it when I moved to London. I take it this is the first year it's not happening?"

"Like you, our brother inherited his title this year, and he's decided not to host it." Bianca furrowed her brow. "I am trying to change his mind. Everyone looks forward to it, and it's not as if we can't afford it."

Poppy's brows arched as she cast a look at Bianca that seemed to ask, *Are you certain of that?*

Of course she was certain. Before their father had died, he'd told Bianca of her large settlement, which would be her dowry. Unless she didn't wed. Then it would become hers on her twenty-fifth birthday. She doubted she would have such a substantial sum if the dukedom was not in excellent financial order.

"If anyone can change his mind, I'm certain it's you," Ash said encouragingly. He glanced toward the dance floor. "We've missed this dance, but may I request the honor of partnering you in the next one?"

Again, she couldn't really say no without appearing rude, but she didn't want to be trapped in a square with Thornaby or stand next to him in line. "Actually, would you mind taking a promenade instead? I don't think I have the stomach for another dance."

His gaze flickered with surprise and seemed to hesitate before he answered. "Certainly." He offered her his arm and looked toward Poppy who inclined her head.

Bianca placed her hand on his arm, and they started to circuit the drawing room. "This won't be a very long promenade. We'll have to make two circuits."

"At least."

She responded to the humor in his voice with a grin. "How lovely it is to have you back. Did you ever imagine you would be the earl?"

He shook his head. "I suppose I should have after my

uncle died a couple of years ago, but I assumed Lyndon would wed and have sons, and that would be that."

"He called on me early last spring." Bianca recalled Lyndon's attempts to charm her, but she'd been too wrapped up in caring for her father to pay close attention. In fact, she'd asked him not to call again. "I think he hoped to make a match."

"And failed miserably, apparently."

"It wasn't his fault. My father was ill. It wasn't a good time." Oh dear, that sounded as if Lyndon's suit might have been appreciated, and she was fairly certain she would have put him off regardless of what was going on in her life.

He shot her a look of apology. "My condolences. I always liked your father."

"Thank you. Goodness, he and your cousin died within a month of each other."

"Did they?" Ash cocked his head to the side. "I think you're right. It's good you didn't wed my cousin—a double tragedy would have been horrible."

"There was no danger of that, even if my father had been well. I don't think your cousin and I would have suited. Actually, I'm not sure marriage is for me."

He laughed, surprising her. "You swore never to marry."

She laughed too. "You remember that?"

His gaze met hers. "I remember many things."

An unfamiliar heat bloomed in her chest and spread. She turned her head from his. "That's one circuit."

"It is indeed. I should warn you that Thornaby has his sights set on courting you. He means to make himself known at this party, if I'm not mistaken."

She didn't stop herself before pulling a face. "I hope you're wrong."

"I don't think I am."

She thought of her dance with Thornaby and sighed with

disgust. "No, I don't think you are either." She cast him a sidelong glance. "What did he say?"

"You want me to speak freely?"

She lifted a shoulder. "We always did."

"We were children."

"Such a shame that children can say whatever they like to each other, and when we become adults, we must hesitate and consider and censor." She gave him a sly look. "I'm not very good at that, I'm afraid."

He chuckled. "I wouldn't expect you to be—not the Bee I remember."

"Are you going to tell me what Thornaby said or not?"

He grinned. "He said your brother is anxious to marry you off, preferably before he has to pay for a Season. I can't believe that's true—it's just Thornaby being a jackanapes." He flicked her a glance, his eyes widening slightly. "My apologies," he murmured.

"No apology is necessary. Thornaby *is* a jackanapes, as far as I can tell. And sadly, that sounds exactly like my brother. He's actually rather horrid." She waved her hand. "Not that it signifies since I don't want a Season anyway. London doesn't interest me." She peered at him. "You lived there?"

"For ten years."

"And you liked it?"

"Very much."

"Why?" She genuinely wanted to know.

"That is a rather lengthy tale, and we are nearly at the end of our second circuit."

Bianca thrust her lips into a mock pout. "That is hardly fair. Will you tell me some other time?"

"It would be my pleasure."

They arrived at Poppy, and Bianca reluctantly pulled her hand from him and moved to stand beside her sister. What a refreshingly honest and open conversation. "Are you going on the hunt in the morning?" Bianca asked.

He shook his head. "I don't hunt."

Bianca's heart thumped an extra beat. She'd never understood hunting for sport with the hounds and all that nonsense. "Oh?"

"I do like to shoot, however, and ride, and I tried to convince Thornaby to organize an excursion for those of us who aren't hunting. I don't think he listened, however."

"Then allow me," Bianca said, narrowing her eyes. "I will see you tomorrow." She turned abruptly and made her way to Thornaby, who'd just left the dance floor.

In five minutes, he'd agreed to organize a ride during the hunt and a separate shooting competition in the afternoon. As she walked back to Poppy, she realized she could likely manipulate him into hosting the St. Stephen's Day party. If she wanted to.

She wasn't sure she did. He would be a ghastly host. Unfortunately, she might not have any other choice.

Her gaze trailed to where Ash stood talking to a pair of young ladies. He would be a *much* better host. Except his estate was too far away. They'd have to transport everyone over ten miles.

Bianca's brain began to churn...

"You're thinking again," Poppy said, eyeing her speculatively.

A grin slid over Bianca's lips. "Always."

~

The morning was slightly overcast and quite cold. As a result, only two people showed up for the ride—Ash and Bee. There were more grooms to accompany them, three to be exact.

Ash wondered if she'd beg off since it would be just them. Instead, she seemed…pleased?

Bee's eyes sparkled in the midmorning light as she glanced around. "Just us, then?"

"So it appears," Ash said.

She gave him an impish smile. "Lovely." She crossed to the mounting block and climbed atop the horse Thornaby had provided.

Ash mounted his horse and moved closer to Bee. "Is this acceptable? Us alone on a ride, I mean."

She shrugged. "Does it matter?"

He laughed. "You are as audacious as I remember."

"Is that a good thing?" she asked as they started out of the stable yard.

"I think so. It's certainly not boring."

"Is that a danger? Boring females?"

"Anything boring is a danger."

"I wholeheartedly agree. What did you do in London to ward off boredom?" she asked. "You promised to tell me why you liked living there."

He sent her a teasing look. "I don't recall promising you anything."

She rolled her eyes. "Perhaps I exaggerate."

"You? Never." He recalled the time she'd said she'd seen a wolf, but when he'd told her there were no wolves in England, she'd admitted it was just a large dog. "I feel the need to run, then I will tell you about London, all right?"

She nodded, then gave him a coy smile. "Shall we race?"

They were out of the stable yard and cresting the small hill that overlooked the parkland adjoining Thornaby's estate. She didn't wait for his response before kicking her horse into a gallop.

"Bloody hell," he muttered in both appreciation and anticipation. He directed his mount after her and did his best to keep up.

She won in the end, but then he hadn't tried too hard to overtake her. He'd enjoyed watching her far too much.

When he caught up to her, she was grinning, her breath coming hard as she stroked her horse's neck. "Caught me at last?"

"You're an exceptional rider," he said.

"Thank you. I didn't get to see you, but since you kept up, I imagine you are also quite skilled."

He laughed at her hubris. "I'm passable."

"Don't denigrate yourself. You're more than that." She started to walk her horse back the way they came, the grooms trailing behind them. "Now tell me about London."

"You've truly never been?"

She shook her head. "My father never encouraged me to go when I was younger, and it didn't occur to me to ask. I'm quite content here in County Durham. But I imagine there is much to do and see in London."

"Oh yes. The theatre. The British Museum. The Royal Academy Exhibition. Hyde Park. And so much more." He thought of his favorite places—nowhere she could go.

"That's what you liked about living there—the places to visit? To alleviate your boredom?" She asked the last with a flirtatious smile.

Flirtatious? Maybe. He wasn't particularly good at flirting and wasn't entirely sure he'd know what it even looked like. He had no experience on the Marriage Mart or in courtship in general. "It was hard to be bored. I was accepted to the Inns of Court and worked as a barrister."

She seemed impressed, her gaze moving over him with admiration. "Well done. What did you do for fun?"

Hit people.

Thankfully, he didn't say that out loud. Boxing had been

his true love—a way to work through the anger he'd nurtured for so many years at school and to control his impulses. The speech, the coughing and throat clearing, the twitches.

Not long after he'd arrived in London, he'd attended a match. That had led to lessons and ultimately to participating in matches himself. Nothing glamorous, but small bouts that allowed him to hone his skill and learn self-control. And build a reputation as a fearsome pugilist, which hadn't been his intent.

"I, ah, didn't have much spare time. But I enjoyed riding."

She narrowed her eyes at him. "This is not a long story at all. You were bamming me last night."

"Hmm, you may be right. It was ten years, so it felt like a long story." He tried to think of what he could say that wouldn't reveal too much. She was a young lady, after all.

Hell, she was also *Bee*.

"I loved London," he said, reflecting on how much he'd changed in his time there. "It's where I became who I am. I don't think that would have happened if I'd come back here when I finished at Oxford." He hadn't wanted to anyway, not after everything he'd endured there.

"Becoming a lawyer did that?" she asked, sounding skeptical. "I think there's more to your story. Maybe someday you'll tell me."

He wanted to. "Maybe someday I will."

They trotted their horses for a few minutes, then slowed once more as they approached Thornhill.

"I wonder if you might give me your opinion on something," she said, looking at him askance.

"If I can, I will."

"I wager you know Thornaby better than I. Do you think he'd host the St. Stephen's Day party?"

"Why would—" He caught himself before he finished.

Though he worked hard to keep a rein on himself, sometimes things leapt from his mouth. He stretched his neck in reaction. "I don't think I know him well enough to say."

"I hope I didn't anger you with my question."

Hell, he hadn't meant to give her that impression. "Not at all." He sought to divert. "Why isn't your brother hosting the party?"

"I wish I knew. I mean, *really* knew. He just says he won't do it. He doesn't have a good reason. He doesn't have *any* reason, as far as I can tell."

Ash didn't know Calder Stafford very well—he'd been gone from Oxford by the time Ash and Lyndon had arrived, and Ash had only run into him periodically in London. "I'm sorry he's proving difficult. It's such a shame he won't host it. Or at least give you a good reason."

"Yes, he owes us that, if nothing else."

He blinked at her. "Us?"

"Me. Our retainers and tenants. The villagers. You."

"*Me?*"

"You would have come, wouldn't you?"

"Probably." He hadn't thought about the event at all. It was enough to consider spending his first Christmas season as an earl at Buck Manor.

"Is your mother at Buck Manor now? It seems I haven't seen her in Hartwell the last several months."

"She came to join me this past July. She will be disappointed about the party, now that I think about it."

"We must have it," Bee said as they rode back into the stable yard. "Everyone will be disappointed. Calder will have to come around."

"And if he doesn't?"

A groom met them, and Ash dismounted. He quickly handed the reins to the groom, then went to help Bee down.

She'd been on her way to the mounting block but stopped

when she saw him approach. The groom took her reins, and she turned to place her hands on Ash's shoulders, then slid from the saddle.

Ash clasped her waist firmly. When she stood before him, he could see the cobalt depths of her eyes and smell the sweet fragrance of her floral soap. A surprising heat stole over him, suffusing him in something he hadn't expected: desire.

Taking his hands from her, he stepped back.

She smoothed her hands down her skirt, seemingly unaffected by their brief connection. And why should she have felt what he had? In fact, he was beginning to doubt he'd felt anything at all. He was simply happy to see her after so many years.

"To answer your question," she said, "if Calder doesn't come around, I must come up with an alternate plan. Though it pains me, I think I must ask Thornaby if he will host it."

Thornaby would be delighted to help her. Except he was also incredibly cheap, or at least he had been, and Ash couldn't imagine that had changed. He was, however, eager to establish a relationship with Bee, and Ash wouldn't put it past the man to try to use her request to benefit himself. "Be careful," he advised.

"I always am." She turned toward the house, a breeze stirring the dark curls about her face.

Ash laughed. "Like when you climbed so high in the tree that I had to come up and help you down?"

"Yes, exactly like that."

He laughed harder. "How is that being careful?"

She flashed him a smile. "Because I knew you were there to rescue me."

The laughter stuck in his throat, but he forced it out lest she realize how her words affected him. And how was that?

"Would the woman you are now actually want to be rescued?"

She stopped and pivoted toward him. "No." She stared up at him. "How could you know that?"

He hadn't, but he'd guessed. She'd always been confident, almost reckless, even. And she seemed as outspoken and fearless as ever. "It made sense that you grew into a someone who can take care of herself."

She looked at him with unflinching pride. "Thank you."

They continued toward the house. "Still, if there is ever any way I can be of assistance, I hope you'll ask."

They reached the doorway and she paused. "I will. Unlike you, I will make a promise. And I will keep it." Her gaze turned saucy, and he had to think she was flirting. Again. Maybe.

"I didn't make you a promise," he repeated softly. "But when I do, I will keep it." He opened the door for her.

She held his gaze a long moment, then the edge of her mouth ticked up. "Good."

CHAPTER 3

*B*ianca and Poppy walked from the house toward the lawn where the shooting competition was set up. Bianca hoped they planned to allow women to participate. And if they didn't, well, she'd shoot anyway.

Most of the house party guests were in attendance. Bianca immediately spotted Ash standing on the periphery of a group of gentlemen.

"It looks like the spectators are over there," Poppy said, gesturing to the right where most of the guests were gathered. Everyone else, including a handful of footmen, was clustered near a table. Beyond that stood three targets. "Do you mean to shoot?" Poppy asked.

"I do."

"Papa would be proud." Poppy's voice was soft. She missed their father, but not as much as Bianca, likely owing to the fact that it was Bianca who had cared for him in his final years. Poppy had already been wed to the Marquess of Darlington. And, of course, Calder had been off in London hardening his heart.

"You could shoot too," Bianca suggested, even though she knew her sister would decline.

Poppy laughed with genuine mirth. "No one wants to see that. I never possessed the skill that you do. Frankly, I never possessed the desire to learn."

"No, you are a much more proper female."

"Because I like to sing and play music?" Poppy gave her a teasing look.

"Because you are good at both and at needlepoint and all things domestic. All the things at which I am abysmal." Bianca grinned with pride.

"That is not true. You are more than capable of arranging and managing all manner of things. That is an exceptional domestic talent."

"I suppose it is." Bianca fixed her gaze on the target field with great intent. "They better allow me to shoot. I don't see one woman over there."

"I fear for them if they don't," Poppy said drily.

Bianca sent her a wicked glance, then strode toward the target area. Ash noted her approach, a single auburn brow arching along his forehead.

"Good afternoon, Lady Bianca," Thornaby said in greeting, his thin lips stretching back to reveal a patronizing smile. No, that wasn't fair. Bianca oughtn't assume they weren't going to let her participate. "Did you come to wish us good luck?" He gazed at her expectantly.

She rocked forward on her toes. "Not at all. I came to shoot."

Thornaby's eyes widened, and someone laughed. Followed by a second person. Then a third. While the viscount didn't join in, he was clearly trying not to smirk. "I'm afraid this competition is for gentlemen only," he said with mild condescension. "You may watch from over there." He motioned toward the spectators.

Bianca forced a sickly sweet smile. "Are you afraid I'll beat you?"

Her query was met with more laughter.

"It's a danger," Mr. Moreley said from the side of his mouth. "She did beat Ruddy in a race earlier. Sorry, Buckleigh, I mean."

Several gentlemen turned their heads toward Ash and snickered. Moreley had said sorry, but he didn't appear apologetic. And Bianca didn't think he'd been apologizing for mentioning the race. No, he'd corrected himself after calling Ash "Ruddy." Was that a nickname?

"Trounced him, I heard," another gentleman said.

Bianca noted that no one looked at her with admiration or appreciation. They all cast taunting glances toward Ash. He stood silent, his face impassive.

"It wasn't a race," Bianca said, even though she'd absolutely challenged him to a race. She'd sensed he hadn't actually raced her.

How had any of them heard about it anyway? She scowled toward the stables, thinking it had to have been one of the grooms. She detested a retainer with loose lips and was glad to have none of those at Hartwell.

"It was, and you won," Ash said, causing everyone to whip their heads in his direction. "I've no problem losing to a woman." He pinned Thornaby with an expectant stare. "Why not let her shoot?"

"Because the prizes aren't for women," he said crossly. He turned back to Bianca and summoned a pathetic excuse for a smile. "Why don't you demonstrate your skill for us prior to the competition?"

"An excellent notion," Ash said. "Her efforts can still be measured against everyone else's." He looked her in the eye, and Bianca had never felt more included or...present. The moment enveloped her until she forced herself to speak.

She turned to Thornaby. "I accept."

Thornaby looked utterly nonplussed. He exchanged a look with one of the other gentlemen, his brow creasing. Bianca held her breath. Would he allow her to shoot, or would he make an even bigger scene?

He settled his gaze on her. "Which weapon would you like to use?" His voice was tight, as if just asking the question pained him.

She had to bite her tongue lest she laugh. And he hoped to court her? Moving past him to the table, she perused the half-dozen weapons laid out. There was a lady's muff pistol in addition to a Manton flintlock. Her father had given her a lady's muff pistol three years ago. It looked small compared to the others, but she knew it was just as powerful. Still, she was surprised to see it on the table with the other weapons since it wasn't generally used for distance shooting. Why would they include it?

Swallowing her smile, she reached for the muff pistol, then frowned. "It's already loaded."

"Of course," the viscount said.

"I prefer to load my own." She didn't press the issue. It was enough that she was allowed to shoot. *Allowed.* Bitterness rose in her throat, and she swallowed it back as she stepped around the table. "Does it matter which target I use?" she asked.

"No, you just have to say which before you shoot," someone other than Thornaby answered.

"The middle one." She lifted the pistol and fixed her aim. Eyeing the target—a piece of crockery atop a post—she squeezed the trigger.

The crockery splintered and flew from the post to a chorus of cheers—from the spectators. And from one of the gentlemen. She turned. It was Ash, of course. He grinned and applauded.

A rush of pleasure swept over Bianca. She dipped a curtsey.

"Lucky shot," Keldon said, staring at the pottery she'd ruined that now littered the ground around the post. He sounded shocked, as if he couldn't believe what he'd seen.

Irritation pricked her neck. "It wasn't luck. Shall I demonstrate again?" she asked with mock innocence. "Perhaps the Manton?"

Thornaby came toward her. "I think that's enough for today. Thank you for the...demonstration."

Bianca bit back a retort. This was why marriage held no interest for her. She'd yet to meet a man who truly valued a woman as a person of equal merit and ability. Her gaze flicked to Ash, who was frowning at Thornaby.

Feeling slightly mollified by Ash's attitude and seeming support, she retreated toward the spectators, though she didn't go all the way. It was a small rebellion at least.

Thornaby looked at where she stood and frowned, but he didn't tell her to move. Good, because she wasn't going to.

One of the footmen reloaded the lady's muff pistol as Thornaby addressed the gentlemen. "We'll have a first round, and everyone who hits the target will proceed to the second round in which we will all fire at the same target. Our shots will be marked, and the one who is closest to the center will be declared the winner."

There were six gentlemen and six pistols. Everyone moved toward the table and plucked up a weapon. Ash was the last to get there and was left with the lady's muff. She so wanted him to best them, but she had no idea if he was a good shot.

Thornaby inclined his head. "I put the lady's pistol out for you. Thought it would be easier for you to manage. Didn't realize an actual woman would want to shoot." He pursed his lips with disdain, and though he'd lowered his voice for the second part, Bianca had still heard him. She was glad she'd stayed relatively near.

"We're willing to let you stand closer, Ruddy," Moreley said toward Ash before looking at the other gentlemen and laughing.

There was that name again. Ruddy had to be Ash, but why? His last name was Rutledge. Was it a nickname? She looked at his temple where his dark red hair peeked from beneath his hat. Ruddy—red.

Ash checked his pistol. "That won't be necessary, but I appreciate your thoughtfulness."

The gentlemen took turns, and it happened that Ash went last. Bianca held her breath as he took his stance toward the target.

"The one on the left," Ash responded.

Bianca had to listen carefully to hear all that they said. She was glad she hadn't gone to stand with the others, for she wouldn't be able to hear them at all.

"That's all that remains," Keldon said with amusement.

Ash turned a stony stare toward Keldon. "I am following the rules as directed."

Moreley chuckled. "You always did, even when it wasn't to your benefit."

Ash's jacket rippled across his shoulders, and his head tipped briefly to the side. Then he coughed.

"Oh dear," Keldon said. "Moreley, you've disturbed him. You know better than to do that."

Before anyone could say anything else, Ash fired, and the small pot shattered.

Bianca exhaled and smiled in relief. "Well done!"

Ash turned to look at her, but his features were inscrutable. He seemed very focused, which was good. She wanted him to win.

"Looks like all six of us are progressing," Thornaby pronounced.

Three of the footmen finished reloading the weapons while the other two went to nail a target—a large piece of wood with a small mark in the center—to the posts. They returned to the table, and all was ready for the final round.

How Bianca wished she could participate. It bloody wasn't fair.

"It's a shame Lady Bianca can't be included," Ash said.

One of the gentlemen, a portly fellow called Tealman, glanced toward her, then lowered his voice to say, "It wouldn't be borne." Bianca had to strain to hear. She didn't bother glaring at him despite the anger bubbling in her veins.

Ash chuckled. "As I said, I'm not bothered by the prospect of losing to a woman."

"Clearly, as evidenced by your pathetic loss this morning," Moreley said with considerable disdain.

Bianca wanted to put Moreley in front of the target.

The first man took his place and fired. He struck several inches from the mark and dipped his head slightly as he turned back toward the others. Even so, they congratulated him.

"You've a steady arm," Keldon said, clapping him on the shoulder. "Better than some." He inclined his head toward Ash.

How dare he say that? Ash had hit the target! And he'd been steady. Bianca's hands balled into fists at her side as she seethed with outrage.

Moreley walked around the table to take his turn. "I have to say, Ruddy's better than he was ten years ago. I daresay he wouldn't have been able to lift the pistol without suffering a fit." He looked back at Ash. "What sorcery have you invited to be so changed?"

"Is he that changed, truly?" Keldon asked. "The speech is better, but I see he still twitches."

"Perhaps he drinks," Thornaby offered.

Moreley shook his head. "Doubtful. He could never hold his liquor at Oxford. Always a pathetic mess." He lowered his voice and said something toward Thornaby and Keldon, smirking all the while. They laughed in response, and the other two gentlemen joined in. Ash, meanwhile, stood stoic. No, not quite stoic. That same ripple passed across his shoulders followed by the tip of his head and the stretching of his neck. And another cough.

Bianca couldn't hear what Moreley said, but was certain it was awful. Yes, he should definitely be the target. It was perhaps a good thing she wasn't shooting.

Moreley took his shot, and the result was slightly closer than the first gentleman. Tealman went next and hit near the edge of the wood. He muttered—probably a curse—under his breath and shook his head as he returned to the table.

Keldon clasped Tealman's bicep. "A good showing. Doubtful you'll be the worst."

He didn't look at Ash, but they all knew whom he was referring to. Bianca doubted anyone else could hear what was being said, but she could. Did they realize? Would they care? How could they treat Ash, who outranked them all, so horribly?

And yet Ash stood there proud and unmoved. Well, almost unmoved. The twitches were coming at intervals now. He cleared his throat several times. She watched as he flexed his hands into fists, loosened them, then repeated the exercise.

Keldon fired and nearly hit the target. The others clapped and cheered. Smugly, Keldon set his firearm on the table and looked to Ash. "Beat that."

"I will." The words shot from his mouth as from one of

the pistols in the competition. Ash twitched again, and this time, his arm shuddered. If that happened when he was shooting...

No, it couldn't. It wouldn't. She willed it not to happen. Her father had often told her she had the will of ten men, that she could do anything she set her mind to. In some ways, she'd thought he was patronizing her, but he'd repeated the sentiment several times as he lay ill, and she knew he'd meant it. His belief in her had only increased her determination.

She wanted Ash to know that someone believed in him too. "Of course you will!" she called, smiling broadly in encouragement.

He looked at her, and she felt the weight of his gaze deep in her belly. It held her a moment, trapping her breath in her lungs, then he broke eye contact and walked toward the table.

"Not yet," Keldon said, holding up a hand. "Thornaby first. You always did try to get ahead."

"You mean when I finished school before all of you?" It was a simple statement, and yet so powerful. Bianca resisted the urge to rush over and hug him with glee.

"We weren't in any hurry," Moreley said. "But then, we enjoyed school and had each other."

Keldon sneered. "Aye, that we did. And we still do." There was no mistaking the way in which their words and demeanor excluded Ash. What on earth had he ever done to them? Or were they just cruel?

"Your turn!" Moreley called to Thornaby.

The viscount took his place amidst words of encouragement and a round of applause from the spectators. Because he was the host, presumably. Bianca hoped the gun misfired. Horribly.

It didn't.

The ball wasn't quite as close to the center as Keldon's, but it put him in second place. This was met with more cheers. Finally, it was Ash's turn.

"Sure you don't need to move closer?" Thornaby asked. "None of us would mind. You seem a mite shaky. Wouldn't want your bullet to go wide."

"Egads, no," Moreley said, shaking his head. "Can't have that. I insist you move closer."

Bianca edged toward them because the volume of their conversation was dropping and she didn't want to miss what they said.

"Or maybe he shouldn't shoot at all," Keldon said, looking at Ash with mock pity. Or maybe it was real pity. Bianca couldn't tell, nor did she think it particularly mattered. Either one was rude and wholly unnecessary.

She stalked to them, uncaring how they might react. "Oh stop it, and let him shoot. If he's shaky, it's because you're all behaving like jackasses."

They all gaped at her. Save Ash, who gazed at her in open appreciation.

"Back away, Lady Bianca," Moreley said sharply. "This is no place for you."

Keldon frowned. "Indeed, there's no call to behave in such a fashion. What would your brother say? Come, step away." He moved toward her, his arm outstretched.

"Don't touch her." Ash growled the words, and the air changed. The taunting and mockery gave way to something far more sinister.

Moreley stepped toward Ash, his lip curling. "And what will you do about it?" He glanced toward Keldon as if urging him to continue.

And that was precisely what Keldon did. He took Bianca's elbow and began to steer her away.

The next actions happened so quickly that Bianca had to

review them in her mind several times to track how it had all happened.

Though he was farther back from the targets than anyone else had been—behind the table, in fact—Ash lifted his arm and shot at the target, hitting it dead center. Then he dropped the weapon on the table and turned to grab Keldon by the arm.

He dragged Keldon, whose jaw dropped, away from Bianca. "I told you not to touch her, you son of a bitch." Again, the words exploded from his mouth. This was quickly followed by the largest tremor yet. His shoulders twitched, and his neck stretched, thrusting his head to the side. This happened three times in quick succession. Or maybe it was four.

Ash opened his mouth, his face turning a shade of red that outshone his hair, then snapped it closed. He let go of Keldon and, without a look at anyone else, stalked toward the house.

Everyone stared after him. Bianca wanted to follow, to soothe him, to tell him none of them mattered. And to celebrate his victory.

She turned to the target and spoke loudly so that everyone, including Ash, would hear. "He won."

"He cheated," Moreley groused.

Bianca swung her head toward him, anger blazing through her. "How?"

Moreley sniffed. "He didn't stand in the right place."

"You were going to let him move closer! Now you take issue with him shooting farther away?" A growl started low in her throat. "You're just angry because he was better than all of you."

Thornaby straightened his coat. "Never mind. He forfeited with his behavior. I'm sorry you had to witness that, Lady Bianca."

"I'm sorry I had to witness *your* ill behavior."

The viscount's eyes widened, and his mouth opened in surprise. He recovered quickly, his lips forming an easy, false smile. "You witnessed a group of old friends having fun recalling their youth."

Bianca snorted in disgust. "You're awful." And to think she'd wanted to ask him to host the St. Stephen's Day party! She couldn't imagine him wanting to, not with his small mind and petty behavior. It didn't matter—she wasn't going to ask. She'd find another way.

Turning on her heel, she started toward the house. A moment later, Poppy caught up to her. "Wait for me, Bianca!"

Bianca slowed but didn't stop. When Poppy came abreast of her, she said, "I want to leave."

"What happened? We couldn't hear what was going on."

"Thornaby and his friends were behaving horribly toward Ash. He, er, lost his temper—as he should have. In fact, it's a wonder he didn't lose his patience sooner. I would have." She thought of his odd twitches and coughing and of what Poppy had told her earlier about how he'd been before he'd gone to school. Bianca didn't remember him doing any of that before.

They went into the house, and Bianca didn't stop. She continued through on her way to the stairs.

"It looked like you did," Poppy observed. "It appeared as though you were lecturing them."

Bianca glanced at her sister. "So what if I was? They deserve to be lectured. They were horrid to Ash."

"You can't keep calling him Ash," Poppy murmured.

Stopping at the base of the stairs, Bianca turned toward her sister. "Why? I've known him since I was a child. We're friends."

Poppy gave her a beleaguered stare. "You know why. It's not…seemly."

Bianca rolled her eyes and started up the stairs. "I want to go home. After I see *Ash*." She stressed his name on purpose.

When they reached the top, Poppy touched her arm. "You are always looking for trouble. In this case, let it be. At least for a while. The earl appeared upset when he returned to the house. And he shot that gun in a rather unsafe manner. I don't know if you should see him at all."

"He knew precisely what he was doing." And yet, he'd clearly been upset, his body twitching, his face turning red. Ruddy... Her heart ached for him.

"I'm not sure that's an endorsement."

Bianca wouldn't stop her defense of him. "He was being perfectly safe."

"Bianca, just take a few minutes. *Please.*"

Groaning, Bianca scowled but relented. She stalked toward their chamber. Once inside, while Poppy went into the dressing room, she asked her maid to find out where Ash's room was located.

Bianca paced while she awaited Donnelly's return. She wanted Ash to know that she stood with him, that she was going to leave the party before dinner and hoped he would do the same. She also wanted to ask why they treated him so poorly. Would he tell her?

She sensed there was more about his life in London that he hadn't revealed. But then why should he tell her everything? Indeed, why should he tell her *anything*?

Because they were friends. Or they had been. She thought about the way in which he'd reacted to Keldon touching her. He'd fired the pistol at the target almost without looking and hit it square. Then he'd pulled Keldon away from her, and she could have sworn she'd seen malice in his eyes. The emotion had flickered so quickly, she couldn't be sure.

Donnelly entered, interrupting her thoughts. "I'm sorry, my lady, but his lordship has left."

Bianca stared at her. "From Thornhill?"

The maid nodded.

Of course he'd gone. He'd been upset and rightfully so. She planned to go too. "Donnelly, pack our things. We're leaving."

Donnelly blinked in surprise, then nodded. "Yes, my lady."

Poppy came from the dressing room. "Did I hear you say we're leaving?"

"Yes, I told you that outside."

"I didn't think you were serious."

Bianca pursed her lips. "I'm always serious."

"Indeed, you are," Poppy murmured. "Let us go, then. I can't say I'll be sorry, especially after what you told me. Did I hear that Lord Buckleigh has also gone?"

Bianca nodded, her mind already moving five steps beyond their conversation.

"It sounds as if he should have. Good for him."

It was, but now Bianca had to find a way to get to Buck Manor. The entire Christmas season depended on it.

Sometimes it was hell to be a young unmarried lady.

CHAPTER 4

*A*s soon as Ash arrived at Buck Manor, he immersed himself in a hot bath and drank a glass of brandy. Both soothed his mind, even while his soul raged. He'd been a fool to think those men had changed. And yet, *he* had.

His disease had been much worse in his youth. He'd mastered the twitches and vocal interruptions as he'd gotten older, with great effort and because the behaviors had just seemed to lessen. Right around the time he'd started fighting.

"Shall I trim your hair, my lord?" Harris offered.

"Yes, I suppose you should." Ash covered himself in a banyan and sat down for the valet to do his work.

Harris set to work with the shears, working quickly and efficiently, as he did with all things.

"You are astonishingly good at your post," Ash said, looking in the mirror situated over the dressing table in front of him.

"Thank you, my lord. I never could have imagined how much I enjoy being a valet. I never quite fit in as a footman, and I definitely didn't suffice as a groom."

"Is that where you started?" Ash asked. "I hadn't realized."

"At another estate, yes. The other grooms weren't very welcoming. When I left, I learned that I'd been given a position they'd hoped would go to one of their brothers. I believe they ensured I wasn't successful at my position. I have no regret since things have worked out rather well." He smiled as he continued to snip and style Ash's hair.

"What estate was that?"

Harris let out a soft chuckle. "Actually, it was Thornhill."

Ash watched his eyes widen in the mirror, then looked up at Harris behind him. "Did you see any of those men while we were there?"

"I recognized the groom when we arrived, but he didn't behave as if he knew me. I certainly didn't greet him."

Ash could understand that. He also had no trouble believing Thornaby's staff was as cruel as he was. Ash was more glad than ever that he'd promoted Harris. "I know what it's like to feel as though you're a misfit," Ash said.

"I can't imagine that, my lord." Harris finished with the shears and set them on the dressing table. Then he went about brushing the shorn hair from Ash's banyan to the floor.

"It's true." Ash hadn't felt like he fit in until he'd started to box. No one in his pugilism circle had seen the small, terrified boy he'd been at Oxford, the misfit who'd been ridiculed and excluded. They'd only seen the fierce, mostly silent, warrior.

"Hard to think of you, an earl, being an outcast." Harris went to set out Ash's evening clothes.

While Ash had overcome the worst of his disease, he was still different from everyone else. But now he couldn't hide in the shadows. He *was* an earl, but to some extent, he still felt excluded. Because he hadn't been born to the title, and he had much to learn.

Now there were new expectations. He had to speak in the

House of Lords and present himself at court and in Society. He also had to wed.

Bee came to his mind, her exuberance, her outspokenness, her staunch loyalty. She accepted him precisely as he was—or so she seemed to. Would she still if she knew he was tainted?

It didn't matter. She'd been quite clear in her desire to remain unwed. Furthermore, she detested London, and since he would spend half the year there, a union with her would be lonely. He'd spent most of his life feeling lonely. When he wed, he hoped it would be to someone with whom he could share everything. Together, they would build a family, and if any of their children suffered his affliction, he would love them and nurture them in ways his father hadn't.

Ash stiffened when he thought of him, how horrified he'd been by Ash's twitches and outbursts, especially when they'd intensified as he'd gotten older. When his father's older brother, the earl, had suggested Ash attend Oxford with Lyndon, Ash's father hadn't been able to agree quickly enough.

Then he'd ignored Ash's pleas to come home. After a few months, Ash had given up and known he was on his own. When his father had died a few years later, just before Ash graduated, Ash had felt relieved. But there was a guilt that came with not mourning one's father.

"My lord?" Thankfully, Harris interrupted Ash's maudlin thoughts.

Ash stood and prepared for dinner.

A short time later, he went down to the dining room, which was set with just two places as usual. His mother arrived a moment later.

"You *are* home," she said, crossing to him.

Ash kissed her soft cheek and noted the crease in her brow. "Yes." He went to his seat at the head of the table.

"You weren't due until tomorrow. What happened?" The footman helped her into her chair to the left of Ash, and then Ash sat.

He shrugged. "I was bored, and I've far too much to keep me busy here." The estate ledgers were a mess, and there were many issues with the tenants to address, from repairs to cottages to plans for increasing sheep herds.

"I'm sorry to hear it wasn't engaging." Martha Rutledge was the kindest person Ash had ever known. Ash had no living siblings—two older sisters had died in their youth—so his mother focused all her attention, and love, on him. She always worried about her son, so much so that Ash had long ago tried to keep her from fretting. He'd kept his troubles at school from her, as well as his frustration and disappointment with his father.

"I'm sure it was nice to see old friends," she said with a smile as the soup was served.

No it wasn't, with one sparkling exception. "Lady Bianca was there. It was lovely to see her after so many years."

Mother's deep brown eyes lit. "Was she there? I've always liked her. She had such a trying time when her father was ill. I used to see her in town regularly, but I saw her less and less as his sickness progressed."

Ash had kept up on the local happenings somewhat via his mother's letters, but admittedly, he hadn't paid much attention. "The duke was ill for some time?"

Mother nodded while she sipped her soup. "My goodness, for a couple of years at least. And Lady Bianca bore the brunt of it. Her sister is married, of course, but you would have thought Chill would have come home to help."

"He didn't return at all?"

"No, but neither did you." She gave him a slightly vexed look. "I had to come visit you in London."

"I was busy." He focused on his soup.

She exhaled. "I know, and quite successful too."

Yes, he had been. Before Lyndon had died, Ash had been deciding between a potential position with the government or purchasing a commission. Two very different paths, neither of which he'd pursue now.

"Do you miss it?" she asked.

"Sometimes." The boxing mostly, but he'd fashioned a large sack that he hung in a corner of the stable to hit. He had to regularly refill the bag with dirt and straw to keep it firm for his practice, but the concept worked. The sack also didn't hit back. Was that what he missed? Or was it the accolades that came with winning a fight?

"There is plenty to keep me occupied here," he said, hoping to turn the conversation. "Especially with the Christmas season almost upon us. Lady Bianca told me Chill won't be hosting the St. Stephen's Day party this year."

Mother had dipped her spoon in her soup and now dropped it in reaction. "How can he do that? The townspeople will be so disappointed, to say nothing of his retainers, I'm sure."

He'd thought his mother might be upset, but her reaction was greater than he'd anticipated. "It will matter that much?"

She nodded. "Oh yes. It's perhaps the most important day of the year. It's a tradition dating back generations." A deep frown marred her features. "Why isn't he hosting it?"

"I don't know, but Lady Bianca is doing her best to change his mind." Or come up with an alternative. Was she still planning to ask Thornaby? Ash couldn't think she would, not after what had happened earlier. She'd staunchly defended him, turning the tables to become *his* rescuer. But then he'd no idea what might have happened after he left.

"Good," his mother said. "We shouldn't discount her abilities."

That much was true. Still, it did sound as if her brother

might be immovable. And then what? Ash didn't want to disappoint the villagers or the people of Hartwood or his mother. Or Bee.

"I'm sure she'll find a way to make it happen." He'd do whatever he could to support her. If she wanted him to. He had no idea what she thought of him after today's outburst.

His gut twisted. He had to stop thinking about that, about the way those men had made him feel. Again.

He'd thought he'd left those emotions behind, that "Ruddy" had died. To think that people judged him for who he'd been and not who he was now was incredibly disheartening.

No, to think that people judged him for an affliction he couldn't control was infuriating.

He took a deep breath to calm his racing pulse. He wouldn't think of them. There was no cause to see them ever again. Except Thornaby in the House of Lords. And potentially all of them at a St. Stephen's Day event, provided Bee was successful.

Of course she would be successful. Even if she wasn't, it was ludicrous to think he wouldn't see them again. How would they all behave after today?

Hopefully, he could simply avoid them. At the party, in London, wherever he might have cause to encounter them.

Or he could beat them all senseless. Yes, that sounded fun.

Ash reached for his wineglass and nearly drained it. He wasn't going to hit anyone. He was better than that. He was better than *them*.

Why, then, did they still have the power to hurt?

～

"Good morning." Bianca sailed into the breakfast room and glanced at her brother. He sat at the table, his plate before him, his nose buried in a newspaper.

He didn't look up. "Why are you home?"

"Good morning, Bianca, how lovely to see you. You're home early from the house party. Is anything amiss?" She glowered at her brother. "It's not difficult to be pleasant."

His gaze lifted slowly from the newspaper and fixed on her with cool irritation. "Good morning, Bianca. Why are you home early from the house party?"

His second attempt was laced with sarcasm, but she'd take it. "Because it was dreadful." She went to the sideboard and served up her plate before taking a seat opposite her brother at the table.

She didn't really want to get into the specifics—the horrid way in which Ash had been treated. "The new Earl of Buckleigh was there. It was wonderful to see him again."

Calder had looked back down at the paper and now he glanced up, his brow creasing. "Lyndon's cousin?"

"Yes. Ash," she said, picking up a piece of toast.

The furrow in his brow deepened as he regarded her. "'Ash'? That sounds awfully familiar."

"I knew him when we were children. I always called him Ash. 'Buckleigh' or 'my lord' is just odd."

"It's also proper." His tone took on an edge of condescension. "He, however, is not. I'd prefer you stay away from him."

Bianca's jaw froze as she chewed her toast. She took a drink of tea to wash it down. "How on earth is Ash not proper?"

"Stop calling him that. He had a reputation in certain circles in London."

The hair on the back of her neck stood up. "What sort of reputation?"

"A dangerous one." He gave her a pointed stare. "He was a pugilist. I saw him fight a few times, and he's brutal. Definitely not the sort of man with whom my sister should associate, let alone be familiar with." He scoffed as he returned his attention to the newspaper and his breakfast.

Bianca stared at the window that looked out over the rolling parkland of the estate. A sloping hill met a stand of bare-branched trees beneath the dove-gray sky. It looked cold and forbidding, not at all like the fire-haired gentleman who'd made her laugh just yesterday.

"I can't believe that's true." She shook her head and cut a bite of ham.

"What, that he's a pugilist or a particularly fierce one?" Calder lifted a shoulder. "Both are true. As I said, I saw him fight. Or do you doubt me?" He pierced her with his frigid stare, challenging her to cross him.

"I don't doubt you think it was him, but I just can't see it." Ash had always been kinder than most everyone. Together, they'd saved animals and insects and talked about how they wanted all the women and children at the Institution for Impoverished Women in Hartwell to have a warm hearth and a full belly. To that end, Bianca had always done her best to support Hartwell House, which was the name everyone called it. Did Ash feel the same as he had in their youth, or had London corrupted him somehow?

She recalled his evasiveness when discussing his time there and the sensation she'd had that he'd left something out. She also thought of how quickly and savagely he'd shot the pistol, hitting the target with almost no effort. Then there was the malice and fury in his eyes. The emotions had been well earned, but was there more buried within him?

"Whether you see it or not, it's true, and I don't want you

associating with him. He's certainly not marriage material—not for you, anyway—and that's where your mind should be. Thornaby would be a good match."

She couldn't keep from snorting in disgust. "Thornaby is a bully. He'd be a good match for a simpleton with no sympathy or capacity to care for others. And what's more, my mind is on St. Stephen's Day and what I shall do if you insist on not hosting the party."

Calder looked at her sharply. "There will be no party. Not here."

She stared at him a long moment, trying to find the caring brother she'd grown up with. "You really mean it, don't you?"

"I don't say things I don't mean." He shifted his attention back to the newspaper.

"Then I shall have to find another way. I refuse to disappoint the people of Hartwood and Hartwell."

"If you think a party has the means to keep from disappointing people, you've a great deal to learn. Life is more than parties and celebrations and tradition."

At least he knew tradition was part of it. But he also didn't seem to care. "Yes, life is more than that," she said softly. "It's also family and duty and loyalty and love."

He glanced toward her briefly, his lips pressed into a flat line. "Duty—at least we agree on that. Consider Thornaby, or, if you'd rather, I'll come up with a list of potential suitors. You should have a few in mind when you get to London for the Season."

"I'm not going to London for the Season." She'd told him that a dozen times, and he never seemed to listen.

"Of course you are."

She sweetly tossed his words back at him. "I don't say things I don't mean. I'm not going to London."

His gaze lifted at a glacial pace. His stare was so cold, so unfathomable, that she imagined he'd scare just about anyone with it. Not her, however. "It isn't up for debate." His lips barely moved. Was he actually carved from ice?

"I would agree. I'm not going, and that's final." She stood from the table, having lost her appetite. "I am, however, going to Poppy's. Perhaps it's warmer there."

"You *are* going to London, and *that's* final." He looked back down at the newspaper. "I doubt it's warmer at Poppy's. She's only seven miles away. It looks like it may snow, which means you'll have to stay the night. Prepare accordingly." He picked up the newspaper and held it up, blocking his face from her.

Apparently, she was dismissed.

A combination of frustration and agitation propelled her from the breakfast room. Perhaps she would ask Poppy if she could move in with her and her husband. They wouldn't mind.

But she couldn't. Poppy and Gabriel had their own troubles, and Bianca didn't think she could live with the tension. With Calder, she could mostly avoid him. However, she couldn't avoid her sister, especially when she suffered such heartache… In fact, that was maybe another reason Bianca should consider at least staying there for a period of time. Such as for the entire Christmas season…

Well, she would discuss it with Poppy next time she saw her. That wasn't, however, going to be today. She had another destination in mind.

Energized, Bianca flew up the stairs to "prepare," as Calder had put it. She wanted to get on the road within the hour, and she would pray it wouldn't snow.

A devilish grin sprouted across her lips, unbidden. Actually, she might not pray that hard.

CHAPTER 5

$\mathscr{T}$he coach slowed in front of Buck Manor. With a tall Palladian façade and sprawling wings to the east and west, the house commanded respect and awe. It wasn't as large as Hartwood, but it was larger than Poppy's home, Darlington Abbey.

Thinking of her sister only reminded Bianca that she'd lied to the coachman upon leaving Hartwood. She'd had him stop the coach after the first two miles, when it had become necessary to change course, and told him of her change in destination. He'd seemed hesitant at first, but that was largely because he was concerned it would snow.

Both he and Calder had proved right. The snow, falling softly at first, was now coming down in earnest. As Bianca stepped out of the coach, she tilted her head up and was promptly rewarded with a snowflake landing on her nose.

She smiled and started toward the house. Donnelly, who'd accompanied her, followed.

"My lady?" the coachman said, causing her to stop and turn. Donnelly paused with her, then stepped out of Bianca's line of sight so she could see the coachman.

"Yes?" Bianca asked.

"Will this be a quick visit?" He glanced up at the sky.

"It won't be terribly long, but why don't you take the horses to the stables where they will be warmer?"

He nodded and returned to the vehicle while Bianca continued toward the house. They didn't reach the door before it opened. The butler ushered them inside.

"Welcome to Buck Manor," he said. "May I take your cloak?"

Bianca pivoted and unclasped the outer garment. "Thank you. Please let his lordship know that Lady Bianca is here to see him. Can my maid warm up somewhere and perhaps have a cup of tea?"

The butler removed her cloak, and she handed him her gloves and hat. "Of course, my lady. I'll see to it. May I show you to the drawing room?"

"That would be lovely. I hope there's a fire."

He smiled as he handed her things off to a footman. "Indeed there is." He looked toward the footman and murmured, "Please see her ladyship's maid to the downstairs parlor."

Bianca nodded at Donnelly before following the butler from the hall into a large reception room decorated in greens and golds. She went directly to the massive fireplace and warmed her hands before the crackling flames.

Would Ash mind that she'd come? Would he ask her to leave? She flicked a glance toward the windows, where she could see the snow was falling at an even greater pace. Could she leave even if he wanted her to?

"Bee?" Ash's voice carried through the large drawing room, sending a surprising dash of heat up her spine. Surprising because her back was away from the fireplace.

And probably she didn't want to consider that Ash was the source.

Turning, she greeted him with a smile. "I hope you don't mind that I've come."

"Not at all." He seemed genuinely happy to see her, coming forward with a welcoming grin. "I'm surprised. And delighted." He looked around the room. "It's just you?"

"Yes. I told Calder I was visiting Poppy. He's being a pain in my—" She inhaled quickly and blew the breath back out. "Never mind. I plan to go to Poppy's after this. Provided the weather isn't too bad." She looked toward the window again.

"It doesn't look good," Ash said. "Perhaps we should be brief."

"That's what my coachman suggested. I can try." Only she didn't want to. Now that she was here, she wanted to stay. No, if she were honest, she'd hoped it would snow so that she would *have* to stay. They had much to discuss—the St. Stephen's Day party first and foremost. Also his reputation and whether he was a brutal, merciless pugilist. She brought up none of those things. Instead, she asked, "Is your mother here?"

"Yes. I already asked Cornelius to fetch her."

"Wonderful." Bianca was looking forward to seeing her. But first, she supposed she ought to broach what had happened the day before at Thornhill. "I wanted to talk to you about yesterday."

He stiffened, and the air between them shifted as if a wall had sprung up. "There's nothing to discuss. I apologize for leaving without bidding you farewell."

She waved her hand. "That's the least of my concerns. Actually, I have no concern about that at all." That wasn't precisely true. She'd felt disappointed upon learning he'd gone. "I wanted you to know that I found the behavior of Thornaby and the others reprehensible. It was my privilege to speak up for you."

"Thank you." His voice was soft but his features hard. He gazed at the window instead of at her.

Bianca moved toward him, eager to unwrap the secrets enveloping him. "Has it always been like that with them?"

"Yes, not that I've seen them in a very long time." He shook his head and finally turned his attention to her. "Anyway, it hardly signifies. I don't plan on spending time with them in the future."

"Me neither," she said with great satisfaction and a supportive smile. "May I ask why they call you Ruddy?"

Unfortunately, she wasn't to receive an answer because his mother arrived. Mrs. Rutledge entered with a swish of lavender skirts and a broad smile. "Lady Bianca!"

She came to Bianca, and they embraced warmly. "How lovely to see you, Mrs. Rutledge. I see becoming the mother to an earl agrees with you."

She laughed. "Being Ashton's mother has always agreed with me." She looked at him with pride and love, and Bianca felt a twinge of regret. She had no parents left to look at her like that, and her brother certainly wasn't going to bestow that sort of care or affection on her.

"Come, let us sit," Mrs. Rutledge said, gesturing toward the seating area nestled close to the fire. She looked outside and shuddered. "What an awful day to be out."

"It wasn't snowing when I left," Bianca said, lowering herself to the dark green settee. "I was on my way to my sister's, but I daresay I may be stranded here."

Mrs. Rutledge took an adjacent chair. "Oh, I think you might be. That snow is starting to pile up."

Ash sat down next to Bianca. Well, not *next* to her—a good foot separated them.

"I do love snow," Bianca said on a sigh. "I may have to go out and traipse through it if it's thick enough."

"Take Ashton with you. He always adored the snow. Did you miss it in London, dear?"

"It snowed in London," he said. "Perhaps not as much, but enough to satisfy my desire."

Something about those three words sent another lick of heat up Bianca's spine.

The butler, Cornelius, arrived with a tray. He set out a plate of cake and biscuits along with a pot of tea and three cups. Mrs. Rutledge said she would pour, recalling exactly how Bianca preferred her tea. The same as Ash—just a splash of cream and a dash of sugar.

When the butler retreated, Ash's mother asked, "What prompted you to stop at Buck Manor today?"

Ash responded before Bianca could. "She came to talk about the St. Stephen's Day party."

Bianca regarded him closely. He'd been careful to answer and had provided a reason she hadn't even brought up. Did he not want his mother to know about yesterday? More secrets. Which only made her more determined to unravel them. To unravel *him*.

In fact, she *had* come to talk about the party, so in that sense, she and Ash were of a mind. "Yes, I was hoping you and Ash might have some thoughts about the party. Did Ash tell you that my brother is refusing to host it?"

Mrs. Rutledge nodded somberly before sipping her tea. "He did, and I'm sorry to hear it. Is there no persuading him?"

"I'm afraid he's proving quite intractable." Bianca picked up her cup with a grimace. "I'm resolved to find an alternate solution. Not having the party is simply not an option. I will not let the people of Hartwell and Hartwood down."

"You've such a kind and generous heart," Mrs. Rutledge said. "But then I've always known that." She looked to her son. "Did you know that Lady Bianca has worked tirelessly at Hartwell House to ensure the residents have proper clothing, food, and opportunity? She even teaches the children to read."

"When I can," Bianca said, feeling a trifle embarrassed for perhaps the first time ever. She busied herself with eating a biscuit.

"That does not surprise me," Ash said with soft appreciation. "We always planned to rescue everyone there and make sure they had jobs and homes and families."

Her eyes met his, and the heat she'd felt along her spine spread through her. "We did indeed." After a moment, she pulled her gaze from his and looked to his mother. "That's why it's so important to me to ensure there is a St. Stephen's Day celebration. If nothing else, there must be a celebration for the women and children at Hartwell House. Christmas should be a joyous time, with plenty for everyone."

"I wonder..." Mrs. Rutledge tipped her head to the side and looked into the fire. "I know Shield's End isn't terribly large, but much of the festivities has always happened outside, weather permitting. We could use the house as the kitchen and repository for all the food and supplies."

Bianca clasped her hands together. Using Ash's childhood home was an excellent solution. "What a wonderful idea!"

"See, there's a reason we didn't sell it," Ash said, smiling.

His mother chuckled. "I wanted to, but you said we should wait. It's a credit to your forethought. Though how you could have predicted this, I'm not sure."

"I didn't. I was just reluctant to let it go." His cheeks turned a faint pink as he sipped his tea.

Bianca understood the sentiment. There was something very special about tradition and roots and the things—both tangible and not—that made one's life special and beloved. "Just as I refuse to let the St. Stephen's Day party die."

"Precisely," Mrs. Rutledge said. "So we'll host it at Shield's

End." She rubbed her hands together, grinning. "I can't wait to get started. There's so much to do in the next month!"

The woman's enthusiasm was infectious, not that Bianca needed any motivation to be excited about this plan. "I will write to all the people who typically support the party with food and drink." She thought of Thornaby and his friends. Asking them was out of the question. And Calder had been plain: he would do nothing. "Now that I think of it, I'm not sure whom to ask." She looked toward Ash, who nodded almost imperceptibly.

"I'll take care of it," he said.

"All the food and drink?" his mother asked with grave surprise. "That's an enormous undertaking. There are plenty of people in the area who can—and should—help."

Ash stood abruptly and went to the window. "I don't think you'll be going anywhere, Bee. The snow is accumulating, and your carriage will be trapped before it leaves my drive."

Pity. Bianca's insides somersaulted. "I have my maid and was prepared to stay with Poppy, so it's no inconvenience to stay here. I hope it's not an imposition."

He turned and met her gaze. "Not at all. I'll have Cornelius prepare you a room. Dinner is at seven. Now, if you'll excuse me, I've some correspondence to finish." He bowed to them and left.

Bianca realized he'd done everything possible to avoid discussing the prospect of asking others to help with the party. It was evident he didn't want his mother to know about the enmity between him and the other gentlemen in the area.

Gentlemen? They weren't gentlemen, they were cads.

"As to whom you should ask for help," Mrs. Rutledge said after nibbling a cake. "I recall Viscount Thornaby always supported the event, as did Keldon. I'm sure there are others.

Regardless of what Ashton says, it's not right that he shoulder the entire burden."

Bianca agreed, but she also respected his desire not to ask for help. His pride was important. Furthermore, she wasn't sure those bullies would provide assistance if Ash was at the center of it. Would they, however, if she asked?

It didn't matter. She didn't want to ask them. She'd go back to Calder and plead with him to at least provide food and ale. He couldn't say no.

He could, and he very likely would. She frowned into her teacup before taking a sip of the now tepid liquid.

"I'd be happy to help with the correspondence," Mrs. Rutledge offered.

"I'll start with my sister," Bianca said quickly. In the past, the occupants and some of the household staff of Hartwood and Darlington Abbey did the bulk of the work. Other estates in the area, such as Buck Manor and Thornhill, would also help. They'd just have to make do without Thornaby and his friends. She gave Ash's mother a bright smile. "You focus on preparing Shield's End."

Mrs. Rutledge nodded. "I'm sure we can find enough people willing to help. I'm so sorry to hear your brother isn't willing to host the party. I own I'm surprised given how important this event has always been to your family."

"No one was more surprised than me." Bianca wondered if she'd ever learn what was going on in her brother's head. She feared she never would. She also feared he was lost to them, that the Calder they'd known and loved was gone forever. If she only knew why, perhaps there was a way they could bring him back.

Cornelius entered the drawing room and looked to Bianca. "If you're ready, my lady, I'd be happy to show you to your room."

Bianca stood. "Thank you, yes."

Mrs. Rutledge also got to her feet. She gave Bianca another quick hug. Then she held her hands as she spoke. "I'm so pleased you've come. I daresay it's not altogether proper, but I am here to act as chaperone." She waggled her brows. "Do I need to act as chaperone? I don't know that my son is looking for a countess yet, but I can think of no one better."

Oh dear. Bianca wasn't remotely interested in marriage. Not to Ash. Not to anyone.

And yet, the thought of being *Ash's* countess provoked a captivating thrill…

Bianca squeezed Mrs. Rutledge's hands before letting them go. "Ash and I are old friends. We don't need a chaperone except that propriety demands one." Bianca rolled her eyes. "Not that it matters out here." This was yet another reason she had no interest in a London Season. Society and its ridiculous rules. She would feel so constrained, so *trapped*.

"Hopefully, your sister won't be worried when you don't arrive," Mrs. Rutledge said.

"She'll realize the weather is to blame. With luck, the snow will stop soon or overnight, and I'll be able to travel tomorrow."

Or not. Bianca could think of nothing better than spending a day in the snow with Ash. She'd pelt him with snowballs, and they could take a ride so they could race, and she would beat him again.

Only maybe she'd let him win this time. Except she suspected he let her win last time. Her pulse quickened at the prospect. Either way, it would be a wonderful way to spend the day.

Goodness, maybe they needed a chaperone after all.

*a*sh managed to ensure the conversation at dinner had veered quite clear of the St. Stephen's Day party. Instead, they focused on stories of their youth. He credited Bianca with supporting his intent to avoid discussing the party—specifically asking people to help. She understood him like no one ever had.

It was, in a word, enthralling.

The snow had continued into the evening, finally tapering off while they'd dined. Now it was nearly midnight, and the house was dark and quiet. He crept downstairs with the plan of stealing outside to see if the snow had started again or if the sky had cleared.

Carrying a lantern, he walked through the hall toward the back of the house to the terrace. A flash of blue from the library drew him to a stop. A candelabrum on a table inside illuminated Bianca. She stood near the flickering light, her head bent as she cradled a book in her hand.

Ash simply stood there and watched her a moment. Her dark hair hung in a loose plait over her shoulder, the end curling against the swell of her breast. Outlined beneath the

Egyptian blue of her dressing gown, her body beckoned him —the elegant slope of her shoulder, the gentle indentation of her waist, the alluring curve of her hip. Good God, when had he become so drawn to her?

Her gaze lifted from the book and turned toward him, perhaps sensing his presence. Smiling, she snapped the book closed. "Ash."

He walked into the library as if he were pulled by a magnet. "I wasn't expecting to find you here."

"What were you expecting to find?"

"Nothing, really. I was on my way outside to see if the snow had started again or if it was truly finished."

She quickly set the book on a table and moved to stand before him, her gaze eager. "I'll come with you."

He offered her his arm, and as her warm hand curled around him, he was painfully aware that they were both barely dressed—she in a dressing gown and he in a banyan over his shirt and a pair of breeches. This was wholly improper, and he didn't give a damn.

This was Bee. They'd known each other forever, it seemed. Friends since childhood. Yet, this was something more. He wondered if she felt it too.

He guided her out to the terrace where the snow was maybe three inches deep. They barely stepped outside, staying clear of the snow.

She looked up into the ink-dark sky. "It *is* snowing."

Surveying the white terrace, she lifted the hem of her gown and waded into the snow. "Ooh, it's cold and wet." She lifted a careless shoulder before tipping her head back.

Light, soft flakes landed on her upturned face. He held up the lantern to see the graceful planes of her cheekbones, the bright, dazzling sparkle of her blue eyes. He'd never seen anything more beautiful. He moved toward her and wiped a snowflake from her cheek.

She brought her head down to look at him, her lips parted in joy. He brought his finger to his mouth and licked the snowflake from the pad.

Her gaze fixed on his mouth, and the desire that had been swirling inside him all day swelled to a crescendo, hardening his cock and making his breath come short.

"We always tried to catch the snowflakes." She tipped her head back and closed her eyes, then stuck out her tongue.

What was beautiful was now also incredibly erotic. Ash told himself to go inside, to tell her she should return to her chamber. But he did neither. He stared at her mouth and thought of her tongue doing unspeakable things. He thought of kissing her beneath the snowy sky.

He didn't do that either.

She caught a snowflake and drew her tongue back between her lips. Her eyes opened, and it was as if he could see straight into her soul—a bright beacon that was now emblazoned in his memory. He wondered if she could have been a light in the darkness at Oxford. He would never know.

Soft, bliss-filled laughter slipped from her mouth. "Too bad it's dark, or I would bombard you with snowballs."

"Not if I bombarded you first."

She gave him a saucy stare. "Is that a challenge?"

"It might be, but it will require boots and appropriate outerwear—and daylight."

She exhaled with regret. "And a hot bath when we're finished."

Hell, now he was thinking of her nude in a bath, steam rising from the water. He nearly groaned with want. Again he wondered how his childhood friend had suddenly become the object of his greatest desire.

Ash coughed and worked to suppress the shudder that threatened to crane his neck and roll his shoulders. "If you're suggesting we engage in a snowball fight and then take a hot bath, I'll have to remind you that propriety would frown upon it."

"I didn't mean together." A faint pink stained her cheeks, but he couldn't know if it was because of their flirtation or the cold temperature. "But remember that propriety is the least of my concerns." She twirled about in the snow, her arms out wide. Flakes clung to her dark hair, making her look like a winter princess.

"Were you really on your way to your sister's?" he asked.

She stopped and dropped her arms to her sides. "Yes, but I knew it was possible I might be stranded here because of the weather."

"And you came here just to talk with me about…yesterday." He didn't really want to bring it up again, and yet he couldn't seem to stop himself. He wanted to know why she was *really* here.

He wanted to know if there was something blossoming between them. No, he knew there was for him. He needed to know if the sensation was present for her too.

"Not just for that, no." Her words prompted his pulse to quicken. "As I said, Calder was being insufferable, so I was anxious to be anywhere but Hartwood. I also wanted to speak with you about St. Stephen's Day—I'm so glad we resolved that."

Mostly. He still didn't want to involve Thornaby or anyone else.

She stepped toward him until there was barely any space between them. "I know you don't want Thornaby or Keldon or any of the others to help. I don't either. I also realize you don't want your mother to know you don't want them involved."

She was incredibly perceptive. And caring. He suddenly acknowledged there had been a dreadful weight on his chest for as long as he could remember. He noticed its presence in this moment because it lightened, and he felt...free. A gentle twitch moved across his shoulders.

The snow was clinging to her brows now, and a shiver jolted her frame.

"Let's go inside." He swept his arm around her waist and ushered her back into the house.

She shuddered, sending snow flying from her dressing gown and her hair. "I didn't realize how cold it was. You distracted me." Her gaze met his, her brow arching. "You also changed the subject. Again."

He laughed softly. "Only because I didn't want you to freeze. You need to get out of that wet dressing gown." He placed his hand against the small of her back. The silk of her gown was damp, and he pulled his hand away. Not because he didn't want to get wet, but because he didn't want to press the cold material against her skin.

"You can touch me." With her words and the impassioned look in her eyes, a different weight settled into him. One that was welcome with its heat and intensity.

He put his hand lightly against her as he guided her toward the stairs. "I don't want you to catch cold."

"I will disrobe as soon as I get upstairs. Will that suffice?" She gave him a heated stare, and he wasn't sure if she was being playful or serious. Did it matter? His body burned hotter at the thought of her removing her gown...

They started up the stairs. "Bee, are you flirting with me?"

"Probably." Her voice had dipped to a lower timbre, one he felt in his bones. "It's just..." They weren't quite to the top of the stairs, but she stopped and turned toward him. "I was so angry yesterday. I wanted you to know that." She searched his face, her lips slightly parted, her chest rising and falling with her breath.

He sensed there was more. "What else did you want me to know?"

"Actually, it's what *I'd* like to know. You said London was a long story, and then you prevaricated—don't pretend you didn't." Her tone was scolding, but with an underlying warmth. "My brother told me you were a pugilist." She blinked. "Is that true?"

He felt his heart beat in his neck along with a rush of excitement. The combination of thrill and trepidation when something so guarded was about to be revealed. "It is."

Her eyes widened slightly with surprise, and her lips parted as she stared at him for a moment. Her reaction was troubling.

"That bothers you," he said.

"I don't know if it does," she admitted, sounding tense. "My brother said you were dangerous, that I should stay away from you."

"I take it he doesn't know you're here?" She shook her head, and he couldn't help a short chuckle. "You really don't care about propriety, do you?"

She shook her head again. Then she took his hand. "I didn't think you could be dangerous—not the Ash I knew. But then you shot that pistol, and you looked so—"

"Angry." That word didn't remotely encompass the emotion he'd felt. The rage, the pain, feelings he'd thought long buried. He gripped her hand more tightly. "I'm not dangerous. Not to you."

He was too aware that they were standing on the stairs, not that he expected anyone to be about. He squeezed her hand and led her up to the landing. Without speaking, he took her to the left toward his private apartments. A few moments later, he ushered her into his outer sitting room, where a low fire burned.

Positioning her in front of the fire, he said, "Stand there and don't move."

Her brows climbed her forehead, but there was humor in her gaze. She nodded mutely and moved closer to the warmth.

Satisfied she would not catch cold, he went to the sideboard, where he poured two glasses of brandy. He returned to her and offered the tumbler. "This will warm you from the inside."

Lurid images of other ways he could warm her from the inside filled his mind. Why had he brought her here of all places?

So he could explain.

He sipped the brandy, and she did the same.

She swirled the amber liquid in the glass. "French brandy?"

"Lyndon had a fair supply of it. Smuggled, I'm sure." He took another sip to steady his nerves and keep from arching his neck. "I've never talked to anyone about why I fought."

Pivoting, she faced him in front of the fire. "Fought as in the past? You don't fight anymore?"

He turned to her, shaking his head. "Not since Lyndon died. It seemed I should stop doing that if I am to be the earl."

"Do you miss it?"

"Nearly every day." A weak smile surfaced from within him, conjured by his regret. "Not as much as before—the earldom keeps me very busy. Before that, I had my work and fighting."

"Nothing else?"

"No. I needed both those things to overcome my…affliction."

The space between her brows gathered. She took a step toward him. "What affliction?"

"Surely you've noticed it. The way I twitch, the vocal-izations?"

She nodded. "My sister mentioned it—she recalls you doing that before you went to school, but I don't."

"You were very young, not quite ten, I believe."

"Yes, but you visited, and although I didn't see you very often, I still don't remember you doing those things." She frowned. "What causes it?"

"I don't know. I've always been that way. It grew more troublesome as I started to mature." The twitches could be almost constant, and the vocalizations, including words and phrases he would never voluntarily say aloud, could happen at any moment. "At school, it was horrible."

"Thornaby and the others taunted you for it," she said flatly.

"Lyndon was the worst. When we had lessons together in our youth, he often mocked my efforts—the symptoms have always displayed when I am nervous or tense." He glanced from her toward the fire. "Or afraid." Conquering his fear through fighting had been his primary goal after Oxford. Admitting it aloud to another person was, he supposed, another victory.

"Is that why they called you Ruddy?" she asked.

"Because my face would grow red, both from embarrass-ment and my efforts to control myself."

"You seem to be in control now."

"Mostly." He tipped his head to the side, and a small smile flitted across his lips. "Like that. It seems innocuous, but I can't control it."

She reached up and cupped her hand against his jaw. "How does it feel?" The question was soft and rife with concern as well as a genuine need to understand.

"I don't know that I can explain it. When I was younger, it was as if I was standing outside myself watching it happen to someone else. Now, it's simply who I am. Along with my red hair—that's the other reason they called me Ruddy. And my name, Rutledge."

She slipped her hand back behind his ear and ran her fingers through his thick strands. "I have always adored your hair. I wanted it for myself. It's so vivid and full of fire and energy."

Anticipation continued to build inside him. "Like you." The words tumbled from his mouth, not that he would have stopped them. If he was losing control where she was concerned, he wasn't sure he wanted to rein himself in.

But he should.

"Yes," she whispered. "Your hair is how I feel inside—it isn't fair that it belongs to you."

He grinned, utterly charmed by this woman. And yes, she was very much a woman and not the girl from his youth. "Bee—Bianca—I'm going to kiss you unless you tell me not to."

She stared up at him, then dropped her hand from his hair. Turning her head, she set her glass atop the mantelpiece before returning her gaze to his. Her lips didn't part, and the look she gave him overflowed with expectation. With invitation.

Ash set his unfinished brandy next to hers. He cupped his hands against her cheeks and moved closer until their chests touched. "Last chance," he murmured just before his lips grazed hers.

Her palms flattened against his chest, her heat seeping into him through the damp of his banyan. He took that as encouragement and pressed his mouth to hers. She moved beneath him, tentative at first. He went slow, both to give her time to adjust and to decide if she wanted to stop.

Then her fingers curled into the silk of his banyan, and she leaned into him. So much for going slow. Still, he kept control. He tipped his head to the side—completely on purpose this time—and opened his mouth against hers. Gently, he slid his tongue along her lower lip.

"Open," he whispered against her.

She parted her lips, and he slipped his tongue inside. Again, her fingers dug into him, this time the tips pressing into his flesh through the fabric. Her tongue moved against his, her mouth blooming beneath his, and the concert between them began.

The song lifted his soul, and he cradled her nape with one hand while he trailed the other down her back and pressed against her lower spine. He withdrew from her mouth only to begin again from a new angle so he could learn every part of her. She met him eagerly, greedily, her hands clutching at his neck, her body straining against his.

He moved his hand lower to her backside and pulled her flush against his erection. A low groan rumbled in his chest, and she pulled away.

What am I doing?

This was Bee. Not some London trollop. He stepped back and lifted his hand to his mouth, horrified. "I'm so sorry."

She glared at him, and he'd never felt worse in his life.

Then she untied the sash at her waist and let her dressing gown fall to the floor. Beneath the garment, she wore only a thin chemise, through which he could see every curve and slope of her body.

His mouth went utterly dry, and he had to know if this was all in his mind. "What are you doing?"

"Encouraging you not to stop. Is it working?"

Wait, she didn't want him to stop?

He blinked at her, trying to make sense of what was happening—between them and within himself. He'd never wanted anything more than he wanted Bianca.

Blowing out an exasperated breath, she drew her chemise

over her head and kicked her slippers from her feet. "How about now? Please tell me this is enough to tempt you, because I can't take anything else off. I suppose I can try seduction, but I haven't the faintest idea what to do—"

He would never know if she meant to say anything else because he swept her up against his chest and kissed her fiercely. It was some minutes later before he came up for a breath.

He stared down into her eyes. "I am seduced."

CHAPTER 7

*G*lee mixed with excitement and anticipation as Bianca clutched his neck. This was not at all what she'd envisioned when she'd decided to come here today, and yet she couldn't say she was surprised. It felt—to her, at least—like the inevitable conclusion to their acquaintance. As if their childhood had been a precursor to this so that they would have a shared background that would bind them together as nothing else could.

Or maybe it was just that when he kissed her, she felt as though she was going to melt into a puddle. Not *just* when he kissed her. The way he looked at her. The way he spoke to her. The way he valued who she was and how she lived her life. No one else made her feel so…right.

"Show me what to do," she whispered.

His warm brown eyes held hers. "You're certain?"

She nodded. "Never more."

One of his auburn brows arched high on his forehead with a hint of humor. "You have always been a woman of conviction." He lifted her and carried her through a doorway.

Into his bedchamber. The room was large, but the four-poster bed sat in a place of prominence on a raised dais against the wall opposite the fireplace. Heavy dark blue drapes edged with gold hung about the bed, and the bedclothes were even more opulent—rich, deep blues and golds swirling on the coverlet.

"It's a bit ostentatious for my taste," he said, setting her down. "However, I've other things I prefer to spend money on. Such as hosting a St. Stephen's Day party."

She came up on her knees and put her arms around his neck. "Oh, Ash. You are so very wonderful."

Their lips met once more, and she surrendered to his kiss. No, not surrendered, for she was an equal instigator. In fact, it seemed she could do more to further her cause.

She slid her hands into the opening of his banyan and pushed it from his shoulders. There was a sash, she recalled, but he was already undoing it, and the garment slid to the floor.

Dipping her gaze to his shirt and breeches, she frowned slightly. "You are wearing far more clothes than me."

"An unlikely situation since women are typically far more clothed than men. However, we can easily rectify the situation."

"Yes, please." She found the hem of his shirt, which was loose from his breeches, and pulled the garment over his head. He provided assistance, casting it away as soon as he could.

She studied his bare chest in the firelight. "Here are your freckles." A light smattering of pale brown spots dotted his upper chest. "I was afraid they'd disappeared."

"I was glad when they did."

"I was thinking that I missed them." She ran her fingers over his flesh, glorying in the heat and firmness of him. Then she dipped her head and kissed the largest freckle she could find.

"*Bee.*"

"You're still wearing breeches."

She closed her eyes and kissed upward, along his sternum and neck. He cast his head back as she felt him working open his fall. A moment later, they were gone from him, or at least they sounded like they were.

Bianca skimmed her hands down his chest, relishing the ripples of his ribs and abdominal muscles, in search of his waistband. There was no garment to block her passage. There was, however, his cock.

Her hands stilled, and she pulled back slightly, looking down at his sex. She'd never seen a man like this in person. Oh, she'd seen drawings—hidden in the bottom shelf of the library at Hartwood—but nothing could compare to this. To Ash.

"Do you wish to stop?" he asked. The words were so lovely, like a verbal caress.

She lifted her gaze to his and shook her head. "No."

"I may keep asking, in case you change your mind."

"I won't." She couldn't imagine stopping now. She wanted this—she wanted *him*. "But that you would accept that is lovely."

"Of course I would. I don't want you to regret this."

"I couldn't. Now, tell me how to seduce you."

He laughed softly. "As I said, I am already seduced. You, on the other hand, require my attention." He brought his hand to her breast, sliding it up beneath and lifting the weight of her.

The sensation was simple but incredibly decadent. She'd never imagined she could feel such desire. It started where he touched her and spread outward, spiraling down through her belly and pooling between her legs. When he'd first kissed her, a spark had lit there, and now he kindled the flames, stoking a fire within her that begged to burn.

His hand closed over her, and he captured her lips once more. She kissed him back, but her focus was fixed on him touching her breast. He stroked her gently, drawing his fingers over her nipple. It was both too much and not enough.

She pressed into him, offering all that he could possibly take. He left her mouth, his lips blazing a path down her neck and across her collarbone. Pushing her breast up, he held her captive to his mouth. And then he sucked.

The sensation between her legs intensified. She felt like an utter wanton, desperate for him to touch her there to ease the ache growing inside her. She clamped her legs together, seeking something to satisfy her need.

His free hand skimmed along her belly and out to her waist, then lower to her hip. His touch was soft and subtle, but she was aware of every graze of his fingers and brush of his palm. He curled his hand behind her, stroking the curve of her backside.

The flesh between her legs began to throb. "Touch me."

He dragged his hand back along her hip and down her thigh, coasting inward as he went. "Here?" he murmured just before he stroked her sex.

Oh yes, but much, much more. "You're teasing me."

He lifted his head and gave her a sultry smile. "That's part of sex. The teasing, the anticipation." He skimmed his fingers over her, a light caress designed to torture her, she was certain.

"If you are trying to heighten my awareness, I should tell you that I am keenly aware in ways I have never been before. I do think I may die if you don't touch me."

"We wouldn't want that." His thumb found the top of her

sex, and he pressed. "I believe this right here is what you want me to touch."

She gasped as lights danced before her eyes. Every sensation seemed to gather and tighten in that very spot. "*Yes.*"

"And if I continue to do so, your desire will climb." He stroked his thumb and fingers over her, doing exactly as he said. "If I go faster, the pleasure will build until you're unable to stand another moment."

Everything he described was true. Her legs felt weak, and she began to crumble. He eased her back on the bed until she lay before him. She wanted to watch him, to share this with him, but as her body began to shudder, her eyes closed.

"Now come for me, Bee." He moved his fingers faster, then slid one inside her. She *couldn't* stand another moment. Every one of her muscles was pulled tight as her body gathered into a storm. She wasn't sure what he was doing, just that pleasure was raining down on her. It was a torrent of lightning and thunder that broke suddenly free into a bright and roaring crescendo.

"Shhh," he whispered against her ear.

Vaguely, she became aware of his body against hers, of his hand stroking her sex, calming her after the storm. She opened her eyes and looked at him. His face was taut, his jaw clenched.

"That was magnificent." She snuggled toward him and felt the brush of his sex against her thigh. She felt foolish. He hadn't participated. "It also wasn't fair. What about you?"

He kissed her temple. "This was about you."

She shook her head. "I want you to experience what I did." She rolled to her side. "May I?" She gently touched his cock. It was soft and smooth and incredibly hard. "Show me."

He put his hand over hers and curled her fingers around his flesh. Then he guided her to the base. "Up and down," he rasped. "Slowly at first."

At first. She did as he described, gripping him gently as she moved her hand up his shaft. "As you did with me?" At his nod, she continued, setting a modest pace. "Then faster, also as you did with me?" She increased her speed.

He rolled to his back. "Dear God. Yes."

"When do you put this inside me?" Her sex began to pulse again. Was that normal? She wanted to feel that same release he'd given her once more.

He closed his eyes, his face a mask of need. "After we're married."

Her hand stilled, and his eyes opened. He turned his head to focus on her, his pupils dilated.

Married? Had she heard him right? "But we aren't getting married."

He blinked, then flicked a glance down at where she still touched him. "I think we must."

She withdrew her hand and scooted away from him. "Why?"

"I should think it's obvious."

Because of what they'd done. And yes, she supposed that would be the normal course of things. "I don't think it's obvious, actually. I think that's what most would expect, but I am not most people. On the contrary, I've no wish to marry."

Color started to rise in his face, and he twitched twice in quick succession. "Hell." The word shot from him, and the resulting frown gave her to think he hadn't meant to say it.

His "affliction" was surfacing. And it was her fault. "I'm sorry. I don't mean to upset you. It's just...I have enjoyed tonight between us, and I would continue. But I understand if you would rather not."

He turned his head, his neck stretching—another twitch. "My honor will not allow me to."

She'd said she understood—and she did—however, that

didn't mean she wasn't disappointed. She slid from the bed. "I'll go."

He sat up. "Bee."

"It's fine." She summoned a smile. "Thank you. For what you gave me. I'll treasure tonight always." Feeling suddenly emotional, she darted from his bedchamber back to the sitting room, where she quickly donned her clothing. The dressing gown in particular was still damp, and she began to shiver as she worked to stuff her feet into her wet slippers.

Quick, before he comes out and sees that you're upset!

Bianca hurried from the sitting room and made her way across the upper floor to her chamber. She moved quickly, praying no one would see her—especially Ash's mother.

At last, she reached her room. Once inside, she went to the fire, which was quite low.

"My lady?" Donnelly's sleepy voice came from the dressing chamber, and a moment later, she appeared, wiping a hand over her eye. "I'm sorry. I dozed off."

"That's fine." Bianca preferred to be alone right then anyway.

"I'll just stir the fire," Donnelly said, already applying herself to the task.

A bigger fire and the warmth it would provide would not come amiss. Bianca was still feeling chilled. And she wasn't sure it was entirely from her clothing.

She walked past Donnelly toward the dressing chamber. "I need to change." A moment later, she was garbed in a fresh night rail. She rushed back to the fireplace and curled herself onto the chair before it.

Donnelly fetched a blanket from the bed and wrapped it about Bianca. Warmth began to soothe her—at least on the outside. Inside, she still felt cold.

"Can I get you anything else?" Donnelly asked.

Bianca tried to smile at her and failed. "No, thank you. Go

on back to bed. I went outside to look at the snow, and I just need a few minutes to warm up."

Donnelly nodded. "Of course, my lady." Then she turned and retreated to the dressing room, where her cot was located.

Gradually, heat pervaded Bianca's body, but it wasn't the kind Ash had stoked within her. She tried to identify the reason for the cold, hollow feeling inside her, a feeling that trapped unshed tears at the back of her throat.

She thought of how generous and kind Ash had been all evening and of how she'd stirred his infirmity. The ache inside her intensified. She hated that she'd caused him to be upset.

What a tangle. She considered going back to his room to apologize, but reasoned that would only keep the matter festering between them. Wait, would it agitate and disrupt their friendship? She hadn't considered that. She hadn't considered anything except embracing the delicious moment that had sprung up between them.

And if she went back, could that moment continue? Did she want it to?

Yes.

Groaning, she knocked her head against the cushion of the high-backed chair. She was a wanton, clearly. She wanted Ash, her oldest and dearest friend, but she didn't want to marry him. It wasn't him, it was shackling herself to someone who would control her life. Living with Calder and his dismal behavior was bad enough.

Then there was the fact that Ash was an earl, and he had to be in London part of the year. She would hate being away from her home. On the other hand, Ash had obviously loved it—and it had changed him for the better. Or so he said. Could she grow to appreciate it too?

She opened her eyes, startled, and sat up in the chair. Was she considering his proposal?

She wasn't entirely rejecting it. She couldn't. Not when she thought of the way he'd made her feel. For a while, she'd lost control and for someone who liked to manage everything, it had been a surprisingly heady feeling. Because she knew she could trust Ash.

What's more, if she didn't marry him, she'd never know what happened next. She wasn't sure she could go a lifetime with that sort of frustration.

After staring into the fire for she didn't know how long, Bianca rose from the chair and padded to the bed. Burrowing under the covers, she closed her eyes and tried to make sense of how quickly and drastically her life seemed to have changed. All because she'd found Ash again.

The boy who'd rescued her. And maybe the only one who ever would.

❧

*A*sh purposely went down to breakfast later than usual the following morning. Aside from having been up half the night tortured by thoughts of Bianca and the future he now desperately wanted and apparently couldn't have, he didn't particularly want to see her or his mother.

So it was with hope that he entered the breakfast room, only to stop short at seeing both women seated at the table. He took a deep breath and counted to three, but a shudder passed over him nonetheless, twisting his neck and cresting across his shoulders.

They swung their heads toward him, one with a tense, expectant expression, the other smiling. His mother spoke. "Good morning! I was wondering if you'd perhaps taken ill.

You didn't go out in the snow last night, did you? I know how much you love a snowfall, especially the first one."

"I did, in fact." His gaze connected with Bianca's, but just for a moment, because he abruptly turned to fetch a plate from the sideboard. A twitch pricked his frame, and he rolled his shoulder.

The footman was at the sideboard, a mild look of confusion marring his brow. Typically, he would serve Ash's plate and deliver it to the table. Today, however, Ash shook his head, and the footman retreated.

After filling his plate, Ash went to sit down. He stared at the food and wondered why he'd taken so much. He wasn't sure he could eat. Not with his fondest desire sitting across from him.

"Alas, the snow has stopped," his mother continued. "But that means Lady Bianca can go to her sister's house today."

"We'll see," Ash said, picking up his knife to spread jam on his toast. He willed his body to behave, but his head tipped to the side. "The snow does not appear to be melting, and if the temperature doesn't warm quickly enough, she won't be able to leave. Not in a carriage, anyway. I suppose she could ride to her sister's."

"Surely it's too cold for such a journey," his mother declared. She turned her head to Bianca. "You may have to stay another night."

"I won't mind," Bianca said.

Hell. One more night under the same roof with her? Last night had been agonizing enough.

Ash couldn't look at her. Instead, he focused on eating his toast, which tasted and crumbled like sand in his mouth.

His mother pushed back her chair. "If you'll excuse me, I'm going to repair to my sitting room to work on plans for the St. Stephen's Day party. There are so many lists to make." She beamed at both of them. "I'm so thrilled to help."

Ash was glad to see her so happy. He knew it had been hard for her to leave their home in Hartwell, but she'd insisted on coming here to support him as he learned how to be an earl. This would give her the chance to spend time in Hartwell and see Shield's End put to good use. "I daresay it will end up benefiting everyone that the duke decided to forgo hosting the party. I can think of no one better to lead the charge." He smiled at her and forced himself to take another bite of toast.

"Not me," his mother said. "Lady Bianca is leading things. I am a happy soldier." She started to rise, and Ash got to his feet. He was having even more trouble chewing and swallowing this bite of toast. He was also having difficulty avoiding Bianca's gaze.

Perhaps he should quit the room too. "Do you need help, Mother?" he asked.

She waved him back down. "No. Finish your breakfast. I'll see you later." With a final cheerful nod toward both of them, she turned and left.

Ash gave up on the toast and moved on to his eggs. They tasted like...nothing. At least he could swallow them down without much effort.

Bianca glanced toward the footman, her eyes furtive. After the fourth time, it was evident she was hoping the footman would leave.

Ash turned toward the retainer. "Would you go and speak with the head groom and ask if he thinks Lady Bianca will be able to travel today?"

"Yes, my lord." The footman spun about and departed.

"Better?" Ash only looked briefly at her before taking another bite of tasteless eggs.

"I'm sorry I can't leave," Bianca blurted.

"We'll see if that's true."

"Please don't be angry with me."

Now he pinned her with a direct stare. "I'm not."

"Well, I am."

He cocked his head—on purpose—and blinked. "You're angry with me?"

Her eyes widened in horror. "No! I'm angry with *me*. I never meant to cause you…distress last night. I feel awful."

"You mustn't. It wasn't your fault."

Her expression turned dubious, her brows briefly arching. "I'm not sure I agree with you, but I won't argue."

"I'm the one who must apologize," he said. "I never should have allowed things to progress."

"It wasn't your fault at all. I'm to blame. I'm the one who took my clothes off and tried to seduce you. Then I touched your—"

"*Bee.* I'd rather you didn't talk about it." Reliving their torrid encounter was bad enough, but hearing her describe it was a torment he wasn't prepared to endure. A tremor worked through his neck and down his arm.

Quiet reigned once more. Ash surrendered the eggs and moved on to the kippers. After one bite, he decided he was finished. He looked toward her as she gazed out the window, her face in profile. The gentle slope of her nose and the strong jut of her chin were so distinctive. He could identify her at fifty paces from among a field of women. And the rest would pale in comparison.

She abruptly stood, and Ash quickly got to his feet. "I think it's time for our snowball fight."

"I'm not sure that's a good idea."

She laughed gaily. "Come on." She gave him a tart, teasing look, and he was helpless to resist her allure. "I think you will feel better if you can throw a snowball at me. Or ten."

He would feel better if he could marry her. If he could claim to the world that she belonged to him—that he loved her beyond measure.

He loved her?

Of course. That was what the empty ache in his chest signified—the loss of something he'd only just realized he wanted more than anything. A countess was necessary, but Bianca was absolutely vital. He couldn't imagine anyone else sharing his life or his bed.

Suddenly, the idea of throwing snowballs—maybe not at her—sounded exactly perfect.

CHAPTER 8

*D*espite her tall boots, heavy cloak, and extra-thick gloves, Bianca was quite wet. Making and throwing snowballs would do that, she supposed. Still, she wouldn't trade it. Seeing Ash laugh was worth any price. Being the one to provoke that laughter was a gift.

She'd seen the disappointment and sadness in the rigidity of his body the moment he'd walked into the breakfast room. Knowing she was the cause of his upset had nearly torn her in two.

Then, when she'd apologized and tried to take responsibility, he'd been an utter gentleman. He was, she realized, without compare.

She looked askance at where he was building his snowman. They were having a contest to see whose would be taller without falling over—he'd promised not to go higher than her head to keep things fair.

Only he wasn't there.

Too late, she heard the soft squish of snow behind her. Just before the coldness seeped down the back of her cloak.

Gasping, she spun about, her jaw gaping. His eyes danced as he shrugged. She promptly burst out laughing.

He joined in, and a good minute passed before she could speak. "I deserved that." She'd crept up on him earlier and pressed a small snowball on the back of his neck. He'd nearly jumped out of his skin.

"You absolutely did," he said.

She realized she still held snow in her hand. She'd scooped it up to add to her sculpture. Curling her hand around the cold mass, she started to throw—

Only to have him launch toward her. She tried to back out of his reach, but her foot slipped in the snow, and there was nothing she could do to keep from going down. Her legs slid out from beneath her, and she fell back into the soft snow.

Ash's eyes widened, and then the heavens made things right, and he slipped too.

His arms windmilled, and he fell forward, managing to pivot so that he landed beside her. Unfortunately, he got a face full of snow.

He lifted his head and turned it toward her. Snow clung to his brow, his nose, his chin making him into a living snowman. Bianca dissolved into laughter once again.

He grinned. "Do I look absurd?"

Bianca caught her breath. "You look like my brother if his outside matched his inside." She immediately grimaced. "I probably shouldn't have said that."

"It's not as if I will tell him. Your secret—all your secrets —are safe with me."

She wasn't sure she had any secrets. Except for last night. And he knew about that one. What he didn't know was how deep her regret went or how conflicted she felt, especially in this moment.

She enjoyed being with him. He made her feel cared for

and respected. If she was going to wed, he was the type of husband she would want.

Propping herself on her elbow, she turned to her side. She was immediately sorry as the cold wet saturated the clothing covering her hip. There was no help for it now. She was going to need a bath no matter what.

She watched as he wiped the snow from his face. "Is your offer from last night still available?"

His hand froze, then jolted—a tremor, she believed. He finished clearing the snow away and pierced her with the warm chocolate of his eyes. "It will be until you decide to marry someone else."

Her breath tripped in her chest. "I wouldn't. It isn't that I don't want to marry you." On the contrary...she *might*. "It's that I don't want to marry anyone."

"Then we may both die unwed." He said it in a wry way, but it was an incredibly sad thought.

"Well, that's depressing."

He laughed softly as he turned to his side to face her. "It's the truth. Sometimes the truth isn't what we want, but it's what we must live with."

She thought of his infirmity and the pain it had brought him—and how he learned to cope and survive. Admiration crested within her. "You're an extraordinary man. That's why I want you to know it isn't you."

He nodded. "I understand." He lifted his voice to a higher pitch, mimicking her. "*If* I were to wed, I would wed you!" He lowered his tone once more. "Is that the right of it?"

He grinned, and she scooped up another bit of snow and tossed it at his chest. His eyes widened, then narrowed. His jaw clenched just before he launched forward and pushed her to her back once more.

Grabbing her hands, he held them above her head. She

gasped again, but it had nothing to do with the cold at her back and everything to do with the way he straddled her.

"Has anyone ever told you that you're diabolical?" he asked.

"My siblings, I'm sure." Heat and joy rushed through her, along with a jolting heat given the way he held her arms and the manner in which their pelvises touched. Why was she declining his marriage proposal? "It's not just that I don't wish to marry. If I *were* to marry you, I'd have to live in London, and I don't want to. I like it here. No, I love it here." Especially *here*. With him.

"We're back to that?" He lifted a shoulder, and she wasn't sure if it was a twitch or not. No, she knew—this one was on purpose. "Only part of the year, or you can stay here year-round. Though I would miss you dreadfully."

She would miss him too. When he left after the new year, she feared her heart would break.

"What if I bought you a house outside London? Then we could see each other regularly and you wouldn't have to live in the city. I'm sure there's a local cause we can find for you to dedicate your time and passion to."

The sun emerged from behind a cloud, its rays already working to melt the snow around them, just as her resolve was suddenly faltering. He was too perfect. Too wonderful. No, he was simply Ash.

"Together, we could choose a house and make it feel like here," he continued. "Like home."

She already knew what home felt like. Ash.

"My goodness, what are you doing?" Mrs. Rutledge's voice rent the air and was followed by a nervous laugh.

Ash nearly jumped off Bianca, springing to his feet and quickly helping her to stand. "Nothing. We slipped."

"That explains it," his mother said with another awkward

laugh. "I think you both need a bath right away. Even though the sun is out, you must be freezing."

"Now that I am wet, yes," Bianca admitted.

As they started toward the house, Mrs. Rutledge said, "I came to speak with you about the party. I do think we should ask Thornaby and Keldon for support."

"No," Bianca and Ash said in unison. Their gazes met around Ash's mother, who walked between them.

"Whyever not? They'd be more than happy to help, and Keldon's mother is a friend of mine. She'd be disappointed if I didn't ask."

"We don't need to trouble anyone," Ash said with a flick of his shoulder. "Let us surprise everyone with what we come up with."

Bianca nodded enthusiastically. "Exactly. I'm sure Poppy and Gabriel will help—we can manage it between us."

Mrs. Rutledge frowned slightly as the footman opened the door. "If you say so."

"We do," Ash assured her.

His mother went in first, followed by Bianca, and then Ash.

"They both need warm baths," Mrs. Rutledge said to the butler while he closed the door. The retainer nodded and took himself off.

Bianca moved to Ash's side and whispered, "Too bad we can't take one together."

He gave her the most scalding stare she'd ever received, and the unfulfilled ache inside her began to grow again. "You're going to ruin me completely." His voice was barely audible next to her ear above the pounding of her blood.

Today, Bianca had had a glimpse of what their life together could be like. The prospect was beyond tempting.

~

*I*f there had ever been a more perfect day, Ash wasn't aware of it. Not in his life. Not in anyone's life. He'd dare anyone to best the sheer joy and delight of spending time with Bianca. And that was *after* she'd declined his marriage proposal.

Oh, it still stung, but he possessed something tonight he hadn't the night before: hope. She'd been flirtatious and provocative as well as apologetic and possibly plagued by regret. He didn't wish her to feel bad, truly, but if that remorse moved her to change her mind, he would consider himself fortunate indeed.

Reality—and cynicism—crowded his buoyant thoughts. If he hoped to persuade her to alter course, he was nearly out of time. Tomorrow, she would be on her way to her sister's. The snow had melted considerably that afternoon, but not quickly enough for her to arrive at Darlington Abbey before the sun went down. She would, however, be able to leave in the morning.

He had a choice—he could lie here in bed and wait for something to happen, or he could get up and pursue the future he wanted. Put like that, there was no choice at all.

Ash threw the covers off and reached for his banyan, drawing it closed over his nightshirt. Before he could think better of his intentions, he went from the bedchamber into the sitting room. In a trice, he opened the door.

And immediately stopped cold.

Standing there in her dressing gown was Bianca, her dark hair hanging in a thick plait over her right shoulder. Her brilliant blue eyes regarded him with surprise. "I didn't even knock," she said.

"I was coming to see you."

"Were you?" She sounded slightly breathless.

He clasped her elbow and drew her inside, quickly closing the door behind her. "Bee—"

She put her finger against his lips. "Shh. I came to see you. I get to speak."

With her touching his mouth, he wasn't sure he would hear a word she said. His cock was already at full attention, his body thrumming with keen desire.

He answered by nodding.

"Good." She lowered her hand, and he resisted the urge to snag her fingertip between his teeth. "I've changed my mind. I will marry you."

Joy burst in his chest, and he just barely caught himself from yelling an expletive. At the worst of his affliction, that had been a rather common occurrence when he was excited. And since this was potentially the most spectacular moment of his life, it made sense he would react in the same manner. He was just glad he'd stopped himself before he drove her away for good.

The reality of what she said settled into him. "Do you mean it?" he whispered. Fear edged out his happiness. What would she do when he inevitably didn't control himself? When something leapt from his mouth, or he suffered a fit of twitching that would draw all manner of attention?

"I do."

"I think I might have changed *my* mind."

Deep lines furrowed her brow as she stepped closer to him until they almost touched. "Why?" She shook her head. "No, never mind. You can't."

"Yes, I can. You shouldn't marry me. I'm...broken." He turned away from her.

But he didn't get very far. She rushed around him, blocking his path. "You are not." She put her hands on her hips and glared at him. "Don't ever say that. You are perfect."

He laughed. The reaction was partly beyond his control,

but it was also fitting. "I am anything but that. I don't want to subject you to this—to me."

She raked him with her gaze from the top of his red hair to the tips of his bare feet. "Too late. You already subjected me to you, and I'm rather fond of you."

His chest constricted as his heart swelled. "You've seen… It can get much worse. Sometimes things come out of my mouth, things I can't control."

Her lids drooped over her eyes. "Is that all?"

"The twitching can be…violent. I've been known to frighten people, though not as much now."

She touched his face, her soft hand caressing his stubbled jaw. "How have you borne it? When I think of what you must have endured at school and in London, I am filled with outrage."

"London was not so terrible, but as you know, school was horrendous. If I hadn't scored such high marks and earned the care of the head of my college, I am confident they would have sent me home."

"You have survived." She stroked his cheek. "As I said before, you are an extraordinary man. I would be proud to call you my husband, if you'll let me."

His fear began to ease, but he was still confounded by her reversal. "Why did you change your mind?"

She cupped his face in her hands and stared earnestly into his eyes. "I didn't change it—you did. You showed me what I would be missing, what I would regret. When you said today that you wouldn't marry until I did, I knew that I couldn't consign you to a life of being alone."

He barked out a laugh. "So you took pity on me?"

She grimaced, letting her hands slide down his neck to his collarbones. "That didn't come out right. I don't want you to be alone. More than that, I don't want you to be with anyone but me."

He wrapped his arms around her and pulled her against his chest. "Good, because I don't want anyone other than you. You're certain you can live with my disease?"

"Since I don't think I can live without you, I would say, definitively, *yes*."

"Bee." He lowered his head and brushed his lips against hers. Before he could say he loved her, she kissed him in wild abandon, her mouth opening beneath his.

Her tongue touching his was the spark that set his entire world aflame. Lifting her, he carried her into his bedroom and laid her gently on the bed.

"This seems familiar," she murmured.

"This night is not going to end the same," he pledged.

She reached for him as he shrugged out of his banyan. "Good."

In a flurry of limbs, they disrobed. Ash paused to take in the sheer beauty of her body. He bent his head to worship at her breast, taking her nipple into his mouth and suckling until she threaded her fingers through his hair and cried out his name.

He slid his hand down her belly until he found the curls cloaking her sex. She was hot and wet for him already. The moment he touched her clitoris, she shuddered.

"Please. Ash."

He stroked her, increasing speed as she moved her hips in concert with his touch.

"Fill me. Now." The plea was dark and desperate. She grasped at his shoulders as she rose off the bed to meet his caresses.

He slipped his finger into her sheath, filling her as she asked. She whimpered, and he felt her muscles clench around him. He pressed on her clitoris, and she flew apart, her legs shaking as her cries grew higher. He covered her mouth with his, taking her passion into himself.

He didn't wait for her to return from beyond. Sitting back, he positioned himself at her sex.

Her eyes opened, and the blue of her irises was so clear, so vivid in her wonder, that he paused. He leaned forward and kissed her softly, then eased slowly into her sheath. She sucked in a breath and held it. Her eyes slitted but didn't close as he continued on. When he was buried completely inside her, he paused, waiting for her to adjust.

"Do you feel all right?" he asked. He hadn't ever done this with a virgin, and he didn't want to cause her undue pain.

She finally exhaled. "I think so. It feels strange."

"My apologies. From what I understand, the next time will be much better for you."

"Lucky for me, I will have many, many next times with you."

Love swelled within him. Then she moved, a slight hitch of her hips.

Her eyes widened briefly. "I didn't mean to do that! I think I twitched." She giggled.

"You mean my disease is catching?" he asked in mock horror.

"Perhaps, and I don't care. It's who you are, and I wouldn't change a thing about you. Maybe one thing, actually. I think I might like you to move."

"With pleasure." He withdrew and thrust gently forward, again and again until her breath began to shorten and her eyes closed in what looked like ecstasy. He clasped her thigh and guided it to his waist. "Wrap your legs around me, love."

She did just that, opening herself to him so that he sank even deeper into her. She moaned softly. "I think this time is quite nice." Her legs tightened around him, and he lost conscious thought.

They moved together in an ever-quickening pace, their bodies finding a magical rhythm. He felt the blood rush to his cock and knew he was close. Reaching between them, he stroked her clitoris again, determined to coax another orgasm from her or at least try his damnedest.

Just before he came, her muscles clamped down around him. He cried out her name and thrust deep, spilling himself into her. Pleasure spiraled through him, tossing him into unparalleled bliss.

Some moments later, when he was fully back within himself, he shifted his weight from her. He kissed her cheek, her jaw, her mouth.

She sighed into him as he left her body. He tried to move away, but she held him close. "I'll be right back," he whispered. "We should clean up."

Her eyes opened, and he saw what he felt: bone-deep satisfaction. And, maybe, love.

"I don't want to go," she said softly.

"Then don't. We are betrothed."

Her lips curled into a smile. "As good as wed. Will I really be the Countess of Buckleigh?"

He nodded, still thinking how strange that sounded.

"I would have been just as happy as Mrs. Rutledge." She yawned.

Her proclamation warmed him as he left the bed to get a cloth. When he returned, she took the cloth and tidied herself then he tucked her beneath the coverlet. By the time he returned to snuggle beside her, she was already asleep.

Smiling to himself, he pressed his lips to her temple and whispered, "I love you."

Though it was melting, snow still dotted the landscape as they traveled to Hartwood. Bianca nestled closer to Ash in his coach, not only for the warmth he offered but because she found she simply liked to be next to him. Her maid and his valet rode behind them in Calder's coach. Ash had decided to bring his valet in case Calder invited him to stay. Bianca would do everything she could to make that happen.

Now that she decided she couldn't live without Ash, she wanted their life together to start immediately. "Do we need to have the banns read?"

They'd discussed the timing of the wedding that morning at breakfast. His mother had been overjoyed at the news of their betrothal. She'd also said she wasn't surprised given their behavior yesterday. Then she'd said the sweetest thing: "It will be so lovely to have a daughter again."

Fighting back tears, Bianca hadn't known what to say. She'd never had a mother before.

"Would you rather I buy a license and we marry tomorrow?" Ash asked.

"Could we?"

He laughed. "Not tomorrow, but how about this Thursday?"

"Hmm." She tapped her finger against her chin, pretending to consider. Dropping her hand to her lap, she grinned at him. "As luck would have it, I am free."

"Brilliant." He kissed her as he'd done a dozen or more times on the journey so far. Too bad they were pulling up the drive to Hartwood, or she might have tried to coax him into more than kissing…

The coach rumbled to a stop, and Bianca exhaled in resignation. "I'll apologize now for my brother's behavior." She was a trifle nervous he would say something about Ash's fighting, but resolved that it didn't matter.

When they were out of the coach, she took Ash's arm and gave him an encouraging smile that was as much for him as it was for her. They walked toward the house, and Truro, the butler, opened the door to greet them.

"Welcome home, Lady Bianca," he said.

"Thank you, Truro. This is the Earl of Buckleigh, my betrothed." Saying that out loud sparked a rush of joy and excitement. She wanted to shout it from the turret in the northwest corner so all of Hartwood and Hartwell could hear.

Truro was quite possibly the most unflappable butler in the history of butlers. He didn't register even an inkling of surprise nor did he demonstrate any other emotion. He inclined his head and said, "May I offer my deepest congratulations?"

She beamed at him and at last saw the barest hint of a smile. "Thank you. Will you ask my brother to meet us in the drawing room?"

"Certainly." He took her cloak and other accessories while a footman took Ash's things.

Bianca relooped her hand through Ash's arm and led him through the entrance hall into the inner hall and then right into the drawing room. "My brother is going to be ecstatic to be rid of me."

"You think so?" Ash asked.

"I know so. He keeps grumbling about me having a Season, and now neither of us has to bother with it."

They stood in the middle of the drawing room, and Ash turned to her. "Will you be coming to London with me?" They hadn't gotten to discussing that in the coach.

Bianca hated the prospect of leaving her home, but she hated the prospect of not being with him even more. "Yes. Anywhere we're together is my home now."

Smiling, he leaned down to kiss her again, but Calder's arrival interrupted them.

"What the devil is going on?" His angry voice carried through the drawing room. It was the most emotion she'd heard from him since he'd come back to Hartwood. "Truro referred to Buckleigh as your betrothed." He glowered at Ash.

"You really need to work on polite greetings," Bianca said with impatience. "It's nice to see you, Calder. Allow me to present my *betrothed*, the Earl of Buckleigh."

"I bloody well know him," Calder growled. "And he is not your betrothed. I haven't given you permission to wed. But that is beside the point right now. How is it that you went to Poppy's and returned home with him?"

Bianca felt Ash stiffen and then a tremor shuddered through him. "I didn't go to Poppy's. I was trapped by—"

His eyes snapped with fury. "You didn't go to Darlington Abbey? You lied to me?"

"I took a detour. I wanted to speak with Ash about where to have the St. Stephen's Day party." She sniffed and notched up her chin. "Which we have resolved, thank you very much.

Or not, actually, since you're the reason we had to come up with an alternate location."

"I don't give a damn about the bloody party." He clenched his jaw as he continued to glare at Ash. "And there will be no wedding."

"There *will*." She clutched Ash's arm and tried to imbue him with her support and love. *Love? Oh yes.*

Ash twitched several times in quick succession, as well as coughed and cleared his throat.

Calder's lip curled. "There will *not*. I won't allow you to marry Buckleigh. He's too volatile. Just look at him. It's as if he can't control himself."

"Shut up!" Ash pulled away from Bianca, and for a brief moment, she worried he might go after Calder. Which Calder wholly deserved. "I have a disease, and sometimes— particularly when I'm provoked—it's beyond my control." His chest rose and fell rapidly as he fought to regain command of himself.

Bianca touched Ash's arm but looked to her brother. "I'll marry whom I choose. I'm of age."

Calder's eyes narrowed with distrust as he regarded Ash. Then he turned his attention to Bianca. "While that is true, your settlement is under my control until you are twenty-five. If I don't approve of your husband, you don't receive the money."

Her jaw dropped as outrage curled through her. "You would keep what Papa intended me to have?" Why had her father even set things up in that fashion? Because he'd trusted Calder not to be a coldhearted monster.

"He gave me the management of it—and you—for a reason. I would be remiss if I didn't do my duty."

Bianca threw her hands up. "You and your duty. Forget family or loyalty or *love*." She glared at him and fully surrendered to her anger and disappointment toward him. "I don't know who you are, but you aren't my brother. I don't need your approval, and I don't want it either. Keep my settlement. It seems money is all that concerns you anymore. I hope it will make you happy."

Calder frowned deeply. "You're making a mistake marrying him."

"I'm not the one who will regret this day, Calder. I'm going to stay with Poppy until the wedding on Thursday. If you can't at least be polite to the man I love, I ask that you stay away—from the wedding, from us, and from St. Stephen's Day."

He exhaled with exasperation. "I've told you I've no interest in—"

She held up her hand. "Don't bother. We're leaving now. You can finally be alone, which I think is what you want." Bianca took Ash's hand and pulled him from the drawing room through the inner hall to the main stairs.

"I need to tell Donnelly to pack my things as quickly as possible," she said, starting up the stairs.

"Did I hear you right?" he asked, tugging on her hand as they reached the landing.

She turned to him, her mind whirring through her ire and frustration. "What?"

"Did I hear you say that I'm the man you love?"

All the negative emotions crowding within her faded away. She glanced down at the floor, suddenly feeling rather shy. "Yes."

He touched her chin, lifting it. "Of all the times for you to become timid." He laughed, then cupped her cheek. "I love you, Bianca, and I'm overjoyed you love me in return."

"Of course I do. I'm just so sorry my brother ruined our happiness." She straightened her shoulders. "No, he *tried* to ruin it. And he failed."

"He did manage to take your settlement from you,

however." The muscles in Ash's neck flexed, and his head cocked to the side as he coughed. "I'm sorry it came to that."

"I'm not. It doesn't matter, so long as we're together."

Ash pulled her against his chest. "I am the luckiest man in the world."

She twined her arms around his neck. "Then I am the luckiest woman." She stood on her toes and kissed him, but kept the contact brief. She wanted to leave Calder's toxic orbit as soon as possible.

Tugging him up the stairs, she said, "Come, let's hurry. I want to visit Shield's End before we go to Darlington Abbey." She paused just before she reached the first floor and looked up at him. "On second thought, maybe I should just go back to Buck Manor." She narrowed her eyes suggestively.

He let out a soft growl. "You are incredibly wicked, my lady."

"I'm not your lady yet," she teased.

He pulled her to the top step and into his arms once more. "Oh yes, you are. You're mine. For all time."

～

*a*s Ash helped Bianca into his coach, he cast a final disappointed look at Hartwood's imposing manor house. He wondered if they would ever return. The rest of Bianca's things would be sent to Buck Manor, so there was really no need for her to come back. Not until her brother apologized.

If he apologized. Right now, Ash couldn't see that happening.

They settled into the coach and started toward town where they would stop at Shield's End to speak with the caretaker about the St. Stephen's Day party. Tucket had taken care of the property since long before Ash had been born, and though he was now nearly deaf and not nearly as spry as he'd once been, they wouldn't replace him. His son was a cabinetmaker in the village, and he checked in regularly.

"We should also stop and speak with Alfie Tucket in town," Ash said, thinking he should be made aware of the party along with his father.

"Oh yes, we must." Bianca shook her head. "I'm afraid I'm not thinking quite clearly."

Ash took her hand and gave her a comforting squeeze. "That's to be expected. Let me do the thinking today."

Her answering smile glowed bright with gratitude. "Thank you. I'm still so sorry about Calder."

"You've nothing to apologize for. He'll come around—or he won't. Either way, we will live our lives." Ash cleared his throat as a ripple ran down his neck.

Ever determined, Bianca pressed her lips together. "Yes, we will." She turned her head to look out the window and almost immediately gasped.

Ash bent his head to try to glimpse whatever she saw. "What's wrong?"

"There's smoke."

Leaning forward, Ash craned his neck and caught sight of a plume of smoke rising into the gray sky. He frowned as he conjured a map of the town in his mind. Unease slithered through him as a shudder twitched his shoulders. It couldn't be...

Bianca turned her head toward him, her eyes wide. "That isn't Shield's End, is it?"

Ash's stomach dropped straight through the bottom of the coach as a wave of fear assaulted him. "I'm afraid it might be."

For the next several minutes, his anxiety grew. Bianca clutched his hand ever tighter as it became evident that the smoke was definitely coming from Shield's End.

The coach stopped at the end of the lane, and Ash didn't wait for the footman to open the door. He bounded out and gaped in anguish at the smoke billowing from his childhood home.

"Ash!"

He turned to help Bianca down. Her face mirrored his pain. "Go," she urged, pushing him toward the house. "I'll send the coach to get help."

"Stay back," he said before letting her go and dashing down the lane toward the house.

The fire hadn't consumed the structure, but Ash could see flames licking from the side of the ground floor. He hoped Tucket wasn't inside. He lived in a small cottage next to the stable. Ash raced there in the hope of finding him. When he wasn't there, ice-cold fear lodged in the center of Ash's chest.

Running toward the back of the house, Ash stopped as he caught sight of a pair of men standing in the yard, staring at the burning structure. When he neared, he saw exactly who they were, and his fear blackened into rage.

"Moreley! Keldon! What the devil are you doing here?" he thundered, his hands curling into fists.

They turned in surprise. "Ruddy!" Moreley said, wiping a hand over his mouth. "Ah—"

"There's been an accident," Keldon said quickly. "Thornaby's inside."

"Where is my caretaker?"

Both men blanched, and Keldon responded, "There's a caretaker?"

Ash swore vehemently as a series of tremors and twitches sailed through his body. "Bianca has taken my coach to get help. Make yourselves useful and fetch water from the well at least, for pity's sake."

Taking off past them, Ash raced into the house and was instantly overcome with a wall of smoke. He coughed and put his hand over his mouth. Untying his cravat, he pulled it from his neck and fashioned a mask, which he tied over his mouth and nose.

Blinking, he tried to assess the situation—where the fire was located and where it was going. At the same time, he called out for the caretaker. "Tucket!" He did this repeatedly as he moved farther into the house. Desperation curdled in Ash's chest.

How was Tucket ever going to hear him?

Satisfied that he'd searched everywhere he could down-stairs away from the flames, he went to the stairs. If he went up, he could become trapped. But if he didn't go up and Tucket was up there… Not to mention Thornaby. Much as Ash despised the man, he wouldn't let him die.

Ash started up the stairs and nearly stumbled as he heard the bleat of a goat. A *goat*?

Yes, a goat, being pulled along by Tucket. Ash dashed up to the top. "Thank God, Tucket," he yelled, hoping the man could hear him. "You go down. I'll get the goat!"

Tucket scowled and pulled on the animal's lead. "He's being stubborn."

Ash picked the goat up and was rewarded with several loud bleats. "Go!" he called to Tucket.

The caretaker grasped the railing and started down. Ash walked down the other side of the staircase and reached the bottom first. He waited to make sure Tucket made it to the ground floor. The goat, however, did not appreciate their proximity to the fire as flames were licking the room adjacent to the hall. The animal tried desperately to jump free and to destroy Ash's hearing as well.

Ash clutched the goat more firmly and hurried from the house straight to the yard. He quickly deposited the animal onto the grass, then removed his mask to take several lungfuls of air. Tucket emerged from the house, staggering, and Ash rushed forward to help him.

"Sit down," Ash urged, guiding him away from the structure. "Catch your breath." He spoke loudly and clearly and was glad when Tucket nodded in response.

Ash looked back at the house as he settled the caretaker onto the grass. Why was Thornaby still inside?

"There's another goat upstairs," Tucket said between deep breaths. "And a fancy gent. He was trying to get the goat down, but she was even more stubborn than this one." Tucket threw a disgruntled scowl at the goat who was now grazing.

Another goat? Why the hell were there goats in his house? Ash swore loudly—he couldn't help himself—and went back to the house. And where the hell were Keldon and Moreley with the water?

Ash's second trip inside was much worse than the first. He affixed the mask over his face, but the smoke was thick and acrid. He ran to the stairs and registered that the fire was edging closer. The other staircase was on the side with the raging fire, so this was their only way out aside from jumping out a window.

Spurred by desperation, Ash darted up the stairs. "Thornaby!" Ash called his name several times and was answered by the distant bleating of a goat. Following the sound, Ash found them in the bedchamber that had belonged to his parents. Smoke filled the room. Thornaby stood near the bed, bent over and coughing.

Ash grabbed the goat and went to Thornaby. "Let's go. I have the animal."

Thornaby lifted his head. His eyes were rimmed with red. He tried to speak between coughs, but Ash had no idea what he was trying to say.

"Just go!" Ash ordered, pulling on the man's bicep.

Thornaby stumbled but began walking toward the door. Ash picked up the goat and hefted her over his shoulder. She protested, kicking her legs and making a horrendous racket.

Ash went as fast as he could. Between the smoke and the weight, he was beginning to flag. At the top of the stairs, he looked back and saw that Thornaby was following, but very slowly.

"Come on, Thornaby! You have to move faster. The fire is spreading!"

Ash dashed quickly down to the ground floor, where the goat renewed her fight, landing a nasty kick against Ash's back. His body jolted, and he nearly dropped the idiot animal.

Threading his way outside, Ash set the goat down as hastily as possible. The animal dashed to join her friend who didn't even look up from his grassy meal.

Keldon and Moreley had returned. They stood there with two buckets of water.

"What are you doing?" Ash demanded. "Throw it on the bloody fire!"

"Where's Thornaby?" Moreley asked, his face a ghostly pallor.

Ash swung around and didn't see the viscount. "Bloody fucking hell." Letting out a string of invectives, he stalked back to the house and went inside before he could think better of it.

The smoke was impossible to see through now. Ash bent over to where the visibility was slightly better and looked for Thornaby while calling his name.

The fire was now in the hall, and there, lying at the base of the stairs, was an unconscious Thornaby. Ash swore again, then bent to pick the man up. Grunting, Ash lifted him over his shoulder as he'd done with the goat. God, he hoped he could make it outside. His head was beginning to swim, and he felt as though he couldn't draw breath.

Staggering, he slowly made his way outside. Heat and smoke enveloped him, and the moment he emerged, he dropped to his knees. Thornaby tumbled from his shoulder.

Ash was vaguely aware of voices and of being dragged over the grass. Someone pulled the mask from his face, and sweet air poured into his lungs. A beautiful face floated above him with a halo surrounding her dark hair.

"Am I dead?" Had that come from his mouth?

That was the last thing he recalled before darkness descended.

"*A*sh, wake up, please," Bianca tried not to panic completely. He was breathing, even if his face was the color of his name.

She was aware of the others gathering around them, just as she vaguely registered the group of villagers that had rushed to help. They worked to try to extinguish the fire, but Bianca paid no attention.

Her entire world was suddenly centered on the man lying in the grass, his eyes closed, his dark red lashes still against his face. Though he wouldn't want to, she whispered, "Twitch, jerk, do *something*. Anything." Her voice broke.

At last, his forehead wrinkled. His eyelids fluttered. Then he stared up at her, his beloved brown eyes softening. "Bee." The word was a soft croak, but it was the sweetest sound she'd ever heard.

"Oh, Ash." Tears tracked down her cheeks as she bent over and kissed him—his brow, his cheek, his mouth. Joy rushed through her and washed away the fear.

After a long moment, she sat back. Someone handed her a

damp cloth, which she used to wipe the grime away from Ash's face.

"Why were there goats in my house?" he asked. He moved his gaze from her and squinted up at the people surrounding them.

"I'd like to know what Thornaby and his friends are doing here," Bianca said, turning her head to stare at Moreley and Keldon, who stood near Ash's feet.

"We should go see about him," Moreley said, his face turning the color of a persimmon. He spun about and marched off. Keldon hesitated but eventually followed him.

"Where's Thornaby?" Ash asked.

Bianca pointed a few feet away. "Just there. It appears he's still unconscious."

Ash blinked up at her. "Tucket?"

"He's here," Bianca said, touching Tucket's leg.

The caretaker had stood beside her and now knelt down. "My lord, you're the hero of the day."

Ash didn't react to what he said, instead asking, "What happened?"

"I'm not sure how the fire started," Tucket said. "I smelled smoke and saw that the house was burning. When I went closer to investigate, one of those gentlemen," he jabbed his thumb toward Thornaby, Moreley, and Keldon, "ran from the house as if he was on fire." Tucket scoffed. "He wasn't."

"Tell me about the goats," Ash rasped.

"The gent that ran out—the bald one, I know that because his hat fell off—said there were goats in the house and that they started the fire. He said his friends were inside trying to coax them out." Tucket snorted and wiped his hand under his nose. "They sounded like idiots, so I ran in to rescue the animals myself. But damn me if those aren't the most stubborn goats." He threw the pair of animals a glare before adding with regret, "And I'm not as young as I used to be."

"You did what you could," Ash said. "How did these goats start the fire?"

"One of them knocked over a lantern."

Bianca looked toward the trio of bullies and saw that Thornaby was now sitting up.

"We didn't notice until the room was already ablaze—we were busy with the other goat." Thornaby grimaced.

Ash struggled to sit up, and Bianca helped him. "Why the hell were there goats in my house?" he repeated.

Thornaby started to answer. "It was—"

Keldon cut him off. "Thorn!"

Shooting an angry look at Keldon, Thornaby continued. "It was a prank. Like the one we pulled at Oxford."

Bianca felt Ash tense and the pair of tremors that shook his body and made him cock his head to and fro. She put her arm around his shoulders and tried to support him.

"When you let a goat into my room," Ash said flatly, "it made a mess."

Thornaby's face was red, but he didn't falter as he spoke loudly and clearly. "That was our intent. We heard you were going to host the St. Stephen's party here."

"Why would you want to ruin that?" Bianca asked as anger flooded her.

"It wasn't so much to ruin it as to cause trouble for Rud—Buckleigh," Thornaby said, his head dipping in what Bianca hoped was shame.

Ash cleared his throat. "How did you hear about the party?"

"Your mother sent me a note asking if I would help."

Bianca and Ash exchanged a look. Why had she sent a letter after they'd said no? Was there a chance she'd sent it before asking them?

"She shouldn't have," Ash said coldly. "We don't want your help."

"I don't blame you." Thornaby sounded as if he felt remorse. "I wouldn't want my help either. We never meant to cause a fire."

"It's not our fault!" Moreley cried.

Thornaby glared at him. "It is—we brought the bloody goats. Haven't you acted cowardly enough today? Own up to what we've done." Thornaby looked to Keldon next. "You too. I can't believe you both abandoned me." He gestured toward Tucket. "That old man has more courage than both of you put together."

"You owe Ash an apology," Bianca demanded.

"They owe him restitution," Tucket said. "The house will have to be rebuilt."

It was true. Though the villagers were working on passing water from the well to the house, they couldn't keep up with the flames.

Thornaby struggled to stand, but Keldon and Moreley helped him. He weaved his way over to Ash, who also got up with Bianca's and Tucket's assistance.

"Words cannot convey how sorry I am about your house," Thornaby said. "How sorry all of us are." He indicated the men flanking him.

"I want to hear them say it," Bianca pressed. "And you'll apologize for everything. The shooting competition and everything you ever did or even thought about doing at Oxford. You all make me sick."

None of them could look at her. To a man, they dropped their gazes to the ground.

After a moment, Thornaby lifted his toward Ash. "We've treated you awfully—from Oxford until today. But no more. I owe you my life."

"Yes, you do," Bianca spat, thinking he didn't deserve to be rescued by Ash.

Ash touched her arm, and she looked up at him to see that

he did not appear as furious as she was, at least not anymore.

"I'm sorry too," Keldon said. "Truly. We just meant to cause trouble, nothing serious. When you left the house party the other day, several of the guests were upset. They believed we'd somehow driven you to go."

"You did." Bianca growled low in her throat.

Thornaby nodded. "I was angry that people were siding with Buckleigh."

"There are no sides," Ash said quietly. "That's all in your imagination."

"Yes." Thornaby sounded utterly defeated, and Bianca wanted to dance with glee.

"Moreley?" Bianca prompted. "I believe it's your turn."

"I, ah, I'm sorry. For everything. We won't bother you again."

"Except for rebuilding his house and supporting his St. Stephen's Day party," Thornaby said, his eyes gleaming with determination.

Bianca fixed each of them with a stony glower. "Only we have no place to hold it now."

"You can use Thornhill," Thornaby readily suggested.

"I'd rather not," Bianca said coolly.

Ash shook his head and coughed. "It's too far. I would host it at Buck Manor, but that's also too far."

"It's a pity your brother won't host it," Keldon said.

Yes, it was. Bianca's anger at him sprouted anew. "That is not an option."

"Is Thornhill really too far?" Thornaby asked. "It's only five miles. We can transport people, and whoever needs to stay overnight can do so. We'll make it work. Just tell me what we need to do."

"You'll let my wife and my mother manage everything, and I mean *everything*. You will take their orders, and you won't complain or rebel."

Thornaby nodded, then blinked, cocking his head to the side. "Your wife?"

Ash put his arm around Bianca's waist, and she pressed into his side, reveling in his warmth and basking in the joy of being alive—with him. "Bianca. We will be wed next week. Forgive us for not inviting you to the breakfast." He said the last with more than a hint of sarcasm.

"I wish you both a hearty—and heartfelt—congratulations." Thornaby tried to smile but gave up. "I wouldn't expect to be invited."

"It's settled, then." Ash exhaled, and his shoulder twitched against Bianca.

"Come, let's get you to the coach. I want to take you home so you can rest."

"I won't leave the house. Not until the fire's out." He looked at the burning structure, and she felt his body go rigid. "My mother is going to be devastated."

Bianca flicked a glance toward the trio of miscreants. They hung their heads in shame.

Ash kissed her temple. "I'm fine now, my love. Let me help with the effort to put out the flames."

"I'll help too," she said.

"So will we." Keldon started toward the line passing water. Moreley and Thornaby joined him.

Bianca encircled Ash's waist and squeezed him tight. "I'm just glad you're safe. When I think of what could have happened…"

"Shh, my love." He brushed his lips against her cheek. "I am here with you, where I plan to stay for a very, very long time."

She looked up at him with love and admiration. "Forever, I hope."

His lips curled into a happy smile. "Forever."

CHAPTER 11

The day of Bianca and Ash's wedding dawned cold and gray. Ash would have loved snow, but he also wanted to be able to get from Buck Manor to the Hartwell Church and back to Buck Manor for the wedding breakfast without incident.

And so it was with great delight that he and Bianca emerged from the coach at Buck Manor only to have a dusting of snowflakes settle upon them.

Laughing, Bianca looked up to the sky. "What a perfect gift for our wedding day."

Ash smiled down at her. "I arranged it special."

She slid him a glance of sheer disbelief, then laughed again. "I shouldn't put it past you, actually. You have been an absolute hero for everyone, so why not for me?"

He curled his arms around her waist and brought her against him so he could kiss her. The contact was brief, but incredibly heady. "I only care about being a hero for you."

"They're here!" the Marchioness of Darlington called from the doorway. She'd left the church with her husband and Ash's mother as soon as the ceremony had finished so they could be here to oversee the wedding breakfast preparations.

Ash and Bianca had visited with the vicar for a while, primarily to discuss plans for rebuilding his house. The entire village was eager to see his property made whole again.

And no one was more eager than Thornaby.

Ash guided his wife into his house—no, *their* house— where a line of guests was waiting in the hall, Thornaby among them. Moreley and Keldon were also there. Bianca hadn't wanted to include any of them, but Ash had persuaded her that it was time to truly put the past behind him. He only hoped they were as committed to that as they professed to be.

He and Bianca spent the next half hour greeting people, followed by a joyous wedding breakfast in the dining room. Afterward, they withdrew to the drawing room, where they drank champagne. Ash watched with pride and love as his countess laughed and spoke with everyone in attendance. Perhaps she didn't laugh with Thornaby and the others, but she was polite and they were effusive in their kindness and praise.

"You're a lucky man, Buckleigh." Thornaby came up behind him, prompting Ash to turn.

"Thank you. I am." While Ash appreciated the man's reversal, he was also incredibly puzzled by it. "I hope you'll forgive me for asking, but after so many years of you torturing me, I find myself wondering what led you to make such a change in your behavior."

"I would forgive you anything," Thornaby said earnestly. "And I mean that. You saved my life. There is something rather clarifying about nearly dying. My life came into a focus I'd never seen before." He glanced at the floor, then sipped his champagne. When he looked at Ash again, there was a weight in his gaze Ash had never seen before.

"I've always felt inadequate," Thornaby admitted. "You didn't know this, but I struggled at Oxford. Reading was very difficult for me. Words and letters—and numbers, even—would jumble in my vision."

"I didn't know that. You always behaved as if you knew and excelled at everything." Ash didn't mask the wryness in his tone.

A small smile flitted across Thornaby's mouth. "It's terrible to say, but I understood your...challenges."

As if provoked by Thornaby's mention of his disease, a shudder rippled across Ash's shoulders, and he tipped his head to the side. "Why is that terrible?"

"Because I was horrible to you because of them." Thornaby grimaced. "It made me feel better about my weaknesses to exploit yours. If that isn't abhorrent, I don't know what is. That you could forgive me for how I treated you, especially for causing your house to burn—"

Ash saw the tears in Thornaby's eyes despite the man quickly blinking them away. "I do forgive you. Because what good would it do to continue to hold a grudge? That certainly doesn't benefit me. As you said, I'm a lucky man, and I intend to be grateful."

"What a beautiful sentiment," Thornaby said in soft wonder.

Ash considered Thornaby's revelation. "I do understand your coping behavior. I chose a different path—I used to hit people."

Thornaby's eyes widened. "You never hit me."

"I was too small." Ash chuckled. "You—or more likely Moreley—would have pounded me into the dirt. Actually, Moreley did do that once."

"So he told me." Thornaby dipped his chin in apology. "I think I missed that. Whom did you hit?"

"Many people. Men, I should clarify. I was a pugilist in London."

Thornaby gasped in surprise. "Were you? How extraordinary. And that helped your affliction?"

Ash nodded. "Boxing gave me strength, obviously, but also courage to face others as well as myself and my limitations. It also showed me that I wasn't as limited as I'd thought." He grinned. "I was quite good at hitting people."

"I think I'd like to see that." Thornaby cocked his head to the side. "Could you teach me?"

"I don't see why not." Ash marveled at how far they'd come in such a short time.

"Thank you." Thornaby lightly clasped his bicep. "I'm grateful for your forgiveness and, dare I say, friendship."

Ash waggled his brows at him. "Go ahead and dare. Now, if you'll excuse me, I need to go and speak with my brother-in-law."

Thornaby inclined his head with a smile and let go of Ash's arm. Ash lifted his glass in a silent toast, then strode toward the Marquess of Darlington, who stood near the windows, his focus trained on the champagne in his hand.

"Darlington," Ash said. "You look as though you're in need of cheer."

The marquess shook his head and blinked. "'Tis nearly the season for that, I suppose. Sorry, I was ruminating."

"May I ask about what?"

"Mostly about Hartwell House and how badly it's in need of repair." Darlington grimaced. "Never mind. After the fire, you are up to your eyeballs in repairs."

"Reconstruction, you mean," Ash said wryly. "Bianca and I are looking forward to St. Nicholas Day tomorrow at Hartwell House."

"Yes, it should be quite...cheerful."

Ash laughed softly. "Indeed. As you said, it is the season for it. Come, let us join our wives." A thrill danced up Ash's spine. He loved referring to Bianca as his wife.

When they arrived, the third woman had left so that it was just Bianca and her sister. They were animatedly discussing their brother.

"I still can't believe he refused to give you your settlement," the marchioness said crossly. "I plan to speak with him as soon as possible. It's bad enough he didn't come today."

"To be fair, I didn't invite him," Bianca said.

"I did." Ash had reasoned that as long as he'd changed his mind and decided to include the men who'd bullied him and burned his house to the ground, he ought to also invite Bianca's brother, even if he'd behaved in an utterly wretched manner.

"You did?" A host of emotions flitted across Bianca's face. Her features finally settled on irritation. Ash just wasn't sure where it was directed. He coughed gently and rolled his shoulder. "And he didn't come," she said in flat disappointment.

At the duke, then.

Ash exhaled. As long as he was admitting what he'd done, he'd be completely honest about what had happened next. She deserved the truth, and he planned to never keep secrets from her. "I wish I could say he at least responded, but he did not."

Bianca scowled, and her sister let out a surprising description of their brother, complete with a curse. Gasping in surprise, Bianca swung her gaze to the marchioness. They and the marquess promptly dissolved into laughter.

His mother joined them. "You look as though you're having a jolly time. Everyone is, I think. I should know, as

I've spoken to everyone about St. Stephen's Day. Support for the event is overwhelming. Even from the viscount." She cast a look toward Thornaby, and Ash knew her well enough to recognize a thread of anger and distrust in her gaze.

The emotions stuck out to him because she rarely displayed them. However, Thornaby was a special case. When she'd learned Thornaby and the others were behind the house burning down, she'd been inconsolable. She revealed that she'd written to him and Keldon, sending a rider with the missives before speaking to Ash and Bianca. Then when they'd said no to requesting help, she hadn't wanted to admit she'd already done so. While Ash was ready to forgive, she hadn't yet reached that point. But Ash knew she would. She was far too kindhearted not to.

"Let us drink to the earl and his countess," Thornaby called out, raising his glass. "Buckleigh is a true hero—in every way. Without him, we would not be celebrating St. Stephen's Day this year as we ought."

Keldon lifted his glass. "Hear, hear!"

Ash felt the need to correct them. "Actually, if not for my lovely wife, there would be no St. Stephen's Day celebration this year. It is her passion and her drive that will continue this tradition." He gazed at Bianca with all the love overflowing his heart.

She smiled in return, her eyes promising a future filled with that same passion and drive. She lifted her glass in appreciation, and the room erupted in a chorus of "Hear, hear!" and "Congratulations!" and "To the earl and countess!"

Pride and joy filled Ash's chest as he drew Bianca against his side. As he looked around the room, he counted his blessings. "I wish the same happiness for all of you."

∾

*S*t. Nicholas Day was the official start to the Christmas season. Everyone celebrated in different ways, but the people of Hartwell had long made the day special by exchanging gifts among immediate family members. Bianca and Ash, along with her sister and her husband, spent the morning distributing gifts to the women and children who were not just in need of things but of good cheer. Bianca's heart swelled as she watched a young boy play excitedly with a half-dozen toy soldiers.

"This was a wonderful idea," Ash said softly as he came up beside her. "May I suggest we do it every year?"

She beamed up at him, glad that he shared her desire to help those in need. "Oh, I insist."

He chuckled. "Of course you do. I can imagine what you might say to my next suggestion."

"Please allow me to speak first," she said. "And I hope you don't think me too forward. I realize Shield's End was your house, but it was sitting empty, and Hartwell House is in horrible disrepair." A light sparked in his eyes, and she watched as his lips curled into a warm smile. "Is my proposal the same as yours?"

He lightly clasped her waist. "If you were going to suggest we rebuild Shield's End as the new Institution for Impoverished Women, then yes. We are of the same mind. Again."

She laughed gaily. "I shouldn't have been surprised. We seem to want precisely the same things."

"Which is why we were destined to be."

She sighed, moving closer to him as he moved his hand around to her lower back. "Yes."

"I look forward to having the plans drawn up when we go to London next month."

"You're going to send inquiries before that?"

He nodded. "Next week. I know you're anxious to get started."

She glanced toward the people who would benefit from the new institution. "Now more than ever. And there should be a dedicated school with a teacher and a larger farm that will feed the occupants." She tipped her face up to meet his eyes. "Perhaps we could even build individual cottages for families."

"I couldn't agree more. Your heart is as beautiful as I remember." He brushed his lips across her brow. "Keldon has offered to oversee the building while I and Thornaby are in London for Parliament."

She riveted her gaze back to him, still in awe that he'd forgiven his tormentors so easily. Well, perhaps not easily. They'd discussed it at length, and she understood his reasons —they had everything to do with him and his sense of peace, not absolving the others' guilt. "You are the best of men."

"You make me want to be." He grimaced slightly. "I do wonder if you'll still think that when I tell you that I don't have a gift for you today. It's coming. I'm afraid that between the wedding and preparing for today, we've been quite busy."

Bianca laughed with relief. "Good, because I don't have your gift yet either." She lowered her voice. "But let me just say that I am confident we can think of plenty to give each other later. In our bedchamber."

He drew her into a shadowy corner and kissed her until they were both breathless. He stroked his finger along her cheek. "My love, you are the only gift I'll ever need."

Keep reading for Poppy's story in The Gift of the Marquess! Then find out what happens with the St. Stephen's Day party and why Calder is such a Scrooge in Joy to the Duke!

AUTHOR'S NOTE

One day, I thought it would be fun to write a Christmas trilogy and base the stories on classic holiday tales. What is more classic to a Gen X child like me than the stop motion TV special, Rudolph the Red-Nosed Reindeer? I had a lot of fun crafting a story that captured the moral of Rudolph and adding some romance. (Not that Rudolph and Clarice didn't have their thing!) You met Cornelius the butler who borrowed Yukon Cornelius's name and Harris the valet who I didn't name Hermie, but who wasn't right for his old job just like Hermie wasn't meant to be an elf. I loved incorporating them.

The Institution for Impoverished Women is something entirely of my own creation. It's based on workhouses of the time, but I didn't want a "real" workhouse which separated men and women (and children—they didn't see their parents often) and was typically more like a prison.

Thank you Catherine Kenner for the GORGEOUS rendition of The Red Hot Earl, sung to the tune of Rudolph the Red Nosed Reindeer (lyrics by me - spoiler: they are not as fabulous as her voice). Listen to it here. Also thank you to Julie Kenner for, well, far too many things to list.

I hope you enjoyed this inspired story! And Merry Christmas. :)

THE GIFT OF THE MARQUESS

THE GIFT OF THE MARQUESS

The Marchioness of Darlington wants nothing more than a houseful of children, but after three years of marriage Poppy has given up hope. When she learns her husband doesn't share her sense of loss, Poppy tries to soothe her aching heart by helping at a local institution for single women and mothers. But the arrival of an expectant mother only reignites her longing, driving the wedge between her and Gabriel deeper.

After losing his mother and sister in childbirth, Gabriel, the Marquess of Darlington, is secretly glad his wife hasn't been able to conceive. He can't bear the thought of losing her, not even to achieve their dream of having a family. Desperate to prove his love, Gabriel makes a shocking proposition. It's a risk, but if he can overcome Poppy's fears and hesitation, he can give her what she wants most for Christmas.

For Banana Cat
for giving all the snuggles

CHAPTER 1

County Durham, England
November 1811

A child's squeal rent the air, making Gabriel Kirkwood, Marquess of Darlington, pause in his hammering. Two small boys ran toward the open doorway where Gabriel was repairing the broken hinge. They stopped short, the taller boy ramming into the shorter one, whom he was chasing.

"Beggin' your pardon, my lord," the younger boy, named Matthew, said, looking up at Gabriel with wide blue eyes.

"Careful there," Gabriel said with a smile as he glanced down the corridor over their heads. "Don't let Mrs. Armstrong catch you running inside." The overseer of the Institution for Impoverished Women, which everyone referred to as Hartwell House, expected order and discipline.

Matthew looked over his shoulder while his older brother

John shook his head. "We're careful, my lord. She's busy," he added, as if to prove their diligence.

"Good." Gabriel went back to his work and finished hammering the new hinge into place.

"What're you doin'?" Matthew came up beside him, his curious gaze riveted on Gabriel's repair.

"I replaced the hinge so this door will close properly." Gabriel stood back. Hartwell House had been converted into the institution some fifteen years ago when the owner and his wife, the Armstrongs, had started taking in impoverished women, many with small children and no way to feed them. The only alternative for most of them was a workhouse, and that was no place to raise children, not if you wanted to spend time with them. Hartwell House allowed mothers and children to stay together, to build a life—together. "Go on, give it a try and see if I did a good job."

The boy shot him a dubious glance, and Gabriel nodded in encouragement. The lad swung the door closed, slamming it in his brother's face.

Giggling, Matthew put his hand over his mouth.

Gabriel kept himself from laughing. "Looks like it works fine."

The door pushed open to reveal the glaring eyes of John. "You didn't have to shut it in my face."

"I didn't mean to." Matthew looked up at Gabriel. "I'm glad you fixed it. It was too loud in here the other night." He made a face, then walked out of the room, which was the women-only dormitory.

Gabriel looked to John. "Why was it too loud?"

"Cryin', because someone died." John made the statement without a shred of sadness, which pulled at Gabriel's heart. What sort of tragedy had this boy already endured to be so unmoved by death?

Or, perhaps more accurately, the perspective of mortality

had not yet visited the child. It wasn't until Gabriel was ten and he lost his mother that the unmanageable grief of death had forever altered his view. Life was precious and could change—or be gone—in a moment.

"I'm sorry to hear that," Gabriel said softly.

"There you are." Mrs. Armstrong's lilting voice carried down the corridor. "You boys are late for your midday meal. Get on with you, then." She arrived at the dormitory and gave them a warm but firm stare.

They didn't spare a parting glance for Gabriel, telling him just who held the higher rank here at Hartwell House—and it wasn't a marquess. Suppressing a smile, Gabriel turned to the formidable woman who ran the institution. Tall, with brown hair that was beginning to gray at the temples and a thin mouth that might have been cruel if she didn't laugh so much, Mrs. Armstrong was the heart of this place, especially since her husband had passed away the year before.

"I hope they weren't bothering you," she said, eyeing the door.

"Not at all. They were helping, in fact. It occurs to me that I could teach them some useful skills. If you think they're old enough."

"I do, and that would be wonderful." She beamed at him. "You and the marchioness are so lovely with all that you do for us here. I've been meaning to ask—and I hope you don't think me too forward—if her ladyship is all right. We haven't seen her in nearly a fortnight."

"Has it been that long?" Gabriel realized she hadn't come with him the last few times but hadn't counted the days. He read the concern in Mrs. Armstrong's eyes and sought to put her at ease. "Poppy is fine, thank you. Just busy with things at home." Gabriel didn't know if that was true. He'd find out—Mrs. Armstrong's worry was now his.

"I'm glad to hear it," she said. "The children miss her."

A sharp pang sliced briefly through Gabriel's chest. Of course they did. Poppy spent most of her time here with the children, reading to them, playing with them, teaching them while their mothers sewed or worked in the garden. Hartwell House provided opportunities for the residents to work and earn money in the hope that they would eventually be able to leave and have their own household. Since he and Poppy didn't have children of their own, she enjoyed spending time with the youngest residents. She would have been a wonderful mother, but after nearly three years of marriage and no pregnancy, it seemed that was not to be.

Gabriel shook the thought from his head. "I heard someone died." He hoped the boy was mistaken, but the dark shadow that fell across Mrs. Armstrong's eyes told him he wasn't.

"So sad, but not surprising, unfortunately. The girl was so undernourished. Not really a girl, I suppose." Mrs. Armstrong shook her head, then frowned. "No, she *was* a girl who'd been about to become a mother."

Gabriel's breath stuck in his lungs as a tremor of dread snaked through him. *Oh no…*

He recalled the young woman—the girl—who'd arrived several weeks ago. She'd been nearly starving, and Mrs. Armstrong had done all she could to help her. "The babe?" Gabriel asked.

"Stillborn. The mother fell into an exhausted sleep and never woke up." She glanced toward one of the beds. "Already filled her space, though."

It was hard to think of that as a bright spot, but what else could the woman do? This was her life—assisting those she could and letting go those she couldn't.

Gabriel couldn't help but think of his wife, of his beloved Poppy, and their inability to have children. And how bloody *grateful* he was for that. For knowing he'd never lose her the way that poor girl had died. Or the way his mother had died. Or his older sister. Or Poppy's mother. All around him, women died in childbirth, and he had every expectation the same would happen to Poppy.

He couldn't bear the thought of it.

"Mrs. Armstrong?" A young woman named Judith who had worked for Mrs. Armstrong as long as Gabriel had been coming here stuck her head into the dormitory. "There's a new arrival."

"It never ends," Mrs. Armstrong said with a shake of her head. She started to turn, but hesitated. "I hope you don't think me impertinent, but if her ladyship is having trouble because of her condition, I'd be happy to talk with her about it."

Gabriel blinked at her, not certain what she meant. "Condition?"

"That she doesn't have children of her own." Mrs. Armstrong's voice was soft, her forehead creased with empathy. "You've been married, what, three years now?"

"Almost."

"That's right around the time I realized Mr. Armstrong and I weren't going to be blessed with children. The following year, we took in our first young woman. Helping her and her young son gave us joy and…purpose."

A small knot formed at the base of Gabriel's throat. He swallowed to keep it from rising. "I believe that's how Poppy feels about coming here—it brings her joy." And probably purpose. He wasn't sure.

Mrs. Armstrong's mouth bloomed into a caring smile. "That's good to hear. I hope she'll come back when she's ready. Now, if you'll excuse me."

"Of course," Gabriel murmured.

Alone once more, Gabriel cleaned up his tools and left the dormitory. He'd done all he could today, but there were always things to be done. The building was in sore need of rehabilitation. The roof might not even last the winter.

"You have to let me stay!" A woman's voice carried from the back corner where Mrs. Armstrong's office was located.

"I'm afraid we don't have accommodation for someone in your condition," Mrs. Armstrong said. "You're too ill. I'm so sorry. There is a workhouse—"

"No!"

The sound of coughing filled the air followed by a thump, as if someone had fallen.

"Good heavens!" Mrs. Armstrong declared, prompting Gabriel to stride toward the noise. Arriving at the office, he saw a crumpled form on the floor. Mrs. Armstrong and Judith knelt beside a woman whose coughs faded into a groan.

"Why didn't you say you were with child?" Mrs. Armstrong asked, aghast.

The woman on the floor answered with a cough.

"Can I offer assistance?" Gabriel asked.

Mrs. Armstrong looked up, relief flashing in her eyes. "Yes, thank you. Can you help us lift her to a chair?"

Gabriel moved farther into the office and looked down at the pale, unkempt woman. Her blonde hair was falling from its pins, and she wore a ratty cloak that opened to expose her clothing, which was dirty and torn. It also didn't fit well, stretching taut over her round belly.

He squatted down and gently lifted her to a sitting position between Mrs. Armstrong and the other woman.

"Let's get you to the chair," Mrs. Armstrong said.

"Why?" The woman tried to shrug her helpers away. "I need to find another place to stay."

Mrs. Armstrong looked at her with kind determination. "We'll make room. I'll give you my bed. You're not well, and you need to take care of yourself for the sake of the babe."

"I don't even want the brat," the woman said, scowling.

Mrs. Armstrong gave her a serene smile. "You might think that right now, but once you meet the babe, you'll change your mind."

She shook her head vehemently. Then promptly dissolved into a coughing fit. "I'll find someplace else," she rasped between coughs.

Mrs. Armstrong frowned. "You should stay here."

Controlling her cough, the woman looked at Gabriel. "Help me up, please?"

Gabriel put his arm around her and lifted her to stand. "I have an empty cottage on my estate. Would you like to stay there until you're well?"

Rising, Mrs. Armstrong looked at him in surprise. "She can't be alone. She needs care."

"You can't give up your bed, Mrs. Armstrong," Gabriel said. "I have an empty cottage."

"I'll go to care for her," Judith offered.

Mrs. Armstrong took a deep breath. "That's very kind of you, Judith. I shall miss you here, but of course you must go. If the woman is set on leaving, and if she'll have you." She sent an expectant look toward the pregnant woman.

"I am and I will." She sniffed loudly, a horrible sound that nearly made Gabriel cringe. "Where is this cottage?"

"I can take you there now," Gabriel said, glad he'd brought his cart today instead of riding his horse. It was difficult to deliver several sacks of flour on horseback.

"All right." The woman began coughing again, bending at the waist as she fought to stop.

"You'll need medicine," Mrs. Armstrong said to Judith. "And clothing for her that will fit properly."

Judith nodded. "I'll go see what I can find." She turned to leave.

"I'll pack a basket." Mrs. Armstrong pivoted toward Gabriel. "You'll have food and other necessities for them?"

"Of course." The cottage he had in mind had been vacant since last spring, but a neighbor had kept it clean and in good repair until a new tenant came along. He'd make sure to stock food and linens for them. Plus, he'd ask his steward to have the same neighbor look in on them. Not that Gabriel wouldn't also check on them regularly. He was keenly interested in the woman and the fact that she didn't want her baby.

A dream rooted in his mind… A dream he dared not hope for, and yet couldn't keep from wanting.

Mrs. Armstrong guided the woman to a chair. "What's your name, love?"

"Dinah Kitson."

"Come, Dinah, sit until it's time to go." Mrs. Armstrong made sure she was comfortable.

Dinah lifted her rheumy eyes to Gabriel. "Why are you helping me?"

"Because you're in need of help."

"What about the babe?" Dinah rested her hand on her belly.

"We'll sort that out," Gabriel said, cautioning himself to go slow. The woman was sick, and there was no telling what would happen—whether the babe would even survive. And Dinah could very well change her mind after it was born. She'd see its face and count its fingers and toes, and she'd fall hopelessly in love.

Yes, he had a dream, but he didn't really expect it to come true.

CHAPTER 2

*P*oppy Kirkwood, Marchioness of Darlington, sat before the fire in the sitting room adjacent to the bedchamber she shared with her husband. Her hand moved with quick precision, filling in the pattern of greenery on her needlepoint.

The piece was large and would look lovely hanging in the drawing room during Christmastime. Provided she finished it in time.

Gabriel came in after staying in the dining room to share port with his steward, who'd taken dinner with them. Charlie's wife was at home with their young children. The hollow ache that seemed to always reside in Poppy's chest sharpened briefly before she shrugged the sensation away.

"What are you working on?" Gabriel asked as he moved to sit beside her on the settee.

She spread it out across her lap as best she could so he could see it. "It's a wall hanging for the drawing room."

Gabriel angled himself toward her and surveyed the needlepoint. "Is that mistletoe?"

A smile teased her lips. "It is."

He pressed a quick kiss to her mouth. "I don't think it matters that it isn't real."

"Or hanging over us, apparently," she said wryly.

Grinning, he returned his attention to the hanging. "It's lovely. You've quite a hand for embroidery. Didn't you make a tablecloth for Hartwell House recently?"

Poppy stiffened. "A couple of months ago, yes."

"I was there today, as you know," he said, lifting his gaze to hers. "Mrs. Armstrong asked if you were all right. She's missed seeing you there."

Poppy carefully folded the needlework and set it aside as unease curled through her. "I've been busy."

"That's what I told Mrs. Armstrong. However, when I try to think of what you've been busy with, I'm afraid I don't know what could be keeping you from Hartwell House."

"You are occupied with your own endeavors." Indeed, it seemed he was more consumed than ever with estate matters —and with helping at Hartwell House. He enjoyed building and fixing things. When he wasn't in his workshop here, he was at the institution repairing something or other.

"I miss going there together," he said, reaching for her hands, which she'd folded in her lap after moving the needlework. "Perhaps you'd like to go with me tomorrow or the next day?" His lips curved into a soft smile that was so at odds with the square set of his chin and the chiseled line of his jaw and cheekbones. It was that smile that had claimed her attention three years ago at a local assembly. But his humor and concern for others had won her heart.

Straightening her spine, she answered, "I'm afraid I won't be able to."

His smile dipped, turning to a slight frown. "Is there something amiss? Some reason you don't want to visit Hartwell House anymore?"

The concern in his eyes unraveled her closely held

composure. She stood from the settee, nervous energy spiraling through her. "No." She stepped toward the hearth, her suddenly cold body seeking the heat of the fire.

He rose behind her—she could feel his presence as he moved close. "I wondered if perhaps…if it bothered you to spend time with the children there?"

She turned toward him, surprised by the accuracy of his query. "Is that what you think?"

He lifted a shoulder. "Mrs. Armstrong mentioned it. She's happy to speak with you—to lend support—if you wish."

"You discussed our problems with her?" Poppy liked Mrs. Armstrong very much, but this wasn't something one talked about with those outside the family. In Poppy's case, it wasn't something she talked about ever.

"She brought it up. She's concerned about you." His brow creased. "As am I."

Emotion bubbled inside her—sadness and frustration—but she refused to surrender to despair. She'd cried too many tears. "I don't want your pity. I don't want anyone's pity, not even my own. I am trying to find a way to accept that this is what my life will be, and I can't do that with children running about. You seem to have no problem being there." She tried to keep the irritation from her tone, but feared she failed. "How have you accepted our fate?"

He blinked, then glanced toward the fire. When his gaze met hers once more, she saw something odd, something she'd never seen before. "I will admit it wasn't as difficult for me as it seems to be for you."

Poppy's jaw nearly dropped to the floor. She felt as if all the air in her lungs had been squeezed out and that it might never return.

He continued, "While I would have liked to be a father, I can't say I'm sorry you won't suffer the risks of pregnancy and childbirth."

Now she knew what was in his eyes—relief. He was glad they hadn't conceived. He hadn't accepted anything. He'd welcomed their lot while she wallowed in sadness and disappointment.

"You're *happy*?" the question came out small and so soft, she wondered if he even heard her, because it took him a moment to respond.

"Not happy, no. But it's not the end of the world to me."

The end of the world… "That's a bit hyperbolic." She tried to make sense of what he was saying. He'd never revealed this to her before, and she almost felt…betrayed. "You don't understand how I am affected."

"Of course I do," he said, the furrows in his brow deepening while his eyes narrowed. "But perhaps you don't comprehend how *I* feel."

"Oh, I think I do." He had the blessing of feeling *relieved* while she suffered. And here she thought he'd suffered too.

He edged toward her, his height making him tower above her. "Do you? Do you know the anguish I feel when I hear of another soul lost to childbirth? Just today, Mrs. Armstrong told me of a girl—a *girl*—who died along with her stillborn babe."

She insulated herself to the pain in his tone. It was nothing when compared with her torment. "Yes, it's tragic, but it's also life."

"And death. I don't want to lose you the way you lost your mother, the way I lost my mother and sister."

She notched her chin up, bothered that he would mention *her* mother, whom she'd lost at the age of two when her mother had given birth to Poppy's younger sister and whom she didn't even remember. Her memories were all things she'd been told by their father and by their older brother, Calder. She was also sensitive to how deeply Gabriel grieved the loss of his own mother when he was young. "You can't go through life fearing death. It awaits us all."

Anger flashed in his eyes. "I know that. But not yet. Not *now*."

She wanted him to understand her sorrow. "I'd risk it. Don't you want to leave something of us behind? If you fear death, think of how children, how a family makes us immortal."

He stared at her, his jaw working as his teeth clenched and unclenched. "I've lost too many people, and losing you would be a living death."

The ache inside her leapt, hungry for a kindred soul. "You've described precisely how I feel. Empty. Cold. Alone."

His pulse beat in his throat. He lifted his hand and cupped her cheek. "How can you feel alone with me? Am I—is my love—not enough?"

It wasn't. And yet it was. Mostly. Maybe. She didn't know. All she knew was that she needed to banish this heartache.

She brought her hands up and gripped the lapels of his jacket. "Make it enough. Make it *everything*."

Gabriel stared into her eyes as expectation grew between them. She feared he would walk away.

He didn't.

He thrust his hand back into her hair, dislodging pins as he cupped her scalp. Then his lips devoured hers in a searing kiss.

She tightened her hands on his coat, holding him against her as she thrust her tongue into his mouth, claiming everything he would give her. Wrapping his other arm around her hips, he drew her to his body, pressing her pelvis to his.

Desperate need sparked within her. This was unlike anything she'd ever experienced. She wanted this—*him*—to take her away from the pain in her heart. Casting thought aside, she gave all her attention to him, to the storm gathering between them.

Anger and hurt and desire swirled together as she pushed at his coat, eager to strip him bare and lose herself in the only thing that would make her feel whole. Maybe not whole, but not completely hollow either.

Gabriel pulled at her hair, freeing the tresses until she felt them cascade down her back. Then he helped her get his coat off, discarding it to the floor. She flicked at the buttons of his waistcoat, and that garment quickly followed the first. With a grunt, he picked her up and carried her the short distance to their bedchamber. There, he set her down beside the bed and began undressing her, his movements quick and efficient.

Ruthless.

He tossed her shoes away and spun her around to pluck at the laces of her gown. In a trice, the garment pooled at her feet. He pushed her petticoat down over her body to join it.

His lips and tongue rained pleasure on the back of her neck as he loosened her corset. A moment later, it fell from her as the rest had done, leaving her clad in her chemise and stockings. He kissed along the back of her shoulder, his teeth gently scoring her flesh while his hands came around and cupped her breasts through the cotton of her undergarment.

She gasped at the roughness of his touch, his thumbs and fingers drawing on her nipples. Raw lust shot straight to her sex. She wanted him now.

"Gabriel, I need you."

"You'll have me." He pulled her chemise up, baring her backside. "Bend."

She did as he instructed, bracing her hands on the bed in front of her as she bowed at the waist. One hand moved between her thighs while the other dove beneath her chemise, rending it slightly at the front, to further torment her breast. He cupped and squeezed, teasing more sensation from her than he ever had before.

He stroked her sex, and she arched back, seeking more of his touch. He slid his finger into her, filling her. She closed her eyes and curled her fingers into the coverlet.

He kissed the side of her neck, then nipped her earlobe. "Do you feel empty now?" He thrust up into her, and she pressed forward, rubbing her clitoris against the bed.

"No." She gasped as ecstasy curled inside her.

"Good." He put two fingers in her, pumping in and out, driving her toward a mad climax.

She clutched at the bed and snapped her hips back and forth with his rhythm. His hand left her breast, moving down between her and the mattress to flick her clitoris, again and again, sending her over the top of the mountain as she came apart in his arms.

Without waiting to fully recover, she turned and pulled at the buttons of his breeches. As soon as they were unfastened, he bent to pull off his boots, grunting and swearing with the effort. Then he stripped the stockings from her legs while she whisked the chemise over her head and threw it aside.

Casting the rest of his clothing off with vocal impatience, he climbed into the bed, pushing her onto the mattress. He kissed her savagely, and she gloried in the heat and despair of their joining. No, she wouldn't think. She would only feel.

He moved down to her breasts, his lips and tongue blazing a path of stark rapture. She reached down between them and found his sex, curling her hand around the base of his cock. He groaned, and she squeezed, milking him as she tugged up and slid back down. His hips moved against her, and moisture slicked her hand.

He found her clitoris again, stroking wildly as he suckled her breast. She cried out as pleasure built within her once more.

"Fill me," she begged. "Now. Take away the emptiness."

He rose up and looked down at her. "You are never alone, not so long as I am here."

The anguish inside her split as he drove into her. She pulled him down on top of her, seeking his weight and the security he gave her—an anchor in this tumult. Moisture wetted her cheeks, and she prayed he didn't feel it or see it. She didn't want to think. She only wanted to feel.

And the feelings had taken over.

Yes, he filled her, but she knew nothing would come of it. Never mind the ecstasy flashing within her as he thrust toward her barren womb. Or the way her body responded by meeting him, her legs curling around him and drawing him deeper and deeper, as if this time would be different. As if the ferocity of their passion could change their fortune.

She knew it would not.

Still, she flew. Higher and higher until she stood at the precipice. Then he kissed her, bringing them together even more completely, filling her as she'd demanded.

The climax rushed over her, sending her falling into darkness. Only this time, she knew the darkness would win.

This time, she welcomed it.

CHAPTER 3

*T*ime was not Poppy's friend. She counted days and tracked her cycle, always aware of when her courses should start. And painfully disappointed when they did. It was a vicious game that she invariably lost, and she wondered what would happen if she stopped playing.

Maybe she would stop feeling disappointed. Maybe she would look to other aspects of her life besides her inability to have a child.

That was what she *should* do, but finding the strength, the courage, to do so was incredibly difficult. Particularly when she felt so alone.

Only she wasn't alone. Not really.

The parchment in her hands—a note from her sister Bianca—was proof of that. As was Gabriel. He'd told her last night that she would never be alone.

After he'd revealed that he did not share her sorrow regarding their childlessness.

Learning that had torn a hole in her heart. She'd always thought they were united in their desire to conceive, but all along, he'd been relieved she hadn't. Had he also been hopeful? It was a minor distinction, but it mattered. To her, anyway.

Setting aside the note from her sister, she stood from her desk in the sitting room outside her bedchamber and strolled to the window. The day was gray and nondescript, mirroring the way she felt inside.

One would think she would have felt better following their coupling last night. That had been an extraordinary experience—the physicality, the emotion. But in the end, the emptiness had remained. Now she wished he hadn't told her his true feelings. Sometimes ignorance was a far more desirable state.

Oh hell. She didn't want to be ignorant. Nor did she want to wallow in grief any longer. It was time—the word provoked a short, harsh laugh—to stop playing this unwinnable game. Time was precisely what she needed. Time to accept and move on.

Turning from the window, she strode from the sitting room in search of Gabriel. She found him downstairs in his study. The door was slightly ajar, but she knocked lightly anyway.

"Come in," Gabriel called. She pushed open the door and stepped inside. He smiled at her, his gaze dipping over her in warm appreciation. "You look lovely today."

She didn't return his smile, nor did she approach his desk. She wasn't ready to talk with him about last night and about putting this all behind them. *Time,* she reminded herself. "Thank you."

"I was hoping we might go for a ride later since the day is quite fair." It had rained the last few days.

"I'm afraid I already have plans." She didn't really. She was simply stealing time. "I came to tell you that I'll be attending Lord Thornaby's house party with my sister on Thursday."

Gabriel leaned back in his chair. He'd declined the invitation. He didn't care for Thornaby or his friends. "You're a kind sister to chaperone her. Why on earth does she even want to go?"

"A variety of reasons. She is, as you know, rather sociable. She is also, as you know, unmarried. That is a situation I'm sure my brother wishes to rectify as soon as possible."

Gabriel snorted. "Your brother is a toad."

"Sometimes, yes." Poppy exhaled. "He is still my brother."

"Chill is *always* a toad—or worse." Chill was the name he'd been called since childhood, for he'd been the Earl of Chilton until their father's death. "Since the moment I met him, before he inherited the title, he was a blackguard. His progression from careless rake to haughty churl was certainly interesting. How one can actually alter their character for the worst is beyond me. Especially someone with such lovely sisters. It's as if he was raised by different parents."

"In a way, he was," she said softly. She didn't disagree with Gabriel, but today she didn't want to agree with him either. "He had our mother for much longer than I did, while Bianca didn't have her at all. Calder wasn't always the way you describe him."

"That's what you say. It seems he keeps devolving. We can only speculate how unpleasant he'll be in another decade."

Irritation curled along Poppy's spine. She didn't want to listen to Gabriel insult her brother, even if Calder deserved it. "The house party lasts until Saturday." Aside from chaperoning Bianca, Poppy thought the time away from Gabriel might help. She might even decide to stay at Hartwood with Bianca for a few days.

He frowned. "Are you angry with me?"

Her tongue twisted as she searched for the right answer. She wasn't sure she *had* an answer, right or otherwise. "I don't know what I am. I just need...time." She straightened, pushing her shoulders back. "I told you—I'm trying to accustom myself to disappointment."

He stood and started around the desk. "It doesn't have to be like that—"

She held up a hand, cutting him off. "Please don't. I'd rather not listen to you offer comfort. Clearly, our perspectives couldn't be more different."

Spinning on her heel, Poppy stalked from the study back up to the sitting room. She went to the desk and dashed off a response to Bianca saying she would accompany her to Thornaby's house party.

After folding the parchment, she stood to take it to a groom for delivery to Hartwood. While downstairs, perhaps she ought to apologize to Gabriel. He was trying to be supportive, even if he *was* relieved that her dreams wouldn't come true.

She flinched at the characterization. Yet it was precisely their situation.

This breach would take time to heal. Even so, she shouldn't snap at his efforts.

Taking the letter, she went back to his study to apologize. However, he wasn't there, so she went in search of the butler and asked if he knew where Gabriel had gone.

"For a ride, my lady," Walker answered. "He just left a few moments ago if you'd like to catch him."

"Thank you, Walker. Will you have this letter delivered to Hartwood, please?"

He nodded. "Right away."

Poppy quickly fetched her cloak, hat, and gloves before dashing out toward the stables. Almost immediately, she realized she should have changed into boots, but she didn't plan to be out long, and the stable wasn't far.

Hurrying along, she strode toward the stable and caught sight of Gabriel on foot up ahead. However, he altered course, veering right onto a path that led toward one of the roads on the estate.

Poppy followed him but didn't try to overtake him—he walked too quickly for her. She'd do her best to keep him in view and when he stopped, she'd join him.

They continued for quite some time, and she wondered why he was walking instead of riding. Had she ruined his plans by declining his offer?

He approached a cottage. Smoke curled from the chimney, and a woman stood outside. Poppy tried to recall who lived there but couldn't. In fact, if pressed, she would have insisted it was vacant.

Clearly, it wasn't.

Gabriel strode toward the woman, his movements full of purpose as he stopped before her. She lifted her face, and Poppy recognized her from Hartwell House. Mrs. Armstrong had taken her in as a girl.

Why was she at the cottage? And why was Gabriel going to see her? A knot of unease twined in Poppy's gut.

Judith laughed—a warm, gentle sound that carried to Poppy on the wind. Gabriel joined in. Jealousy knifed through Poppy's chest, and she told herself she was being ridiculous. But then he touched Judith's arm, and she turned, leading him into the cottage.

Poppy ought to go and confront them, but she was rooted to the ground. A dozen scenarios swirled in her mind, but she kept coming back to one—they were having an affair.

The roots came free, and Poppy walked toward the cottage. With each step, the knot in her belly tightened.

When she reached the door, she froze, her resolve weakening. What was she going to do? If he *was* having an affair, this was going to be a very ugly—and awkward—confrontation. Did that mean she should walk away?

No, she was not going to endure one more thing. She lifted her hand and loudly rapped on the door.

A moment later, Gabriel answered, his eyes widening as he saw her standing outside. "Poppy?"

"What's going on here?" She hadn't meant to ask so forcefully or indelicately, but her patience was simply gone. Pushing through the doorway, she looked around the small main room. "Where is Judith?"

The young woman came from the back of the cottage. She tucked a strand of blonde hair behind her ear. "Lady Darlington!"

Gabriel and Judith glanced at each other, lending them an air of guilt or conspiracy. Poppy folded her hands over her chest. "Judith, why aren't you at Hartwell House?"

"I—"

Gabriel cut her off. "She's here taking care of a woman because there were no more beds at Hartwell House. Rather than allow Mrs. Armstrong to give up her bed, I insisted the woman come stay in the empty cottage. Furthermore, she is ill, and this way, she can't spread her sickness to anyone else."

"Except for Judith." Poppy pursed her lips at him. "And you, apparently."

"Who's there?" a feminine voice called from the back room. This was followed by a coughing fit. Whoever was there was truly ill. There was no affair, then. Poppy felt foolish for even thinking it—Gabriel wasn't that type of husband.

"My goodness," Poppy breathed, striding past both Gabriel and Judith and making her way into the single bedroom.

The woman in the bed struggled to sit, but Poppy was frozen by the sight of her round belly. Forcing herself to take a deep breath, Poppy went to the bed. "Let me help you." She grasped the woman's arm and slid her other hand behind her back as she shimmied up against the headboard.

"Who are you?" The woman narrowed her eyes at Poppy.

"This is Lady Darlington, my wife." Gabriel came into the bedroom with Judith on his heels. "Poppy, this is Dinah Kitson. As you can see, she is expecting, as well as being sick. She went to Hartwell House, but Mrs. Armstrong didn't have room for her. I offered to let her stay here, and Judith volunteered to come and nurse her until the babe comes."

Poppy turned her head toward him. "How long has she been here, and why didn't you tell me?"

His jaw tensed, and his gaze flicked toward the bed. "Only since yesterday. You've been busy."

Except she hadn't been, not really, and he'd called her on it last night. Which meant he'd kept the information from her on purpose. Because Dinah was pregnant.

She returned her attention to Dinah. "Perhaps you should come stay in the house so I can look after you. Then Judith can return to Hartwell House, where she is needed." Poppy could only imagine that Mrs. Armstrong was now short-handed. And here Poppy had avoided going there. She suddenly felt very selfish.

"What if she gets everyone in the household sick?" Gabriel had a point.

"Very well, but I can come stay here to care for her so Judith can return," Poppy offered.

Gabriel came forward and gently clasped her elbow, then guided her from the room. "Poppy, I don't want you to fall ill."

She pulled her arm from his grasp. "You can't protect me from everything. This woman needs help, and Mrs. Armstrong needs Judith."

"Mrs. Armstrong had no problem with Judith coming here. It won't be for very long anyway. Dinah is already showing improvement after taking medicine, and her time is likely near."

There was that word again.

His gaze was cool. "Since you're so concerned about Mrs. Armstrong, perhaps you should start visiting Hartwell House again."

"I plan to. After the house party. In the meantime, I'll make sure Dinah is well situated. The physician should come see her."

"He will be here tomorrow," Gabriel said, the muscles in his jaw working. He lowered his voice. "Poppy, I didn't want to expose you to her."

"Because she's sick?" Poppy asked innocently, knowing she was likely pricking his ire and unable to stop herself.

"You know why. You said so just a little while ago—you're trying to become accustomed to disappointment."

"Yes, I am. Oddly, I think helping Dinah—and returning to Hartwell House—is exactly what I need." Yes, devoting herself to others would make the time pass. And maybe time would cease to be her enemy.

"If you think so." He didn't sound convinced. But it wasn't up to him.

"I do. Now let me make sure our patient is comfortable. Then we must prepare for the babe."

The thought of having a baby to care for, if only for a little while, filled Poppy with joy. Gabriel's brow creased, and Poppy turned away from his worry. She went back to the bedroom, to the woman who had finally pulled Poppy from the pit of grief.

Poppy removed her hat and smiled at Dinah. "I'm so glad you came. Is there anything I can bring for you?"

～

*T*his was not going the way Gabriel had planned.

He stood in the corner of the room as Poppy talked with Dinah and Judith about fetching more blankets and pillows from the house.

"How about books?" Poppy asked.

Dinah looked suddenly…shy. That wasn't a word Gabriel would have thought to attribute to her. "I like books about nature if you have any of those. And maybe plays?"

Poppy nodded, then turned to Judith. "Before I go, why don't you tell me what I can bring to supplement the kitchen here? Food, cookware, whatever you need."

"Thank you, my lady." Judith listed a few items, and Poppy said she'd have them delivered before the end of the day.

A few minutes later, she and Gabriel departed. Gabriel felt as if he were being swept out on a whirlwind. It was thrilling to see Poppy so engaged, but also frustrating since he wasn't able to accomplish his goal of speaking to Dinah about the baby.

And he wasn't about to do it in front of Poppy. What if Dinah rejected his proposal out of hand? What if she accepted it and then changed her mind? *If* Dinah decided to give her baby to him and Poppy to raise, Gabriel wanted to be certain it happened. As certain as he could be, anyway.

As they walked from the cottage, Gabriel looked over at his wife. The lines of her face were incredibly delicate, from the arch of her cheekbones to the tilt of her nose, but the lush fullness of her lips anchored the whole. She appeared serene, her slate-blue eyes trained forward as dark curls grazed her temple. He marveled at how her beauty could still make his heart pause and then speed before taking flight.

But what was going on behind that beloved façade? Was she still upset with him? Based on her irritation in his study earlier, he'd assumed she was. Then she'd come to the door of the cottage and had seemed even angrier.

"How did you come to be at the cottage?" he asked.

"I followed you. I went to your study to apologize for snapping at you, but Walker said you'd gone for a ride." She slid him a quick look. "Clearly that was not the case." She still sounded annoyed.

"I changed my mind." He decided it was better to clear the air between them. "What were you thinking when you came to the cottage?"

"I was wondering why you would come here to meet Judith of all people. I also wondered why she wasn't at Hartwell House. Seeing the two of you together…" Her lips pressed together, and her jaw tightened.

They had just walked out onto the narrow road. He stopped and gently clasped her forearm, turning toward her. "You thought I was meeting her for an assignation?"

She pivoted, facing him, her brow creasing. "I didn't know what to think. And since you didn't tell me she was here—or about Dinah—I had to ask."

He let go of her arm. "I'm sorry I didn't tell you. I wanted to help Mrs. Armstrong. After last night and what you said, I worried Dinah's presence might upset you."

Her gaze held his for a long moment, her face tense. "I wish you'd told me straightaway, but I understand why you didn't."

Gabriel moved, lessening the distance between them. He cupped her face, tracing his thumb along her cheekbone. "I would never have an affair. You have to know there is no other woman anywhere who could take me from you."

Desire pulsed through him. He wanted to show her how true those words were, how deeply he wanted her. Needed her. Loved her. He lowered his mouth to hers, sliding his hand back to her nape and holding her firm as he kissed her.

Tension arced through him as he awaited her reaction…
She didn't pull away. Her hands lightly clutched his waist,
and she tipped her head to mold her lips to his.

Overcome, he deepened the kiss, sliding his tongue
against hers. She met him eagerly, her fingers digging into
his sides. He pressed forward, and she moved her hands
back, pulling him against her. His cock rose, hardening. He
wanted to make sure she knew…

He pulled his lips from hers and grabbed her hand.
Without a word, he glanced about, then stalked the way
they'd come toward a stand of trees that would offer at least
a modicum of privacy.

When he veered from the road toward the trees, she
stopped. "Where are we going?"

He inclined his head. "There."

She looked at him as if he were mad. "Why?"

He pulled her against him. "Because I want you to know
that you are the only one for me. Now and forever." He
kissed her again but wasn't gentle about it. He claimed her
mouth, clashing lips and tongues and teeth.

She drew away with a gasp. "I am not wearing boots, and
the ground—"

Kissing her again, he didn't need her to finish. He swept
her into his arms and carried her behind the trees so they
weren't openly visible to the road. She curled her arms
around his neck as he surveyed the area. One of the trees had
a large exposed root system.

He set her on the root with the tree at her back.

"You don't have to do this," she said.

He brought his hand up beneath her cloak and grazed his
thumb across her breast. The nipple was impossible to feel
beneath her clothing. He cupped her instead, squeezing
gently. "I think I do. I want to banish any question you could

ever have." He looked into her eyes. Her pupils were starting to dilate.

He bent his head and kissed her neck just beneath her ear. Licking along her flesh, he moved down her throat, then cursed her cloak. "You're mine, and I am yours." He nipped her and sucked, making her cry out.

Lifting his head, he stared at her with naked need. "Tell me to stop. If you want to."

She shook her head. Then she splayed her hand against his neck and dragged her thumb over his mouth. "Don't stop."

He sucked the digit between his lips. She closed her eyes and moaned softly, her head falling back. With a low growl, he kissed her again, this time with a savage, desperate need. Her fingers curled into his flesh, and he wished she wasn't wearing gloves. Or anything else.

His gloves were going to be a bloody nuisance. He quickly stripped them away, then lifted the hem of her skirt. Grasping the layers of her clothing took effort, but he managed to bunch them up at her waist.

She gasped into his mouth, pulling back slightly. "Cold."

"I'll make you warm." He skimmed across her thigh and found her sex. God, she was so wet. As he sank his finger into her heat, he was glad he'd abandoned the gloves. Her hips moved, drawing him deeper as she clutched at his shoulders.

This was insanity, but he was past the point of rational thinking. "Hold your skirts," he rasped as he withdrew from her body and worked to unfasten his breeches.

She did as he asked. "Hurry." Compounding matters—in the best way—she lifted one leg and wrapped it around his hips.

He freed his cock and pressed himself to her sex. She let go of her dress and clasped his hip, pulling him forward. He thrust up into her, and her moan filled the air with erotic promise.

Grabbing her backside, he lifted her. "Wrap both your legs around me and don't let go."

Pinning her between his body and the wide trunk, he prayed this would work, that they wouldn't tumble to the ground in an ungainly tangle. But with the second thrust, he realized this wasn't going to last terribly long. Pleasure raced through him, and her muscles were already beginning to contract around him. Letting go, he drove into her as an overwhelming feeling of passion and possession seized him.

He stared into her enraptured face. "Look at me."

Her eyes came open, the gray blue a haze of seductive desire. "You are mine, and I am yours," he repeated. "Say it."

"You are mine, and I am yours."

He drove deep, hating her womb in that moment—or his cock, whatever was preventing her dream. Even if it was a dream that scared the hell out of him. "Now and forever."

She moved her hand to cup his face. "Now and forever." Her lids fluttered, and her long, dark lashes brushed her cheeks as she closed her eyes. "Preferably *now*."

Her muscles clenched around him fiercely, and her cries rent the air. He grunted, then cried out as he came apart inside her. They both held on as if the power of their climaxes would do what he feared and send them to the ground.

He buried his face in her neck, inhaling her sweet honeyed scent. She held him to her, her hands a powerful anchor for his trembling body.

Easing her down, he withdrew from her and drew deep breaths of air into his lungs. Her skirts fell between them, and she pressed back against the tree, taking deep breaths.

While he refastened his breeches, she turned from him and put herself to rights for a moment. When she faced him once more, she was again the serene beauty who'd left the cottage. His wild, ardent lover was gone.

Tension stretched between them, and he began to wonder if it would ever go away.

Guarded, he asked, "What's wrong? Are you still upset about Judith and Dinah?"

"Sexual gratification doesn't solve anything."

"I'd argue with that," he said, feeling supremely satisfied. He sobered. "I'm sorry I didn't tell you."

"Thank you." She pressed her lips together and sucked them in briefly before exhaling. "I need some time to adjust —to what you told me last night. Not having children has been—is—incredibly painful for me. To learn that it isn't for you, that you're content to remain childless is also painful. I need...time."

He offered a faint smile. "We have forever."

She didn't smile, but she didn't frown either. "Yes, we do."

He offered her his arm and was glad when she took it for the walk back to the house. "Content isn't the right word. It isn't that I don't want children, especially because I know what a wonderful mother you would be."

She stiffened, and he wished he hadn't said that. Actually, no, he didn't. It was the truth. And if he'd learned anything in recent days—and today—it was that he should always tell her the truth, even when it was painful.

They walked for several minutes in silence. He wondered what was going on in her mind. Was her melancholy taking hold again, or was she focused on Dinah? Perhaps he could help her do the latter despite the fact that he didn't particularly want her involved with the woman. On second thought, maybe it was for the best. Maybe Dinah would offer the babe to Poppy.

And perhaps *he* should focus on repairing the rift

between him and his wife. "How much time do you need?" he asked softly.

"I don't know. Let's talk again when I return from Thornhill."

Gabriel hated the uneven ground between them, but acknowledged that he alone couldn't make it smooth. He'd have to be patient. There was simply nothing else he could do.

CHAPTER 4

*a*fter Gabriel left the following day for Hartwell House, Poppy walked to the cottage. She carried a basket with biscuits from the cook and a play she hoped Dinah would like.

Though Judith had told her the day before that she needn't knock, Poppy did anyway. A moment later, Judith answered. "You don't have to—"

"Knock, I know. But I don't think I can break the habit. I brought biscuits from the cook." She handed Judith the basket as she stepped into the cottage.

"How lovely!" Judith peeked inside. "What else is there?"

"A play. I thought I might read to Dinah if she's amenable."

Judith's fair brows arched briefly. "She's a bit disagreeable since Dr. Fisk's visit earlier."

"Oh, he's already been?" Poppy had hoped to be here when he arrived.

Judith nodded. "He told her to rest as much as possible, so the play, whether she allows you to read it or not, will not come amiss. He also left some milk of sow thistle to help with her cough. I was just about to make some tea with it. I'll fix you a cup—without the sow thistle," she added with a grin.

"Thank you. I'll come back for the play if things go well." She winked at Judith before walking back to the bedroom. "Good afternoon, Dinah," she called in warning before stepping over the threshold.

Perched on the edge of the bed, Dinah, her dark blonde hair swept onto her head save a few strands that grazed the left side of her face, grunted in response.

"Are you going somewhere?" Poppy asked.

"Just to the chair. I can't stay in this bed all the time."

"Of course you can't. Do you need any help?"

Dinah silently glared her response, her dark brown eyes snapping. Poppy snagged her lower lip lest she say something, then turned to deposit her cloak and bonnet on a hook.

As she pivoted back, Dinah was just settling into the chair, lowering her small frame slowly so that she looked far older than her perhaps twenty years. Dinah angled her round belly toward the fireplace, which sat between this room and the main room where Judith was preparing the tea.

Poppy tugged her gloves off and tucked them into the pocket of her cloak. Since there was only the one chair, she went to the narrow bench that stood at the end of the bed and moved it closer to the fireplace so she could sit by Dinah.

"How are you feeling today?" Poppy asked conversationally.

"Fine."

"I brought biscuits, and Judith is making tea."

Dinah's eyes narrowed. "What kind of biscuits?"

"Lemon." A light sparked in Dinah's eyes. "Do you like lemon?" Poppy asked.

She blinked the gleam of interest away, and the stoic young woman returned. "Yes."

"You've had lemon biscuits before, I take it?"

"A few times."

Poppy had tried to glean information from Dinah about her background, particularly the circumstances that led to her condition. She wasn't married—that much she'd admitted. "Do you know how to make them?"

Dinah shook her head. "The cook said it wasn't hard." Her eyes widened briefly, and she turned her head to frown at the fire.

Judith came in with a small tray bearing their two cups of tea and a plate of biscuits. She looked about, clearly wondering where to set the items.

Poppy patted the empty space on the bench beside her. "Put the tray here. Thank you, Judith."

After depositing the refreshments, Judith departed. Poppy picked up the plate and offered it to Dinah with a smile. "Here you are."

Dinah tentatively took one, her eyes as wary as they'd ever been, as if she expected Poppy to snatch the confection back from her fingers. She took a bite, and her expression relaxed into a joy Poppy had never seen on her face before.

"I'll have Cook make another batch," Poppy said before taking one for herself and setting the plate back down.

"Yes, please," Dinah said before she had swallowed. "They're delicious."

"I'm glad you like them. The cook you mentioned—was that your cook?" Poppy didn't think that was the case but didn't want to make any assumptions.

Dinah laughed as she reached over the arm of the chair for another biscuit. "No, my mother did all the cooking when I was young. Until I went to work in the scullery in the—" She cut off whatever she was going to say by taking a bite.

Poppy picked up her tea. "You were a scullery maid?"

"For a few years." She continued to nibble at her biscuit.

"Did you like that?"

"Not particularly. I was relieved to be promoted to upstairs maid."

But then she'd become pregnant. Poppy wondered by whom and why the jackanapes hadn't married her. "Did you leave the position when you became pregnant?" she asked softly.

"In a manner of speaking." Her response was terse, her eyes blazing with fury.

"They let you go?" When Dinah glared at the fire, Poppy softly added, "Because of the babe?"

Dinah riveted her angry gaze to Poppy. "It wasn't my fault. My employer made me, said I would lose my job if I didn't let him."

The rage radiating from Dinah sparked in Poppy and caught fire. "Who did this?" she asked, her tone low and furious.

Dinah clenched her jaw and viciously picked up her teacup, sloshing droplets onto the bench and floor. "Doesn't matter."

"It does." Poppy wanted to confront the man herself.

"And what would you do?" Dinah asked, arching a dark blonde brow.

Shoulders drooping, Poppy frowned. Sometimes being a woman made one feel utterly helpless. If she were a man, she could at least call the blackguard out. She turned to Dinah in sympathy. "I'm sorry."

"I went home, but my parents didn't want me either. A neighbor took me in until everyone started to shun her." Dinah sniffed, then coughed. It took her a moment to control the spasms, but not as long as when she'd first arrived. She sipped her tea and set the cup back down. "I don't want the babe. It's been nothing but a burden to me."

Poppy stared at her. She didn't want the child? "You can't mean that. A child is a gift."

Dinah blinked at her. "What has this wretch given me but heartache and poverty? I lost my job, my place. I have no prospects."

Hearing her refer to the babe in such a way twisted Poppy's heart, and yet she could see the woman's perspective. The man—and the resulting child—had robbed her of what little choices she'd had.

"Hartwell House is the place for you. Mrs. Armstrong helps women just like you."

Dinah's eyes flashed with challenge. "There's no room."

"We'll make room." Poppy was determined to help this woman. "When the babe is old enough, you can go back into service. Perhaps we can even hire you here at Darlington Abbey."

Dinah shook her head vigorously. "No. I won't work in domestic service ever again."

Poppy couldn't blame her, but it would be different if she was employed here. "You'd be safe at Darlington Abbey. And you could have your babe." Poppy wasn't sure how they'd work that out, but they would. She had a vision of taking care of the child herself. The resulting ache was strong—and dangerous. She pushed it away.

"I said *no.*" Dinah stifled a cough and grabbed another biscuit and thrust it into her mouth.

Poppy flinched inwardly. She didn't want to upset Dinah and perhaps provoke a coughing fit. "All right, then. You could learn a trade at Hartwell House. Perhaps sewing."

"I don't want to sew. Or cook. Or clean." She gritted her teeth. Poppy was keenly aware of how trapped this poor woman felt.

Poppy angled herself toward Dinah and leaned forward. "What do you want to do?"

The fire behind Dinah's eyes dwindled. She looked down at her belly. "You'll laugh."

"I won't. I promise."

"Since I was a little girl, I wanted to be an actress." Her voice had turned soft and shy. She lifted her gaze but quickly averted it to some spot beyond Poppy. "My father took me to see a traveling troupe once. The actors were so beautiful, and they told such a magical story." She looked as if she were back there, reliving that moment.

"What was it?" Poppy asked, enchanted by Dinah's reverie.

Dinah blinked and looked at Poppy. "I can't remember, but I think it was Shakespeare. It was about a fairy queen and a king and lovers." She exhaled into a smile, and Poppy smiled too.

"Sounds like maybe *A Midsummer Night's Dream*."

"It was lovely. I wanted to be a fairy. Then I realized there are no fairies, so I'd have to be an actress so I could pretend to be one." She rested her hand on her belly. "I can't see how I'll ever do that now. It was a silly dream."

"No, it wasn't. Dreams aren't silly, and you shouldn't give up." She thought of her own, which would never happen, her gaze straying to Dinah's belly. *You shouldn't give up.* This was different—she couldn't make herself become pregnant, no matter how hard she tried or prayed or wished. She could, however, realize her dream another way. Right in front of her was a woman who said she didn't want her baby…

"Is there a good orphanage in the district?" Dinah asked, breaking into Poppy's selfish thoughts.

Orphanage? Then Poppy could volunteer to raise the child… *No.*

"I don't know, but I don't think you should consider that.

I know this seems overwhelming to you now, but when you have the baby and see his or her face, you'll change your mind. You'll fall instantly in love." At least that was how Poppy imagined it would be. Her lungs contracted, and she fought to take a breath.

"I can't imagine it," Dinah said.

"That doesn't mean it won't happen. Give yourself—and the child—the chance. Doesn't he or she deserve to know its mother?"

Dinah picked up her cup and sipped the tea.

Poppy took her silence as an opportunity to continue her persuasion. "You could stay at Hartwell House, maybe even for a few years, until the babe is a bit older. You could learn a trade—something to do while you are trying to be an actress." Poppy had no idea how she would even go about that, but she was determined to encourage this young woman who'd been robbed of so much. "You could spend time reading plays. Perhaps you could organize the children there to perform something."

Dinah's eyes widened with horror. "Organizing children to perform? Is that even possible?"

A giggle escaped from Poppy, and she clapped her hand over her mouth. Then the most remarkable thing happened —Dinah started to laugh too.

After a long moment, their laughter abated, and Dinah yawned.

"You should get some sleep," Poppy said, rising. She picked up the tray, and Dinah nabbed the last biscuit with a smile. "I'll be right back to help you settle into bed." Poppy took the tray to Judith in the other room.

When Poppy returned, Dinah was already in bed with the covers pulled up to her chin. "I suppose you don't need me," Poppy said.

Dinah looked at her shyly. "Thank you. No one has ever

made me feel like I mattered or that I could hope for things." She shook her head. "Never mind."

Poppy offered her a kind smile. "I understand. You *do* matter, especially to the babe you carry. I hope you'll think about what I said."

Closing her eyes, Dinah didn't respond. Poppy stood there for a moment, wishing there was something she could do to ease this woman's plight, but some parts of a journey were solitary. Poppy was learning this as she tried to find her way back to where she needed to be. Where she wanted to be. Whole and happy.

Poppy turned and grabbed her cloak and bonnet, then tiptoed from the room. In the main room, she set her bonnet on her head and pulled her cloak over her shoulders.

"Is she asleep?" Judith asked, coming to help Poppy don her cloak.

"Thank you," Poppy said. "Yes." She fastened the cloak, then tied the ribbon of her bonnet beneath her chin.

"I heard what you said to her. You're a kindhearted person, my lady."

Judith might not think that if she could see inside Poppy. She wanted to be incredibly selfish, and she'd had the chance... Why hadn't she taken it? More importantly, how badly would she regret not turning this to her benefit, to doing what she'd advised Dinah—to pursue her dream?

Maybe she wouldn't have to. Dinah seemed quite committed to not raising her child. Giving her another option would be so easy and maybe even welcome. But Poppy wouldn't take advantage. Dinah was the child's mother, and Poppy would do everything she could to keep them together.

～

*T*he early afternoon sun disappeared behind a cloud, lowering the already near-freezing temperature. Gabriel hastened his pace toward Dinah's cottage.

Though Poppy had only been gone a few hours, Gabriel missed her. Not for the time since she'd left to fetch her sister for the house party but for the past several days. She'd been sleeping in another bedchamber and spending a great deal of time at the cottage with Dinah.

He looked forward to when Poppy came home, to when they could return to the way things were. If that was even possible.

A lingering discomfort pervaded Gabriel's mind when he thought of what had caused the rift between them. *He* had caused it, with his lack of understanding for what Poppy had suffered and continued to endure. His relief was her pain. The unfairness of it nearly tore him in two.

Still, he found small comfort in knowing he wouldn't lose her the way he'd lost his mother and sister. The way she'd lost her mother.

Turning from the road, Gabriel made his way to the door of the cottage. Before he reached the threshold, Judith welcomed him inside.

"I saw you approaching from the window," she said.

He stepped inside, and she closed the door behind him. The interior of the cottage was warm and cozy, and it smelled of baking bread.

Gabriel inhaled deeply. "How long until the bread is done?"

Judith smiled. "Not long. I'll cut you a slice."

"If you insist." He grinned, then glanced toward the back room. "How is Dinah?"

"She's reading."

Gabriel blinked at her. "Is she?"

"Shakespeare. Lady Darlington brought *A Midsummer Night's Dream* the other day. She's had quite an effect on Dinah. She's actually considering keeping the babe now."

She was doing *what*? Gabriel masked his shock and disappointment. "What changed her mind?"

"Lady Darlington did."

She had? Gabriel was utterly confused. "I'm surprised. Dinah has been clear from the moment we met her that she doesn't want the child."

Judith nodded. "Lady Darlington has convinced her that she'd regret the decision, that as soon as the babe is born, Dinah will fall irrevocably in love."

That sounded like his wife. While Gabriel wanted the child for Poppy, he was moved by her selfless behavior. Taking the child would benefit them, but what of Dinah? What if she did regret not keeping him or her?

He'd come here intending to talk to Dinah about him and Poppy raising the baby. Now he couldn't do that, especially since Poppy had worked to persuade Dinah to keep it.

"I thought I heard voices."

Gabriel turned and saw Dinah standing in the doorway to the bedroom. She wore a loose gown, but nothing could disguise the advanced state of her pregnancy. Dr. Fisk had told Judith the babe could come at any time.

"Good afternoon, Dinah," he said.

"Did you bring lemon biscuits?" she asked.

"I didn't." He glanced toward Judith. "Should I have?"

"Yes," Dinah answered. "Lady Darlington always brings them now."

"I didn't realize. I'll make sure you have some before nightfall." He walked toward her. "Judith said her ladyship also brought you something to read."

"She did. I like her. She's very kind."

"She is indeed. I am the luckiest of men."

"I'm going back to bed." Dinah turned and waddled back into the bedroom.

Gabriel followed her, not yet certain what he meant to say.

She climbed into the bed and looked slightly surprised, her brows arching, as she pulled the coverlet over her belly. "I thought you were going to get biscuits."

He smiled. "I will. Judith tells me you've changed your mind about keeping the babe."

Deep creases furrowed Dinah's brow. "I'm considering it. I asked Lady Darlington to stop bothering me about it, so if you're here to continue her assault, I'd ask that you don't."

"I won't." Conflict warred within Gabriel—he wanted to support Poppy, but he also wanted this baby for them. For Poppy.

For himself. Maybe he wanted to be a father more than he'd realized. His gut tightened, and he did his best to ignore the sensation.

"Dinah, I want you to know that whatever you decide, your baby will be cared for. We'll make sure."

"You and Lady Darlington are the kindest people I've ever met, and that includes my own family." She shook her head. "I don't understand why."

And now Gabriel felt like a charlatan. His own desires and motivation aside, he did want to help her, even if she did keep the babe. "We don't turn our backs on those in need."

"You spend a great deal of time at Hartwell House from what I gather."

"We do."

"How long have you and Lady Darlington been married?" she asked.

"Three years in February."

"And you don't have any children of your own?"

He shook his head. "We do not."

"I wasn't sure. I assumed if you did, they were with a nurse or a governess. That's what you folk do."

Gabriel knew she was speaking from experience—with "you folk." "Were you a nurse? Or a governess?"

"No, I worked in a scullery. And as a maid."

"Did you?"

Dinah narrowed her eyes. "Lady Darlington didn't tell you?"

Gabriel kept himself from wincing. Poppy hadn't shared much with him of late. He decided there was no good answer to Dinah's question so he ignored it. "I'll make sure you have lemon biscuits."

"Hand me my book before you go, please."

The tome, from his library, sat on the bedside table. Well within reach, but she'd have to push up to get it. Gabriel handed her the play. "*A Midsummer Night's Dream* is my favorite Shakespeare."

She set the book on her belly, for she had no lap. "I saw it performed once when I was a child—by a traveling troupe of actors. Reading the words, I can see the play again in my mind."

For the first time, he saw joy in the depths of her usually apprehensive gaze. She looked like that talking about a play, but he'd never seen that when she spoke of her baby. He wondered if Poppy knew how Dinah had come to be pregnant. Hopefully, he'd be able to ask her. When she returned, and they went back to normal.

"Then I will leave you to it," he said, nodding toward the book.

He turned, and as he hit the threshold, she called, "Don't forget the biscuits! Please."

He looked back over his shoulder, but she was already reading. He watched her for a moment, thinking—shamefully—for the first time of her as a person with hopes and dreams and a baby she maybe didn't want. Or maybe she did. Either way, she was alone, impoverished, and without prospects. Yes, he must speak to Poppy about her. Whatever happened with the baby, they couldn't turn Dinah out without offering support. That wasn't who they were.

Assuming she survives.

The dark voice surfaced from the back of his mind. The petrifying fear that came when he thought of losing his mother and sister bubbled up. He was able to keep it at bay for the most part, but he'd come to know Dinah, and if she died… *When* she died. For he had every expectation that she would. And damn if that—his expectation—wasn't horrible.

Trying to banish the darkness, he strode into the main room. Judith handed him a plate with a thick slice of bread slathered in butter. He didn't think he could force it past the lump in his throat. Still, he took the plate.

"I heard her ask about biscuits," Judith said.

"Yes, I'll have a groom bring some down later." First, he had to see if Cook even had any on hand.

Gabriel's insides roiled with unease. "How do you manage loss at Hartwell House? When people die, I mean."

Judith's eyes widened briefly. Lines creased around her mouth as she seemed to ponder his odd question. He was on the verge of telling her to forget he'd asked when she said, "It's difficult, particularly when we've come to know them well. However, we always see it as a blessing for them for they are no longer suffering. And, we hope, they passed in a place of comfort and love."

Tears stung the back of Gabriel's throat. He swallowed, praying he wouldn't humiliate himself in front of Judith. He took a bite of bread, not because he wanted to, but because it gave his body something to do besides surrender to grief.

The bread was delicious, and Gabriel was surprised when he eagerly finished the entire slice. The flavor, the simplicity, the care with which Judith had prepared it for him gave him comfort.

The room around him came into sharper focus as he saw with a clarity he'd never managed before. He handed the empty plate back to Judith. "Thank you. For everything." He smiled at her then turned and left.

He'd spent so many years fearing death that he'd failed to realize what he was truly afraid of, what he'd worked so hard to avoid—grief. The thought of losing Poppy had precluded him from living the way he ought, without preoccupation about things that he could not control.

He finally understood Poppy's perspective. Or, at least, he hoped he did. He loved her beyond measure, and that she'd suffered in her grief without him beside her—*truly* beside her—threatened to break his heart.

Thankfully, he could fix this. He could show Poppy that the loss, the *grief*, was theirs together. She wasn't alone.

And neither was he.

"*A*re you upset we left early?" Bianca asked as the coach carried her and Poppy away from Thornhill the day after the party began.

"Of course not. I only came to chaperone you," Poppy said. That wasn't exactly true. She'd also welcomed the chance to spend some time away from Gabriel. By leaving early, she was shortening her respite, but if she were honest with herself, she'd admit that she missed him.

Bianca smoothed her hand over her skirt. "And I appreciate it. Since you are already being so helpful, perhaps you can provide assistance with Calder. We are now in dire need of him to host the St. Stephen's Day party after today's debacle with Thornaby and the others."

"It was a debacle?" Poppy hadn't heard what precisely had gone on at the shooting competition that had been held at Thornaby's house party—she'd been too far away—but Bianca had said the host and his friends had bullied the Earl of Buckleigh. Whatever had happened had been enough to drive the Earl of Buckleigh away, as well as Bianca and Poppy.

"It was for Ash—and for me."

"You're calling him Ash again," Poppy murmured. They'd known the earl since they were children. He'd lived in Hartwell until he'd gone off to Oxford, after which he'd moved to London. He'd just come back this year upon inheriting the earldom from his cousin, something he'd never expected to do.

Bianca slid her an exasperated look. "You're pointing it out again."

Poppy smiled to herself. How she loved her sister. And how nice it was to be with her away from her own worries.

"It was especially awful because of St. Stephen's Day," Bianca said. "I'd hoped Thornaby could host the party at Thornhill—it's the closest estate to Hartwell after Hartwood."

"He won't host it?" Poppy asked, having missed that fact from earlier.

"I didn't ask him to. I *can't*." Bianca made a face. "He's horrid."

Poppy turned her head and stared at her sister. She'd jumped rather quickly and passionately to Ash's—*Buckleigh's*—defense. Was there something between them?

"Bianca, do you have a tendre for the earl?" she asked softly, her lips curving into a slight smile. How wonderful it would be if her sister fell in love. Poppy doubted Calder would be so fortunate. He was making himself rather unlovable with his stinginess and frigidity.

Bianca blinked, then turned her attention to the window. "Don't be absurd. We're old friends."

It seemed more than that based on Bianca's behavior, but Poppy wouldn't press the matter. She remembered falling in love with Gabriel. They'd danced at the holiday assembly, and she'd been immediately smitten by his charm and good looks. He'd made her laugh, and she'd counted the days—two —until he'd called on her at Hartwood.

The three-year anniversary of their meeting was almost upon them, she realized with a bittersweet ache. Would they celebrate? Or would they still be at odds? She hoped not.

"Are you all right?" Bianca asked, fixing Poppy with an anxious stare. "I mean, I know things aren't—" She abruptly stopped and shook her head. "It's not for me to ask. I just want you to know that I'm here if you need me."

Poppy appreciated her sister's concern. It wasn't as if she was trying to keep anything from her, but why burden anyone else with her troubles? Especially when there was nothing to be done about them.

"Thank you." Poppy gently touched Bianca's arm. "You are the sweetest sister."

"Calder wouldn't agree," she said wryly, provoking a welcome laugh from Poppy.

"No, I suppose not. I do wonder if he will come around," Poppy mused. "To be more like how he used to be."

Bianca exhaled. "I can't see it happening, unfortunately, especially with him refusing to host the St. Stephen's Day party as all the other Dukes of Hartwell have done before him. I'm still going to try to persuade him, mind you."

"Of course you are. And if anyone can, it's you. But you're right. I do fear he's hardened into a forbidding shell, and that breaks my heart."

"He needs a wife," Bianca said, straightening her spine. "Someone who will manage him and make him feel again. What I should like to know is what made him this way." She looked over at Poppy. "Or do I just have a rosier idea of who he was before he went to school? I was rather young."

"No, you remember him correctly. He was kind and caring. He used to make jokes, if you can imagine."

"I can, actually. I remember giggling with him." Bianca

frowned. "Which makes his behavior all the more maddening. And distressing." She turned her head toward Poppy. "What happened, do you suppose?"

Poppy thought she knew—or had a good idea, anyway. "I'm sure it was at least partly due to Felicity."

Bianca cocked her head to the side. "I'd forgotten about her. See, I *was* young. What happened?"

Felicity Templeton, now Garland, had lived in the village of Hartwell with her parents. When Poppy thought of how different her brother had once been, she always thought of him with Felicity. "Calder wanted to marry her. However, for reasons that have never been made clear to me, they didn't wed. She and her family moved to York."

"Her mother came back to Hartwell last year, after her husband died, I believe." Bianca glanced out the window. "I don't see her very often. In fact, I should look in on her. Perhaps I'll do that."

Poppy smiled. "You've such a caring heart. Let me know when you go, and I'll join you."

"Like when we used to visit Hartwell House together," Bianca said, grinning. "Do you remember when we first started going there?"

Poppy nodded. "Father said we read too many books and suggested we do something else."

Bianca giggled. "So we took our books to Hartwell House and read to the children."

"And then taught them to read," Poppy said with a hint of pride. They both still did those things, just not together. Of late, however, Poppy hadn't done them at all.

They fell silent for a few minutes before Bianca spoke up again. "Do you think Calder has had a broken heart ever since?"

"I suppose it's possible, but I'm not sure that's the case. Gabriel has told me all about Calder's behavior in London when he was younger. It doesn't sound as if he was pining for Felicity."

Bianca's brows arched. "I see."

Just like that, the mention of Gabriel drew Poppy back to her own problems. As much as she wanted to aid Bianca in her dealings with Calder, she needed to go home. All this talk of Calder and who he was before made her realize she was ready to be who *she* was before—who she wanted to be now.

Still, as they drove up the lane leading to Hartwood, she didn't want to abandon her sister's cause regarding the St. Stephen's Day party. "Bianca, do you want me to come in and talk to Calder with you?"

"I don't think it would matter," she said with resignation. "Anyway, he's often busy in his study—there's no telling if he'd even see us."

"Surely he'd come to dinner," Poppy said.

"To be honest, I'm not sure I have the patience for dinner with him tonight. Not after the events of the day."

The business with Ash had affected Bianca quite profoundly. Poppy kept that observation to herself.

After bidding her sister farewell, Poppy urged the driver to make haste so they would reach Darlington Abbey before it was fully dark.

~

*D*espite a succession of clouds, the light of the moon guided Gabriel back to the house. His belly was delightfully content from dinner at the cottage. Aside from making excellent bread, Judith also crafted a mouthwatering stew.

As he walked into the house, a giddy anticipation filled him. Tomorrow, Poppy would return. His excitement reminded him of the night before St. Nicholas Day when his family would exchange gifts. He'd barely been able to sleep, wondering what he'd receive on the morrow.

Deciding to have a glass of port before heading upstairs, he went toward his study and ran into the butler on the way.

"Good evening, my lord," Walker said. "Lady Darlington has returned."

The anticipation thrumming through Gabriel expanded. "Where is she?"

"Upstairs, I believe."

Gabriel was already striding toward the stairs before he remembered to thank Walker. As much as he'd enjoyed dinner at the cottage, Gabriel now wished he'd been at home instead. He took the stairs two at a time.

The fire in their sitting room burned low, and a single lantern flickered on the desk in front of the window. Gabriel went into their bedchamber and stopped short. Standing before the fire, her body silhouetted beneath her cream-colored night rail, was the woman he dreamed of. The woman who held his heart in her hands—precisely where he wanted it to be.

She turned, and he held his breath—both because of her beauty and because he didn't know what to expect. Would she turn him away? No, she was here, in their bedchamber, unlike the nights before she'd left.

"You're here," he whispered.

"I'm here. Bianca wanted to leave Thornhill early."

"Did something happen?"

"Thornaby and his friends—the ones you don't like—bullied our old friend Ash." She shook her head. "The Earl of Buckleigh."

Gabriel knew Buckleigh. They'd met on a few occasions in London, and Gabriel had encountered him in Hartwell since he'd become the earl. "I'd been meaning to invite him to dinner."

A half smile tilted her mouth, and Gabriel's heart flipped. "Have you? I suppose we've been busy. Or distracted." Gabriel's throat constricted, and she continued before he could gather himself to speak. "There was a shooting competition, and while I couldn't hear what was being said, Bianca could."

"Why is that?" Gabriel interrupted.

"Because she insisted on shooting and remained somewhat close to the competition after they deigned to allow her to have a turn—not *in* the competition, of course, but to demonstrate her skill."

Gabriel chuckled. "I'm not surprised she demanded equal opportunity. And good for her." His sister-in-law was perhaps the most fearless and self-possessed person he'd ever met.

"Whatever happened between the gentlemen upset Buckleigh enough that he left the party. Bianca insisted we do the same."

"To show solidarity?"

"I'm not sure. She says that she and Buckleigh are just friends, but she referred to him repeatedly as 'Ash.'"

"You just did the same," he noted.

"So I did," she said with a laugh. "We have known him forever, it seems. Beyond that, however, she was very upset by what happened. Passionately so, I would say." She gave Gabriel a direct stare. "The only man I feel passionately about is you."

Gabriel's pulse sped. His heart thudded, sending blood crashing through his ears. Had he heard her right? In a handful of steps, he stood before her. "Poppy, I think I understand what you've been going through. I didn't before. Or at least, I didn't want to. I should have shared in your grief—*our* grief—but I couldn't."

She took his hands in hers. "I know. I shouldn't have

expected it of you. I know how deeply your mother's and sister's deaths affected you."

He didn't deserve her understanding. "Don't. I left you alone to deal with what was happening. Or not happening, as it were. I was too scared." He squeezed her hands. "I'm still scared."

She moved closer and brought her hands to his face, holding him as she looked up into his eyes. "I know, but you don't have to be."

He clasped her waist, holding her against him. "I wish I could change things. I wish I could fill you with a child. With ten children." She arched a brow at him, and he laughed softly. "Too many?"

"At once, yes," she said drily.

He grinned. "Not at once, then." Sobering, he wrapped his arms around her. "Scared as I am, I want to be a father, and I'm heartbroken I can't make you a mother."

Poppy stood on her toes, whispering, "My love. We are still a family." She kissed him, her lips soft and warm beneath his.

A dam of emotion broke inside him. He swept her up against him and deepened the kiss, desperate to show her how much she meant to him and how sorry he was. But it was she who showed him—her hands twined in his hair as she pressed her body to his, offering herself in sweet surrender.

After a thorough, toe-curling kiss, she undressed him piece by piece, her lips pressing into his skin each time she revealed a new part of him. He cupped her head as she unfastened his fall to strip him of his last garment. "What did I do to deserve you?"

"Don't be silly," she said with a soft smile. "We deserve each other." She peeled his breeches away, exposing his cock. Then she dropped to her knees as she pulled the garment completely down his legs. Her hand encircled the base of his shaft as he worked to kick the breeches away.

Before he could tell her to stop, that he wanted to be the one to worship her, she took him into her mouth. Her dark curls fell across her cheeks as her head bobbed forward, her lips sliding over his flesh.

Gabriel thrust his fingers into her hair, holding her lest he spin away into darkness. He was aware only of her—the clasp of her hand, the gentle pressure of her thumb, the glide of her tongue, the heat of her mouth. His hips moved, and he had to work to keep from thrusting into her.

Suddenly, it was too much. He withdrew from her and bent to scoop her into his arms. He bore her the few steps it took to reach the bed, then he laid her down and climbed between her legs.

He reached for the hem of her night rail, but she was already tugging it up, revealing herself to him inch by inch. He smiled to himself as she went slowly on purpose. It had been a long time since she'd seduced him.

The moment she bared her sex to him, he bowed forward. She spread her legs to him, but he put his palms against her thighs and pushed them farther apart, opening her to his gaze completely. She was so beautiful with her bright pink lips and glistening folds. He was humbled by the offering of her body and just knew that the fault of their childlessness had to lie with him.

"Gabriel?" she asked softly.

He looked up her body where she had the night rail gathered at her waist. She'd brought her head up to look down at him, her gaze heavy with desire but also tinged with concern.

"Take it off," he rasped.

She pulled the garment the rest of the way up her body, lifting from the bed and then whisking it over her head. The cotton floated away, but he was fixed on her breasts, so full and round and tipped with soft, blush-pink nipples. They tempted him, but he was already committed, the scent of her arousal luring him back to her sex.

He buried himself in her, using his tongue and fingers to tease and fill her. Her whimpers were a song, urging him to give her more. He curled two fingers into her, finding that sensitive spot that sent her spiraling into ecstasy. Her legs quivered and her muscles clenched around him, signaling her release. She cried out, and he suckled her clitoris, drawing out her pleasure until she begged him to stop.

He looked up at her as she tugged on his hair. "You really want me to stop?"

"I want you inside me," she said.

"I was," he argued with a smile.

Her heavy-lidded eyes slitted with impatience and lust. "Not that part of you. Your cock."

She didn't often use coarse language, but God, when she did, he nearly came undone. He prowled up over her body, lavishing kisses upon her flesh at intervals until he reached her breasts. There, he stopped and feasted on her until she writhed beneath him.

"You're taking too long," she said, breathless.

"The best things are worth waiting for." He drew her nipple into his mouth, sucking hard for a moment before licking along her pearlescent skin. "I like it when you talk to me. And say things like 'cock.'" He lifted his head and grinned at her.

One of her brows arched in that playful fashion he loved. Then she shoved at his shoulders, pushing him over and pinning him to the bed as she straddled his hips. "Put your *cock* in me now."

"Yes, my love." He grasped his shaft and positioned it at her sex. She lifted off him and covered his hand with hers, guiding him into her wet sheath. Bearing down, she covered him completely, drawing him deep into her sex. She closed her eyes, her body growing taut as he filled her.

Then she began to move. How he loved watching her like this—the slender column of her throat, the lines of deep pleasure etched into her face, the sway and bounce of her breasts as she pumped herself on him.

And then rapture claimed him. He gripped her hips and thrust up into her, losing himself in her sweet heat. She fell forward with a cry, grinding against him, bracing herself over him. He licked at her nipple, drawing her breast into his mouth, and she came apart around him.

Over and over, she bore down on him, her moans and whimpers driving him toward a climax that threatened to rip him in two. He held her tight as she collapsed over him, finishing with a rapid series of strokes and then cradling her close to his heart.

He kissed her temple, her cheek, her jawline. "I love you, Poppy."

She lifted her head and looked at him. "I love you too, but is that enough?"

CHAPTER 6

*T*he look of distress in Gabriel's eyes spurred Poppy to lean down to kiss him. She pulled back and caressed his cheek.

"That didn't come out quite right," she said. She drew in a breath and tried to formulate the words she needed to say to properly convey her emotion. "What you said earlier—" She couldn't bring herself to ask if he was truly heartbroken. "About having children—"

He slipped his hand into her hair and cupped her head. "Loving you, and you loving me, is all I need. If this is all we ever have, it is more than enough. More than anyone can hope for."

Emotion clogged her throat so she could only nod. She kissed him again, finding comfort in his embrace. It had seemed so long since she'd done that. He turned with her so they lay facing each other on the bed.

She nuzzled close against his chest. "I don't want to be melancholy about it anymore. I may always feel sad, but that can't be the ruling emotion in my life. Hearing you say that just the two of us is enough makes me so happy."

He tensed, and she wondered if she'd said something wrong. She pulled back so she could see his face. "What is it?"

"Would you consider fostering a child?"

Dinah and her baby instantly came to Poppy's mind. "Yes. Did you have a child in mind?" She held her breath, wondering if he'd thought the same thing as she.

"I do. I did." His brow creased. He pushed up and pulled the bedclothes back so they could slide beneath them. Then he sat against the headboard. "I need to tell you the entire truth about Dinah."

She sat up and faced him. The covers settled around her waist, and a shiver twitched across her shoulders. "Can you reach my night rail?" she asked.

He slipped from the bed to fetch her garment, and she took the opportunity to marvel at his firm, rounded backside.

He helped her don the night rail before resituating himself in bed and continuing. "When I met Dinah at Hartwell House, it's true that Mrs. Armstrong didn't have space and that I wanted to help. What I neglected to tell you is that I'd hoped to persuade Dinah to allow us to raise her child. She'd already said she didn't want it, so I thought I would be offering her a welcome alternative." His gaze was heavy with regret. "That's why I didn't tell you about her coming to the cottage. I didn't want to get your hopes up in the event she declined. Or worse—if something happened to her and the baby."

"Oh, Gabriel." She took his hand in hers, wanting to draw his anxiety away. "I considered this too. But I felt selfish even thinking of it."

"Is it selfish if our need solves her dilemma?" he asked.

"I wouldn't want her decision to be based on our need."

"But she'd already decided she didn't want the child."

Poppy didn't think she could make that decision, not

before giving birth. "I have to think she'd regret giving the babe away. How can she not look at his or her face and fall instantly in love?"

He traced his thumb over her hand. "That's what you would do."

"I would already be in love," she said softly. "From the moment I knew the babe was growing inside me, I would be lost." She watched as apprehension darkened his eyes and lined his forehead. Reaching up with her free hand, she brushed her fingertips over his brow. "I know that frightens you—the specter of what could happen. But I can't live in fear. *We* can't."

He nodded slowly. "I know that. Here." He tapped his temple. "But here..." He lowered his hand to his chest and pressed his palm against his heart. "Anyway, I don't think it matters as I believe she's changed her mind. You were quite persuasive."

She couldn't tell from his tone how he felt about that. "Are you angry?"

"How can I be when my wife is the most thoughtful person in the world? That you would ignore your own desire to save a woman from a lifetime of possible regret is the epitome of kindness and selflessness."

Poppy chewed her lower lip, suddenly worried about Dinah's future, and more importantly, that of her baby's. "I fear I will be the one to have regret," she admitted quietly. When he looked at her in confusion, she explained. "Dinah wants to be an actress. How can that be a good life for her or her child?"

Gabriel's dark gaze flickered with surprise. "I know nothing about the profession, but I imagine it's difficult."

"I tried to persuade her to stay at Hartwell House until the child is a bit older."

"You're hoping she'll change her mind about becoming an actress in that time?"

"Or at least wait." Poppy shook her head. "I don't know. I just didn't feel right trying to take the child, even with her saying she didn't want to raise it."

He tipped his head to the side, his thumb stilling on the back of Poppy's hand. "What if we offered her an option? If she knew that her child would be well cared for—*loved*—she may choose that over bearing the burden on her own."

His suggestion made perfect sense, but uncertainty lingered in her mind. "It still feels rather self-serving to me."

He gently squeezed her hand, conveying his understanding and concern. "Whatever happens with Dinah, I want to help her. We will see her and the babe settled. Are we in agreement on that?"

She loved him so much. "We are."

"And if Dinah does decide to raise her child, there are many other children who are in need of help. We will undoubtedly find one—or ten"—he flashed a smile—"to foster."

Poppy leaned toward him and pressed her lips to his for a soft, lingering kiss. "Thank you," she whispered as she pulled away. "I love you."

"Not nearly as much as I love you, and don't try to dispute that."

She laughed softly. He always told her that. "I never do. Which isn't to say I agree." She gave him a saucy smile.

"Keep looking at me like that, and I'm going to roll you over and show you just how much more I love you."

Desire curled through her. "Promise?"

With a growl, he wrapped his arms around her and tumbled her back until she was flat against the mattress, his body covering hers.

"Wait," she said, suddenly breathless and quite happy to

be. "I'd like to go to Hartwell House tomorrow. It's been too long."

His eyes, dark with passion, softened. "Of course. I would love to take you—if you want me to."

"There's no one I'd rather go with." She curled her arms around his neck and pressed her breasts up against his chest. "Now kiss me and whatever else you have planned."

"With pleasure." He grinned before claiming her mouth and stealing away thoughts of tomorrow.

~

*A*s it happened, the weather did not allow them to visit Hartwell House the next day. Or the day after. Trapped inside due to snow, they had no trouble making the best of their time. Though they did venture out for a walk in the snow—and a snowball fight that deteriorated into rolling around in the snow, which necessitated a shared bath. It was a delightful two days, truly the best Poppy could recall in recent memory.

Before going to Hartwell House, Poppy made a visit to the cottage to see how Judith and Dinah had fared in the snow. Plus, she'd wanted to speak with Dinah about her choices.

Poppy waited for Dinah to eat the first of the lemon biscuits she'd brought before launching into her proposal. "Gabriel tells me you've changed your mind about raising the baby. That's wonderful news."

Seated in the chair by the fire, Dinah looked as though her belly was taking over her body. Though it had only been a few days since Poppy had seen her, she seemed markedly rounder. "Did he?" Dinah plucked up a second biscuit. "I said I was thinking about it. I haven't decided for certain."

"I still think you should," Poppy said, choosing her next

words carefully. "However, if you decide for any reason that you cannot be a mother to the child, Gabriel and I would be—"

Before she could finish, Dinah spoke. "You want my baby."

Poppy hated the way that sounded, but it was true. She wanted a baby, and Dinah was going to have one. "We want to help you. And if that means raising your child as our own, we would be honored."

"You made a rather persuasive argument as to why I should keep him." Dinah laid her hand atop her belly. "Or her. But now you want me to give it to you?"

"No." Poppy shook her head. "I still think you should keep him. Or her."

"But if I don't want to, you'll take him. Or her." She picked up a third biscuit and held it between her thumb and forefinger. "What sort of help will you give me?"

Poppy and Gabriel hadn't discussed anything specific. "What would you want?"

"I've been thinking about what you said, about how being an actress might make motherhood difficult, especially since I don't have any money to fall back on. I have to think of the babe as well as me."

She really *was* changing her mind. Poppy's stomach dropped through the floor. She hadn't realized until that moment that she'd actually been hoping Dinah wouldn't listen to her, that she'd want to leave the child. And, oh, didn't that make Poppy the worst sort of person?

"Yes, you do," Poppy said. "I'm glad to hear you're considering it. As I said before, I'm sure you could live at Hartwell House. We'll make room." Or she could live here. Poppy would talk to Gabriel about it.

"I'm still not sure I want to live there. I'd rather do something more than learn to sew. I actually know how to sew…"

She thrust the biscuit into her mouth and stared into the fire as she chewed.

Poppy had spent enough time with Dinah to know the young woman was smart. Judith had just told Poppy that Dinah had read *A Midsummer Night's Dream* three times and was starting on her fourth. "Shall I bring you more Shakespeare to read?" Poppy offered.

Dinah swung her head back to look at Poppy, her eyes momentarily wide. "Yes. Please."

An idea came to Poppy. "Dinah, do you know how to do sums?"

"I do." Her brow furrowed. "Why?"

"I've long thought that Hartwell House should have its own school. Perhaps you could be the teacher."

Dinah's gaze moved from Poppy's and became slightly unfocused. After a moment, she blinked. "I'll think about it."

Every time Poppy glimpsed what was probably the real woman buried beneath the burdens of her young life, Dinah shuttered herself. It was as if she'd practiced hiding and didn't dare emerge.

Kindness. That was what she needed. And Poppy was determined to give it to her.

"Yes, you think about it," Poppy said sunnily as she stood. "There are more lemon biscuits if you want them."

Dinah sniggered. "Of course I will want them." She looked up at Poppy. "Thank you."

"You're welcome. I'll have a groom bring some Shakespeare." Poppy would make a few selections from the library before leaving for Hartwell House. She bid farewell to Dinah and then to Judith.

A while later, she and Gabriel were on their way to Hartwell House. "Thank you for delaying our departure," Poppy said, drawing the woolen blanket more securely about their laps as Gabriel drove the gig.

"What were you doing in the library?"

"Gathering more books for Dinah. She's on her fourth reading of *A Midsummer Night's Dream*, so I offered her something new."

"Thoughtful of you, but that is unsurprising." He tossed her a smile. "They were not troubled by the snow?"

Poppy shook her head. "Judith said Dinah even went outside."

"That's something." It was, for she mostly stayed in the cottage even though her cough was completely gone.

"I spoke to her about the babe. She is strongly considering keeping it now. I encouraged her to do so." She hesitated as she recalled her feelings of disappointment. She didn't want to bring that up to Gabriel, not when she was trying so hard to have a positive outlook. Focusing on that instead, she continued, "I came up with an idea for Dinah. She is not keen on living at Hartwell House and learning to clean or cook or sew. She's already worked as a maid, and that ended horribly."

He slid her an inquisitive glance. "She told me she was a maid, but I don't know what happened to her."

"After being elevated to upstairs maid, she drew the unwanted attention of her employer. He didn't give her the option of declining his advances."

Gabriel's jaw flexed, and his voice dropped to a low hum. "Who is he?"

"She didn't tell me." Poppy touched his sleeve. "Anyway, what would we do? It's not as if he would wed her, and I can't say I'd want him raising the child."

"I could call him out. Or beat him silly." He nodded. "Either would be satisfying."

"My beloved to the rescue." They exchanged a heated look.

"What was your idea?" he asked, turning her mind back to their conversation instead of how much she loved him.

"I was thinking about how much she likes to read, and how astounding it is that she loves Shakespeare. So I asked if she knew how to do sums. She does."

"What's going on in your shrewd mind?"

"We've discussed Hartwell House's need for a teacher. Perhaps she could take the position."

Gabriel looked over at her in open admiration. "Never say your sister has all the cleverest ideas. That's positively inspired."

Poppy sat taller in her seat. "Thank you. I hope Mrs. Armstrong is supportive."

"I'm sure she will be. As you said, we've been talking about this for a while now. This is a perfect solution—Hartwell House has a need and so does Dinah."

"She hasn't agreed to the position yet. She's thinking about it. I think she will." Poppy couldn't see how she could turn her back on such an opportunity.

"I'm sorry," he said softly, his gaze trained on the road ahead.

"Why?"

"Because it truly seems the baby will remain with her. Are you disappointed?"

"Yes," she admitted. "I don't want to be, but there's no help for it. Still, I think it's the right thing. And you're right, we'll find a child who needs us, and everything will turn out as it should."

Gabriel didn't respond, and they rode in silence the rest of the way to Hartwell House. When they arrived, Mrs. Armstrong was overjoyed to see Poppy.

"I'm so pleased to have you back again, my lady." Mrs. Armstrong beamed at her. "We've much to discuss. But first, I must speak to his lordship." She turned, grimacing, to

Gabriel. "The snow caused a few new leaks. I just don't know how much longer this poor house is going to keep standing. You do your best to fix what you can, but a refurbishment is needed, and there's just no money." She waved her hand. "Never mind that for now. Can you please take a look at the corner in the dining hall? It bore the worst of the damage."

"I'll see to it." Gabriel took himself off.

Mrs. Armstrong turned to Poppy, her smile bright. "You are looking quite well. Are you?" Though her smile remained, lines fanned from her eyes and furrowed her brow.

"I am, thank you. I must apologize for staying away for so long. It was incredibly selfish of me."

Mrs. Armstrong looped her arm through Poppy's and led her from the entrance hall to her small sitting room to the left. Releasing Poppy's arm, the older woman took her hand instead as she faced her. "You are anything but selfish. I can well imagine what you've been enduring."

"You can?" Poppy had never talked to her about her troubles.

With a nod, Mrs. Armstrong motioned for Poppy to take one of the chairs near the hearth where a fire blazed. When Poppy was seated, Mrs. Armstrong sat in the other chair.

"Mr. Armstrong and I never had children."

Poppy knew that, or at least that she and her husband didn't have any living children. She realized she didn't know the particulars. "Have you never even been pregnant?"

Hands clasped firmly in her lap, Mrs. Armstrong shook her head. "And it wasn't for our lack of trying." She winked at Poppy. "Sometimes, however, we are meant to do other things. We were meant to open our home to women, including those with children, in need. Through that endeavor, we fostered a few children ourselves, including Judith."

"I didn't realize she was your foster child."

"She and her mother came to us when Judith was four. Her mother passed a few years later, and Judith remained. While we aren't an orphanage, in some instances, when the child had nowhere else to go, Mr. Armstrong and I kept them here. With Judith, I was just so attached to her, as she became attached to us when her mother was ill."

"I'm so glad you were there for her. Judith is a lovely young woman."

"She is," Mrs. Armstrong noted with pride. The pride of a mother. In that moment, Poppy glimpsed a future in which she didn't feel sad or…less. She wanted that future to start right now.

"I tell you this," Mrs. Armstrong continued, "because there are so many children who need a home and security. They need a family."

"I was just thinking that," Poppy said softly. "Thank you. Gabriel and I have discussed fostering a child." Or children. Why would they stop at just one?

"I'm glad to hear it." Mrs. Armstrong's blue gaze turned hesitant. "Dare I ask if that's why he took Dinah in?"

"Partly. He also just wanted to help—her and you. We know you are out of empty beds at present."

"We are, and the condition of the house is becoming a problem. I fear we need some big repairs." She looked as though she was going to say more but then snapped her mouth closed.

Poppy knew what was on her tongue. The same thing was in her mind. "Things have become more difficult since my brother withdrew the support of the dukedom after he inherited." She clenched her jaw as she thought of how he'd ceased giving the money their father had given to Mrs. Armstrong for Hartwell House. He'd said he needed to review the ledgers to determine if such charity could truly be afforded. As far as she knew, he hadn't made a final decision. "I will press him on the matter. In the meantime, we will pledge more support." Gabriel wasn't as wealthy as Calder, but he was committed to helping those less fortunate.

Mrs. Armstrong shook her head. "You both already give so much—money and time. Now, back to Dinah. Is she going to let you raise the baby?"

The blunt question took Poppy slightly off guard, but why shouldn't Mrs. Armstrong speak plainly? "I don't think so. I've been working to convince her to keep the child."

"You have?" Mrs. Armstrong asked with surprise.

"As someone who seeks and values motherhood, I worried she would regret not keeping the child."

"She didn't strike me as particularly motherly, but then Judith's missives have painted a picture of a young woman who fell victim to unfortunate circumstance."

"Judith has been writing to you about Dinah?"

"Yes. It sounds as though Dinah has perfected quite a bravado." Mrs. Armstrong cocked her head to the side. "Do you share that sentiment?"

"I can certainly see it. She hides her true self quite deep, I think. She's read *A Midsummer Night's Dream* several times."

Mrs. Armstrong laughed softly. "Judith mentioned that."

"She's good at sums too," Poppy said. "I wonder if she might fulfill the role of schoolteacher here at Hartwell House."

Mrs. Armstrong stroked her cheek in thought. "Oh, to finally have a school… Do you think she could?"

Poppy lifted a shoulder. "It's worth trying."

"It certainly is." But Mrs. Armstrong's expression dimmed. "I just don't know where we would house the school or her—and her child. We are fair to bursting at the seams."

"Let me discuss it with Gabriel." And Bianca—she would

likely think of something. While Gabriel had noted she didn't have *all* the ideas, she did conjure a great many of them.

"Mrs. Armstrong!" A boy ran into the sitting room, his face pale. "There's a fire!"

Mrs. Armstrong leapt to her feet as the color drained from her face. Poppy rose, legs trembling and heart pounding.

"We need to get everyone out," Mrs. Armstrong said, sounding dazed.

"Not here," the boy, who was perhaps eight or nine, said. "It's over at Shield's End. Lord Darlington just left to go help. He told me to come tell you."

Shield's End was a house—and former farm—that belonged to Ash. It had been his family home before he'd become Earl of Buckleigh. "At least no one is living there right now," Poppy said with relief. Still, it was horrible.

Mrs. Armstrong laid her hand against her chest and closed her eyes briefly. "You gave me a fright, Michael. Round up the boys, and we'll go to see how we can help."

He nodded, then dashed out of the sitting room.

"I'll take them," Poppy offered. Since Gabriel had gone, she wanted to go too.

Lowering her arm to her side, Mrs. Armstrong gave her a grateful smile. "Thank you."

Despite the effort it took to herd the half dozen boys who joined her to walk over to Shield's End, they arrived fairly quickly. Smoke was visible from Hartwell House, which sat a half mile away, but now, as they walked up the lane to the house, she could see flames licking up from the structure. Her heart ached at the sight. Ash would be devastated.

Poppy cautioned the boys to stay close behind her and not go near the house. She led them to the back, where a line of villagers were passing buckets from the well to try to put the fire out. It seemed a losing battle.

Then she caught sight of her sister standing with Ash as they watched the house burn. Though she wanted to go to them immediately, Poppy took the boys to the water line and put them into service first.

After ensuring they were well organized, she hurried across the grass. "Bianca!"

Bianca pivoted. Her eyes lit, and she threw her arms around Poppy. In her haste, she knocked into Ash. The hug didn't last long as Bianca turned back to Ash and clutched his arm. "Sorry, are you all right?"

He gave her a wry look. "I'm fine. You can hug your sister. I should go see how things are progressing. I fear it's going to be completely ruined." He nodded toward Poppy. "Lady Darlington."

"Lord Buckleigh, I'm so sorry," Poppy murmured.

He ducked his chin, his eyes sad, then took himself off.

Bianca frowned after him. "I hope he doesn't overtax himself. He already rescued those who were inside."

Poppy gasped. "I didn't think anyone was living there."

"They aren't, but—" Bianca groaned. "It's a long story that I shall tell you later. Suffice it to say that Thornaby and his pack of rascals are responsible for this disaster in the name of a *prank*."

Poppy gasped again, this time, lifting her hand to her chest in much the same way Mrs. Armstrong had. "Despicable."

"Indeed," Bianca said darkly.

A dozen questions ran through Poppy's head. She chose what seemed the most pressing. "Whatever are you doing here?"

"Ash and I happened to be passing by." She opened her mouth to continue, but Poppy cut her off.

"You and Ash. Happened to be passing by. How?" She put her hand on her hip. "Why?"

"We're betrothed!" Bianca's bright blue eyes gleamed with excitement despite the disaster happening a short distance away.

"You're what?" Poppy was surprised and yet she wasn't. "That was fast."

"Faster than you and Gabriel, yes, but as I think you told me at the time, when you know it's right, why wait?"

She *had* said that. Or something like it. Joy coursed through her, and she hugged her sister again, this time for longer as happiness flowed between them. When they parted, Poppy caressed her younger sister's cheek. "I'm so thrilled for you. I want to hear everything. How you 'happened' to be passing by with Ash, how he proposed, all of it." She glanced toward the burning house and then at the water line where Gabriel stood with Ash surveying the fire. "But perhaps later."

"Yes," Bianca said somberly. "Definitely later."

Poppy looked around again. "Why isn't Calder here? Or any of his retainers? Surely they can see the smoke from Hartwell."

"Maybe. The clouds have thickened since we arrived. We didn't see the smoke until we were close to the village." Bianca snorted. "I am not excusing him, by the way."

"Me neither." Poppy gritted her teeth. "Later, after you tell me all your good news, we need to discuss him."

"We do." Bianca's tone held a note of foreboding—for Calder. Poppy might have felt sorry for their brother if he hadn't become a complete and utter blackguard. "I'm afraid he was quite horrible today, and I was actually on my way to stay with you until the wedding. If that's all right."

"Of course it is." Poppy didn't know what Calder had done now, but was certain he deserved a good shaking.

Bianca turned her attention from the house and looked to

Poppy. "Let us go and speak to the men and try to soothe them."

"Bianca, I am truly sorry for Ash's loss."

"I am too, but I am just grateful he is fine. The loss of timber and furniture is nothing when compared to the loss of a loved one."

Hearing her sister speak of her love for Ash and seeing the emotion evidenced in Bianca's eyes made Poppy smile. "Well said, sister. Well said."

CHAPTER 7

"It's good that it started raining," Gabriel said, thinking of the largely burned Shield's End as he joined Poppy in bed that night. "What a day."

She snuggled up beside him, laying her hand on his chest, as he sat against the headboard. "It felt like a week."

Gabriel stroked his wife's shoulder and back. "Bianca is all settled?"

"Yes, though I wonder if she will actually sleep. She's rather worked up."

"The fire or the wedding?"

"Both. I told her to focus on the latter. I don't think that will be a trial."

Gabriel smiled through his weariness. "They seem very happy."

"They do."

"It happened rather quickly, didn't it?"

Poppy chuckled, her body vibrating against his. "That's what I told her. She reminded me of something I told her after we became betrothed. Something to the effect of when it's right, it's right."

He gazed down at the top of her dark head. Her curls were tamed into a plait for sleeping, but he knew from experience that he could unwind it in a trice. Perhaps he would if he wasn't so bloody exhausted… "Is that how it was for us?"

She looked up at him, her lips curling into a heart-stopping smile. "Yes. Don't you agree?"

"Right doesn't adequately describe how I felt. To me, it was destiny." Perhaps he wasn't as exhausted as he thought.

She pressed a kiss to his chest, and though he wore a nightshirt, he felt the connection as if his flesh were bare to her. Sighing, she lowered her head to his chest. "Is Shield's End completely destroyed then? It looked as though the newer wing survived."

The addition made in the last century to the medieval-aged manor still stood, but Gabriel had to think it was greatly weakened. "I'm not sure it can remain without the support of the rest of the structure, particularly with the winter ahead of us."

"I hope he'll be able to rebuild soon. I'm glad Thornaby is paying for it."

Gabriel snorted. "That's the least he can do." Upon learning the fire had been caused by a goat, which Thornaby and his friends had brought into the house as a prank on Buckleigh, Gabriel had wanted to force the man to make restitution. That he apparently didn't have to be made to do the right thing was a small victory.

"Yes, after putting goats in the house. Bianca said they did that to Ash at Oxford and thought it would be amusing to repeat the prank."

"Makes me glad I went to Cambridge."

She glanced up at him. "No one stooped to such idiocy at Cambridge?"

Gabriel let out a sharp laugh. "Not that specifically.

Perhaps I *should* have gone to Oxford. I would have stood up for Buckleigh if I'd been there."

"Of course you would have. You're the most thoughtful man I know." She tipped her head back to look him in the eye once more. "Thank you for agreeing to stand up with Ash at the wedding."

"It's my honor. I'm just sorry your brother is being such a miserable pig." He flinched. "Forgive my description."

She patted his chest once. "In this case, I'll allow it. I may even call him that myself since he refuses to approve of Bianca's marriage." Bianca and Ash had gone to tell Calder of their betrothal, but he'd refused to grant permission for her to wed him. Legally, Bianca didn't need it, but she did if she wanted the settlement their father had left for her. "He's still denying support to Hartwell House. When did he become such a cold, unfeeling blackguard?"

Gabriel didn't have an answer. As long as he'd known Calder Stafford, he'd always been heartless. "Please don't think poorly of me, but I'm beyond caring about him when so many are affected by his cruelty."

"I can't disagree with you, but I do plan to talk with him about Hartwell House. It's unconscionable that the building is in need of repairs, there isn't enough room for everyone who needs shelter, and it's past time we founded the school."

Hearing her speak so passionately warmed Gabriel's heart. It seemed she truly was breaking free of her melancholy, and for that he was exceptionally grateful. He leaned down and pressed a kiss to the top of her head. "You can talk to him, but I daresay it won't matter."

"I have to try. The fact that he refuses to host St. Stephen's Day is bad enough." She sniffed. "Bianca and I will do our best to ensure the celebration at Thornhill meets everyone's expectations, despite it being so far away."

It was only five miles, but for many of the villagers, it might as well have been London. Thornaby had apparently offered to transport people, and Gabriel planned to do the same. If Darlington Abbey weren't even farther from the village, he would have insisted on holding the party here.

"I'm glad that's sorted, at least," Gabriel said. "As for Hartwell House, I will do my best to complete the necessary repairs. Some help would not come amiss." He could use both hands and financial support. He already donated a noteworthy sum to Mrs. Armstrong annually.

"I was thinking we should raise funds at the Yuletide Assembly. Bianca and I can surely persuade people to donate. We should squeeze Thornaby until nothing comes out."

Gabriel laughed. "You're vicious when you're on a mission. And that's a splendid idea—raising funds at the assembly, I mean."

She rotated her body so that her breasts were pressed against his chest and side and looked up at him with a saucy smile. "You don't agree with us bleeding Thornaby dry?"

"I'd actually pay money to see that."

Her eyes sparked. "Another way to raise funds!"

He laughed again. "Yes, though none of this solves the issue of providing additional room for Dinah and anyone else who comes along, nor does it address the school."

Her mouth tipped into a half frown. "I know. Watching Shield's End burn, I was thinking it could have made a marvelous extension of Hartwell House."

"Indeed it would have." He lightly massaged her neck.

"You're assuming Dinah wants to stay," she said softly, laying her head back on his chest.

He assumed nothing. He *hoped* she wouldn't, actually, that she would give her baby to them to raise. But he didn't voice that. "You've done your best to convince her."

Poppy ran her fingertip along the neck of his nightshirt. "You sound a bit disappointed."

Damn. "I'm not." *Yet.* "We should invite her to reside in the cottage for as long as she needs, though I'm sure Mrs. Armstrong would like to have Judith back at some point."

Sliding up his body a few inches, Poppy pressed a kiss against his collarbone. Exhausted or not, his cock didn't care as it stirred to attention. "You're the sweetest man. I'll let her know tomorrow. I plan to visit in the morning because I don't know how much time I can spend there over the next few days. There's much to do to prepare for Bianca's wedding."

Gabriel worked to ignore the desire swirling through him. They were both tired. "Mmm."

"I wanted to tell you what Mrs. Armstrong said to me today," she said softly, stirring him from his preoccupied haze.

"What's that?"

She pushed up to a sitting position beside him, her body angled to his. "She encouraged us to foster a child—or children. That's what she and Mr. Armstrong did. I didn't realize Judith has been with her since she was four."

"I didn't realize it was that long either," Gabriel said.

"She believes we'll have a family when it's meant to be." Poppy's entire face beamed with warmth—and love. "I believe that too."

He clasped her waist and pulled her atop him so she straddled his hips. "I believe I married the most spectacular woman who will undoubtedly make all my dreams come true."

Her eyes narrowed provocatively as she pressed her pelvis down against his. "And what is your dream right now?"

He held her tight and moved her over his rigid erection. "I think you can probably tell."

She curled her arms around his neck and gave him a smoldering smile. "Good, because that's mine too."

∼

*B*ianca's wedding the day before had been lovely and wonderful, even without the presence of their brother. Or maybe because of it. Poppy thrust him from her mind. Thinking of him only made her angry, and she was determined to be positive and pleasant. It was, after all, Christmastime.

Today was St. Nicholas Day, and already Darlington Abbey was adorned in greenery. Poppy made sure mistletoe was hung in key places, including Gabriel's study and the doorway between their sitting room and bedchamber. Plus at least a half dozen other places Gabriel would least expect. She'd done the same last year, and it had led to a rather memorable afternoon in the orangery.

Poppy stood back and surveyed the greenery she'd just festooned around the drawing room at Hartwell House in preparation for the St. Nicholas Day party that would commence shortly.

"What's that smile for?" Bianca asked as she breezed into the room.

"Oh, nothing, just remembering something in years past." Poppy noted that her sister was positively glowing today, and why shouldn't she be? Seeing her thus made Poppy so happy.

To think that just a fortnight ago, Poppy had been dreading the season because finding joy had just seemed impossible. Facing her disappointment and working through her grief—with Gabriel at her side—had made all the difference.

Bianca climbed onto a chair, and Poppy handed her one end of the pine garland the children had made that morning. "Last night, I was thinking about the space issues here at Hartwell House."

"On your wedding night?" Poppy shook her head while expelling a light laugh. "Of course you did."

"Can't turn my brain off, I'm afraid," Bianca said cheerfully. "Thankfully, Ash loves that about me. Now, I hope you don't find my proposal too forward, but I would think not since you are already giving shelter to someone for whom there wasn't room here."

Dinah. Poppy and Gabriel had visited the cottage briefly yesterday on their way home from the wedding festivities. Dinah had barely spoken to them, for she'd been extremely uncomfortable and had ultimately asked them to please leave her in peace. Judith had whispered that she suspected Dinah's time was coming soon.

A tremor of anxiety coursed through Poppy when she thought of the baby coming. Decisions would have to be made. There would be no more postponing the future—not for any of them.

A bead of hope worked its way through Poppy's nervousness, but she refused to embrace it. She didn't dare.

She couldn't.

Poppy focused on her sister. "What's your idea?"

"Ash and I plan to open up a portion of Buck Manor to anyone who needs it. We have several rooms that aren't used, and they could provide a temporary home for a few souls until Shield's End is rebuilt."

"What a wonderful plan," Poppy said. "I wish we could do the same, but Darlington Abbey is not as large as Buck Manor. We should ask Calder to take people in."

Bianca nodded. "There are entire wings at Hartwood that he doesn't even step inside."

"He'll refuse," Poppy said flatly. "Though I suppose we should still ask."

"I don't think I've ever seen you so angry with him," Bianca said.

"I don't know that I ever have been. His behavior is deplorable."

"Can I presume you're speaking of your intolerable brother?" Gabriel strode into the drawing room, his arms full of packages, with Ash trailing behind, his arms also full of gifts for the children.

"What gave it away?" Bianca asked drily. "Poppy wants to ask him to help with housing people from Hartwell House as we plan to do at Buck Manor."

"A pointless endeavor," Gabriel said as Poppy moved to help him unload the gifts onto a table. "We should make him, however."

Ash deposited his armful of packages next to Gabriel's. "Is that possible?"

"No," Poppy and Bianca said in unison.

"Oh, let me try." Gabriel's whisper was soft and dangerous, his eyes gleaming with challenge.

Bianca set her hands on her hips and frowned. "He should be here. Our father would have been."

"He is not our father." And that made Poppy sad. Their father hadn't been perfect, but he'd been an excellent duke, a dedicated and admired leader in the community and in London. Calder, on the other hand, was feared. She supposed he *was* dedicated, but to only one thing: himself.

Gabriel looked to Bianca and Ash, who stood close together, their arms touching. "You plan to house people?"

Bianca nodded. "If it becomes necessary."

"It may. Mrs. Armstrong typically sees an influx of women in the winter, and, frankly, I'm concerned about the physical structure of Hartwell House. Three rooms are currently uninhabitable, and I can't see them being repaired until spring."

"Damn, if only Shield's End hadn't burned." Ash took Bianca's hand and addressed Poppy and Gabriel. "Bianca and I decided the house will be rebuilt specifically for the Institution for Impoverished Women."

Poppy gaped at him. "You can't be serious?"

"Never more," Ash said. "The house was sitting empty, and my mother will be staying with us. We were going to host the St. Stephen's Party there—before it burned—and I was glad to see it used for something that would benefit others. We'll consult with Mrs. Armstrong regarding what she'd like the new building to contain."

"That's just…" Gabriel shook his head. "It's incredibly generous."

"I know Mrs. Armstrong would like to have a school for the children who live there," Bianca said. "Ash would take that into account when he meets with the architects."

Poppy had an idea. "Or, and this may not work, we could use Hartwell House as the school since Shield's End would be the new institution. If we can repair Hartwell House adequately."

Bianca beamed at her. "That's a marvelous suggestion."

Gabriel grinned as he regarded her with keen admiration. "You're just full of amazing ideas. And yes, we should be able to repair Hartwell House, especially if we're able to raise funds at the assembly next week."

"Oh yes, that is our intent." Bianca's gaze turned shrewd. "I'm thinking Thornaby and his friends should give until it hurts."

"As should Calder," Poppy said sourly. "Bianca, we're going to have to pay him a visit."

"Yes, we are."

"We'll come with you for fortification," Ash offered.

"I'm not sure if that would help. In fact, it may hinder us."

Mrs. Armstrong bustled into the drawing room, her dark gray skirts swirling about her legs. "Can you help bring in the refreshments? The children are beside themselves with anticipation. I think we need to begin the party." She smiled broadly. "Oh, to be young again!"

They went to help immediately, and soon the room was filled with laughter and gleeful conversation. Women and mothers and children alike opened gifts that Poppy and Gabriel and Ash and Bianca had provided. Watching their joy filled Poppy with contentment. She looked forward to the future and all they had planned.

Later, when everyone began to play games, Mrs. Armstrong drew Poppy aside. "Where is Dinah? I thought she was coming to the party."

"She wasn't feeling well. Judith thinks it may be almost time for the babe."

Mrs. Armstrong inclined her head. "I own I'm sad Judith isn't here. This is the first St. Nicholas Day we haven't spent together. I have a gift for her—perhaps you could deliver it?"

Poppy's heart pinched. "Of course. I should have sent someone to watch over Dinah so that Judith could come." She felt terrible she hadn't thought of that.

"Don't fret yourself. Judith would have said something if she thought it wise for her to come. I wager she thought she was needed with Dinah."

At that moment, one of the grooms from Darlington Abbey appeared in the doorway. He held his hat in his hand, and his face was reddened as if he'd been riding in the wind.

Gabriel went to speak with him, and Poppy watched as his features tensed. He nodded then turned, his gaze searching for Poppy, but she was already walking toward him.

"What is it?' she asked, her entire body swirling with apprehension. With expectation.

He clasped Poppy's hand, his fingers tight around hers. "Dinah has gone into labor. The babe is coming."

*B*y the time they reached the cottage at Darlington Abbey, Gabriel's anxiety and apprehension were so high that he wanted to climb right out of his skin. He prayed Dinah and the baby would be fine. And then he prayed she would decide to let them raise her. Or him.

He shared neither of those hopes with Poppy.

It was nearly dark when they arrived. Another vehicle was parked along the lane. Gabriel recognized it as belonging to Dr. Fisk. Knowing the physician was here should have made him feel better.

It did not.

Gabriel helped Poppy from the gig. They hurried inside to escape the cold, but mostly to discover what was happening.

A wave of dread crested over Gabriel as they reached the front door. He hesitated.

Poppy must have sensed his fear. She turned to him and put her gloved hands on his cheeks, as she looked earnestly into his eyes. "Whatever happens, my love, we will be fine. *You* will be fine."

"I'm not worried about me," he said quietly, his voice a thin thread.

"I know." She gave him an encouraging smile and pressed her palms gently against his face. "And that is why I love you so. One of the many reasons." She stood on her toes and kissed him just as a scream rent the air.

Gabriel gasped against her mouth, his eyes flying wide as panic sliced through him. He remembered his mother screaming when she gave birth to his youngest sibling, a still-born boy his father hadn't wanted to name.

Poppy opened the door and preceded him into the cottage. It was warm—warmer than usual—with a large fire blazing in the hearth. The flames were so high that Gabriel couldn't see through to the back bedroom.

"Good evening, Dorothy," Poppy said.

Who was Dorothy? Gabriel blinked and realized one of the maids from Darlington Abbey was tending the fire.

She turned and bobbed a curtsey to Poppy and Gabriel. "Good evening, my lord, my lady. Dr. Fisk stopped and picked me up on the way here. He said he needed an extra pair of hands because Mrs. Fisk wasn't able to come."

"Where's Judith?" Poppy asked.

"In the back with Dr. Fisk. I don't think it will be long now."

"We heard a scream." The words came from Gabriel's mouth, but he sounded as if he were standing outside his body listening to someone else speak.

"She's done that a few times now," Dorothy said, wincing. "I heard Dr. Fisk tell her that was all right."

Poppy moved to stand in front of Gabriel. She'd removed her hat and cloak, as well as her gloves. "Try to relax, my love," she whispered, removing his hat. "Why don't you sit?" She unfastened his great coat and moved around him to help him doff the garment.

He watched as she hung the items next to hers on a hook near the door. He felt as if he couldn't move. God, if this was how he behaved when a woman he barely knew gave birth, how would he be if Poppy were in this situation? He was immensely glad he'd never find out.

Before he realized what she was doing, Poppy had removed one of his gloves. After he removed the second, she took his arm and guided him to the settee near the fire. A few moments later, she returned with a glass of brandy, which she pressed into his hand.

Grateful, he lifted the drink. Another moan followed by a high-pitched wail filled the cottage. He jerked, and half the liquid in his glass splashed over his hand and onto the floor. "Bloody hell," he muttered. He needed to pull himself together.

Poppy rushed to wipe up the brandy from his hand and wrist, then did the same with the droplets on the floor. "Drink."

He didn't have to be persuaded. Downing the contents of the glass in one gulp, he welcomed the spiced fruit flavor. But it wasn't enough. He held the empty glass up for her to refill it. A moment later, she pressed it back into his hand. This time he sipped. And managed not to spill when a long, loud, shuddering moan seemed to shake the very walls of the cottage.

"Do you want me to go look in?" Poppy asked him softly.

He looked up at her and nodded. "Please."

She left him, and then he heard it—the beautiful, unmistakable sound of a baby's cries. The tension in him released, and he sagged back against the settee. He stared at the fire, unseeing, as he listened to the sounds from the other room— bustling feet, Dr. Fisk giving orders, that melodic cry.

Melodic?

He wiped a hand over his face and laughed at his pathetic

state. After a few minutes, Poppy returned. "It's a girl," she said, grinning. "Dr. Fisk said the birth went well. Dinah is resting now."

"And the babe?" All the tension that had left Gabriel gathered once more, curling and tightening within him.

"Suckling." She quickly added, "There is no wet nurse." Had she read his mind? His first thought was that Dinah had made her decision, that she was going to keep her baby.

Her daughter.

Suddenly realizing he would never have a daughter who looked like her mother, Gabriel's insides turned to mush. His throat squeezed, and he forced himself to breathe.

Poppy sat down beside him. "Do you want to go, or would you rather stay for a while?"

"Stay." He had to know what Dinah meant to do. And he wanted to see the babe.

Gabriel sipped his brandy and Poppy sat quietly next to him, her thigh pressed against his. Dr. Fisk finally came from the bedroom, his ruddy face dappled with sweat.

"Good evening, my lord," he said with a bow. In his fifties, the doctor was a kind and generous man with a large family of his own, including a son who planned to become a physician. Dr. Fisk, often with his wife and a few of his children helping, cared for the women and children at Hartwell House without accepting payment.

Setting his glass down on a small table, Gabriel rose and shook the man's hand. "Good evening, Dr. Fisk. Thank you for attending Dinah. I hear everything went as it should." He heard the note of question in his voice, despite Poppy already telling him things went well.

"Quite! Though rather, er, vocal, Miss Kitson was an excellent patient."

"She'll recover?"

"I have every expectation, my lord," Dr. Fisk said jovially

as he glanced toward the glass of brandy. "I don't suppose I might trouble you for a nightcap?"

"I'll see to it," Poppy offered with a smile.

Gabriel suffered through a good half hour—at least—of chatting with Dr. Fisk before the physician returned to the bedroom once more. Then he took his leave with the promise to check in on the mother and babe in a few days.

The moment he left, Gabriel's anxiety climbed even further, and it took a great deal of effort not to ask him to come back. What happened if Dinah or the babe took a turn?

Dorothy came from the back room bearing a basket with soiled linens. "My lord and lady, if you'd care to visit briefly, you are welcome."

Poppy started toward the bedroom, then stopped, perhaps realizing that Gabriel hadn't moved. He stared toward the chamber in fright, unable to make his feet move.

Coming back to him, Poppy took his hand. "Are you all right?"

Somehow, he nodded. Then he took a step. And another. As they reached the threshold, he recognized a scent in the air, something he couldn't describe. Something he associated with despair. A memory came rushing over him.

His mother lying in the bed, her face pale, her body cold. He wasn't supposed to be there. But he'd wanted to see his beloved mama and tell her how sorry he was that his baby brother had died.

He took her hand. She usually squeezed his fingers and called him her "sweet boy." She did neither.

"Mama?" he whispered, standing on his toes so he could lean toward her form.

She didn't stir. He let go of her hand and found the stool to climb onto the bed. Just as he put his hands on the mattress to boost himself up, his father came in and yelled at him to get away.

"She's gone, boy!"

"Gabriel? Gabriel, can you hear me?" Poppy stood in front of him, her hands on his cheeks, her eyes wide, her words a desperate plea.

He blinked as he returned to the present, to this smell that wasn't quite the same but close. It could so quickly turn...

"She's going to die," he whispered, his gaze moving past Poppy to the bed where Dinah lay cradling her babe. Swaddled in blankets and nuzzled to her mother's chest, the girl was barely visible. Perhaps she was already gone...

Poppy pulled his head down, forcing him to refocus on her. "Look at me, Gabriel. You mustn't think like that. She's fine. And the baby is fine."

"Now. But you know as well as I do that can change."

"It can change for all of us," she said, keeping her voice low. But her tone was harsh. Honest. Fucking unavoidable. "You and I can leave tonight, be set upon by highwaymen, and killed. Or contract an ague and die in a fortnight. Or perhaps there would be a fire, and Ash won't be here to save us. Bad things happen, my love. They happen all the time. But so do good things. We must focus on those, pray for those, celebrate those. If we don't... What is there?"

He heard what she was saying and came to the same question—what is there? He watched as Dinah bent her head and kissed the babe, holding her to her chest. She smiled and whispered to the girl, every part of her radiating joy and love.

She was not going to abandon her daughter.

So much for good things. Steeling himself, Gabriel stepped around Poppy toward the bed. "You look well," he said, sounding surprisingly normal.

Dinah tipped her head up. She looked pale, but not dangerously so. Her eyes were tired, but her mouth seemed glued into a half smile. Indeed, he'd never seen her in such fine spirits.

"I have a baby girl," she said.

There was his answer. But he'd already deduced it. "So I heard. Have you chosen a name for her yet?"

Dinah looked down at her and shook her head. "I never allowed myself to think of a name. I didn't think I should."

Poppy had joined them at the bed, standing on the other side. "Why?"

Glancing toward Poppy, Dinah spoke in a soft, almost sad voice. She didn't sound quite like herself—at least not the woman Gabriel had come to know. "I didn't think I would be a mother. I didn't think I should."

He had to strain to hear the last part. He looked over at Poppy, saw the flash of pain and disappointment in her eyes, and felt the emotions echoing in his heart. She covered them quickly, smiling at Dinah with warmth and understanding.

"Of course you should," Poppy said with honest encouragement. Gabriel knew that as badly as she wanted a babe, she would support this woman's choice to be a mother.

"I know you hoped—" Dinah snapped her mouth closed, her jaw tightening, and returned her attention to her daughter. She held the girl close, as if she were afraid to lose her. Gabriel would do the same if the babe were his.

Poppy touched Dinah's arm. "I hoped for you to find peace, to make a choice that you feel is best for you and the babe."

When Dinah looked back up, her eyes were full of tears. "You were right, my lady. I am in love. I can't ever let her go."

"Of course you can't."

Gabriel couldn't believe Poppy's voice didn't catch. He didn't think he could speak if his life depended upon it.

"I'm so glad we could help you become a mother and provide a safe haven," Poppy said, stroking Dinah's arm.

"When you are recovered, we can talk of the future. Your future—yours and your daughter's."

Dinah nodded and dashed her hand over her eyes. "I've been thinking about what you mentioned before, about becoming a teacher at Hartwell House. I—I would like that very much."

Poppy's eyes lit with joy—true happiness amidst this crushing disappointment. "Wonderful! We will need to work out the specifics, but we have so many plans for Hartwell House, and now you will be a part of them."

"Thank you." Dinah looked from Poppy to Gabriel, her eyes welling once more. "I can't thank you enough—ever. You have changed my life. You have *given* me life. How fitting that this is St. Nicholas Day." She smiled down at her daughter. "If she were a boy, I would name her Nicholas."

"Why not Nicola?" Poppy suggested.

"Oh, that's perfect." Dinah tapped her finger lightly against her daughter's nose. The babe snuffled, and Dinah laughed softly. "Nicola, my love."

Gabriel needed to go. "Poppy, we should allow them to rest."

"Yes, we should." With a final pat to Dinah's arm, Poppy said goodbye and they left.

They spoke briefly with Judith, who planned to stay with Dinah for a few more days at least. Poppy said she would speak with Mrs. Armstrong about moving Dinah and Nicola to Hartwell House. Gabriel heard them discussing ideas about how to make that happen but wasn't listening to the words. He'd gone back to that room with his mother.

Somehow, he and Poppy were soon ensconced in the gig. He plucked up the reins and started toward the abbey, his muscles moving as if he were an automaton. After several minutes, Poppy exhaled as she pressed close to his side. "What a long day."

"I found my mother dead."

The words cascaded from his mouth like an avalanche of rocks that would crush him if he didn't flee. Gabriel had nowhere else to run.

Poppy stiffened beside him. He didn't look at her but could feel her gaze on him like the rays of the sun on a hot summer day. But he wasn't warm. The night was cold, and he was even colder on the inside. Absurdly, he wondered if this was how Poppy's brother felt.

"You never told me that," she said quietly.

"I only just remembered it tonight."

She put her hand on his thigh beneath the blanket she'd drawn over their laps. "That's why you went so deathly pale. I worried you were going to faint."

"It was the smell. Of birth, I suppose." He shook his head the faintest amount, his gaze trained on the dark road, barely illuminated by the lanterns hanging from the sides of the gig.

"That triggered the memory?"

He swallowed as the recollection filtered back in small pieces—he didn't want all of it. "I only wanted to see her, to tell her how sorry I was that my brother had died."

"He was stillborn."

"Yes. My father told me I couldn't visit her, that she was tired and not feeling well. But I just had to see her. " His voice started to break. He gripped the reins, glad the journey was short and they were nearly to the stable.

"Gabriel." The anguish in his wife's voice nearly undid him.

"Please don't, Poppy," he barely whispered. "I can't."

He drove her to the side door and stopped the gig. "Go inside. It's cold."

"I'll go to the stable with you, and we can walk to the house together."

"No. Please go."

She turned toward him—he could feel her movements. "I'm not leaving you. Not like this. You're upset."

"Poppy, *go*."

The sound of her breath drawing sharply into her mouth and the feeling of her body going ramrod straight beside him did nothing to ease the ache inside him. On the contrary, he only felt like more of a failure. She deserved a child, and he couldn't give her one.

She got out of the gig and walked inside, turning to look at him as she reached the door.

Gabriel couldn't meet her gaze. He should at least have helped her out of the vehicle, but he was too entwined in himself. In the painful past.

In the dismal future.

He drove to the stable and cared for the horse himself while the grooms managed the tack and vehicle. Moving slowly, he didn't care how long the task would take. He had nowhere he wanted or needed to be.

Yes, it was St. Nicholas Day. A day for giving and sharing. He'd never been more bereft.

$\sim$

"Tell me how you're enjoying being married," Poppy said to Bianca as they drove to Hartwood. If she could manage to keep the conversation diverted away from herself, she would be able to keep from breaking down. And yet, she wondered if it might do her good to discuss her problems with someone. No, not with someone. With her sister.

Bianca laughed, and Poppy seized onto the glorious sound, basking in its joy and warmth. "It's only been a week. But it's quite lovely." She gave Poppy a knowing glance, and Poppy couldn't help but laugh too.

"I see," Poppy murmured. "I am glad you are content. You chose very well. Ash is perfect for you."

Grinning, Bianca situated her cloak around herself, almost preening. "Yes, he is. He's quite excited about the new Shield's End." She cocked her head to the side. "It will be strange not to refer to the Institution for Impoverished Women as Hartwell House. Perhaps we should keep the name."

"Except Hartwell House will still exist as the school."

Bianca exhaled. "That's true. We shall simply have to adjust. Shield's End will be the institution and Hartwell House will be the school." She shook her head, smiling. "How lovely it will all be when it's completed." She looked over at Poppy. "I was so pleased to hear Dinah has agreed to teach the children."

The mention of Dinah sliced through Poppy, reopening the wound she'd been trying to heal over the past six days. Doing so was proving difficult, particularly because Gabriel barely spoke to her. He barely spoke to anyone. And he didn't sleep in their bed.

Poppy had visited Dinah and Nicola several times. They were doing quite well. Dinah was already managing her cottage, and Nicola was a large, healthy babe. Dr. Fisk was very pleased with their recovery. Judith would return to Hartwell House in a few days.

"She'll be wonderful in the role," Poppy said. "We've discussed how she means to proceed, and she's given the position a great deal of thought. She would like to begin after Epiphany, but I cautioned her to take things slow."

"Indeed. She has her hands full, I imagine." Bianca fell quiet a moment, but her gaze was fixed on Poppy. "Has it been difficult?" she asked softly. "Spending time with Dinah and her babe?"

Poppy tensed. "No." That was a lie. Why should she lie to

her sister? "Yes. But I'm very happy for her—I'm glad she decided to stay and be Nicola's mother."

"That doesn't make it any easier." Bianca's brow creased, and her mouth turned down as sympathy clouded her eyes. "I'm sorry."

"I'm most worried about Gabriel, actually." So much for avoiding the topic. "The birth brought up memories of his mother's death. He's been incredibly upset."

"Did it do the same for you?" Bianca asked.

Poppy shook her head. "I was not reminded of our mother. I don't remember her at all. Gabriel was much older than I was when he lost his mother." She stopped before she revealed how worried she was.

"You'll work through this," Bianca said with a confidence Poppy didn't feel. "I pray my marriage to Ash will be as loving and caring as yours is with Gabriel. You support and love each other." She gave Poppy a small, admiring smile. "It's lovely to behold."

Poppy blinked and then looked out the window. She knew Bianca was trying to help, but her words only reminded Poppy of how they weren't supporting each other right now. And how she wanted to be there for Gabriel. If he would let her.

Poppy sniffed and straightened her spine. "Let us discuss how we mean to proceed today. What do we hope to gain from our visit with Calder?"

They'd discussed paying a call on their brother and had decided it was past time. "We've so many things to talk to him about," Bianca said, pursing her lips. "Where to begin?"

"I should like to lambaste him for not attending your wedding."

Bianca curled her lip. "He did not approve."

"What palaver," Poppy said in disgust. "After I scold him about that, let us castigate him for refusing to support

Hartwell House. It's in a shambles, and he could help fix it tomorrow."

"*Castigate?*" Bianca sniggered. "Why, Poppy, am I rubbing off on you?"

"It was bound to happen." Besides, Poppy had enough strife. She didn't need any more from her idiot brother.

"We should also mention the assembly. He really ought to attend."

"Why, so he can cast his dark cloud everywhere?" Poppy grunted softly. "My apologies. I am taking my frustration out on Calder."

"I can think of no one who deserves it more," Bianca murmured.

They arrived at Hartwood, and Truro, the butler, welcomed them warmly. "May I say marriage agrees with you, Lady Bianca?" He shook his head. "Forgive me, Lady *Buckleigh.*"

"It does, Truro," she answered gaily. "And please do not worry over propriety with *me.*" She waggled her brows at him, and he couldn't help but chuckle.

"And Lady Darlington, may I say how nice it is to see you."

"Thank you, Truro. I'm delighted to see you as well. I hope our brother isn't causing you too much distress."

Truro's gaze flickered with surprise and maybe...appreciation. "Not at all, my lady."

"You can be honest with us," Bianca said conspiratorially, leaning toward the butler. "We know how His Grace has been. And we're here to fix it."

"Well, you can try, my lady." His eyes widened briefly and he nodded once, keeping his head bowed for a slight moment.

Bianca inclined her head with determination. "We'll do

just that. Will you let the duke know we're here? We'll await him in the drawing room."

Poppy and Bianca gave their outerwear to a footman, then showed themselves to the drawing room. Bianca looked about as if she'd never been there before. "It's strange to be here as a guest."

"Yes, it took some getting used to for me." Poppy wasn't sure if it was her current situation or Calder's frigidity, but she'd never felt more uncomfortable here.

"He hasn't even decorated," Bianca noted as she crossed to the hearth. "There should be boughs here. And mistletoe."

"My sisters have arrived."

The deep voice of their brother made them both turn toward the doorway. He filled it impressively with his towering height and wide shoulders. His frosty gray eyes surveyed them briefly, as if he wasn't entirely pleased to see them. No, "pleased" wasn't a word one would use to describe Calder, especially given the harsh lines around his mouth and the near-constant furrows cutting across his brow.

Bianca frowned. "You still need to work on your greetings."

"You need to work on a great many things," Poppy added, then inwardly winced. She hadn't meant to start like that—what was wrong with her?

She was angry. And sad. And in need of something she could *fix*.

Calder sauntered into the room and went to sit in a high-backed chair situated near a settee. He didn't invite them to sit. "Out with it, then. Since you came all this way. But do be brief. I am rather busy."

"With what?" Bianca demanded, marching toward him and dropping onto the settee. "You don't have a wife. You aren't helping Hartwell House. You aren't hosting St. Stephen's Day. What are you *doing*?"

"Being a duke." His ice-gray gaze was colder than a shard of ice, his tone supercilious.

Poppy moved to sit beside her sister. "Well, I am a married marchioness, and I still manage to dedicate time to Hartwell House. And St. Stephen's Day." And a host of other things.

"You're a woman."

Bianca narrowed her eyes at him. "Careful, Calder, or I'll chuck something at your head."

"If you both truly came to berate me, you've wasted your time." He started to rise.

"Do sit down," Poppy said. "Please. We want to speak with you about Hartwell House. It's in grave disrepair, and if you reinstated the support Papa gave, we could—"

"No."

Bianca reached over and clutched Poppy's hand, squeezing it. "Why not?"

"Because I haven't the funds."

"Nonsense," Bianca argued. "If Papa could afford it, why can't you? Have you mismanaged things so quickly?"

Calder's gaze grew—impossibly—colder. "How do you know he could afford it?" His voice was dangerously soft.

Poppy had the feeling she didn't know this man at all. Her anger began to give way to alarm. "Are you saying Papa mismanaged things?"

"I'm saying you don't know anything about the estate or what I can afford. Furthermore, you shouldn't be bothering me about it. You're both married now." He gave Bianca a terse look. "I should think you would pay all your attention to your husbands."

Poppy couldn't keep quiet. "Yes, we're married. Why didn't you come to Bianca's wedding? We know you were invited."

"I didn't approve of her choice of husband. He's a brutal

pugilist who can't seem to control himself. Why would I support something which I cannot endorse?"

A low groan of frustration bubbled from Poppy's throat. "What has happened to you? Why are you so horrid, so unfeeling?"

He began to stand again, this time rising fully. "If there's nothing else…"

"There's plenty else," Bianca snapped. "Such as not hosting the St. Stephen's Day party. Did you know we were going to have it at Shield's End?"

"It burned down."

Bianca let go of Poppy's hand and stood, glaring at him. "Yes, and Ash thanks you for your concern." She took a step toward him. "Why won't you answer Poppy? What has made you like this? How can you turn your back on those in need? Several of the rooms at Hartwell House are leaking. The institution is bursting with residents. Until Shield's End is rebuilt, we have to make Hartwell House more habitable. You *must* help."

"I mustn't do anything. If you and your husband"—he tossed a glance at Poppy—"as well as you and yours want to waste your money on an endeavor that will provide no return, you are featherbrained indeed."

Poppy rose on shaking legs as she exchanged an incredulous look with Bianca. "Featherbrained?" they asked in unison, their voices climbing.

He shrugged. "There is nothing to be gained from coddling those less fortunate. The institution should be turned into a formal workhouse. In fact, I am looking into how to make that happen."

Their jaws dropped, and it was Bianca who found her voice first. "You can't. Mrs. Armstrong will never let you turn it into a workhouse."

"Well, I am the magistrate, and it's up to me to ensure our

community is orderly. Hartwell House may not be allowed to continue as it is. The institution should be run by the parish."

"Hartwell House is not disorderly." Poppy sounded as if she were choking. And she supposed she was—on her brother's cruelty and disregard for those less fortunate.

Bianca touched Poppy's forearm. "Poppy, don't bother. I fear he's lost to us. Just look around you. There's no cheer. No warmth." She gave him a pitying look. "And to think I wanted to convince you to come to the assembly."

He twisted his lips into a frown. "What assembly?"

"The holiday assembly *in two days*," Bianca said. "We hold it every year. But then, you aren't usually here. You haven't been here in more than a decade. Now you're back, and you've completely destroyed our family's legacy."

Bianca went to him, standing just in front of him so he had to look her in the eye. "What happened to you?" she asked softly, trying to infuse her voice with care. It wasn't difficult. He was her brother. Somewhere in there was the boy who'd led them around the estate playing pirates.

He looked at her, but the connection was brief. His discomfort, his *antipathy* radiated from him like a stench that couldn't be scrubbed away. "Nothing."

"Felicity Garland is back," Poppy said, searching for the faintest reaction.

There. A slight flicker in his eyes. It faded so quickly she could have imagined it.

He blinked at her, tipping his head slightly as if annoyed. "Felicity who?"

Now she knew he was just lying. Poppy scoffed and turned away from him. "Yes, I daresay he's a lost cause. Come, let us go. It is far warmer outside than it is in here."

"Yes, do. Go on back to your husbands. To your *happy* lives."

Poppy had turned but now swung her head back toward

him. Bianca did the same. They both studied him a moment before linking arms and departing the drawing room.

"Why do I wonder when we'll see him again?" Poppy asked.

"Because it may be a very, very long time," Bianca said darkly.

Poppy feared she was right.

*a*fter bidding farewell to Truro—and apologizing for failing to make any progress with the duke—Poppy and Bianca climbed into the Buckleigh coach and started toward Hartwell House. Unfortunately, they would not have good news to share. Poppy wanted to go back inside and throttle her brother.

"Now you're the one who looks as though she wants to commit murder," Bianca said. When Poppy looked at her in alarm, Bianca laughed. "You accused me of that the day you came to take me to Thornaby's house party."

Poppy relaxed against the squab. "So I did. Well, now I understand." She understood many things, including the effect of Felicity Garland.

"I think Felicity must have something to do with his change," Bianca mused, tapping her finger against the side of the coach.

"I was just thinking the same thing. Do you suppose she would tell us if we asked?"

"It's worth trying," Bianca said. "In the meantime, we must come to accept that our brother may be gone."

"I'm not ready to give up on him." Poppy couldn't believe she was saying that. However, since she couldn't have children of her own, she was aware of how small their family was. They needed to be there for each other, even when one of them was, to quote Gabriel, a miserable pig.

They arrived at Hartwell House and carried in the baskets of treats from both the Buckleigh and Darlington kitchens. Mrs. Armstrong greeted them and ushered them into the drawing room, where the children were gathered for their afternoon story.

A small girl, perhaps five years old, named Susan ran to Bianca and threw her arms around her legs. "Lady Bianca! Did you come to read to us?"

Bianca laughed. "Why, yes." She looked over at Mrs. Armstrong, who nodded.

Mrs. Armstrong glanced sideways at Poppy. "I never read to them when Lady Buckleigh is here. Why would they want me when they can have her ladyship?"

"Yes, Bianca is quite good at doing all the voices and imbuing her oration with excitement."

"This also allows me a chance to speak with you about Judith. And Dinah." Mrs. Armstrong led Poppy into the sitting room. "I'm so looking forward to having Judith back. Are you certain Dinah is well enough to be on her own?"

Poppy removed her cloak and hat, setting them on the edge of the settee. "I think so. Dinah has taken to motherhood quite naturally."

"That's what Judith said in her last letter. I'm delighted to hear it—shocked, but delighted. Judith also said Nicola is a darling babe."

"She is indeed," Poppy agreed, somewhat bracing herself should Mrs. Armstrong wish to discuss their shared inability to bear children.

Mrs. Armstrong took a seat near the hearth. "And you

think she'll make a good teacher here?"

Poppy set her gloves on her cloak. "I do. I've spent a great deal of time with her over the past weeks, and I like her very much. Her transition since giving birth has been nothing short of extraordinary. If her behavior with Nicola is any indication, she will be wonderful with the children. She was merely afraid. She didn't think she should be a mother."

"The poor dear. I shall like having her here—and the babe. I'm glad things have all worked out where she's concerned." Again, her gaze lingered on Poppy in such a way that Poppy anticipated she would say something about Dinah having a child while Poppy could not.

Hoping to avoid the topic, Poppy went to the fire to warm herself. "It's cold today."

"Yes, it's good of you to come out."

Relaxing, Poppy redirected the conversation. "We visited our brother in the hope of persuading him to reinstate his support of Hartwell House. I'm sorry to say we were not successful."

Mrs. Armstrong sighed. "I do appreciate you trying. We shall have to continue to make do. I learned long ago not to expect things."

A current of frustration whipped through Poppy. She pivoted toward Mrs. Armstrong. "It's not right. You should be able to expect support from the community, especially from those most in a position to help." Though Poppy had no knowledge of the Duke of Hartwell's accounts, she couldn't believe that Calder couldn't afford to help, nor could she believe their father had mismanaged anything.

"Your outrage on our behalf is heartwarming."

The more she thought about her brother's unaccountable stinginess, the angrier she became. "My father would not be pleased. I don't understand Calder. He didn't display even a bit of remorse." Poppy began to pace, just a few steps, back and forth in front of the fireplace. "When I think of him alone in that huge house while your rooms are leaking and you have barely enough beds—not enough when Dinah comes."

A wave of light-headedness washed over Poppy. Her legs wobbled, and she had to grab the mantel for support.

Mrs. Armstrong was beside her in a trice, her arm clasping around Poppy's waist. "Here, sit down." She guided Poppy to the settee. "Are you all right?"

"Just a bit dizzy." A flush rose up Poppy's neck. "And perhaps overheated. I think I was too close to the fire."

Placing a hand on Poppy's forehead, Mrs. Armstrong pressed her lips together. "You don't feel too warm. Should you lie down?"

"I think I'm fine." The dizziness returned along with a surge of nausea. Poppy slapped her hand over her mouth and closed her eyes, leaning back against the settee.

"Oh dear, I'll be right back." Mrs. Armstrong bustled toward the door.

"Would you mind bringing a few biscuits or cakes?"

"You want to eat?" Mrs. Armstrong asked in surprise.

"A nibble, perhaps." She'd felt unsettled like this yesterday and the day before, and a few bites of a biscuit had set her to rights.

Poppy closed her eyes as she waited for Mrs. Armstrong to return. After a few minutes, the sound of the woman's shoes on the floorboards drew Poppy's eyes open.

"Here." Mrs. Armstrong placed a cold cloth on Poppy's brow. "This should help. And here's a Banbury cake." She handed Poppy a small triangular cake dotted with currants.

Taking a bite, Poppy chewed slowly then took another bite. After four nibbles, she set the cake on the plate Mrs. Armstrong had placed on the table next to the settee. "Thank you, that's better."

Mrs. Armstrong sat back in her chair, her gaze never leaving Poppy. "How long have you been feeling like this?"

"A few days, but the sensation is mostly fleeting, occurring in the afternoon for a short while. I haven't been sleeping particularly well." Because of Gabriel. He wasn't sleeping in their bed, and she knew he was suffering.

"That must be it, then." Mrs. Armstrong sounded almost…disappointed. She turned her gaze to the fire.

"Did you suspect something else?"

"It was silly, and I shouldn't mention it." She slid Poppy a nervous glance. "It's just that…as soon as you arrived, you seemed different. I didn't want to think anything of it, but then after this…" She waved her hand. "Please pardon me."

Alarm pricked at Poppy's neck. She sat straight, taking the cloth from her forehead, then leaned toward Mrs. Armstrong. "Should I be worried?"

"I don't think so, but it can't be. I mean, it could, I suppose…"

Now Poppy was beginning to grow frustrated, and with that came another wave of nausea. She pressed the cloth to her cheeks.

Mrs. Armstrong's eyes sparked with concern. "Are you feeling ill again?"

"A bit. If you have information that would help me avoid this, I would appreciate you sharing it."

"Forgive my audacity, but when did you last have your courses?"

Thinking back, Poppy counted. The illness faded from her belly, and a strange tingling spread through her limbs. The room became a bit fuzzy, then snapped into sharp focus. "Too long ago," she whispered. She'd counted and tracked her bleeding for well over a year now. Her cycle was always the same. *Always.*

Until now.

Mrs. Armstrong moved to the settee next to Poppy, taking her hand. "Do you feel different in other ways? Tired? A tenderness in your breasts?"

Yes, but again, she'd attributed that to Gabriel. She was tired because she wasn't sleeping well. And her breasts ached a bit because she missed him touching them. But that was absurd, she now realized.

She was, after all this time, with child. She knew it as clearly as she knew Mrs. Armstrong was sitting beside her.

Poppy lowered the cloth to her lap, careless that it was making her skirt damp. "What do I do?"

"Rejoice." Mrs. Armstrong grinned, then wrapped her arms around Poppy in a fierce hug.

Hugging her back, Poppy began to laugh. Then Mrs. Armstrong joined in. Soon they were fighting to draw breath and dabbing at their eyes.

"Lord Darlington is going to be thrilled," Mrs. Armstrong said, beaming.

Poppy couldn't wait to tell him. This would draw him from his melancholy, and they could look to the future together.

The future. The birth of their child.

Gabriel would be terrified.

She thought of how Nicola's birth had affected him, the memories it had coaxed forth, the damage those had done. "I don't know how to tell him," she whispered, feeling his fear as if it were her own.

Mrs. Armstrong blinked in surprise. "Why?"

"He's...afraid. His mother died after giving birth. As did his sister."

"As did your mother." Mrs. Armstrong nodded. "Obviously, you will have to tell him." Her tone was wry but caring.

Poppy wondered if she could wait until she *had* to, until her condition became evident. She didn't want to worry him, especially if she wasn't truly pregnant. Or worse—if something happened and she didn't stay pregnant.

Now his fear *was* her fear. She couldn't tell him.

And yet, when she thought of how he'd kept Dinah from her for fear of causing her pain, she knew there could be no secrets between them. Pain and fear and loss and grief, they were part of life and they'd promised to share them with each other, to face and fight them together.

Poppy nodded at Mrs. Armstrong. "I'll tell him. Soon." In the meantime, she would confide in Bianca, who would be thrilled. Poppy prayed everything would turn out right.

Mrs. Armstrong gave her an encouraging smile. "You've been through so much. You deserve this happiness."

While that might be true, Poppy couldn't help but think Mrs. Armstrong had deserved it too, but hadn't been so fortunate.

Yes, there was pain and disappointment, but there was also love and acceptance. She looked around at the magnificent home Mrs. Armstrong—and her husband—had built, and she knew no matter what happened, she would be fine. No, she would be wonderful.

Life was a gift, and she would be eternally grateful for it.

～

*B*rooding had never been Gabriel's strong suit, and yet of late, he felt as if he could win a prize for gloominess. He stared into the fire, a glass of brandy dangling from his fingertips.

Poppy was home after spending last night at her sister's. He'd been disappointed when she hadn't returned after visiting Hartwood and Hartwell House, but could he blame her? He wasn't exactly good company. In truth, he oughtn't be surprised if she never came back.

But she had.

Grumbling, he lifted his glass only to find it was empty. *Hell.*

Pushing up from the chair, he went to the table next to the bed in the chamber he'd moved into a week ago. After Dinah had given birth to Nicola, simultaneously raising his worst demons and killing his last hope.

Was it any wonder he'd spent the past week in a stupor?

And how much longer do you plan to continue?

The voice in his head sounded like Poppy. He snorted as he reached for the bottle only to find it was empty. *Bloody hell.*

He set the glass down with a clack and crossed the room. Opening the door, he sucked in a breath at the sight of his wife standing over the threshold.

She wore a red velvet dressing gown that hugged her curves and outlined them to perfection. Her dark hair was gathered into a loose plait that hung over her right shoulder, the end of it curling against the swell of her breast. He wanted to tease her nipple with the silken strands. The erotic thought brought his cock to a half stand.

"May I came in?" She gave him a tentative look that made him feel like a beast.

He moved to the side, and she slowly walked in. He held the door as he watched her backside sway beneath the rich fabric. Mouth watering, he closed the door.

He was worse than a beast. Lusting after his wife when he wasn't even worthy of her.

She turned to face him, her chin high. "When are you returning to our bed?"

He blinked. She meant to cut right to it, then.

"Soon." What the hell did that mean?

She tipped her head to the side. "Why did you leave it in the first place?"

"You know why." The words were little more than grunts. The kind a beast would make.

"If I knew why, I wouldn't have asked." She gave him a perturbed stare and crossed her arms over her chest. "I know you're upset about what you remembered. And probably about not being able to raise Nicola as our own. I'm upset about those things too." She moved toward him, and he tensed. He'd successfully avoided thinking too long about either of those things. The brandy had helped.

"I'm deeply troubled," she continued, her body swaying toward him and not stopping until she nearly touched his chest. "And I don't want to be troubled alone."

"Poppy." He said her name haltingly as he fought to keep hold on his equilibrium—and his sanity. "I can't do this."

She arched a brow at him. "I demand you do. You are my husband. You promised to be with me in sickness and in health, in good and bad. We are in this *together*."

Emotion roiled inside him—he gave in to the easy one: anger. "You didn't want to share your grief with me. Weeks you moped around here without talking to me. We weren't *together* then."

She flinched, and he felt horrid. "No, we weren't. I wish I had talked to you. Talk to me, Gabriel. Tell me what you're feeling."

"No." The denial squeezed past the rock in his throat.

"Then tell me something else. Tell me you miss me. You love me. You want me."

"All of those things," he rasped, his fingers itching to touch her, to claim her.

"Show me."

She'd said that to him weeks ago when he'd finally broken through her grief. Neatly, she'd turned the tables on him. God, he loved her.

He clasped her back and brought her roughly against his

chest. His gaze held hers, riveted on the way her dark pupils enlarged into the blue-gray irises as her arousal grew.

"I've missed you." He reached between them and plucked at the clasps holding the gown closed.

The fabric fell open, and his mouth went dry. Her curves were so discernible because she wore nothing beneath the scarlet gown. "I love you."

He pushed the garment from her shoulders, sliding it down her arms, as he drank in her loveliness. From the column of her neck to the generous swell of her breast to the dip of her waist to the flare of her hip, he was entranced.

Picking up her plait between his thumb and forefinger, he dragged the end across her bare nipple. It rose to a stiff peak as she moaned, casting her head back and closing her eyes.

His cock raged with need, his body coursed with desire, his mind raced with passion. "I want you."

Her eyes came open, and she took his free hand. "Then take me."

She led him to the bed, where she climbed on top of the mattress and spread herself before him like a sumptuous buffet. There were too many delectable courses. He didn't know where to begin.

He still held her hair. Watching her, he swirled the end of the plait around her nipple, going in wider circles with each rotation. She came up off the bed, arching for more. He leaned down and kissed her other breast, his lips and tongue laving and sucking her flesh.

Then he abandoned her hair and cupped her breast, taking her in his hand and squeezing as he drew her other nipple into his mouth. Her cries grew louder. He gave her more, tugging on her and sucking hard.

She gasped, her hand clasping his neck. "Softer."

He lightened his touch—hands, fingers, mouth. Gently, he cupped both breasts and skimmed his thumbs across the nipples. She cried out his name and dug her fingers into his scalp.

There was something…off. She felt different, and she was behaving slightly…different. Her breasts felt heavier, almost larger, and she was so sensitive. Almost too sensitive…

He stilled. "Poppy, are you all right?"

She blinked her eyes open, taking a moment to focus on him. "Yes."

"Are you certain? Your breasts are different."

Her eyes widened. "You can tell?"

"Tell what?"

She hesitated, and panic began to bloom in his chest. "They *are* different. Because I'm with child."

The room went sideways. Gabriel reached for something and found the post of the bed. Clasping it tightly, he waited for the world to right itself. Only it couldn't.

She was pregnant.

The day he'd feared, the day he'd been relieved would never come, had arrived. He was going to lose her.

She sat up on the bed and put her hands on his waist, holding him tight. "Gabriel, it's going to be all right."

He shook his head. "You can't know that. How…"

"I think you know how." Her mouth curled into a smile, and all he could think was *How can you smile right now?*

"But why, after all this time?"

She shrugged. "I don't know. And I know you're scared. I am too. I'm also thrilled. Gabriel, this is a gift—"

How was losing her a gift? It was the exact opposite. He backed away from the bed. She made to follow him.

"Don't." He shook his head. "I can't. You can't be… No."

There would be no happy ending. Just misery and grief. And an empty, gaping hole before him where his beloved wife had been.

Gabriel turned and fled.

CHAPTER 10

*A*fter dozing—to call it sleeping would be generous—on the small settee in his study, Gabriel had taken a ride around the estate. Then he'd gone into the town of Darlington. Now he was back on the estate, having wandered the day nearly away. He squinted up at the sky where the sun had just moved behind a high cloud on its way toward the horizon in just a couple of short hours. The day was cold and breezy, but he felt nothing inside or out.

Not that he *hadn't* felt something.

Last night's revelation, that Poppy was going to bear their child, still ricocheted through him. However, after spending most of the night pacing, tossing, and pacing again, he'd come to a sort of numb acceptance. After all, there was nothing he could do about the situation. She was pregnant, and her life was now at risk.

He blinked, realizing he'd found his way to Dinah's cottage. A figure walked about the front yard, and he recognized her—because she carried her babe.

What the hell was she doing?

Fury and fear unraveled within him, banishing the numbness. He rode to the yard and dismounted, letting his horse graze. Then he stalked toward Dinah, who lifted her head toward him.

"What in God's name are you about?" he growled. "You and the babe shouldn't be out here. You'll catch your death of cold." He moved toward her, but she took a step back, her eyes narrowing.

"We won't either. I only just came out, and we won't stay long." She pursed her lips at him. "I needed a bit of exercise, if it's any of your concern."

He could barely see Nicola's head amidst the mass of blankets swaddling her, and he supposed she was warm enough. Still, why invite illness? "You must take better care."

"I beg your pardon, my lord, but did you stop just to lecture me?" she asked.

"No." Maybe? He hadn't really intended to come here, and yet here he was. Then he'd seen her outside with the babe and...lost what little composure he'd possessed.

"I notice you haven't visited at all since Nicola was born." She squinted up at him. "You don't like babies?"

He didn't know any babies. Why would he? "I've been busy."

"You weren't busy before she was born." She took a deep breath, and her gaze warmed with sympathy. "I know you and Lady Darlington hoped to raise her. I know you don't have children of your own, and given how long you've been married, it seems unlikely you will."

Gabriel wanted to laugh, but he feared he would cry instead. "As it happens, Lady Darlington is expecting." Why had he told her that?

Dinah's entire face lit up with joy. "How wonderful!" Then she immediately frowned. "Why has she been upset, then?"

"What do you mean?" Gabriel asked, though he suspected he knew.

"Every time she's visited since Nicola was born, I sense she's unsettled. Something is bothering her quite profoundly." She studied him intently. "Are you not aware?"

"I'm aware." He exhaled. "It's my fault."

Dinah blinked at him, her lips twisting into a frown. "Then why don't you fix things? Lady Darlington is one of the kindest, loveliest people I've ever met."

"It's rather, er, complicated."

"How can that be? If you say her upset is caused by you, uncause it." The babe stirred in her arms, and Dinah adjusted her hold. "You're both so lucky to have each other. What I wouldn't give to have a husband to help me. To support me. To love me."

Her words were a series of arrows piercing through his fear and anxiety. Yes, they were lucky. To have each other. And now to have a child coming. God, he was already so in love with him or her, and it would be months and months until he met the child. He just prayed he would get the chance.

"I'm terrified," he whispered.

"Could you be more terrified than a young woman who was attacked by her employer, cast out by him and then her family, and who, without the kindness of strangers, would have birthed her babe in a filthy workhouse or worse?" She made it seem as if he shouldn't be frightened, but his fear was real and paralyzing.

"You're a brave young woman," he said quietly. "I am a man who expects to lose his wife and likely his child after she gives birth. Tell me, how do I live with that apprehension every day?"

"You do because the alternative is that you don't live at all. When I said I would give anything to have what you do, I would take it if even for a short while. Any time is better than none." She stepped closer to him as the baby began to make soft noises. "Lady Darlington may die, but the odds are against it. Only you can decide if you want to cower in fear or walk straight into the future with courage and purpose. I had no choice, and right now, I can see that was a good thing."

She was right. He had a choice. He had the luxury of being a self-centered lout. A wave of disgust washed over him.

"What will you choose? Fear or joy?" Nicola began to cry, and Dinah excused herself before walking back into the cottage.

Fear or joy…

Gabriel conjured an image of Poppy's belly swelling, of her laughing in the summertime as she stroked the roundness of her midsection. Her dream had come true, and he realized his had too—to see her happy.

There was no choice to make, not when Poppy was the base of everything he was and everything he wanted to be. Gabriel strode to his horse and quickly mounted. He raced back to the stables and dashed into the house in search of his wife.

"She's already left for the assembly, my lord. Lord and Lady Buckleigh came and conveyed her to Hartwell."

Bloody, bloody hell. "Walker, I'll need a bath." Gabriel ran upstairs, intent on the fastest toilet of his life. He had to pursue his wife.

And joy.

~

*T*he assembly dripped with pine boughs and ribbon. Lanterns flickered, and mistletoe hung in the corners. Arrack punch, like the kind they served at Vauxhall in London, graced the refreshment table, as did a variety of sweet confections. A huge blancmange in the shape of a Yule log and decorated with pine sat in the center.

The scene should have filled Poppy with cheerful expectation. But without Gabriel at her side, she felt sad. Particularly since this assembly was where they'd met three years before. Being here without him didn't feel right. In fact, she'd almost decided not to come, but Bianca and Ash had already been en route to fetch her, and she didn't want them to have gone out of their way for nothing.

So she'd pretended to be happy and made up a story about Gabriel being ill.

"There's Felicity," Bianca whispered, inclining her head toward a tall blonde woman garbed in a blue gown.

Poppy picked Felicity out of the crowd. "Should we go and speak with her?"

"Of course." Bianca took Ash's arm, and the three of them crossed the assembly room to where Felicity stood with her mother. Mrs. Templeton looked a bit frail. She clung to her daughter's arm.

"Come, Mama. You must sit. Otherwise, I will rethink my decision to allow you to come. You are still recovering."

"Oh, pooh. I'm fine, dear. But yes, a chair would not come amiss." Mrs. Templeton smiled up at her daughter and the change in her expression made her look much more robust, if that were possible.

Felicity saw them then, her green eyes lighting with recognition. "Good evening, Lady Darlington and Lady... Buckleigh, is it?"

"Yes," Bianca answered. "Allow me to present my

husband, the Earl of Buckleigh. Ash, this is Mrs. Felicity Garland."

Ash inclined his head. "Of course I remember you, Mrs. Garland."

Felicity rose from her curtsey with wide eyes. "Ash, as in little Ashton Rutledge? I would not have recognized you."

"None of us did," Bianca said with a laugh.

"How marvelous to see you all." Felicity glanced around. "Where is your brother? I've yet to encounter him since I returned to Hartwell."

Poppy and Bianca exchanged a wary look. "I doubt he'll be here this evening," Poppy said smoothly. "He's not very social these days. The dukedom keeps him quite busy."

"That's too bad," Felicity said. "I'd looked forward to seeing him. I suppose I'll just have to pay a call."

Bianca's gaze snapped to Poppy, and she opened her mouth. Poppy worried that nothing helpful would come out, so she rushed to say, "Perhaps send him a note asking when he receives visitors." She added a placid smile.

Ash sucked in a breath, his eyes fixed on the entrance. "He's here."

All four women turned their heads to see Calder standing just inside the threshold. Indeed, a hush fell over the entire assembly.

Calder surveyed the large room, his gaze moving quickly until settling on them. No, not on them. On Felicity Garland. He strode toward their group, and the crowd magically parted as if he were an ancient river carving its way through a hillside.

"Good evening," he announced as he arrived, standing next to Poppy.

"Good evening," Poppy said, eyeing him with disbelief. He was garbed in unforgiving black save his white shirt and cravat. Gentlemen typically dressed up their assembly attire with something festive. Calder did not.

Felicity curtsied and helped her mother do the same. "Your Grace, I was just telling your sisters how I looked forward to seeing you."

"Did you? How surprising after all this time." Calder's voice carried an edge—not the same obnoxious tone he'd had of late. This was something different, something that cut far deeper.

"Yes, it's been many years," Felicity said. "I do hope we'll find time to visit. If you'll excuse me, I need to see my mother to a chair."

It was a perfect invitation for Calder to step forward and offer to help. Given how he'd immediately spotted Felicity and walked straight to her, Poppy would have expected him to provide assistance. Instead, he stood there, his gaze cold as he regarded her mother.

"Allow me to help," Ash said, presenting his arm. He sent a glance toward Calder as Mrs. Templeton accepted his assistance.

"Thank you, Lord Buckleigh."

"I'll be right there, Mama," Felicity said. She watched as they walked away, then looked to Calder.

"Why are you here?" he asked sharply, his voice low so that only the four of them could hear.

Poppy suddenly felt as though she and Bianca were intruding. She edged close to her sister and grazed her elbow against Bianca's arm.

Felicity drew back, her features tightening with confusion. "Everyone comes to the assembly."

Not everyone. Poppy was painfully aware of her husband's absence, particularly now that Calder of all people was here.

"Not here at the assembly, here in *Hartwell*." There was an accusatory note to his statement. Poppy tensed.

"My mother returned last year, and several weeks ago, she became ill. I came to take care of her."

"So your visit is temporary."

She narrowed one eye at him very briefly. "I haven't yet decided." Casting a smile toward Poppy and Bianca, who'd linked arms, Felicity continued, "I'm especially glad to be here for the holidays. No one celebrates better than the people of Hartwell. I am so looking forward to St. Stephen's Day, but I was sad to hear Hartwood would not be hosting the event. I'd feared you were ill." She regarded Calder closely as if she could discern some sort of malady.

Would that she could, for there was absolutely something wrong with him. This was not their brother!

"I am not, as you can see."

"You don't appear to be, and yet you aren't quite the man I remember." Felicity shook her head. "But then it's been over a decade."

"Yes, people change over time. And some people change overnight." Calder gave Felicity a haughty stare. "I'm not sure the woman I remember ever existed."

Oh dear, this was not the place to have such a conversation. Poppy moved toward her brother, reaching for his arm. "Calder, perhaps we should—"

He swung his gaze toward her, glowering. "Don't touch me. I will say what I like."

"Not to my wife, you won't." Gabriel inserted himself between Calder and Poppy. She stared at him, shocked he was there. She'd been so intent on her brother that she hadn't noticed his entry. Glancing about, she realized the entire assembly was focused on Calder.

"Calder, you're causing a scene," Poppy whispered.

Calder's gaze darkened, and his lip curled. Before he

could speak, Gabriel edged toward him. "Careful, Chill, don't let this scene escalate into something else."

Calder glared at all of them, but his most hateful stare went to Felicity. "I've come to see what I needed to. And now I am free." He spun on his heel and stalked from the assembly.

Bianca smiled broadly and looked urgently at Poppy and Ash, her eyes asking them to join her in appearing pleasant. As if their brother hadn't just behaved like a horrendous boor in the middle of the holiday assembly.

Except Poppy couldn't quite bring herself to do anything but stare at her husband. He was here.

Gabriel turned to her. "I didn't mean to drive him away."

"It was for the best," she said.

He offered her his arm. "Shall we take a turn?"

She ought to introduce Felicity and ensure the situation was truly settled, but she was too wrapped up in wanting to know why Gabriel had come. Wordlessly, she put her hand on his sleeve, and he led her to the periphery, where they began a promenade around the hall.

He spoke first. "I'm sorry. That I wasn't at home when you left for the assembly. That I've been distant and self-absorbed. That I reacted like an idiot when you told me about the babe."

Her heart leapt, and she squeezed his arm. He steered her into a corner, well away from anyone else.

She turned toward him, standing close, her eyes searching his face. "You were scared."

"There is no past tense." His tone was dry, and she was so grateful for even a modicum of humor. "I am terrified, but I am also overjoyed. I realized I prefer the latter, so I'm going to focus on that."

"You 'realized'?"

"I might have had some help from Dinah. Perspective is a powerful thing."

"It is." She rested her palm on his lapel. "So is sadness and fear. I know what that feels like," she said softly.

"Of course you do, my love. We are on this journey together—for better or worse. I think we are both due for some of the better." His mouth ticked up, and her heart somersaulted.

"I think so too. I promise I won't die. And neither will the babe." She touched her other hand to her stomach.

His smile took on a sad tinge, but only for a moment. "You can't promise that. However, I believe everything will work out as it should, and I plan to spend every day basking in the love we share and the joy of thinking about tomorrow."

"Even if that tomorrow doesn't come?" She almost wished she hadn't asked that. He'd come so far already.

"But it will, whether we want it to or not, whether we are here or not. So why not plan for the best?" He winked at her. "I'm still working on this, so bear with me."

She grinned up at him. "As you said, it's a journey. I will be with you every step of the way."

The first strains of music started. "Speaking of steps," Gabriel said. "I believe it's time for you to dance with me."

A laugh bubbled up from deep inside her. "That's what you said to me three years ago—you didn't really ask. I thought you were so arrogant."

"It was all bluster."

"It worked."

"If I'm correct, there was also a bit of mistletoe involved." He waggled his brows at her.

She glanced up. "Look."

Hanging above them was a bouquet of mistletoe.

"I didn't kiss you three years ago."

"You couldn't. And you shouldn't now."

"Hmm, this seems like a question of perspective. For me, I have no problem kissing you here."

She giggled. "Then who am I to quarrel?"

He bent down and brushed his lips over hers. "Consider that a prologue to the story I'll tell you later. Now, let us dance."

As Gabriel swept her into his arms on the dance floor, an encompassing joy washed over her. This was a holiday season she would never forget.

EPILOGUE

August 1812

*P*oppy's anguished cries filled the chamber. Gabriel had weighed whether to be present for the birth, and now he was beginning to question his decision.

"There's the head!" Dr. Fisk called.

Mrs. Fisk looked up at Poppy with warm encouragement. "One more push now, love."

Red-faced, Poppy bore down. She squeezed Gabriel's hand so hard, he feared it would never have blood flowing through it again.

But he'd give up anything for her, including his hand.

"Please let her be all right, please, please, please." The silent plea played over and over in his mind, a chorus of hope.

A loud squall filled the chamber. Poppy exhaled loudly, and her grip on his hand finally loosened.

"We have an heir," Dr. Fisk said, grinning. He glanced over at Gabriel as he handed the babe to Mrs. Fisk. She did something with him, but Gabriel's attention was entirely focused on the exhausted but beaming face of his wife.

She looked up at him. "Did you hear that? You have a son."

"*We* have a son." He was glad his voice didn't sound as shaky as he felt. He lifted her hand and kissed the back before tucking it against her side. Leaning down, he kissed her dewy forehead. "As long as I live, I will never do anything as miraculous or spectacular as you did today."

She laughed. "I can't say I disagree with you."

Mrs. Fisk appeared at his side. "My lord, may I present your son." She handed him the swaddled babe, his pink face scrunched and crying. "I do think he may be hungry." She turned to attend Poppy, but Gabriel was now entirely focused on his son.

He touched the boy's tiny button nose. His cries faded, and his eyes opened. They were blue with a bit of gray—like his mother's, though he'd heard they might not stay that way. He decided they would. Of course they would.

Love, fierce and all-encompassing, assaulted Gabriel, nearly stealing his breath. He'd loved this child for months, but this was different—richer and more complete. He now understood how Dinah had completely changed her mind the moment she'd held Nicola.

"Her ladyship is ready for him." Mrs. Fisk took the babe and put him into Poppy's arms. Mrs. Fisk had arranged her so that her breast was exposed and began to show her how to nurse their son. It was the most beautiful thing Gabriel had ever seen.

Enchanted, he watched tears track down Poppy's face, her smile soft and adoring as she cradled their son. She stroked his cheek and whispered words of love. Words that echoed deep in Gabriel's heart. He wiped a hand over his wet eyes, grinning.

A few moments later, he realized they were alone in their bedchamber—just the three of them. He could scarcely believe it.

"Thaddeus, I think," she said, her gaze locking with Gabriel's. They'd discussed several names that meant gift, for that's what this child was.

Gabriel thought of the other names they'd considered but agreed he looked like Thaddeus. "Yes."

A while later, Thaddeus dozed upon his mother's breast, and Gabriel sat, weary but content, in a chair beside the bed. He was fairly certain Poppy was asleep, her eyes closed, her breaths deep and even. All was well. For now.

Stop it.

He refused to worry or be afraid. The birth had gone exceptionally well according to Dr. Fisk. Even so, he'd agreed to stay with them for three days to alleviate Gabriel's concern.

"I know I can't protect you from everything, but I will do my best," he whispered, gazing at his beloved wife and son. "Always."

Her eyes fluttered open, and her mouth curved into a smile. "I know you will. And we'll be right here doing the same for you."

"I made something," he said, his pulse quickening with anticipation. "I'll be right back."

He went into the sitting room and found what he sought —one of the footmen had brought it up earlier in the day. Hefting the piece of furniture, he carried it into the bedchamber and set it next to the bed.

Poppy gasped when she saw the cradle. "It's beautiful. When I asked if you planned to make something, you said you would…later. I thought you were afraid," she said softly.

"I was, but I told you I wasn't going to surrender to fear."

He'd crafted the piece with love and hope. Made of oak, he'd carved greenery and mistletoe into the wood.

"It reminds me of Christmas," she said, smiling.

"The season of joy and hope." Gabriel leaned down and kissed her, his lips lingering softly against hers. The future stretched before them—bright and long. A peace settled over him.

"Thank you, my love," she whispered. "This is the most perfect gift."

He shook his head in gentle disagreement, love coursing through him. "No, that would be you and our son."

Keep reading to find out what happens with the St. Stephen's Day party and why Calder is such a Scrooge in Joy to the Duke!

∾

AUTHOR'S NOTE

One day, I thought it would be fun to write a Christmas trilogy and base the stories on classic holiday tales. The Gift of the Magi by O. Henry is a lovely story and served as the inspiration for The Gift of the Marquess. This was my first foray into writing a romance where the hero and heroine had already fallen in love and were married. As someone who's been married for nearly twenty-eight years (as of this writing), I can attest to the fact that marriage does not end the conflict—or the romance! It was very rewarding to write Poppy and Gabriel's moving journey.

The Institution for Impoverished Women is something entirely of my own creation. It's based on workhouses of the time, but I didn't want a "real" workhouse which separated men and women (and children—they didn't see their parents often) and was typically more like a prison.

Thank you Julie Kenner for the countless phone calls it took to get this just right.

I hope you enjoyed this inspired story! And Merry Christmas. :)

JOY TO THE DUKE

JOY TO THE DUKE

Denied the woman of his dreams by his father's meddling, Calder Stafford, has spent the last decade proving himself to be self-sufficient, austere, and utterly uninterested in joy. Now that he is the Duke of Hartwell, he'll enact his revenge by abolishing the holiday traditions his father loved so well. His sisters will not sway him and neither will the woman— newly returned to town—who was stolen from him.

Returning to Hartwell to care for her mother, widow Felicity Garland is delighted to be back home, especially for the holidays. However, the jolly festivities she expects are nowhere to be found. When she goes to the source of the problem— the duke—she's astonished to see how much the young man she once loved has hardened. It's up to her to break through the impenetrable fortress around his heart—not just to save Christmas, but to save *him*.

For my children, who are the very definition of joy

CHAPTER 1

County Durham, England
December 1811

Felicity was back.

Calder strode from the drawing room at his estate, Hartwood, via the same doorway his younger sisters had just used to depart. But he didn't follow them. He went in search of a footman and sent him to the stables to see that a groom saddled his horse. After sending another footman to fetch his greatcoat, hat, and gloves, Calder made his way outside. A short while later, he raced toward the village of Hartwell.

Founded in the Middle Ages, Hartwell was built around a center market square. The spire of St. Cuthbert's, the twelfth-century church, stood sentinel over the quaint gathering of shops and cottages.

With the holiday season upon them, doors and windows were decorated with festive greenery. There was, all around, an aura of good cheer. It did not, however, permeate Calder's carefully constructed exterior. Words such as "quaint" and "festive" and "joy" had no place in his heart.

The mere thought of that organ made his squeeze. Or, more likely, it was the knowledge that Felicity Templeton— no, she was Felicity Garland now—was near.

Calder knew her mother had returned to Hartwell last year, but he'd gone out of his way to avoid her. Even so, he was aware of precisely where she lived. How else could he be certain to steer clear of her?

Turning his horse down Kingston Street, he eyed Mrs. Templeton's cottage farther down the road. Like its neighbors, the home was festooned with pine boughs. Smoke wafted from the chimney, rising above the thatched roof.

Now what?

He realized he didn't know what he meant to do. Speak to her? He shuddered inwardly at the thought. Felicity had run off over a decade ago, breaking his heart.

Yet, he had plenty he wanted to say to her. His mind raged with questions and anger. Why had she left without a word?

Except he knew why. His father had paid her family, securing their future so that marriage to the heir to a dukedom wasn't necessary. It appeared that had been her only motivation in attaching herself to him in courtship. Not love or attraction or affection of any kind—she'd been driven purely by avarice.

Calder took a deep breath. Cold winter air filled his lungs, freezing his insides the way everyone presumed they were. He had a heart of ice and a hollow soul. So they said.

And they weren't wrong.

A figure stepped out of the cottage, followed by another. Calder moved his horse to a side lane, positioning himself behind a tree.

The two women passed through the gate into the street and linked arms. Even from this distance, Felicity was precisely as he remembered. Tall and graced with curves that could make a man weep with want, her features were so finely honed, surely every artist in the kingdom should want to paint her. Blonde curls peeked from beneath the rim of her bonnet. She laughed at something her mother said, the lilting song of her voice somehow easing the ache inside him.

Only for a moment. As she moved along the street on the other side, he saw her face more clearly—the delicate arch of her brows, the gentle sweep of her nose, the sculpted beauty of her cheekbones and jawline. But his gaze settled on her mouth, with its lush pink lips that could kiss and seduce him like no one else.

Not that she'd *actually* seduced him, not completely. He'd anticipated taking her to bed when they wed. That dream had died. Or, perhaps more accurately, had been stolen.

Still, he feasted on her, his gaze moving hungrily over her to memorize every new detail—the crinkles around her eyes when she smiled, the air of confidence and perhaps wisdom, the smart way she surveyed her surroundings.

Bloody hell. She was looking this way.

Calder turned his horse and cantered down the lane toward Shield Street, the main thoroughfare that cut through the village. His heart beat quickly, and, if he were honest, he would realize it wasn't due to the ride. But he refused to allow it to be because of Felicity. He'd seen her, and that was enough.

Except, knowing she was near was likely to be a fracture in his mind.

"Good afternoon, Your Grace."

Calder had slowed his mount as he'd turned onto Shield Street. Blinking, he pulled himself from the dark pit of his thoughts and focused on the man addressing him. Alfie

Tucket, the cabinetmaker, stood outside his shop. He bowed, bending his tall form before straightening once more.

"Good afternoon," Calder said. He might be a blackguard, but he was also polite. Sometimes.

"On your way to Shield's End?" Tucket asked, blinking as he looked up at Calder on his horse.

Calder realized he'd been riding in that direction—the old house stood at the end of Shield Street, hence its name. Rather, it *had* stood. The structure had burned over a week ago.

"No," he answered, even as he considered going to see it. Beyond his curiosity, he should care about the destruction since the property belonged to his brother-in-law. The man he'd forbidden his sister to marry.

And whom she'd wed last week.

Tucket shifted his weight, looking slightly uncomfortable. His father was the caretaker at Shield's End. It was possible, if not likely, that Tucket knew that Calder hadn't visited the damaged house and that he hadn't attended his sister's wedding.

There it was again. That sharp, brief twinge in his chest. Though he didn't react, Calder never failed to register the sensation.

Calder turned his horse once more and rode in the opposite direction from Shield's End, toward Hartwood, which stood atop a hill that overlooked the village. The dukes of Hartwell had lived there for centuries. Would they still?

Only if Calder married, and though he was now thirty, he couldn't be moved to take a wife. Not when Felicity still lived in the recesses of his mind.

Time to evict her, his mind chided.

He thought he had, but now that she was here… He shook his head. Perhaps he could find a way to make her leave again. Or, if he were lucky, her stay would only be temporary.

Arriving at the Hartwood stable, Calder turned the care of his horse, something he typically saw to himself, over to a groom. A ripple of unease ran through him. He needed to walk. Curling his tongue, he whistled. A moment later, his dark red-brown greyhound bounded to his side.

Calder stroked the dog's head, scratching her behind the ears. As Calder set off from the stable yard, Isis fell in beside him. They walked past the gardens to where the hill began to slope. Nestled at the base was the family crypt, a place Calder never went.

There lay tragedy and pain—a parent he missed with every fiber of his being and another he loathed with equal vehemence.

The question that had come to his mind earlier returned: would there be any more dukes of Hartwell? He ought to ensure there weren't, at least not from his line. There had to be a cousin somewhere who would inherit. It would serve Calder's father right to have the title pass to some distant relative. Or to pass to no one at all.

The chill in Calder's heart hardened to stone as he thought of the man who'd raised him. The man everyone else remembered fondly, particularly his sisters. They hadn't been subjected to his high expectations, his ruthless demands for perfection at all costs. He hadn't paid the men they'd fallen in love with to leave and then crowed about how right he'd been about them all along.

The twinge pinched his chest again. Perhaps he should have supported his sister's marriage. He barely knew her husband, the Earl of Buckleigh, but from what he'd seen, the man was a volatile fighter, a pugilist regarded for his efficient brutality in the ring. And yet, he couldn't see his sweet, fierce youngest sister, Bianca, marrying someone like that.

Calder ran his gloved fingers over Isis's head. "It doesn't matter, does it, girl?" he asked softly. "He wanted me to be a beast, and so I am."

Isis nudged his hand in response then sat down beside him, content just to be next to him. She might be the actual beast, but she was far kinder and more loving than he.

"I don't really deserve you," he murmured.

He looked down into her large brown eyes that gazed at him so adoringly. Squatting, he stroked her neck and sides with both hands. Then he looked back toward the crypt and spoke to the man he despised.

"I am alone, and I shall probably remain that way. I hope that taunts you for an eternity."

Calder rose and turned, striding back toward the house with Isis trotting alongside him.

Yes, his father had raised him to be ruthless and unyielding. And since Calder strove to excel in everything, that meant he was as cold and unforgiving as one could be.

~

"*Y*ou look lovely, dear."

Felicity donned her cloak just before opening the door for her mother. "Thank you, as do you, Mama." She picked up the small bag, which held her dancing slippers—Mama wouldn't be dancing since she was still somewhat recovering from her illness—and followed her mother out into the cold, dark evening.

"I'm so looking forward to the assembly," Mama said as Felicity linked arms with her. "How many years has it been?"

"Ten." Felicity recalled the last assembly she'd attended in Hartwell. She'd been eighteen and so eager to see her love when he came home from Oxford for the holiday. They'd spent the prior summer together, enjoying every moment possible in each other's company, dreaming of the future in the warmth from the sun and from the passion of their stolen kisses.

Only, he hadn't come. His father had explained that he wouldn't be returning for the holidays, and he'd given her a letter. Brief and cold, the words written by her love had stated in plain terms that they had no future together.

When her father had suggested they move to York where her older brother would be practicing law, she'd leapt at the chance to leave Hartwell—and her broken heart—behind. She hadn't been back since.

"You came last year, didn't you?" Felicity glanced over at her mother, whose white-blonde hair was swept into a fashionable style, though it was partially obscured by the hood of her cloak, which she'd pulled up as they'd left the house. It was important she keep warm after having been ill. Her ailment had been the only thing that could draw Felicity back, and so here she was. She had to admit she'd missed the village and its people, especially at this time of year. Christmas in York couldn't come close to the charm and tradition of Hartwell.

"I did, but it wasn't the same without your father." She summoned a smile as she looked at Felicity. "And you." Mama reached over and patted Felicity's hand.

Papa had died last fall—it was hard to believe it had been over a year already. Awash in grief, Mama had wanted to escape from the house she'd shared with her husband for the past decade, where he'd fallen ill and died. Coming back to Hartwell, where she still had friends and a cousin, had made sense despite Felicity trying to dissuade her.

But that had been selfishness on Felicity's part. Hartwell, for all the good memories it held, would always be the place where she'd lost her innocence, where she'd been a fool to give her heart so completely.

"I'm so glad you're with me this year," Mama said, smiling. "And I do hope you're here to stay."

That was an ongoing debate. Felicity had a home and friends back in York. Yet, it was hard to deny her mother's request. Felicity had begun to hope she could talk *her* into returning to York and living with Felicity.

"Or you're going to come back to York with me. I know you miss your friends." Felicity flashed her a smile, and her mother laughed.

"Don't try to sway me with your father's charm. I am immune."

She wasn't either, but Felicity only chuckled in response.

Mama slid her a probing look. "Are you looking forward to seeing anyone in particular? You've kept to yourself for the most part since returning."

It had only been a handful of weeks, really. "I've been busy helping you."

"Yes, and I'm delighted to have you here with me. I know you are the reason for my recovery."

"Not entirely." Felicity knew her presence had helped. "Dr. Fisk had a great deal to do with it."

"You're right, of course. In fact, I wonder if he might have been able to help your father." Her voice turned sad. "We should have returned to Hartwell when he became sick."

Felicity squeezed her mother's arm gently. "You mustn't think like that. You told Dr. Fisk about Papa's illness, and he said there was likely nothing he could do, that you'd done your best to care for him."

"It's hard not to feel regret," Mama said softly. "But then you seem to be unaffected by that emotion."

Hardly. Felicity regretted more than she admitted, all of it to do with Calder Stafford. She'd almost thought of him as "Chill," the nickname from his youth when he'd been the Earl of Chilton. Now, however, he was the Duke of Hartwood.

She'd never liked calling him Chill—the cool moniker hadn't made sense to her, not when she thought of him as so warm and caring.

How wrong she'd been.

They reached the assembly hall, where a line of carriages dropped off elegantly clad attendees. Light and conversation poured from the building, lending a festive air. A tremor of anxiousness rippled across Felicity's shoulders. She wasn't sure she was ready to face Calder.

She chided herself internally. She refused to be intimidated by him or the prospect of seeing him again. She was ten years older, widowed, and she'd lived on her own the past two years. The young girl he'd so callously hurt was long gone.

Holding her head high, she escorted her mother into the hall. In the vestibule, a footman took their outer garments, and Felicity swapped her boots for her dancing slippers.

They strolled into the ballroom, which was already quite full. Young ladies giggled in the corner, while a group of young bucks tried to appear composed as they surveyed the room, their gazes continually returning to the young ladies.

Felicity smiled to herself. She remembered what it felt like to be youthful and excited, anticipation for the future—the unknown—coursing through her.

They walked to an area on the other side of the ballroom that had been arranged with seating that provided an excellent view of the dance floor.

Eyeing a chair, Felicity inclined her head. "Come, Mama. You must sit. Otherwise, I will rethink my decision to allow you to come. You are still recovering."

"Oh, pooh. I'm fine, dear. But yes, a chair would not come amiss."

Turning her head slightly, Felicity saw a pair of familiar faces—Calder's sisters. Her heart paused as she glanced around in search of him. Not seeing him, she exhaled with relief as his sisters, along with a gentleman, came toward her. Felicity dipped into a curtsey. "Good evening Lady Darlington and Lady...Buckleigh, is it?"

"Yes," Bianca, Calder's youngest sister who had very recently wed the Earl of Buckleigh, answered. "Allow me to present my husband, the Earl of Buckleigh. Ash, this is Mrs. Felicity Garland." Her blue eyes glowed with warmth.

Ash inclined his head. "Of course I remember you, Mrs. Garland."

Surprise leapt through Felicity as she rose from her curtsey. "Ash, as in little Ashton Rutledge? I would not have recognized you."

"None of us did," Bianca said with a laugh, a dark curl grazing her temple.

"How marvelous to see you all." Felicity allowed her gaze to briefly scan the ballroom once more. "Where is your brother? I've yet to encounter him since I returned to Hartwell." She wasn't asking because she wanted to see him, but because if he were here, she wanted to know. To be on guard.

Poppy, the older of the two and the Marchioness of Darlington, and Bianca exchanged a wary look. "I doubt he'll be here this evening," Poppy answered. "He's not very social these days. The dukedom keeps him quite busy."

Felicity was shocked to feel a spark of disappointment. "That's too bad. I'd looked forward to seeing him. I suppose I'll just have to pay a call." The words came out because Felicity always endeavored to be polite. She had no intention of calling on him.

It appeared his sisters didn't think visiting was a good idea. Bianca snapped a look toward Poppy and opened her mouth to speak. However, Poppy cut her off, saying to Felicity, "Perhaps send him a note asking when he receives visitors." Her lips curved into a serene smile, likely meant to smooth any upset Felicity might have detected. Clearly, she wasn't imagining their discomfort.

The sound of the Earl of Buckleigh inhaling sharply drew Felicity's attention. But the earl was fixated on the entrance. "He's here." His tone was flat and yet the two simple words sliced through Felicity with the quick, terrifying efficiency of a long sword from days of old.

Felicity felt her mother pat her arm, but her gaze was trained on Calder. Tall, with broad shoulders that had once made her swoon, he filled the doorway. His crystalline eyes swept over the assembly, his expression impassive.

Had the ballroom gone quiet? Not entirely, for there was a faint buzzing in Felicity's ears as she beheld her former love for the first time in over a decade.

Then she felt the full force of his attention as his gaze settled wholly and purposely on her. Heat danced along her skin. Her pulse sped.

He started toward them, and she felt utterly torn. Part of her wanted to flee. Another part of her wanted to rush to meet him. The largest part of her wanted to stand firmly and call him out for his reprehensible behavior ten years ago.

She opted for the latter. Rather, part of the latter. Or maybe it was really that she couldn't seem to move beneath the weight of his stare. Blast, she hoped it wasn't that, and yet feared that was precisely the case.

He came to a stop next to Poppy. "Good evening." His voice, so deep and silky, like rich, plush velvet, glided over her, eliciting an almost physical response. She felt as though she might sway toward him, her body reacting to his familiarity. But no, he wasn't familiar. This man was a stranger.

She noted the changes in his appearance. His shoulders seemed even broader, if that were possible. His face was more stark as evidenced by the lines around his mouth and the stern set of his jaw. He looked like a man who rarely smiled. The black of his evening clothes gleamed with importance and wealth beneath the flickering chandeliers. He looked every bit a duke and nothing like the young man who'd chased her across a meadow, his dark hair falling across his forehead as he laughed when he caught her.

Poppy turned toward him. "Good evening."

Felicity dropped into another, deeper, curtsey and then assisted her mother in doing the same. "Your Grace, I was just telling your sisters how I looked forward to seeing you." Again, politeness seemed to have taken over her tongue.

"Did you? How surprising after all this time." Calder sounded every bit as cold as she'd imagined him to be given the way he'd rejected her, not at all the young man she'd actually known.

"Yes, it's been many years. I do hope we'll find time to visit." Felicity allowed a bit of sauce into her tone. "If you'll excuse me, I need to see my mother to a chair."

Calder looked at her mother, and for a brief moment, Felicity thought he meant to say something to her—something obnoxious. Before she could think of how to respond if he did, Buckleigh moved toward them, presenting his arm to Felicity's mother. "Allow me to help."

"Thank you, Lord Buckleigh," Mama said, taking his arm.

"I'll be right there, Mama." Felicity watched as they walked away, then looked back to Calder.

"Why are you here?" he asked her sharply, his voice low, but she feared at least Poppy and Bianca could hear.

How dare he question her like that in public? Felicity stiffened. "Everyone comes to the assembly."

"Not here at the assembly, here in *Hartwell*." The outer edge of his lip curled slightly.

"My mother returned to Hartwell last year, and several

weeks ago, she became ill. I came to take care of her." Why did she feel so defensive? She didn't have to explain herself to him. On the contrary, if anyone was owed an explanation, it was her.

"So your visit is temporary." There was a hopeful edge to his tone.

It seemed he would like her to say yes. So she said, "I haven't yet decided." She sent a smile toward his sisters, making it clear the expression was for them and not him. "I'm especially glad to be here for the holidays. No one celebrates better than the people of Hartwell." Schooling her features into a mask of concern, she shifted her gaze back to Calder. "I am looking forward to St. Stephen's Day, but I was sad to hear Hartwood would not be hosting the event. I'd feared you were ill." She couldn't think of why else he wouldn't be hosting it. The dukes of Hartwell had done so for generations.

"I am not, as you can see."

Since he'd decided to speak plainly, so would she. "You don't appear to be, and yet you aren't *quite* the man I remember." Felicity shook her head. She supposed she'd hoped there was a good reason for his rejection ten years ago. A part of her hoped he'd gone on to be happy. She had—as well as she could. She'd loved her husband, but it hadn't ever been the same as what she'd felt for Calder. In fact, she often wondered if their time together had been a dream, that her recollections were somehow a delusion. "But then it's been over a decade."

"Yes, people change over time. And some people change overnight." Calder's eyes burned with a cavalier intensity. "I'm not sure the woman I remember ever existed."

Felicity stared at him, her insides stalling as if she were turning to stone. What was he going on about? That was what she would have said about him.

Poppy reached for her brother's arm. "Calder, perhaps we should—"

He snapped his gaze toward her. "Don't touch me. I will say what I like."

"Not to my wife, you won't." Poppy's husband, the Marquess of Darlington—at least that was who Felicity believed him to be given that he'd referred to Poppy as his wife—stepped between brother and sister.

Poppy seemed surprised to see the marquess but quickly recovered. She glanced about, whispering, "Calder, you're causing a scene."

Calder's gaze darkened, and the marquess took an infinitesimal step toward him. "Careful, Chill, don't let this scene escalate into something else."

What would happen? More importantly, what had become of Calder? For the first time, Felicity felt something she never imagined feeling toward him—concern and maybe a flash of pity.

Calder glared at all of them before settling a particularly horrid stare on Felicity. "I've come to see what I needed to. And now I am free."

He turned abruptly and stalked from the assembly. Felicity snapped her jaw closed before she could gape after him, her mind and body coursing with agitation. What had just occurred?

Darlington turned to Poppy. "I didn't mean to drive him away."

"It was for the best," she murmured.

He offered her his arm. "Shall we take a turn?"

Felicity barely acknowledged that they'd left as she worked to understand why Calder had behaved in such a fashion. He'd said the woman he knew had never existed. She tried to recall the letter he'd written her, words she'd once committed to memory but had since wiped from her mind.

He'd said he wouldn't be courting her or proposing marriage as they'd discussed. He'd said his duty required him to find a more suitable wife. As the daughter of a farmer, she'd feared they had no future, but he'd assured her endlessly that he intended to make her his wife.

Until he'd written the letter and failed to come home for Christmas.

That was when she'd realized it had all been a lie.

CHAPTER 2

"*I*'m sorry about that," Bianca said quietly.

Felicity tried to make sense of Calder's behavior just as she tried to reconcile the blissful time they'd spent together followed by his complete dismissal. It had been more than a lie. It had been a betrayal. And for what? A handful of stolen kisses?

Buckleigh returned from escorting Felicity's mother to the seating area. "Your mother is situated with a few friends." He looked to his wife. "Everything all right?"

"I don't know." She addressed Felicity. "Are *you* all right?"

Felicity mentally shook herself. People were conversing once more, but she was still aware of inquisitive looks drifting in her direction. She blinked and looked at Bianca. "Yes, thank you for your concern. Your brother disturbed me a bit, but I'm fine." She smiled to mask her remaining unease.

Bianca's eyes narrowed. "He's a cad. He didn't even come to my wedding last week."

Felicity was shocked to hear it—in their youth, he'd always spoken highly of his sisters. "You're joking."

"I wish I were." Bianca exchanged an expression of disappointment and frustration with her husband, though the earl also looked…angry. Felicity could understand that. She was angry too. But she was also baffled. It would be easy to simply walk away and return to York. Why then did she want to find out why Calder held her in such disregard?

Because then she could stop wondering what had happened, what she'd done to drive him away from her. Perhaps her comment that she would pay him a call wasn't merely courtesy. Beyond his behavior toward her—now and in the past—she was curious as to why he wasn't continuing Hartwood's holiday tradition. "Why won't he host the St. Stephen's Day party?"

Bianca scoffed. "He doesn't really have a reason except to imply he can't afford it."

Felicity heard the skepticism in Bianca's voice. "You don't believe that's true?"

Bianca shook her head. "I don't, especially since he kept the money my father left for my dowry."

Felicity gasped, then abruptly lowered her voice lest she draw further attention to them. "Why would he do that?"

"Because he doesn't like me," Buckleigh said. "He refused to give his permission for us to wed."

"Not that I need it." Bianca glowered toward the door as if Calder were still there.

Buckleigh gave her a sympathetic smile. "You did if you wanted your settlement."

"It would have been nice to have so that we could help Hartwell House, not to mention the rebuilding of Shield's End." Bianca referred to the Institution for Impoverished Women and Buckleigh's home. Rather, his home before he'd become the earl of Buckleigh. His seat, Buck Manor, was several miles from Hartwell.

Felicity turned her attention to the earl. "Oh my goodness, I meant to tell you straightaway how sorry I was to hear of the fire. I'm afraid Cal—His Grace—distracted me." She prayed they didn't notice that she'd almost called him by his given name. However, given the flash of surprised interest in Bianca's blue eyes, Felicity was fairly certain at least she had.

"Thank you," Buckleigh responded. "The bright spot in all of it is that we will rebuild Shield's End as the new Institution for Impoverished Women."

"Will you?" Felicity asked. "How marvelous. What will happen to Hartwell House?" The Armstrongs had started the institution for women, particularly those with children, several years ago. Mr. Armstrong had passed away, but his wife continued their work, and everyone in Hartwell supported the endeavor as a benevolent alternative to a workhouse, which would separate the women from their children.

Bianca frowned. "It's in grave disrepair, unfortunately. That is why—well, one of the reasons why—I'm so frustrated with Calder. He refuses to continue the support our father provided to Hartwell House, much to their detriment."

Calder was much worse than Felicity could ever have imagined. It wasn't just that he'd turned cold to her ten years ago, it sounded as if he had no sympathy or concern for others at all. Had she completely misinterpreted the young man she'd fallen in love with, or had he changed that much?

"So he won't support Hartwell House, and he won't host the St. Stephen's Day party." And he'd failed to support his sister or allow her to take control of the settlement her father left for her. Felicity was torn between anger and despair. What had happened to make him so awful?

"That's about right," Bianca said with an exasperated sigh. "I won't get into how awful he is to spend time with. I think you probably gathered that on your own." Bianca winced as she looked at Felicity. "My apologies. I shouldn't speak so freely, but I know you and Calder were once… Never mind. It's none of my business."

Felicity couldn't deny that she'd cared about him. Even after his rejection, she'd hoped he would find happiness as she had with James Garland. It seemed he hadn't. Beyond remaining unwed, he seemed to have distanced himself from everyone and everything that might bring him joy.

Bianca turned to her husband. "Ash, will you give me and Mrs. Garland a moment alone?"

Buckleigh smiled warmly, the love he felt for her evident in his gaze. "Of course. I'll go check on Mrs. Templeton."

"Thank you, my lord," Felicity said.

"Please, call me Ash. I'm afraid I'm still not used to being a lord, and I'm not sure I ever will be—especially among my friends."

Felicity nodded. "You—and you," she said to Bianca, "must call me Felicity. We've all known each other far too long to stand on propriety."

Bianca laughed softly. "I knew there was a reason I liked you so much. My brother is an idiot."

Felicity couldn't disagree with her there. She watched as Ash joined her mother and a couple of other ladies. Bianca linked her arm through Felicity's as the music started.

"Oh dear, I'm keeping you from dancing," Felicity said.

Bianca walked with her to a quieter spot near the wall. "There will be plenty of time for that. I wanted to ask if you had any insight as to why Calder is the way he is."

"Why would I? I haven't seen or communicated with him in over a decade."

"Right." Bianca exhaled. "Poppy and I had a theory that his change in behavior was somehow due to you and whatever happened ten years ago. I suppose we were looking for an easy explanation that would help us understand—and maybe even bring him back."

Was she suggesting that Felicity could fix him? Or that she would at least have the key to doing so? "I'm sorry I can't help you. I'm as perplexed by him as you are. He is not how I remember." At least not until he'd written her that horrid letter.

"I'm so angry, but I'm even more sad." Bianca withdrew her arm from Felicity's. "I want the brother I remember. I just fear he's gone forever." She said the last with such soft despair that Felicity's heart squeezed.

Felicity really didn't think she could help, but would it hurt to try? He clearly held ill will toward her—for a reason she didn't understand. At the very least, she should get to the bottom of that. "I'll pay him a call."

Bianca's eyes widened briefly, and she blinked. "You will?"

"On Monday. Perhaps I can convince him to change his mind about St. Stephen's Day. It's just not right that the Duke of Hartwell doesn't host it."

"Good luck." Bianca's response was heavy with doubt. "Viscount Thornaby has agreed to host the event. We were going to hold it at Shield's End until Thornaby and his cronies set it on fire."

"What?" The word exploded from Felicity. She modulated her tone. "They set it afire?"

"Not on purpose, but they were stupid. They wanted to play a prank on Ash and set the house ablaze by mistake. To their minimal credit, they are paying for the reconstruction, and Thornaby is falling all over himself to help however he can, including hosting St. Stephen's Day."

"But Thornhill is, what, five miles away? That's an awfully long way for the villagers to travel."

"Yes, but Thornaby and others, including us and Poppy and Gabriel, will provide transportation. It's not ideal, but it's the best we can do in the face of Calder's refusal to hold the party."

"What of the people at Hartwood?" Felicity hated thinking of the estate's tenants and retainers not being able to celebrate a day that had always been specifically about them and their families.

"We'll transport the tenants, but I don't know about the retainers." Bianca's brow furrowed. "I should speak to Truro about that."

Felicity recalled that Truro was the butler. "I'll ask your brother about it when I call."

"Are you sure you want to subject yourself to his rudeness?" Bianca asked.

"I'm not afraid of him." Felicity squared her shoulders. She was suddenly eager for a fight. He'd broken her heart, and she was finally going to call him out for it. "This has been a long time coming."

"You're a brave woman," Bianca said with a chuckle. "I'm not afraid of him either. He's disagreeable and frigid, but he isn't abusive. And he certainly isn't violent."

That was good to know. While Felicity had a hard time reconciling this Calder with the one she'd originally known, she really couldn't imagine him raising a hand to anyone.

"I do hope you'll let us—me and Poppy—know how your visit goes."

Felicity nodded. "Certainly. Now, if you'll excuse me, I should check on my mother."

"Of course. I'll go with you." Bianca smiled, and they linked arms before crossing back to the seating area.

Determination—and a perverse anticipation—curled through Felicity as she contemplated her visit to Hartwood on Monday. She had a litany of things she wanted to say and ask. Perhaps she should make a list...

At last, the time for reckoning was at hand.

*T*he bottle of gin on the sideboard in Calder's study beckoned him. Perhaps tonight he would down the contents so that he could find sleep, which had eluded him the past two nights since the assembly.

Since he'd seen Felicity up close.

He closed his eyes and leaned his head back against the chair and greedily devoured the image in his mind. She was even more beautiful than he remembered. The planes of her classically beautiful face were a bit more angular, as if honed by the experiences she'd lived during the years since he'd seen her. Her eyes were still a dark, sparkling green, almost jewellike in their intensity. Her blonde hair looked as silken as ever, styled atop her head and dressed with a pearl comb. The Egyptian-blue dress accentuated the curve of her breast and the dip of her waist. He'd been glad to see she didn't wear widow's colors, as so many women did for years after their husband's demise. Did that mean she wasn't sad?

He opened his eyes, cross with himself for trying to discern her feelings. No, for caring about them. She was a greedy, selfish opportunist. She deserved nothing but his undying contempt.

A knock on the door saved Calder from his aggravating thoughts. "Come," he called as he busied himself with the papers on his desk.

The door pushed halfway open, and Truro, his butler, stepped inside. "You've a visitor, Your Grace."

"Who?" Probably one or both of his sisters. They were the only people who dared come to see him anymore. One day, they would stop. He ignored a flash of unease.

"Mrs. Garland. She's awaiting you in the drawing room."

"I'm busy." But Calder's blood rushed, causing a cacophony in his ears. His heart beat so hard, he feared Truro would hear it.

"I did try to tell her that, but she was most insistent." Truro stated this matter-of-factly and without any concern. He was the only retainer who didn't seem to be intimidated by his employer. Calder wasn't sure how he felt about that. While intimidation wasn't his objective, he appreciated the wide berth everyone cut him.

"Fine." Calder stood and took a deep breath. But his pulse still continued its wild race.

"Shall I bring refreshments?" Truro asked as he moved out of the study.

Calder glowered in response before striding past him toward the drawing room.

With high gilt-edged ceilings and an imposing portrait of his father over the fireplace, the drawing room was intended to be the most luxurious room at Hartwood. Calder hadn't changed a thing since his father had died. It wasn't that he didn't want to—he despised everything his father liked, and the man had loved this room. However, Calder's commitment to frugality was greater than his desire to destroy everything his father had cared about. His father would have expected him to "waste money" refurbishing the room, and so he hadn't.

Pausing at the threshold, Calder's gaze moved immediately to Felicity. She stood before the windows that overlooked the gardens and parkland beyond. Her form and profile looked regal in her dark green velvet costume. A jaunty cream-colored feather curled up from her hat, irritating him. She shouldn't look so fresh and lovely.

"I can't credit why you would come here," he said as he stalked into the center of the room. He realized he did want to intimidate *her*. Maybe because his heart was still crashing as if it wanted to escape his body.

She turned from the window, a half smile arresting her

mouth. Her gaze raked over him slowly before settling on his face.

He couldn't tell what she thought of her perusal. That irritated him too.

"Good afternoon, Your Grace."

"If you came for a pleasant conversation to catch up on the past ten years, you will be sorely disappointed."

"I did not," she said softly, walking toward him but stopping a few feet away.

In addition to her hat, she was also still wearing her gloves. Clearly, she didn't mean to stay. Good.

"I came to discuss the St. Stephen's Day party."

He grunted. "My sisters sent you."

"Bianca and I discussed it, but I wanted to come." Now her lips curled into a full smile, but it wasn't the kind that held joy. It was the kind a predator unfurled just before moving to strike its prey.

Calder was no one's prey. "You've made a grave mistake."

She lifted her shoulder in a thoroughly elegant fashion. "Probably, but I'm here nonetheless. Before we discuss the party—and I mean to before I leave—I think we should perhaps clear the air between us. You are angry with me, but I can't fathom why."

She sounded so calm, so reasonable. He almost believed she had no idea. "Have you forgotten what you did? I can't see how that's possible given how drastically it changed your life."

Her eyes narrowed in confusion. "What *I* did?"

He wanted to laugh, but there was nothing humorous about the situation. In fact, he found her attempts at forgetting the past infuriating. "You left."

"*I*...left?" She shook her head. "You didn't come home for Christmas."

"Why would I, knowing that you'd gotten what you wanted and fled?"

She took a step toward him, her eyes dark, the muscles of her jaw tense. "I didn't get what I wanted at all. All I wanted was you." Her words sliced through him, arousing the pain he'd thought long buried. "But you said I wasn't good enough, that you couldn't make me your duchess."

No, that wasn't what had happened at all. His mind raced back to that time, to the visit his father had paid him in Scotland, where Calder had gone to spend the fall at a friend's hunting lodge. The news he'd delivered ricocheted through Calder's brain.

His father had met him in the gathering room of the lodge, his expression foreboding. *"I know you'll think poorly of me, but this is a case in which the ends thoroughly justified the means."* Calder couldn't have begun to imagine what he'd said next. *"I offered Miss Templeton and her family a great sum of money to leave Hartwell. She was more than eager to accept. She never wanted you, just your title and, more importantly, money. I didn't even have to convince her—she was relieved to be free of any promises she made you."*

Calder responded to her, his voice eerily quiet and strange to his own ears. "I *never* said that. Do you deny your family took money from my father and left Hartwell?"

"Money? No!" She set her hands on her hips, her eyes blazing with anger. "We left Hartwell because my father thought I would want to be away from you. He sold his farm, and we moved to York, where my brother lived."

She had to be lying. Calder had no other explanation.

Except he did. His father hadn't been pleased to learn that Calder wished to court Felicity. But then his father had rarely been pleased with anything Calder did.

He managed to find his voice—barely. "My father said he

offered you money to leave and that you gleefully accepted it, that you were glad to be free of me."

Her face went pale, and Calder wondered if she might faint. Then he saw her shoulders stiffen. "I did no such thing, nor did your father offer me anything save a letter from you that said you had no desire to marry me, that I was not an appropriate wife for a duke."

Calder felt light, as if he were floating, as if the earth beneath him had been jerked away. "I didn't write you a letter."

She moved closer, her hand stretching toward him. "Are you all right?"

He stepped back, out of her reach. "I'm fine." But he wasn't. Everything he'd believed for the past decade had been a lie. His father had driven a wedge between him and Felicity. No, not a wedge. He'd burned their dreams to the ground.

And Felicity had wed someone else while Calder had gone to London and raised merry hell until he'd lost everything but the clothes he was wearing and the set of emerald jewelry his mother had left him. The necklace, earrings, and ring had been intended for his wife. Instead, he'd sold them and used them to rebuild himself without a drop of help from his father.

"Well, *I'm* not fine," Felicity said, her brow creased and her mouth turning down. She crossed her arms over her chest, looking bereft. "I thought you didn't want me. To know you did…"

"Don't." Calder couldn't follow that path. That was the distant past. He was not the same man who'd been easily manipulated. "We can't change what happened." And to even think about it would welcome a barrage of hurt he didn't think he could manage. Nor did he want to.

"You can simply forget about it?" She blinked at him, then

stared into his eyes for a long, uncomfortable moment. "We can't change the past, but knowing the truth changes everything."

"It doesn't." It couldn't. He refused to open himself up to…anything. "I need to get back to work." He started to turn, but she came forward and clasped his arm.

Though she wore gloves and the layers of his clothes separated her touch from his flesh, he felt the connection down to the very marrow of his bones. The sensation sizzled through him, reawakening a yearning he hadn't felt in forever.

Or, more accurately, in ten years.

He pulled his arm from her grasp and stared at her hand. She dropped it to her side and looked up at him. "I told you I wasn't leaving until we talked about St. Stephen's Day."

She had said that, dammit. "There's nothing to discuss. Thornaby is hosting it this year."

"Why aren't you?"

Because his father had loved it. Everyone believed St. Stephen's Day was for the retainers and the villagers, that it was their favorite day of the year. While all that might be true, Calder's father had loved it most of all. Everyone heralded him as some sort of king, a benevolent being who deigned to give his people a day of rest and celebration. Everything he did was designed to earn himself praise and adoration. And it worked for everyone, including Calder's sisters.

"It's an expensive event." Even if the cost wasn't his primary reason for refusing to host the party, the statement wasn't a lie.

Her blonde brows arched briefly. "I'm sure you can afford it."

"You know nothing about my finances, nor should you presume." He *could* afford it, but after losing everything and amassing a fortune entirely on his own, he was loath to let any of it go. And the truth was that his father, despite his claims to the contrary, had been a poor financial manager. There was money, but not as much as there should have been. Calder planned to make the dukedom more financially secure than ever before.

"I beg your pardon," she said, but he caught a note of exasperation in her voice. "What if others supported the cost and you merely allowed the event to take place here? It would ease the burden of transporting everyone to Thornhill."

"That isn't my concern."

She blew out a frustrated breath, her brows pitching low over her magnificent eyes. "Of course it is. St. Stephen's Day has been the concern of the dukes of Hartwell for generations."

"Not anymore."

She cocked her head to the side, her expression both curious and pleading. "Why? What has changed?"

"I am the duke now. There is no law saying I must host anything." He narrowed his eyes at her, irritated that she would question him, but also perversely enjoying their exchange. What the hell was wrong with him? "Even if there was, I'm the magistrate."

"So you'd break the law to suit yourself?"

"I *am* the law. However, in this case, there is no law, only your expectation."

She sucked in a sharp breath, and for the first time, he saw something in her eyes he didn't like: pity. Just like that, any pleasure he'd found—and it had been the first in some time—evaporated. "Are you like this because of me? Rather, because of what your father did?"

A thousand emotions exploded inside him, none of which he wanted to address. He was done with this interview.

"You've done what you came to do. We've settled the past and we've discussed St. Stephen's Day. I believe we are finished with each other."

His statement sounded final, and he'd meant it to. With the slight narrowing of her gaze and tightening of her jaw, he wasn't sure she agreed.

"You've yet to provide an acceptable reason for not hosting the party. You don't have to pay for anything."

"It would be an inconvenience. Just as you are being right now."

Her jaw dropped open for a moment before she snapped it shut and pursed her lips. "You bear absolutely no resemblance to the Calder I knew."

Her use of his name was both a balm and a friction. He didn't want either. "Because that man doesn't exist anymore. I'll have Truro show you out." He turned on his heel and quit the drawing room, his heart pounding nearly as hard as when he'd arrived.

"Bloody hell," he swore as he returned to his study. Running his hand through his hair, he tried to banish the encounter from his mind. But all he could see was her heart-shaped face with its stunning—and provocative—emerald eyes. All he could feel was the touch of her hand on his sleeve. All he could smell was the faint scent of bergamot and roses.

Memories he'd worked too hard to bury rose in his mind —holding her hand, laughing with her, taking her lips in the sweetest of kisses…

He'd spent the last decade in some sort of purgatory. Now he feared he would spend the next in hell.

CHAPTER 3

The butler came into the drawing room a moment later. Or perhaps it was longer. Felicity was not terribly aware of the passage of time, not when she'd fallen into a state of absolute numbness.

"Mrs. Garland?" Truro prompted softly from just inside the doorway.

Felicity shook her head and brought herself to the present. If she didn't, she was going to completely lose herself in the past—a past that had stolen her future.

Bitterness stole her breath for a moment. She lifted her hand to her chest and blinked, lest she dissolve into a puddle of tears in front of Calder's butler.

But she wasn't a crier. She was made of stiff, strong stuff, or so her father said.

Her father. Had he played some part in Calder's father's nefarious scheme? Had Calder's father settled some amount of money on them so they could move to York? In hindsight, it was odd how quickly he'd decided to relocate and the ease with which he'd sold the farm.

Her breath caught again, but tears didn't threaten this

time. She felt a wave of outrage. However, there was no one to whom she could direct the emotion.

"Mrs. Garland?" the butler repeated.

"My apologies," she said hastily. "I don't suppose you would tell me where I might find His Grace?"

Truro gave her an apologetic look, his features briefly flinching. "I don't think that's wise."

"Probably not. However, I must speak with him for just another moment. If you don't tell me, I shall go in search of him." She gave him a sly look. "Will you stop me?"

He straightened, and there was a tinge of something in his gaze—admiration, perhaps. "I will not." He lowered his voice to nearly a whisper. "His study is in the northeast corner."

"Bless you, Truro." She flashed him a smile before hurrying from the room.

Good heavens, what was she doing? Calder didn't want to see her. He'd barely stomached their conversation in the drawing room. He also seemed utterly unmovable about St. Stephen's Day.

And yet there was something inside him—something she'd glimpsed when she'd asked if his father had caused him to be the way he was now. Thinking back, Calder hadn't spoken to her much of his father. Now that she knew the man had orchestrated the destruction of their almost-courtship, she wondered how else he'd influenced Calder. What didn't she know?

Probably nothing he would tell her.

Still, she was going to try. She'd loved him ten years ago, and he'd loved her. Through no fault of theirs, save their naïve idiocy in believing the lies his father had spun, they'd been robbed of their chance together. *Then.*

Now, they had another chance. Felicity didn't mean to waste it.

She found his study with ease. However, the door was

closed. Standing outside, she chewed her lip. She ought to knock, but she was rather past following propriety.

Before she could talk herself out of it, she opened the door and strode inside. Calder turned from the sideboard on the right side of the room. A fire crackled in the hearth on the left wall, a chair angled nearby to welcome the heat. His desk, stacked neatly with a ledger and the post, stood before a wide set of windows.

She took all that in very briefly before settling her gaze on her prey. "You seem as if you need a friend. I should like to put myself forward for the position."

He stared at her, his mouth dropping open. He clacked his teeth together. "I do not need a friend, and if I did, it wouldn't be you."

"Why not? We were great friends, I think. More than friends, but we don't have to discuss that. I realize a great deal of time has passed." Her heart squeezed. So much lost time. Yet, she couldn't discount it—she'd been fond of her husband and the years they'd spent together. It had been precisely the type of marriage her mother had encouraged her to embark upon. Their union had been based on mutual respect and shared interests. Mama had said love would come in time, as it had between her and Papa, but Felicity had never truly felt that emotion for James—at least not in the way that she'd felt it for Calder.

Oh, Calder. Her heart ached to see him standing before her, his face drawn, his entire demeanor radiating a seemingly impenetrable cold aloofness.

"An eternity has passed," Calder said. "How did you find me? Am I going to have to terminate Truro's employment?"

"Absolutely not. I told him I was leaving, but I looked for you instead."

"What joy." He poured himself a glass of brandy.

Was that sarcasm? That was far better than abject frigidity!

She eyed the glass in his hand. "You aren't going to offer me any?"

"No. I want you to leave."

"I will if you promise me something."

He snorted, then took a swig of his brandy. He arched a brow at her, and her heart skipped. That was more like the Calder she'd known. And loved.

"Promise me you'll *think* about allowing us to host the St. Stephen's Day celebration here."

"Fine."

She would wager her house in York he was lying. "Excellent. I'll return tomorrow so we can discuss it again." In the meantime, she'd visit Bianca and ensure there were adequate funds to support the event without asking Calder to contribute.

He frowned deeply, his entire face contorting so that she nearly laughed. "Please don't."

"Then you can visit me. I'm staying with my mother in Hartwell. She's leasing Ivy Cottage."

"No."

"Then I'll come here."

"You're incredibly persistent. Even worse than Bianca."

"That is quite a compliment, thank you. I will continue to persist until you agree. I've nothing better to do, you see."

"I do," he said sourly before drinking more brandy.

"You see, or you have something better to do?"

He scowled at her. "Both. Do not visit me tomorrow. I will consider your request and let you know by...Thursday."

"It would be better to know sooner so that we can change the arrangements." She flashed him her most winning smile.

"You actually think I'm going to change my mind."

"If I didn't, I would give up now. I'll come back on

Wednesday, all right?" She didn't wait for him to respond. "I also want you to reconsider your support of Hartwell House. I understand the building is in disrepair and you've ceased the support your father" —she allowed her lip to curl slightly —"gave the institution."

How had the man been so kindhearted when it came to charitable endeavors and his tenants and retainers, and yet absolutely diabolical regarding his son's heart? She longed to ask Calder about that and hoped she'd have the chance. Her persistence wasn't going to be limited to St. Stephen's Day or Hartwell House... She was going to do more than save a holiday and a local institution—she was going to save him too.

His gray gaze darkened like a storm cloud bursting with rain. "Now, you're treading too far. Actually, you've been doing that since you arrived. Be gone with you."

She gave him a pointed stare. "I shall persist." Then she turned and left before he could say anything further.

That had gone better than she'd thought. She'd half expected him to rail at her and banish her from the estate forever. Instead, she'd secured a future appointment with him, even if he didn't really want it.

As her coach rambled from the estate, her bravado faltered. A sense of melancholy settled over her. No, it was something far deeper—a soul-deep sadness over a love not lost, but stolen. There was anger, despair, regret, and just a crushing...grief. She realized a tear had escaped her eye and now made its way down her cheek.

If this was how she was feeling, she could only imagine Calder's response. He was already so broken—at least that was how he appeared to her. Learning that his father had lied about buying her off had to be a staggering blow.

If he hadn't needed saving before, she would say he did

now. And she would be the one to do it—whether he wanted her to or not.

~

The sun was bright against the backs of his eyelids and warm upon his face. The grass was soft beneath him, the smell of honeysuckle rife in the air as the breeze tickled his nose.

"Are you asleep?"

The soft, sweet voice of his love was even more beautiful than the summer day. He opened his eyes and saw her leaning over him. Tendrils of her blonde hair grazed her cheeks, and the sun behind her created a halo around her head.

"You look like an angel," he whispered.

"Then you are surely the devil." She waggled her brows at him, then laughed softly.

"Temptress," he muttered before curling his hand around her neck and pulling her down to kiss him.

Their lips met with a spark of heat and desire. Longing swept through him. It was torture to kiss her like this knowing he couldn't do more. He wouldn't—not until they were wed.

He opened his mouth, and she did the same, their tongues meeting in a clash of hunger and exploration. With his other hand, he clasped her hip, pulling her down on top of him.

She pressed against him, bringing their bodies flush. He groaned, basking in the pure delight of her embrace and this perfect, blissful afternoon. If only it could always be like this... When they wed, it would be. After he returned from Scotland, he'd court her over the Christmas holidays, and they would marry after Epiphany. The future had never looked so wonderful.

He flipped her over to her back, provoking her to gasp into his mouth and then giggle. He pulled back long enough to grin at her. Then the ground began to move.

The blades of grass grew and wound themselves around her, claiming her body as the dirt beneath her gave way. Her green eyes grew wide. She fell away from him, slowly, pulled by the grass and dirt. He couldn't hold her. Terror seized his heart, and he called her name. Over and over.

"Don't let me go!" she cried. "You promised we'd be together."

"Never." The voice of his father boomed all around him like thunder. The sun disappeared, taking its light and warmth. The earth turned gray and barren.

Then the ground swallowed her whole, and he lay facedown in the grass. Only it wasn't grass anymore. It was a carpet pressing into his face.

"You're pathetic." His father again.

Calder blinked as his apartment at the Albany came into view.

"I'm not giving you any more money," the duke spat. "You are on your own. What an embarrassment to me, to our family."

Calder's stomach roiled. "I'm not," he murmured, his voice failing to carry any volume.

"Pull yourself together and come see me. I'll put you on a mail coach to County Durham."

Home…Hartwell…where she'd chosen money over him. He'd never go back.

"No," Calder croaked, lifting his head from the floor and squinting up at the murky figure standing over him.

The tip of a boot crashed against Calder's rib. "Then you are on your own."

Calder dropped his head, but it wasn't a floor. It was soft, like a pillow…

Gasping, Calder turned over and sat up, his chest heaving. Sweat dripped from his forehead as the bedclothes fell away from his upper body. He drew in deep breaths, trying to shake the grip of the nightmare.

It was just a dream.

Except those things had happened. They were memories

—the joyous afternoon with Felicity, his father's cold callousness.

However, now he was viewing them with a different perspective. His father had been even more cruel than Calder had known. His expectations and demands—his abuse—had been bad enough, but now Calder knew what he'd actually done. His father had used malicious deception to separate him from the woman he loved. She'd never taken money from him.

Or so she said.

Calder wiped a hand across his dewy brow. He'd spent ten years hating her, and now he was simply going to take what she said as truth?

The alternative was to believe his father's version of what had happened. Ten years ago, he would have believed her without question. Now...now he was bitter and distrustful, and he guarded himself from everyone and everything.

His heart had slowed, and as the sweat dappling his skin began to evaporate, he became cold. The coals smoldered in the fireplace grate, visible through a gap in the curtain surrounding his bed. Scowling, he lay back and pulled the covers up to his chin.

The truth didn't matter. What had happened a decade ago was in the past, and they couldn't change any of it. He'd dug himself out of despair and failure, and with his father's death, he would build a new legacy for the dukedom. His father had wanted him to be ruthless in his endeavors, whether it was school, marriage, or finances. He'd demanded Calder be the best in everything—there was no time for love or softheartedness. That could all come later, when he'd done all he needed to do to establish himself as a premier nobleman of the realm. Each duke owed it to their heritage to climb higher than the last.

Calder was doing just that. His fortune was greater, his

holdings more vast, his influence without compare. Now would be the time he should take a wife and support the local community—things his father would have demanded he do if he were here.

But he wasn't, and Calder would do the exact opposite. His father would be horrified to learn that Calder would never wed or provide an heir, that he refused to support Hartwell House, that he'd put an end to hundreds of years of tradition.

And that made Calder happy.

Well, as happy as Calder would ever be. That wasn't an emotion he recognized anymore.

But there'd been a flicker that afternoon...when Felicity had visited...

Why the hell had he agreed to consider allowing the St. Stephen's Day party to be held here? And why had he consented to her paying *another* visit that would only upend his carefully wrought façade?

She also wanted him to rethink his decision to no longer support Hartwell House. But he wasn't a hero—not for her, not for anyone. The sooner she accepted that, the better off they would all be.

He'd had a thought about Hartwell House, which he'd mentioned to his sisters. It was time to make that thought a reality. Hartwell House ought to be a workhouse. If they wanted to rebuild Buckleigh's property, Shield's End, as a new institution, it should be as a workhouse operated by the county. Coddling people never did any good—his father had been right about that at least.

Calder closed his eyes and hoped his sleep would not be troubled further. He worked hard to keep memories from surfacing in his mind. Learning what he had today didn't change that. The past needed to stay where it belonged: in the past.

CHAPTER 4

"*G*ood morning, Mrs. Garland," Agatha, their maid of all work, greeted Felicity with a pleasant smile.

Tired due to a rather restless night, Felicity stifled a yawn as she stepped off the last stair. "Good morning, Agatha. Is my mother up?"

"Yes, she just sat down at the table. I am fetching breakfast."

"Thank you." Felicity inclined her head, and the woman, who was about ten years Felicity's senior and lived right outside the center of Hartwell with her husband and son, took herself off toward the small kitchen at the back of the cottage.

Felicity moved toward the parlor where they took breakfast at a two-person round table situated near the window that overlooked the street. She hesitated at the doorway. As Agatha had indicated, Mama was already seated.

After spending the night consumed with thoughts of Calder and the years they'd lost, Felicity was as exhausted in mind as she was in body. Despite that, she knew she must summon the courage to speak to her mother about what she'd learned the day before.

Felicity hadn't been able to broach the subject when she'd returned yesterday. She'd been too overwhelmed with the new knowledge—and with spending time with Calder.

Her heart soared when she thought of him, but only for a moment before the weight of his coldness crushed it down. And then she felt as if she could bleed for him.

"Felicity?" Mama called from the table. Her brow creased as she regarded Felicity with a perplexed expression. "Did you forget something?"

"No." Felicity gave her head a tiny shake, then went to the table and sat across from her mother, who poured her a cup of tea.

"Did you sleep well?" Mama asked.

"Not particularly." There was no point prevaricating. She needed to clear her mind. "The call I paid yesterday was on His Grace." She didn't have to say which duke. There was only one in the vicinity, and there was really only one, period, so far as Felicity was concerned.

Surprise flickered through Mama's gaze before she plucked a roll from the basket between them. "And how did he receive you?"

"Not well," Felicity said.

Agatha came in with two covered plates and placed one before each of them. Removing the covers, she revealed coddled eggs and ham before telling them to enjoy and leaving.

Felicity picked up her fork but didn't eat. Instead, she continued, eyeing her mother with uncertainty. "He holds me in strong disregard. He believes I accepted money from his father and left Hartwell ten years ago to avoid marrying him. Of course I did no such thing." Her insides swirled with anxiety, but she plowed forward. "I wonder, however, if Papa did? Took money from His Grace, I mean." There, she'd said it.

Mama paused in cutting her ham, her body going stiff. When her eyes met Felicity's, there were tears. "I'm so sorry." The apology was soft and low, and it tore at Felicity's battered heart.

"Oh, Mama." The back of Felicity's throat itched, but she swallowed the sensation. Reaching across the table, she briefly touched her mother's wrist. "Why would he do that?"

Sniffing, Mama set her utensils down, then dabbed at her eyes with her napkin. "Your father had talked of selling the farm—he was tired, and neither of your brothers wanted to take it over. When His Grace offered a large sum of money for the property, Percy leapt at the chance. But there was a condition: we had to leave Hartwell and you were not to wed Chilton." She referred to Calder by his former title. "Your father agreed."

"The duke made certain I wouldn't marry his son." Anger rose inside Felicity. She clutched her hands together in her lap, squeezing her frustration through her fingers. "He forged a letter from Calder saying he didn't want to marry me, that I wasn't good enough. But you know that, of course," she said sadly, recalling how she'd sobbed all over her mother for weeks, even after they'd moved to York.

Mama nodded as she dabbed at a fresh wash of tears. "I wasn't sure if it was a forgery, but it seemed clear His Grace was not in favor of your marriage. He was a very powerful man, Felicity. We took the money and left, just as he wanted."

Felicity wanted to understand, but the pain in her chest was nearly crushing. "I loved him."

"You said you did, but you were too young."

"I'm not too young now. I know my mind—now and then. I loved him, and he loved me. We lost a decade together."

"But you loved James!" Mama cried. "You had a good marriage."

"Yes, we did, but I didn't love him. I cared for him a great deal. However, it wasn't the same." There was no comparing the affection she'd felt for her twenty-years-older husband to the wild tide of passion she'd possessed for Calder. A passion that had reawakened yesterday. Part of her sleeplessness was due to remembering the way he'd caressed her, kissed her, and looked at her as if she were the most important thing in the entire world. What she wouldn't give to experience all that again.

"Mama, when I think of what I missed, I am angry and sad. However, I can't change the past." Calder had been right about that, at least, even if he was misled in holding on to those feelings of rage and loss. "And neither can you. I forgive you—and Papa." If Felicity had learned anything, especially after spending time with Calder the day before, it was that life was too short to hold grudges or allow hurt to rule your emotions.

Mama clasped her hand over her mouth and nodded as more tears leaked from her eyes. Sniffing loudly, she wiped her face. "I'm so sorry. I honestly don't know what else we could have done." She blanched. "Is His Grace terribly angry?"

Among other things, but Felicity didn't acknowledge that. Whatever he felt, whatever might be between them would be just that—between *them*.

"He's moved on," Felicity said carefully.

"He has a reputation for being cold and cruel. He rarely comes to the village. And he's never wed. Did we..." Mama shook her head and turned to look out the window, her jaw clenching.

"As I said, we can't change the past. We are here at this moment, and I mean to try to repair things as best as I can."

Mama snapped her gaze back to Felicity, her lips parting as she stared at her a moment. "Are you going to try to pursue a courtship with him again?"

Felicity arched a shoulder. "I don't know if that's possible. However, if I can help him find the joy that seems to be missing from his life, I will consider that a blessing. And it's the least our family owes him."

Nodding, Mama set her napkin back in her lap. "You've a good heart, dear."

Felicity was counting on Calder's being the same—once she cut through the darkness to get there.

By that afternoon, Felicity had listened to her mother apologize dozens of times, and Felicity was more than ready to leave for Buck Manor. The journey was twelve miles, long enough for Felicity to shake off her lingering upset from that morning as well as contemplate her next steps with Calder.

Today, she would speak with Bianca about the St. Stephen's Day party and Hartwell House. Felicity was committed to bringing Calder around on those issues, at least. And if that went well, she'd convince him to apologize to Bianca and give her the settlement he'd denied her.

Goodness, she didn't want much, did she?

It occurred to Felicity—constantly, really—that she'd embarked on a fool's mission. Still, she had to try. Not just for the benefit of the village, the people of the Hartwood estate, and the inhabitants of Hartwell House, but for Calder's very soul. She could see that he was nearly gone, a shell of a man.

Nearly being the key word.

There were glimmers of hope beneath his shell, and Felicity was clinging to those as if her life depended on it. Or his.

When her coach arrived at Buck Manor, she was teeming

with energy and anticipation. She was ready to wipe away the last ten years.

The butler took her outer accessories and showed her to the drawing room. Greenery decorated the mantel and windows, and mistletoe hung near the doorway. Bianca didn't keep her waiting long.

"Felicity! How lovely to see you so soon." Bianca strode toward her, a bundle of vivacity wrapped in a forest-green gown. "My goodness, this is quite a journey for you to take by yourself. Your mother didn't come?"

Felicity shook her head. "She's still recuperating, though she probably would have liked to. Even so, this is a visit I needed to make on my own."

Bianca arched a brow, her gaze curious. "I see." She gestured toward a seating area near the hearth, where a warm fire blazed. "Shall we sit?"

Felicity went to the settee while Bianca took a chair angled nearby. "I visited Calder yesterday." She used his name and decided not to censor herself. He would always be Calder to her, and frankly, she didn't care who knew it.

Now both of Bianca's dark brows climbed her forehead. "You actually went?"

Felicity nodded. "He's really a mess, isn't he?"

Bianca laughed. "How lovely to speak with someone about him openly! Besides my sister and Ash, of course. You're very brave to have gone. How did it go?"

"As well as you can imagine. He said he can't afford to host the St. Stephen's Day celebration, but I can't see how that's possible."

"Thank you!" Bianca crowed. "Neither can I."

"I told him that, but it only made him grumpier. So I suggested he let us—you and whoever else, I mean—host the party at Hartwood without an expense to him."

"Hell, why didn't I think of that?" Bianca asked, tapping her finger against her lip.

"Would you be amenable to that arrangement?"

"I would be *thrilled* with that arrangement. Did he actually agree?" Bianca looked incredulous. "You will have worked a miracle."

"Don't give me credit yet. He's thinking about it."

"That's further than I got with him." Bianca leaned back and crossed her arms. "This is an excellent solution and would be so much easier than transporting everyone to Thornhill."

"Hopefully, he will agree." Felicity doubted he would, which meant she had to find a way to convince him. Perhaps she could circumvent him and go straight to Truro for assistance... The butler was a beacon of hope in that household.

Bianca uncrossed her arms and scooted forward, her eyes alight. "He won't, but perhaps we could trick him."

Felicity laughed, amused they had come to, more or less, the same conclusion. "How loyal is Truro to him?"

"Not as loyal as he is to me," Bianca said with devious glee, her eyes narrowing. "Oh, I must think on this. You're calling on him again tomorrow?" At Felicity's nod, she went on. "I suppose it wouldn't be helpful for me to go with you."

"I don't think so." Felicity was counting on having an advantage that only she possessed—their shared history. Which, unfortunately, included heartbreak. Perhaps what she needed to do was give him new memories... "Bianca, will you be able to coordinate moving the party to Hartwood?"

"Certainly. Ash's mother has been helping me." Bianca tipped her head to the side. "Did you also say you spoke to him about Hartwell House?"

"I did, briefly. You said at the assembly that it's in need of repair."

"Yes, several of the rooms leak, and there really isn't enough space to accommodate everyone. The new Shield's End will support the institution in a much better fashion, but that won't be for some time, so Hartwell House must be fixed. Furthermore, we plan to use Hartwell House as a school for the children who live at Hartwell House and as a day school for anyone else in the area."

"That's absolutely marvelous." Felicity felt a sudden urge to move back to Hartwell so she could be a part of these exciting changes.

Or was it so she could be close to Calder?

She wasn't ready to answer that question. Wanting to restore him to a place of peace and happiness wasn't the same as rekindling their relationship. Except she feared she wouldn't get to decide if she wanted that or not. The passion she'd felt for him in their youth had seemed utterly beyond her control or imagination.

"Poppy and Gabriel already do so much for Hartwell House," Bianca said. "And now Ash and I are focused on rebuilding Shield's End. Continuing the support our father gave to Hartwell House is the least Calder can do. Honestly, even if he would just give my dowry settlement to them, I would be grateful."

Felicity inclined her head. "That's very selfless of you."

"It would be if I were allowed to do it." She exhaled in frustration. "They need the money more than we do, more than Calder does, I daresay. I honestly don't know how he became such a miser."

Felicity thought she knew at least part of the story, but suspected there was more. And she was determined to find out.

∾

*T*hough Calder was expecting Felicity's call, his heart still pounded when her coach stopped in front of the house. He could see the vehicle from the window of his study, but then, he'd been watching for her the past hour or more.

He stood from his desk and went to the window. He'd dreamed of her again last night, but not in the way he had the night before. That had been a nightmare—because of his father.

Calder shoved thoughts of him away. He'd ruined Calder's life once—maybe twice—and he refused to allow him to do it again.

He watched her alight from the coach and then disappear from view. Turning to the door, he took a deep breath and waited for Truro to come fetch him.

Isis sat in front of the fire, her gaze fixed on him as if she were waiting expectantly too.

After several long minutes, Calder began to pace. What was taking so long? He kept himself from going in search of her. Meanwhile, Isis followed his movements, her eyes never leaving his form.

At last, Truro rapped on the door.

"Come," Calder barked, frowning sharply as he stopped and pivoted toward the door.

Truro opened the door and inclined his head. "Mrs. Garland is here. She awaits you in the drawing room."

"It's about bloody time," Calder muttered, striding past Truro on his way to the drawing room. At the threshold, he stopped short and stared at the scene before him.

Felicity sat on a blanket spread across the center of the room, the skirt of her bright blue gown arranged around her like the petals of a flower. A basket sat at the edge of the blanket, and plates of food were arranged, along with two tankards.

"Is that ale?" he asked, a long-ago memory rushing to his mind.

"Yes."

"And blackberry scones." His gaze landed on the plate that held the confection.

"Yes."

He knew everything that was on the blanket—it was a recreation of a picnic they'd had ten years ago. On the very day he'd kissed her beneath the blazing sun. The day he'd dreamed about the other night, before it had become a nightmare.

Wariness crept over him, diluting a shocking rush of pleasure. Even the blanket she sat upon looked the same.

"What are you doing?" The question fell from his mouth, a defense against an onslaught of emotion he didn't want.

"Having a picnic. I'm afraid it's too cold outside. I was worried it might snow."

Calder had been worried about that too. In fact, he'd threatened the sky if it dared prevent Felicity from coming. Which meant he'd looked forward to her visit. Not that he would ever admit it aloud.

"Aren't you going to sit?" she asked.

"I'm not hungry." Except he was. For her.

The years had been more than kind to her. She was even more beautiful now than he remembered. Experience gave her features an alluring wisdom. And her stature exuded confidence and grace—things a girl of eighteen didn't always have in great abundance.

Or a young man of twenty.

God, they'd been young. And naïve. And so foolish. To think they could forge a future—the heir to a dukedom and the daughter of a common farmer...

He went to the blanket, drawn by some invisible thread. Or perhaps the lure of what he'd missed.

He dropped down and reached for the tankard, eager for a fortifying drink of ale. "Did you get this from Tom?"

She nodded. "Of course. Where else would I get it?"

Tom was Hartwell's only brewer. "I have my own here."

"Perhaps we should sample it as well," she suggested brightly as she plucked up her tankard. Holding it toward him, she said, "Let us toast to the future."

He didn't want to drink to that. And yet he *needed* a drink to steady his nerves. He didn't tap his tankard to hers but lifted it and took a drink.

She did the same, then set it down before reaching for the plate of scones. "Would you like a scone? My maid, Agatha, made them this morning. She's a magnificent cook."

"I see what you're trying to do," he said.

"And what is that?" she asked innocently.

"This is disturbingly close to a picnic we shared once."

"Is it disturbing? I should hope not. I have fond memories of that day. In fact, it is among my most favorite recollections."

His pulse racing, he took a long pull on his ale. "Those aren't dedicated to your husband?"

"No," she said softly. "I have lovely memories of our marriage, but they are…not the same."

Something inside Calder unfurled, like a flower blooming beneath the rays of the sun. "I'd heard you were a widow. How did he die?" Calder busied himself with a bite of scone while he awaited her response.

"He was ill for a long time. He was twenty years older than me."

Calder hadn't known that. "You fell in love with him?"

"No. He was kind, and I felt I should marry."

He'd imagined her falling in love with a dashing young man and then pining sorrowfully after losing him. That he'd been utterly wrong was both relieving and...sad. "Were you happy, at least?"

"Yes. He was an excellent husband. We weren't blessed with children, but we had a nice life."

Her description sounded so...pleasant. And while it wasn't what he'd thought their marriage would have been, a "nice life" was still a far cry better than Calder's. "Well, I'm sorry for your loss."

"Thank you." She sipped her ale. "Why haven't you wed?" She eyed him cautiously over the rim of her tankard.

"I've been too busy." He'd completely ignored the Marriage Mart in London. Instead, he'd spent a few years perfecting rakish behavior, conducting liaisons as the mood struck him. The past few years, he'd kept a mistress, but he always terminated the arrangement at the end of the Season. Right now, he couldn't remember any of their names or faces. All he recalled was Felicity. Her winning smile, her gorgeous eyes, her sparkling laugh.

She reached for a fig. "It's good that we're indoors. Do you remember what happened at the picnic?" The edge of her mouth ticked up in a half smile.

For the first time in Calder didn't know how long, he felt his lips tug. How would it feel to smile? To laugh? "You're referring to the bird who defecated on the blanket? Is this the same blanket, by the way?"

She nodded. "You remember." Her tone vibrated with happiness. The sound shot through him like a thousand fireworks exploding in the sky.

He remembered every moment—the bird, their laughter, his scolding of the fowl who had long since disappeared into the beyond. The taste of berries on his tongue, the rush of desire as he'd watched her lick her fingers, the softness of her lips against his.

That she'd kept the blanket and had brought it today

stirred a rush of pleasure inside him. He took another drink of ale, completely at odds with himself. This was at once strange and unwanted while feeling utterly familiar and…wonderful.

"I did try to recreate that day," Felicity said softly. "However, I don't have a dog."

Now Calder did laugh. The sensation was odd and surprising, so much so that Calder transformed it into a cough. The sparkle in Felicity's eyes told him she wasn't convinced he was coughing, that she knew he'd laughed. "You remember the dog?" she asked.

He nodded, then whistled. A moment later, Isis trotted into the drawing room. She came and sat down next to Calder.

Felicity smiled warmly at the greyhound. "Who is this beautiful creature?"

"This is Isis." Calder petted her head, and she nuzzled his hand. "Unlike the dog who interrupted us that afternoon, Isis belongs to me."

That dog, belonging to the owners of a cottage nearby, had prevented their kisses from becoming something more. At the time, he'd thanked the dog to keep him from losing his head. In hindsight, he wished the dog had never found them.

Felicity scooted toward Isis and held out her hand so Isis could sniff her. "Aren't you a pretty girl?" Isis cocked her head, and Felicity stroked her soft, short fur. "Calder, she's lovely." Felicity met his gaze, and he was immediately overcome with a wave of longing—followed by discomfort.

After shunning emotions, particularly pleasant ones, for so long, it was overwhelming to feel so much at once.

"I imagine she must make you happy," Felicity said, continuing to pet Isis as she looked between the greyhound and Calder.

He didn't respond. He never felt *happy*. Isis did, however, make him feel…lighter.

Felicity moved closer to him, her hand resting on the back of Isis's neck. "Calder, why are you like this? What happened? Is this all because of what your father did?"

She was referring to his interference in their relationship, but it was so much more than that. Again, he ignored her. He reached for a slice of cheese and took a bite.

"I wish you would talk to me," she said. "I could help."

He swallowed and fixed her with a frigid stare. "I don't need help. And I don't need to talk to you or anyone else." He ought to toss her out, but damn if he could bring himself to end the nicest afternoon he'd had in years.

He also realized he wasn't helping it stay nice. He was such a beast.

She narrowed her eyes at him before turning her focus to Isis. "I think your master wants me to leave him alone. I don't really want to because I would love to find the Calder I knew before. However, I realize that was a long time ago. So perhaps I should focus on the present." She tipped her head to the side and looked back to Calder. "I'll stop bothering you if you agree to allow Bianca to hold the St. Stephen's Day party here."

"That's extortion."

"Not really. You are in complete control of the situation. You can throw me out at any moment and never speak to me again. I'm merely trying to use any method of persuasion I can. I'll continue to harangue you about your ghastly behavior unless you agree to my terms."

"And how will you do that if I throw you out and never speak to you again?"

She was quiet a moment, then her eyes lit with inspiration. "I'll make signs and post them outside your house and in Hartwell. Their purpose will be to make you laugh—or at least smile."

He nearly did both right then. He had to credit her ingenuity. "So you really aren't going to stop bothering me, despite the deal you offered?"

"I suppose not. However, if you allow the party to be held here, I won't make any signs. Not yet. I do still have other demands, but we can discuss those another time."

"What demands are those?" Why was he asking? It was as if he might consider them.

"Fixing Hartwell House—it's in dire need of repair, and the new Shield's End won't be ready for quite some time. Besides, Hartwell House is to be used as a school, so it must be refurbished."

"Hartwell House is not my responsibility, whatever it's to be used for."

"I would argue it is—you're the leader of this community. Or you should be. And leaders should use their resources to help those less fortunate." She—and Isis—stared at him.

Calder felt rather defensive in the face of both of them. He didn't appreciate his dog siding with the woman who'd broken his heart. Except had she, if his father had orchestrated the entire scheme?

No, but it was far easier for him to continue believing it was her fault. If he didn't...

"You're correct in that I'm the leader in this community. Hartwell House should be a workhouse, not a free boarding-house as it is now. I plan to change that."

Felicity looked at him with affront. "You can't dictate what Mrs. Armstrong does with her property."

Calder ignored her outrage. "You said demands, plural. What's the other one?"

She took a deep breath, her eyes narrowing briefly before she answered, "Giving Bianca her settlement."

How dare she meddle in his family's affairs? He stood and gestured for Isis to come to his side. The greyhound obeyed and moved to stand next to him. "Now I *am* throwing you out."

Felicity pursed her lips. "That's what did it?"

"My family is none of your concern. That you would seek to stick your nose into such matters speaks ill of your breeding."

She snorted, then got to her feet. Calder stepped forward and clasped her arm to provide aid.

Her gaze snapped to his, and a spell fell over him. The picnic from the past was real, the heat of the day, the dazzling joy of her presence.

"That sounds like something your father would have said." Her words jarred him back to the present. Yes, he would have—and often had—commented on her lack of breeding. It was why he hadn't deemed her an appropriate wife.

Was she trying to say he was his father?

It was perhaps the most offensive thing she could say to him. "My father would have given Bianca that money as well as his approval for her marriage simply because Buckleigh became the earl. If he hadn't inherited, my father would have done the same as I did. *My* refusal to give approval is because of who I know Buckleigh to be—a brutal fighter with an inability to control himself. So do not compare me to a man who only cared about a person's position and not their character."

His voice had risen as he'd spoken. He'd actually felt... impassioned. His heart had picked up speed, and a tremor of satisfaction tripped through him.

"I see," she murmured. "I didn't realize those things about Ash. I believe he has a condition that is sometimes difficult for him to manage. I know for certain he isn't brutal and that he adores your sister. He would do anything for her."

Calder didn't wish to hear any of that. He knew his sister was happy, and he didn't care. "It's past time for you to go."

"Yes, I daresay it is," she said on a sigh. "We're settled on the St. Stephen's Day party, then. You'll let Bianca have it here. Thank you, Calder."

He wanted to dispute her, but the words wouldn't form. She continued, "I will return to discuss these other matters after you've had time to think upon them, particularly your sister. If you don't reconcile with her and make things right, you'll regret it. Don't allow a mistake to fester. I wish to God I'd gone to see you ten years ago—after I received that forged letter. Then maybe things would have been different."

Calder couldn't breathe. It was as if a pile of rocks had fallen on top of him and was pressing him into the ground. And the ground would swallow him whole, just as it had done to Felicity in his nightmare.

"Please go." The words came out low and hard. When her gaze dipped to the picnic, he realized all of it belonged to her.

He turned on his heel and stalked from the room, Isis trotting beside him.

"I'll see you soon," Felicity called after him.

Calder wanted to feel dread, but instead, there was anticipation. And that scared him more than anything ever could.

*A*s Felicity's coach bore her back to Hartwell, she couldn't stop thinking of Calder. He'd actually *laughed.* Until he'd tried to cover it with a cough. But she'd caught it, and she was fairly certain he knew she'd caught it. His guard had been firmly in place after that.

The man she'd loved was in there somewhere. She knew it with a deep certainty that filled her with hope—and despair. He kept himself so buried, so cut off from everyone, that she feared he didn't know how to do anything else.

His defense of his actions regarding Bianca had perhaps been the most telling. He'd created a narrative in which he was the opposite of his father and nothing else mattered. At least that was what Felicity suspected. The man had a grip on his son, even in death, and Felicity hoped she could break it. For Calder's sake. Even if they had no future together, and she honestly wasn't sure they did, he deserved to be happy.

Right now, he was decidedly *not.*

She wasn't going to give up, however. Not when she was seeing cracks in his façade. She could also see how much he cared for his sister, even if he'd behaved like a terrible miser.

Thinking of Bianca, Felicity wanted to tell her what Calder had said, but wasn't sure she should. She'd bristled at being thought of as meddling—she preferred to think of it as helping.

She would, however, write to Bianca immediately and tell her the St. Stephen's Day party would be at Hartwood. If Felicity accomplished nothing else, she'd at least done that.

As the coach neared her cottage, Felicity saw another vehicle parked in front. Her coach stopped, and the coachman helped her out before taking the equipage to the stable down the street.

Felicity didn't recognize the coach, but there was a crest emblazoned on the door. She also didn't recognize that, but the presence of a stag gave her an inkling.

She went inside, where Agatha met her, taking Felicity's cloak, hat, and gloves. "Good afternoon, Mrs. Garland. You've two visitors who asked to wait for you. They are in the parlor. Your mother is resting, and I didn't wish to disturb her."

"Thank you." Felicity had given the maid of all work explicit instructions that Mama needed rest in order to fully recuperate. She turned and went to the parlor and was unsurprised to find Bianca and Poppy seated on the settee. "Good afternoon," she greeted them.

Bianca gave her a sheepish smile. "I hope you don't mind us waiting here for you. It's just... I knew you were visiting Calder today, and I'm afraid I was too excited to wait for word about what happened."

"Bianca's excitement can be difficult to contain," Poppy added with a grin. "I should also admit I was eager to hear the results of your meeting. When Bianca told me you'd actually persuaded Calder to reconsider, I was flabbergasted."

Felicity sat in a chair near the fireplace to warm herself

after the ride from Hartwood. "What will your reaction be when I tell you that you may host the party at Hartwood?"

Poppy and Bianca exchanged looks, their mouths dropping open. Then they both laughed with glee.

"Tell us how you managed it!" Bianca said, leaning forward.

"A slight bit of extortion, I suppose. I threatened to continue harassing him if he didn't change his mind."

"And that worked?"

"I might have suggested putting up signs to pester him. In the end, I simply gave him no opportunity to refuse."

Bianca crowed, and Poppy giggled. "Splendid," Poppy said, then sobered. "But I hate that it's come to that."

"I will employ whatever measures are necessary," Felicity said. "I've warned him I am not finished, that we still need to discuss Hartwell House and Bianca's settlement."

Poppy's eyes widened. "You talked to him about Bianca?" She shook her head. "I can't imagine he took that very well."

"He did not, but he wasn't rude either. He actually had a—somewhat—reasonable explanation for doing what he did."

Bianca gaped at her. "He was reasonable?"

"He said he couldn't approve your marriage because he didn't think Ash would be a good husband."

"Because of his fighting and his affliction." Bianca scoffed. "He said the same to me, and I told him it was nonsense. Ash is the best of men. Certainly a better husband than Calder would be."

Inwardly, Felicity winced. She'd once dreamed of Calder being her husband. But she couldn't dispute what Bianca said. "I didn't say I agreed with him. I told him Ash adored you."

"He does," Poppy agreed, sliding a warm smile toward her sister. "And that should be enough."

"I think he could come around," Felicity said cautiously. "I saw a hint of the young man I knew. He's in there still."

Both sisters stared at her as if she'd gone mad. "Truly?" Poppy whispered, sounding hopeful.

"How can you tell?" Bianca sounded dubious.

"He laughed."

The looks Bianca and Poppy exchanged next were beyond incredulous. Poppy spoke first. "Are you sure?"

Felicity nodded. "I mean to continue my assault."

"To what end?" Bianca asked. "Is your goal just to have Hartwell House repaired?"

"And your settlement delivered," Felicity said.

Bianca eyed her with suspicion. "You have no other motive?"

"I think Bianca is trying to ascertain whether there could be a future for you and our brother," Poppy said drily. "We would dearly love to see him happy, and we wonder if you could bring that about."

Felicity clasped her hands together in her lap. "I think Calder will have to be the one to bring it about. But I should like to help him in any way I can."

"Blast it all, I am going to be blunt," Bianca rushed to say. "Is there any chance you might want to marry Calder? You did once, right?"

"I did, yes." Felicity wouldn't—and *couldn't*—commit to anything else. "I don't know what the future holds for me or for him. I will remind you that I don't live here. I live in York."

"Oh." Bianca settled back on the settee, looking disappointed. "I didn't realize."

"I only came to help my mother. However, I am rather excited about the changes coming with Hartwell House and Shield's End. I may decide to stay, at least for a while."

"I hope you will," Poppy said. "Especially if you're

successful in persuading Calder to repair Hartwell House. You will be personally invested in how it all works out."

Yes, she would be. In fact, she wanted to be invested financially too. "I have a bit of money from my husband, and I'd like to give what I can to support the restoration of Hartwell House. Who is managing that fund?"

"Gabriel," Poppy answered, referring to her husband. "I'll tell him you'd like to help. Thank you so much. You should visit Hartwell House."

"I should. It's been years—my father used to take vegetables to Mr. and Mrs. Armstrong."

"Mrs. Armstrong would be delighted to see you," Poppy said before glancing over at her sister. "And she's going to be thrilled to hear about St. Stephen's Day. She was not looking forward to transporting all the children to Thornhill."

Bianca's eyes shone with gratitude. "We can't thank you enough for making this happen. I'll send word to Thornhill straightaway so we can have all the supplies sent to Hartwood." She cocked her head. "Calder still doesn't want anything to do with the event?"

"He hasn't said." But Felicity would ask—he should attend, not just because these were his people, but because he would enjoy it. If he could allow himself to.

"I think we should spend Christmas there," Bianca declared. "That way, we can oversee everything. It's too far to come on the morning of the twenty-sixth, and what if the weather doesn't cooperate?"

"That's been my greatest concern about going to Thornhill," Poppy said. "If it rains too much or snows, no one would be able to attend." She gave her sister a worried look. "Will Calder mind having us there? It would be so lovely to spend Christmas together as a family."

Bianca nodded in agreement. "But only if he accepts Ash and isn't ill-tempered."

"I would love to share my news with him." Poppy's hand drifted across her belly, and Felicity understood immediately what she meant. "I don't know if he'd tell me he was happy for us, but I'd like to think he would."

"You're expecting a child?" Felicity asked. At Poppy's nod, she continued, "My most heartfelt congratulations to you and your husband. You must be thrilled."

"More than I could ever say. After nearly three years of marriage, I'd given up." Pink dotted her cheeks, and her eyes widened briefly. "My apologies. I don't mean to be insensitive."

"You aren't," Felicity said with genuine warmth. "I was married to James for seven years, and we were never blessed with a child." Felicity had become pregnant twice, but hadn't managed to carry the babe long enough. Then, in the latter years of their marriage, James hadn't been able to…perform. She'd accepted the fact that she would be childless. Unless she married again. "I'm so happy for you and your husband."

"Thank you," Poppy said. "It's still very early, but I am surprisingly unconcerned. I just know this child is meant to be, that he—or she—came at precisely the right moment."

Felicity wanted to believe that things happened for a reason. How else could she manage to live with what Calder's father had done? She had to cling to the fact that she was meant to marry James, that the happy times they'd shared were necessary to her life. But what was the reason for Calder? What had happened to him in the last decade that could possibly have been necessary to his life?

Maybe that was a good explanation for what had happened to Calder. He couldn't find meaning in any of it, so he was just…lost.

Well, Felicity had found him. And she wasn't going to let him go.

~

*W*ith Christmas in just five days, an aura of festive jubilance permeated Hartwell. Calder strode along the main street as the shadows grew and the temperature dropped in the late afternoon. It would be close to freezing in a couple of hours, if not below that.

A shiver danced over Calder's shoulders, and he burrowed deeper into his greatcoat. Up ahead, the Silver Goat, Hartwell's coaching inn, beckoned with a warm hearth and lively company.

Not that Calder wanted the latter, nor would anyone seek to have him there. Everyone he passed eyed him with awe and maybe an edge of fear. What else should he expect after removing himself completely from this community? Not to mention everything he'd done to project the notion that he didn't want to be a part of it. He'd refused to host their annual holiday party. He didn't support Hartwell House. He did nothing to endear himself to anyone.

And he'd been fine with that—until Felicity.

She had him second-guessing everything. He'd spent the last two days since her surprise picnic in a foul mood.

Scowling, he strode past the inn, pausing to look in the wide front window. A group of people were gathered around a table laughing. Behind them, near the wall, a couple met beneath the mistletoe. They glanced around to see if anyone watched them, and when it seemed they didn't, their lips met for a sweet, lingering kiss.

An image of him kissing Felicity beneath the mistletoe sprang to his mind. A fierce wave of longing washed over him.

He scowled again and moved on, turning down a side street. A handful of children played up ahead, their shouts and giggles providing a beautiful accompaniment to the charming winter scene.

Calder abruptly turned down a narrow lane and emerged on the next street. He steered to the right and watched as a woman helped an older man into a cottage. The door closed, but Calder watched them through the window as she helped settle him into a chair near the fire. She wrapped a blanket around him, and a younger girl came in to hug him. She sat on a footstool and spoke to him animatedly while the man, her grandfather maybe, laughed.

The woman returned with a tray of refreshments and set it on a table, then began to pour tea. The girl snatched a biscuit from the tray and went to the corner. Music from a pianoforte filled the air. Calder leaned against a tree and listened, the bitter cold of the late afternoon forgotten.

After a few minutes, another man came into the room. He swept the woman into his arms and kissed her cheek before whispering something in her ear. She laughed, and they parted, bowing to each other before launching into a makeshift reel.

The music continued, and the old man grinned as he watched them. Round and round they danced. Calder stood there, utterly enchanted. He'd never seen anything so beautiful. An ache formed in his chest and spread through him. He wanted that. Desperately.

The pianoforte—rather the gifted musician plucking its keys—built to a crescendo, and the dance came to an end. Everyone inside broke into mad applause, and Calder found himself doing the same.

The old man's gaze seemed to find him, piercing Calder with a bright intensity. He lifted his teacup in a silent toast before returning his attention to his family.

Family.

That was what Calder wanted. That was what he was missing.

Darkness swept through him, and he pushed away from the tree, blindly stumbling along until he realized where he was. Felicity's cottage—rather, her mother's—stood across the lane.

Before he could think better of his actions, he strode to the front door and knocked. A moment later, the door opened to reveal Felicity.

Her green eyes widened in surprise. "Calder?" She looked past him. "Is everything all right?"

No. "May I come in?"

"Of course." She opened the door wider and ushered him inside. "Let me take your hat and your coat."

He doffed the garments, handing them to her so she could hang them on a rack by the door. He removed his gloves and shoved them into the pockets of his greatcoat and almost immediately regretted the actions. Why had he come here? He couldn't stay.

She seemed to read his mind, for she took his hand and drew him into the front parlor, a small, cozy room with a blazing fire and bedecked with greenery. He looked about for mistletoe and was disappointed to find there wasn't any. And why should there be? It was her mother's house, and her mother was a widow.

As was Felicity.

He'd never been more aware of that fact. Perhaps because her hand was still clasping his. The feel of her bare flesh against him made the longing he'd felt a little while ago fade into nothingness. He wanted to pull her to him and kiss her, mistletoe or not.

Instead, he let go of her hand and moved to the hearth to warm himself, if that was possible. Sometimes he feared he was frigid at his very core. The name Chill fit him to perfection—or was it that he'd made himself align with the name?

"I'm delighted to see you," she said. "Would you like tea? Or perhaps sherry? I'm afraid I don't have any brandy."

"Nothing, thank you." *Just you.*

She nodded, then clasped her hands briefly in front of her before dropping them to her sides. Was she nervous? Good. He was too.

"What brings you here?" She stepped toward him, and he turned so they could face each other in front of the fire.

"I was just walking through the village and found myself here."

"So you didn't come to speak with me? About Hartwell House or anything else?"

He made a faint sound low in his throat. "I don't want to talk about that. Or St. Stephen's Day." Both his sisters had sent notes thanking him for changing his mind, even though he didn't recall actually doing that. Felicity had managed him rather well.

Poppy and Bianca had also asked if they might celebrate Christmas at Hartwood with him. The thought of them doing so had made him crumple both letters and throw them into the fire.

Family.

He had one, and if he could just... What? He had to do *something*, but he didn't know what. Did he think Felicity could help him? Yes, because she'd reawakened everything he'd buried. Everything he'd thought was dead.

"What do you want to talk about, then?" she asked softly, almost shyly. He was assaulted by the memory of her at eighteen. She'd been shocked when the Earl of Chilton had danced with her at the summer assembly. That had been the single greatest dance of his life.

He suddenly wished they had a pianoforte and someone to play it.

He returned his mind to her question. "I don't know. I just wanted to come inside." To see her. To feel her. "All I do since you returned is feel things. I don't like feeling things."

"Why not?"

"It's easier not to. My father didn't like it when I felt things. He said dukes needed to be above all that."

"Your father isn't here anymore, and even if he was, it doesn't matter what he wanted or what he told you to be. You get to be who you want." She edged closer and lightly placed her hand on his chest, her palm pressing against his lapel. "Who do you want to be, Calder?"

Her touch was sun to the dark landscape of his soul. "I don't know." If she was touching him, perhaps that meant he could touch her. He reached for her face, cupping her gently, then stroking his thumb down her cheek and along her jaw.

Her eyes narrowed seductively, and his body jerked to full sensual awareness. His cock thickened, and he yearned to take her in his arms.

He frowned, glancing up toward the ceiling. "Why don't you have any mistletoe?"

She laughed softly, and it was the music he was missing. "Because I'm a fool. I never imagined I'd need it." She slid her hand up his coat and circled it around his neck. Her fingertips slipped into the hair at his nape. "I was wrong."

"I should say so," he murmured before he lowered his mouth to hers.

This was madness. *This* was wrong. He had no business kissing her, and yet he couldn't have stopped himself if the ocean had washed over him and swept him from the shore.

It was as if no time had passed but also forever. He wrapped his arms around her and held her tight to his chest. She clutched at his neck while molding her mouth to his.

Then she opened, meeting his tongue and ravishing him as surely as he wanted to ravish her.

Groaning softly, he plundered her mouth, telling her in the only way he knew how that he wanted her. Needed her. That she was the very thing his dark heart needed to heal—if it ever could.

Their embrace was thunder and bliss, a joining ten years in the making, a dream he'd never thought would come true. She hadn't abandoned him. She'd been taken from him, and he from her. This was the future they'd promised each other. Or at least, it could be.

Unless he messed it up.

He pulled back, taking his mouth from hers and setting her back to the floor—he'd completely swept her up against him. They breathed heavily as they stared at each other, still so close.

"You're in there," she whispered. "The man I loved."

Loved. Past tense. He loved her in the present and would always love her. But what was love when it came from someone who caused misery?

He took another step back. "I'll consider Hartwell House."

"You should visit," she said softly. Her pulse beat strongly in her throat, just beneath the sweep of her jaw, and her rapid breaths caused her chest to rise and fall in quick succession. She was a woman enraptured. He tried not to stare.

"I'll think about it." He pivoted, his feet like lead. He should go, but couldn't bring himself to.

"Please stop in anytime." She touched him again, her hand on his bicep. The connection galvanized him.

He stalked toward the door. "Thank you." He didn't turn to look at her before going into the entry hall, where he slammed his hat on his head and swept his coat into his arms. He waited to don the garment until he was outside where it was full dusk. The icy cold of oncoming night crashed into him, banishing the heat that had sparked between him and Felicity.

Not banishing it, no. Abating it. He now wondered if he would forever burn for her, if he always had and just hadn't known it.

He buttoned his coat and pulled on his gloves as he reached the street. Turning his head, he saw her standing in the doorway watching him. She was going to catch a chill—and not just from the near-freezing temperature.

He was Chill, or had been all his life until he'd become the duke. The name now seemed prophetic, considering how he'd turned out. She was warmth and light and cheer, everything he was not. For that reason, he should stay far, far away from her.

CHAPTER 6

*B*uilt in the early seventeenth century, Hartwell House was a gorgeous manor home with cream-colored stone and five stately gables. Looking at the structure, one could not discern its disrepair. It exuded charm and warmth, which made sense because it was a home to so many in need of one.

Felicity exited her coach and hurried to the front door. The weather had remained icy cold today. In fact, there had been ice hanging from the cottage that morning. For this reason, Felicity had begged her mother to stay home where it was warm, and she wouldn't risk catching a chill. Mama had been happy to oblige despite wanting to visit Hartwell House.

The door opened before Felicity could knock. Mrs. Armstrong stood inside the threshold, grinning widely. A woman in her late forties with mostly dark hair—there was gray at her temples—she was the overseer of the Institution for Impoverished Women. "My goodness, it's Felicity Templeton! Come in, come in." She ushered Felicity into the hall and quickly divested her of her cloak, hat, and muff.

Felicity pulled her gloves off, smiling. "I'm Mrs. Garland now."

"Of course you are, but to me, you shall always be Felicity Templeton—that's who you were last time I saw you!" She winked at Felicity, then took her gloves. "I'll make sure these are warmed up so they'll be nice and toasty when you go. And I'll fetch some tea. I'm sure that won't come amiss."

"It will not, thank you," Felicity said.

Mrs. Armstrong gestured toward a sitting room just off the entry hall. "There's a nice fire in there."

Felicity left the entry hall with its dark wood paneling and moved into the sitting room. She gravitated toward the fire to warm herself. Despite the warming pan in her coach and the relatively short drive to Hartwell House, she was rather chilled.

A movement to the right caught her eye. She saw a small boot disappear beneath a long settee. Smiling, she held her hands to the fire. "Are you playing hide and seek?" she asked.

"No, but that sounds fun. Can we?"

Felicity laughed, then turned so that her backside was to the fire. A young boy of maybe seven slithered out from beneath the settee. He glanced toward the doorway. "I'm not supposed to be here."

"Oh. Well, then perhaps you should go."

He nodded. "I just wanted to see the carving on the mantel. I'm trying to draw it." He held up a piece of parchment filled with illustrations.

Felicity gave him a questioning look. "May I?"

He handed her the paper, and she gently took it between her hands to more closely see the drawings. "Did you draw these?"

He nodded.

"You are exceptionally skilled. I love this bird." Her gaze caught on a small falcon perched on a fence post. He'd captured the animal's intelligent eyes and the delicate lines of each feather.

She glanced toward the mantel and saw that it was intricately carved with leaves and flowers. She searched the paper and finally found his rendering of some of the flora, but it was very small. "I think you need another piece of paper."

"Parchment is hard to come by," he said matter-of-factly. "I use every last inch. That's what Mrs. Armstrong says to do." He looked toward the door again. "If she catches me here outside of our appointed time, I won't be allowed to visit for a week."

That seemed a trifle harsh, but Felicity had no idea what it took to manage an institution like this with all the women and their children. She imagined it was a challenge to maintain some semblance of order.

"Then, I suppose you better go." She handed the paper back to him. "Could you use more parchment, then?"

He grinned, revealing a gap between his front teeth, which seemed to just be coming in. "Always!" Then he disappeared from the room in a flash.

Mrs. Armstrong returned a moment later with a tea tray, which she set on a table near the hearth. "Do you take any milk or sugar?"

"A bit of both, thank you." Felicity perched on the settee the boy had hidden beneath. "I was sorry to hear about Mr. Armstrong."

Mrs. Armstrong handed Felicity her cup. "Thank you, dear. But then you're a widow now too—and so young. Have you any children?" She fixed herself a cup of tea and then sat on the settee opposite Felicity.

"No, we didn't have any children." Felicity drank her tea, welcoming the warmth of the brew.

"We didn't either, which is how Hartwell House came to

be. We took in a young woman and her baby. Then another." Mrs. Armstrong sipped her tea.

Felicity hadn't realized the Armstrongs didn't have children of their own, but then she'd been rather young when she'd left Hartwell. "It's a wonderful institution, such a necessary alternative to a workhouse, where mothers are separated from their children."

"Yes, though our secret is out, I'm afraid. We've had more women arriving so far this fall and winter than ever before. I tried turning people away for lack of room, but they beg to sleep on the floor if we've nothing else. I don't have the heart to turn them out into the cold. Lord Darlington has temporarily housed a few people in cottages at his estate, which has been a help."

Felicity was more determined than ever to help. "I understand Hartwell House is in need of repairs. I was hoping you might give me a tour? I'd like to donate some money to your cause and see about getting more." Aside from convincing Calder to do his part, she thought of people she could ask in York to contribute.

"You're very kind," Mrs. Armstrong said. "I'd be delighted to give you a tour, and truly, if you have the inclination to come and spend time with the children—reading stories to them or even teaching them skills—we'd all be grateful."

Felicity thought of the boy she'd met and wondered if he could teach her how to draw. "I would be honored to spend time here."

Mrs. Armstrong smiled before drinking more of her tea. She stood and set the cup on the tray. "Shall we take the tour?"

"Yes." Felicity finished her tea and placed her cup next to Mrs. Armstrong's.

Over the next half hour, Mrs. Armstrong showed her the

entirety of Hartwell House, from the uppermost rooms, where a few maids—all women who'd come here in search of shelter and care at some point—resided to the dormitory that housed other women to individual rooms shared by mothers with their children. There was also a schoolroom, an exercise room where the smaller children could run and play when the weather was poor, and a large dining room. Some of the bedrooms leaked, and they were in need of more furniture, namely beds. There was much that could be done, and she was angry with Calder for not continuing his father's support.

At the conclusion of the tour, they neared the small room near the kitchen that Mrs. Armstrong indicated she used as an office. "Is there anything I can readily obtain for you in the near term? Or for the children, especially with Christmas nearly upon us?" Felicity already planned to gather all the parchment she could find in Hartwell.

"We had a lovely St. Nicholas Day party here. The residents received gifts from Lord and Lady Darlington as well as Lord and Lady Buckleigh."

Felicity wished she'd known of it, for she would have come too. She was not surprised when Mrs. Armstrong didn't mention Calder's name. "That sounds as if it was a wonderful event."

Mrs. Armstrong nodded. "Everyone is looking forward to St. Stephen's Day. I'm so relieved it will be at Hartwood. I wasn't relishing having to transport the children to Thornhill. In fact, I'd begun to consider just doing my best to host something here."

Felicity was now doubly pleased she'd arranged for the party to be held at Hartwood. "I'm glad you don't have to."

A figure emerged from the kitchen and stopped short upon seeing them. Poppy grinned. "Felicity, how lovely to see you here."

"Mrs. Armstrong was just showing me all the wonderful things she's done."

"Oh, stop," Mrs. Armstrong said, blushing. "I'm going to my office now before either of you can embarrass me." She flashed them both a grateful smile, then ducked into her office.

"Are you staying long?" Poppy asked.

"No, I was just about to go, in fact."

"I'll walk out with you." Poppy stuck her head into Mrs. Armstrong's office to say she was leaving. Felicity did the same, and they exchanged farewells before Poppy and Felicity started toward the entry hall.

"Felicity, I must thank you again for whatever influence you have with Calder."

Felicity wasn't sure what Poppy could be thinking of. Yesterday he'd refused to talk about anything—he'd been upset. And then he'd kissed her, and everything had gone absolutely sideways. He *had* said he'd think about helping here at Hartwell House…

"Did he reinstate the dukedom's support of Hartwell House?" Felicity asked.

"Not that I'm aware. Did you persuade him to do that too?"

"I didn't think so. What are you talking about, then?"

"He's invited us to spend Christmas at Hartwood." She cocked her head from one side to the other. "Perhaps the word 'invited' is a tad excessive. He wrote and said that if we wanted to come to Hartwood on Christmas Eve so that we could be there to help prepare for St. Stephen's Day, he would appreciate it. Because he doesn't want anything to do with it." She rolled her eyes. "Still the same icy Calder, but it's a move in the right direction at least."

While Felicity was angry with him for turning his back on Hartwell House, she also understood he was a man burdened with pain and loneliness brought on by horrible expectations. She'd begun to suspect that his father's actions toward him ran deeper than verbal cruelty, but she was terrified to learn the truth. "I'm so glad you and Bianca haven't given up on him."

"We never will," she said quietly but fiercely. "And I'm so grateful you haven't either. I know your presence has made an impression."

"I didn't say anything to him about having you for Christmas." Felicity wanted Poppy to give Calder credit, not her.

"Well, I still think you played a part, whether you did so on purpose or not." She took Felicity's hand and gave it a quick, heartfelt squeeze. "Honestly, I'll take any positivity from him any way I can." She smiled before reaching for her cloak.

Felicity was as surprised by Calder's Christmas invitation as Poppy appeared to be. He was so vulnerable, so fragile... The things he'd said to her yesterday about not wanting to feel tore at her heart. He needed care and understanding—and she knew his sisters would give it to him if he allowed them the chance. It seemed he might be ready, or almost ready, to do that.

"You should come too," Poppy said as she pulled on her hat.

Felicity donned her cloak. "I couldn't. I haven't been invited." And she felt strongly he had to invite her. Having his sisters there was likely going to be challenging enough. If he was going to try feeling emotions again, it was probably best if he didn't try to manage too much at once.

Poppy nodded. "I understand. Bianca and I are foolishly hoping you and he will find your way back to one another."

So was Felicity. She sent Poppy an earnest look. "Give him time and don't let go. He needs you, but he'll never say so."

Poppy nodded, and Felicity thought she saw moisture in her gray-blue eyes.

"I nearly forgot!" Mrs. Armstrong's voice rang in the hall, disrupting the taut moment. "Both of your gloves are nice and warm." She handed a pair of gloves to both Felicity and Poppy.

As Felicity drew hers on, she sighed with pleasure. "Oh, these are lovely. Thank you."

Poppy leaned toward her and stage-whispered, "This is my favorite part of coming here in the wintertime."

They all laughed, then went their separate ways. As Felicity's coachman opened the door to her carriage, she asked him to make a slight detour on their way home.

A short while later, they crested a small rise, and her childhood home came into view. She'd managed to be here the last several weeks without seeing it. Why? Because it reminded her of her father and of her lost innocence. Of Calder and the way he'd broken her heart.

Only he hadn't. They'd been victims of his father's machinations. And her father's, somewhat. She had forgiven Papa, but his actions still stung. She wished he were still alive so she could talk to him about it. Maybe that would make what he'd done easier to understand.

Or not. She wasn't sure there was any way to defend his behavior.

The two-story farmhouse looked the same, with its cheery mullioned windows and charming fence with the gate her father had built with the letter T leading up the walkway to the front door.

Her breath caught when the door opened and out bounded a familiar dog.

Isis leapt into the yard and dashed about for a minute before going to relieve herself. Calder came out onto the stoop and looked about, his gaze settling on Isis as she finished her business.

Felicity knocked on the roof of the coach, and the driver knew to pull to the house and stop—she'd told him she might want to. She'd had no idea if anyone lived there. And now it seemed…Calder did?

Not just because he'd come outside with his dog, but because smoke curled from the chimney, indicating it wasn't a quick visit to check on the property. Or maybe it was, and he just preferred to linger. Her heart twisted—he was so incredibly complicated.

Felicity watched out the window as the coach pulled up in front of the house. Calder stepped from the stoop and moved along the path until he reached the gate.

The coachman helped her out, and she told him she'd just be a few minutes. Calder opened the gate for her as she approached, and they walked along the path in silence for a moment. Isis chased a bird who'd had the nerve to land on a fence post.

"What are you doing here?" Felicity asked.

He looked at her askance, a hint of amusement—amusement!—hovering over his mouth. "I could ask you the same."

"I haven't come by since I returned to Hartwell. I was curious. I never imagined to find you here."

"The estate owns it. I didn't know that until I inherited and read through all my father's account books. There was a great deal he didn't tell me." If that was meant to be a veiled comment about the horrible secret the former duke had kept from all of them, she was impressed with how little vitriol Calder's tone carried.

He opened the door to the house. "Do you want to go inside?"

"Please."

He gestured for her to precede him. She walked into the hall, which was flanked by two rooms, one her mother had used for their formal receiving room and the other they'd used as a library and family parlor. She went into the latter and saw that the furniture was the same.

"It looks exactly as I remember," she said softly as she moved about the room, trailing her gloved fingers over a table, the back of a settee, and the mantel. A warm fire heated her as she turned and took in the familiar space. "Why is it the same?"

He stood in the doorway to the hall, Isis at his side, looking distinctly uncomfortable. "I suppose whoever lived here after you left kept everything."

"Where are they now?"

He shrugged. "The house was empty when I inherited." He moved into the room, keeping his gaze from meeting hers. "I like to spend time here when I want to be alone."

Except as far as she could tell, he was *always* alone. Which meant he came here for another reason, at least partially. She wouldn't press him. "I just came from Hartwell House. I have a list of repairs—rather, I can draft one for you. The house requires general maintenance as well as more furniture." She looked around the room. "We could start with what's here."

His eyes met hers with a look of astonishment. "You'd give your family's things away?"

"They're not doing anyone any good here," she said. "At Hartwell House, they will be put to good use."

Calder stood near the window, through which Felicity could see her coach. She couldn't leave the coachman waiting long, not in this cold.

"Calder, I somewhat understand why you stopped giving money to Hartwell House, but you must see that they need it. Surely you can spare enough to see the building repaired at the very least. They are in dire need."

"You 'somewhat understand'? How is that?" His tone held a dark, mocking edge.

"I comprehend that you don't wish to do anything your father did. Since he supported Hartwell House, you will not."

"Or perhaps I'm just a coldhearted monster who doesn't want to help others."

She snorted. "I don't believe that any more than you do." She was fibbing a bit—she wasn't sure if he believed that about himself or not. "I see a man who loves his dog and his sisters." She walked toward him, slowly, as if she could frighten him if she moved too quickly.

He didn't budge as she approached. "Will you ever stop pestering me?"

"No. At least not until you're yourself again. I'll be right here for however long that takes." She stopped directly in front of him so that they nearly touched.

"Felicity, I am not the dream you remember. I am cruel and horrible, exactly the way I was raised to be. As it happens, I *will* repair Hartwell House so that I can then turn it into a workhouse."

She knew he didn't mean it. He was trying to push her away because she'd said she would stay as long as it took. "Mrs. Armstrong will never allow that."

"She will if I offer her a large sum of money. People will do anything for blunt."

The truth hit her hard and fast, particularly standing here in this room—her home—a place her father had forsaken for nothing more than money. "Please don't do that," she pleaded. "You don't have to do that to drive me away. I'll leave if you ask me to."

His jaw worked, and he opened his mouth. But nothing came out before he snapped it closed.

"Do you want me to go?" she asked.

He looked utterly conflicted, his eyes blazing as if a war were being fought just behind them.

Felicity realized she'd pushed him far enough today. He

was making progress—with his sister, and with Hartwell House. Perhaps she could make one more attempt...

She lifted her hands to his shoulders. "Just visit Hartwell House and see for yourself. I agree that you *will* repair it, and the idea of a workhouse will be lost completely."

She stood on her toes and pressed her lips to his. She kissed him once, twice, a third time, her mouth lingering beneath his. "And I'm not leaving Hartwell—or you."

Letting him go was difficult. She wanted to enfold him in her arms and show him how much she cared for him, what it would be like if he let himself truly feel.

But she didn't. She stepped back, gave him a final look that conveyed all the warmth and hope she had for him, then left the house.

She'd come back another day and see the whole thing. Today hadn't been about that or her. It was about Calder and bringing him back. He was so close, and she wasn't giving up until he found peace.

CHAPTER 7

*C*alder's brain hurt. He'd thought and reflected and bloody *felt* more in the past week than he had in the past decade. And what good had it done?

He was allowing the St. Stephen's Day party to happen at Hartwell, something that would have made his father happy, which made Calder decidedly surly.

Then he'd invited his sisters and their husbands to spend Christmas at Hartwood, something else that would have pleased their father. He'd adored them, particularly Bianca, who was the "very image" of their mother, as their father had said a thousand times. And the hell of it was that they adored him. It was a wedge between him and his sisters, invisible to them and insurmountable to him. He could easily tell them why he despised the man they loved, but why ruin their memory of him?

He could hear Felicity now—*See, you are every bit the man I knew you were.*

Maybe. Somewhere deep inside. Somewhere he wanted to keep private and unseen.

And now, here he was at Hartwell House to investigate

their needs. All because of Felicity.

The afternoon was slightly warmer than the day before, but still cold enough that he'd brought his coach. He stepped out of the vehicle, and Isis leapt down beside him.

Calder frowned at the manor house. It looked perfectly fine. He knew he was being foolish, that he likely couldn't see its defects. Plus, Felicity had said they needed furniture. He couldn't decide whether there was a deficit unless he went inside.

He didn't particularly want to.

Postponing the inevitable, he walked around the house, sizing up the exterior as best he could. He noted a broken window and a potential leak judging from the water marks on the stone.

Calder realized Isis was no longer with him. He looked around, then saw the greyhound dash by. She picked up a stick with her mouth and trotted back around the corner to the back of the house.

Following her, Calder saw the reason for Isis's distraction. A girl with bright blonde hair patted the dog's head, then threw the stick again. Hell, she had quite a throw.

"Is that your dog?" she asked as he walked over to her.

"Yes."

The girl's mouth drooped with momentary disappointment. "I was hoping she didn't belong to anyone." She sighed. "She's very beautiful."

"I think so too. Her name is Isis." He glanced back at the house as Isis came back and the girl took the stick once more. "Do you live here?" Calder asked.

The girl nodded. "I'm Alice." She threw the stick again, and Isis ran after it like she was a puppy once more. "I wish I could have a dog. But Mrs. Armstrong says there isn't room for pets. Except her cat, who everyone says is older than any cat should be."

"How old is that?" Calder asked.

The girl's brow creased. "Oh, *very* old. I should say fifteen maybe."

Calder chuckled. "Is that old for a cat or for people too?"

Isis returned with the stick, and Alice took it. Then she blinked up at Calder. "Only for cats, silly. People-old is like you. You must be at least thirty."

Calder's chuckle bloomed into full laughter. "I am in fact thirty. How old are you?"

"Six." She threw the stick. "And a half."

He knew how important that half year could be at her age. "So you'd like to have a dog, but Mrs. Armstrong won't let you have one. What about your mother, what does she say?"

"She wouldn't mind. She thinks my younger brother might like one too."

"You have a younger brother?"

She nodded as Isis ran to her. "Joseph. He's three."

"What happened to your papa?"

"He died." She said this without emotion but managed not to sound cold like Calder did. For her, it was simply a statement of fact, of the reality that was her life.

"I'm sorry to hear that." And he was sorry their little family had needed to rely on the charity of Mrs. Armstrong. Yet it was a far better alternative than a workhouse.

Blast it all, he *was* a monster. He couldn't turn this place into a workhouse. "Do you like living here?" he asked her gently as she continued to throw the stick for Isis.

"Most of the time. Sometimes Mama cries because we can't live in our own house. I only care that we're together. But I wish our room didn't leak." She made a face. "I hate that dripping noise when it rains. I shall be ever so happy when the new institution is built. It won't have a drip." She smiled at him, and the brilliance of it nearly made him weep.

When Isis returned next, she flopped at Alice's feet and let the stick fall to the ground.

"I think that's her way of saying she's tired," Calder said.

"I should go inside anyway. Mama said I shouldn't stay out long because it's so cold." She walked a few feet away and squatted down.

Calder followed her and watched as she picked up a handful of soldiers and a wagon. One of the wheels fell to the ground as she stood.

"Dammit."

Calder blinked at her, his eyes widening. "I beg your pardon?"

She clutched her toys and looked at him, her features frozen. "John says that all the time. It's a naughty word, isn't it?"

"It's not entirely suitable for six—and-a-half—year-old girls."

"Please don't tell Mama. Or Mrs. Armstrong. I won't get any pudding for dessert."

Calder put his hand on his heart. "I swear your secret is safe with me. Dammit." He winked at her, and she giggled. Oh, that sound... He looked at her and saw the future that should have been his—a bright-eyed, blonde-haired little girl with a love for dogs and a penchant for curse words.

He bent and picked up the wheel, then held out his hand for the wagon. "May I try to fix it for you?"

She nodded, handing him the wagon.

Calder studied the toy and realized there was a piece missing. He surveyed the ground and managed to find it. He slid the wheel back onto the axle, then bent to retrieve the missing piece, which he affixed to the end to keep the wheel on. "Here you are." He handed it back to her.

"Thank you, sir."

He noted that the toy soldiers seemed more suited to a

boy. "Would you like to have a doll?"

She shrugged. "I s'pose. But I'd rather have more soldiers. And maybe a gun. I asked for one—and a dog—on St. Nicholas Day, but I got these instead."

Calder couldn't help but laugh again. "You want a gun?"

"Yes, so I can shoot Freddie."

Stifling his laughter, Calder adopted his most serious tone—the fact that she wanted to shoot someone was serious. "Who's Freddie?"

"He pulls my hair and steals my biscuits. I don't like him."

"I don't think I like him either. However, shooting him is rather excessive."

"I wouldn't *kill* him," she said sullenly.

"Well, that's good to know. How about you find revenge in another, more fitting, way?"

Calder's mind worked until he settled on a solution. "You say he steals your biscuits?" At her nod, Calder continued. "Next time, put something in your biscuits that would make him scream."

She stared up at him, rapt. "What would make a boy scream?"

"Maggots." Calder knew this from personal experience. When he'd been around Alice's age, he'd hidden food—he couldn't remember nor could he identify what it was—in his room. Sometime later, he'd stumbled upon it only to see it was crawling with maggots. He'd screamed and then he'd been punished for hiding the food.

"On second thought, perhaps you shouldn't do that," he said. "I don't want you to get in trouble."

She shook her head vigorously. "Oh, I won't. He's the one stealing my biscuits, and if he says anything, Mrs. Armstrong will know he's a thief."

"Perhaps the biscuits should be a gift. That way you have no culpability. I'll bring you some, for Freddie, mind you."

"Oh, would you?" Her voice held a hint of awe that was altogether different from the awe bordering on fear that everyone else treated him with.

"Certainly, plus some for you that are maggot-free."

She grinned widely. "I like you almost as much as your dog."

His heart swelled. "That's the nicest compliment I've ever received."

She rolled her eyes. "It is *not*."

It actually was.

A short while later, after watching Alice go back into the house, Calder left without going inside. He didn't need to see the leaks or the furniture that was needed to decide to support Hartwell House. His interlude with Alice had told him everything he needed to know. That Hartwell House needed his help—and dogs—and that he wasn't entirely broken.

Severely damaged, but for the first time, he had hope that he could be fixed. He smiled, thinking of Alice shooting Freddie. That boy was going to be sorry he ever pulled her hair and stole her biscuits.

When Calder went to the kitchen to discuss his very specific biscuit requirements with the cook, all the retainers in the kitchen and scullery had stopped working and tried not to gape.

"Let me understand, Your Grace," the cook said. "You want a half-dozen biscuits with…maggots?"

"Or some sort of vermin that's available at this time of year," he said, realizing maggots could be hard to find in December unless one visited the privy. And he would never ask anyone to do *that*, not even on his most obnoxious day.

"I know just the thing," one of her assistants said. "Worms are available any time of year. Would that suffice?"

"I should think so. There's a girl at Hartwell House who

says one of the boys keeps stealing her biscuits. I should like him to stop, and shooting him—that was her solution—seemed inappropriate. Worms in the biscuits he pilfers should put an end to his thievery."

Everyone in the kitchen stared at him. Then the cook began to laugh. Others joined in. Calder found himself smiling.

After a minute, the cook said, "We'll come up with something. He won't be stealing her biscuits again."

"Thank you," Calder said. "I'll need them tomorrow afternoon, along with some that are free of vermin for the girl."

"Oh, we'll make something special just for her." The cook and her assistant shared a look, and Calder couldn't remember the last time he'd felt so…satisfied.

What he wouldn't give to make the sensation last. Too bad it was already starting to fade.

～

The weather on the day before Christmas Eve was as cold as the prior two days, with an added bonus: the threat of snow. Felicity looked up at the sky as she arrived at Hartwell House with a stack of parchment.

"I don't think it will snow until later, if at all," her coachman noted as he helped her out of the carriage.

"Well, if it does start, we'll leave at once," she said. "I won't be terribly long anyway."

He nodded, then handed her the stack of parchment that Felicity had accumulated. She'd gathered and purchased as much as she could find. "Thank you. Are you going to the stable to warm up?"

"Aye," he said with a grin. "The other day, I had a mug of fine ale as well."

"I'm glad to hear it," Felicity said, chuckling before she

turned to go to the door. She knocked, but no one came. Then she heard...screaming?

Frightened for whoever was making the noise, Felicity opened the door and went inside. She quickly deposited the parchment on the long, wooden bench that ran along the right side of the entry hall and hurried toward the sound. A moment later, she walked into the dining hall, where a boy was spitting on the floor and dancing around intermittently yelping. He had been the one screaming?

She started forward to ask if he was all right, but then noticed that the other children were not alarmed. In fact, they were...amused. Why were they laughing at him? And why did the one girl look as if she'd just won a very important contest?

Then Felicity noticed the most astonishing thing of all: Calder stood in the corner, his arms crossed, his face alight with mirth. Mirth? She blinked, certain she was imagining his expression. But no, she wasn't. He was *amused*.

Instead of disrupting whatever was going on, she skirted the perimeter of the hall until she reached Calder. "What happened?"

"Freddie's had his comeuppance," he said through a smile.

Felicity regarded the scenario. The boy—Freddie, presumably—had stopped moving. His face was pale as he glared at the girl, who still appeared quite pleased with everything.

"What on earth is going on in here?" Mrs. Armstrong entered, trailed by several women, and Felicity wondered how it had taken them so long to arrive. "We go outside for one minute to take a brisk walk around the house, and this is what happens?" She looked at Freddie and the girl. "What *did* happen?" Her eyes narrowed. "Freddie, did you take someone's biscuits again?"

"In fact, he did," Calder answered mildly. "However, I

daresay he won't be doing so again. Isn't that right, Freddie?" He looked at the boy with a placid smile that should have scared the impudence right out of him. And maybe it did. Freddie looked as if he were horrified to have a duke, or maybe just a man, since there weren't any in residence, speaking to him. It occurred to Felicity that they could benefit from some male guidance. Perhaps she could convince—

Goodness, what was she *thinking*? She'd already pushed Calder well past his limits.

Mrs. Armstrong exhaled, and another woman came forward. She looked quite angry, her dark eyes fixed on Freddie. "I told you if you committed any other infractions, you would miss the St. Stephen's Day party."

Freddie blanched, then hung his head.

"Apologize to Alice," a woman, likely his mother, said, arriving at his side.

"I'm sorry," he mumbled, his gaze still pinned to the floor.

His mother tapped her foot. "Look at her when you say so."

Freddie lifted his head and regarded the defiant Alice. "I'm sorry I took your biscuits. I won't ever do it again."

"Good. You know what will happen if you do," she warned.

Another woman, this one fair-haired and almost certainly Alice's mother, came from behind Mrs. Armstrong. "Now, Alice, vengeance is not ladylike."

Alice sent Calder a smirk then nodded at the woman. "Yes, Mama."

"I think it's time everyone returned to their rooms for quiet time," Mrs. Armstrong said.

The children broke apart, many of them talking and laughing as they departed. Alice went to Calder and hugged him.

Felicity stared in shock as he hugged her in return and whispered something in her ear. She grinned and nodded, then skipped back to her mother, who looked at Calder in bemusement.

A glance toward Mrs. Armstrong revealed she was staring at him in the same fashion. It seemed every adult in the room was as baffled by Calder's behavior as Felicity was. And why wouldn't they be? Until…today, apparently, he had not been a supporter of Hartwell House. To see that he'd somehow befriended one of the residents and had perhaps played a role in a revenge scheme was utterly amazing.

Felicity might not have believed it if she hadn't seen it.

Except she would have. She knew the real Calder was in there, the one she loved. And yes, she still loved him after all this time. This was simply the proof of what she'd already known to be true. She was particularly glad that others could see it too.

When the room was empty save for Calder, Felicity, and Mrs. Armstrong, the latter frowned before addressing Calder. "Your Grace, I am pleased to see you here. However, I must ask that you not encourage disruptions among the children."

"I doubt he was doing that," Felicity said, feeling the need to come to his defense. She moved to his side. "I've been telling him about all the things you need, and I believe he stopped by to see for himself."

"Yes," Calder said. "I would be pleased if you would accept my support to repair Hartwell House."

Mrs. Armstrong's jaw dropped, but she quickly clamped it shut. Nodding, she seemed at a total loss for words.

Felicity jumped in to fill the silence. "Could you also provide a list of furnishings you need? I know you are short beds, and as it happens, we could have a few delivered tomorrow, perhaps."

"On Christmas Eve?" Mrs. Armstrong asked.

Right, maybe not on Christmas Eve. Or Christmas Day. Or St. Stephen's Day. Goodness, this was a busy time.

"I can think of no better time to do so," Calder said. "There are four beds which I will have delivered tomorrow and set up wherever you need them."

Mrs. Armstrong blinked at him. "I— Thank you, Your Grace. I am overcome by your generosity."

"I apologize it has taken me so long to determine how I might continue the support my father offered."

Felicity heard the faint note of distaste when he said "my father," but doubted Mrs. Armstrong would have heard it. It took everything Felicity had not to take his hand and give him a reassuring squeeze.

"I am exceedingly grateful, Your Grace. May I offer you refreshment? Or a tour?"

"I must be on my way, but if you could provide a list of things you require, I will see about fulfilling it. I would also like an itemization of the repairs you are aware of and will provide it to the architectural firm I hire in London next month."

"You're going to hire a firm?" Mrs. Armstrong looked as if she needed to sit down.

"Of course. I am not an expert on such matters."

That would be very expensive. Clearly, money had never been the issue when it came to Calder's miserliness. Felicity's heart ached to hear it, but she knew he was making changes for the better, that he was finding his way back.

Mrs. Armstrong shook her head. "Thank you. Lord Darlington will be so thrilled. I imagine he already knows, since he's your brother-in-law." She smiled. "And now I'm just blathering."

"Mrs. Armstrong?"

The call came from the kitchen, prompting Mrs.

Armstrong to look in that direction. "If you'll excuse me." She gave Calder a final broad grin. "Thank you so much."

When she was gone, Felicity turned to him. "I want to say I'm surprised, but this is precisely what the Calder I know would do. I'm so glad you found him."

His features darkened for a moment. "I had to get you to stop bothering me."

"Oh, is that it?" Felicity put a hand on her hip. "Perhaps you'd like to explain why Alice hugged you? That is the part that has me surprised. No, it has me incredulous."

He waved his hand. "I provided her with a little direction, nothing more."

"Regarding how to exact revenge on Freddie?"

Calder exhaled with exasperation, his gaze at last meeting Felicity's. "He kept stealing her biscuits and pulling her hair."

Felicity smothered a grin. "And how were you even aware of his shenanigans?"

"I came yesterday to see things for myself. Because someone"—he glowered at her—"kept pestering me. I met Alice, and she required my assistance."

"How did you do it?" Felicity edged closer to him, looking up at him with rapt interest.

"My cook prepared biscuits that were intended to be stolen. They were, ah, infested with some sort of vermin."

That explained Freddie's screaming and spitting while hopping around. "I want to feel bad for him," Felicity said, smiling in spite of herself, "but I suppose no harm was done."

"None at all, and it was an important lesson—mostly the humiliation in front of his peers. He won't bother Alice again."

Felicity had a horrid thought. Had Calder's father done this to him? "Please tell me you don't know this from experience."

"No. I would have preferred humiliation in front of my peers to what was—" He clenched his jaw. "Never mind."

She took his hand then and gave him the squeeze she'd been longing to give. "I'm so sorry, Calder. All that is behind you now."

His eyes were sad, desperate almost, and her heart bled. "I want it to be, but sometimes I just don't know." He pulled his hand away. "I need to go."

She wanted him to stay, but to what end? So she could hold him and soothe him? This was neither the place nor the time. "Are the beds you're delivering from my father's house?"

Calder nodded. "Unless you mind?"

She shook her head. "Not at all. I suggested it, after all. I'm delighted you're giving them to Hartwell House. You've a good heart, despite your best efforts to the contrary." She said this with dry humor, but he didn't smile. Those were still few and far between where he was concerned. Perhaps Felicity would ask Alice for her secret in eliciting smiles, laughter, and hugs from the Duke of Hartwell.

"Felicity, you would do well to remember that I don't try to have a black heart—that's simply the way it is. The sooner you realize that, the better off you will be. And maybe then you'll stop bothering me."

He strode from the room, leaving her to stare after him in sad confusion. She'd been certain he was making progress.

Perhaps he was referring to them. Just because he was hosting St. Stephen's Day and supporting Hartwell House didn't mean he was ready to open himself up to personal relationships—to love. To heartache.

Because Felicity knew that with love came heartache. For her, she would gladly risk the latter to have the former. She just wasn't sure Calder would ever be able to share that sentiment.

CHAPTER 8

a light dusting of snow covered the ground on Christmas Eve morning when Calder set out with his sisters and brothers-in-law to find the Yule log. They were all on horseback, while a groom drove a wagon that would convey the tree back to the house. Isis ran alongside Calder.

The sensation of being with his sisters and their husbands was odd, probably because it was the first time. He'd only been back at Hartwell since last spring, and it had been years before that. He felt as though he barely knew them.

"This is a nice copse of trees," Poppy said. "Let's look here."

Her husband quickly dismounted and hurried to help her. He lifted her from the horse very carefully and set her gently on the ground.

Calder didn't particularly care about the Yule log. Before he'd agreed to allow his sisters to come, he hadn't even planned on finding one. The only reason he'd joined them today was to get out with Isis, who loved the snow. He climbed down from his horse, and Isis ran to his side.

"Did we get a Yule log from this copse once?" Bianca asked.

"You've a good memory," Poppy said. "You couldn't have been more than five or so."

That would have made Calder thirteen. He'd been home from Eton, though he would have preferred to remain at school.

They walked as a group toward the trees, surveying them as they went. Everyone but Calder. They could find an old, rotting log on the ground, and that would be fine with him.

"Thank you for inviting us to Hartwell," Buckleigh said. "I'm glad to put the past behind us. Hopefully you are too."

"Ash," Bianca hissed before nudging her husband in the ribs. "Not now."

"Sorry," Buckleigh murmured.

"Now is fine," Calder said, exhaling. "I plan to give Bianca her settlement."

Poppy stepped toward him and touched his arm, smiling. "Thank you."

If he'd been uncomfortable in the face of Mrs. Armstrong's gratitude, this was ten times worse. He felt as if he wanted to crawl out of his skin. He pointed at a tree. "How about that one?"

"Too skinny," Bianca said.

She was right, but then Calder hadn't really looked at it. He'd just been trying to divert the conversation.

Bianca moved toward the one beside it. "This one. It's perfect."

"It is," Poppy agreed. They both looked to Calder, who shrugged. "Gabriel?" Poppy asked.

"Whatever my love desires." Darlington gazed at her with warmth and love, and though Calder tried to remain immune, his insides twisted with envy.

"I'll fetch the axe," Buckleigh said, going back to the wagon.

Bianca walked over to Calder. "This is really starting to feel like Christmas. I'm so glad we're all here together." Her bright blue eyes sparkled in the morning sunlight filtering through the clouds.

Poppy stepped beside her and linked her arm through Bianca's. "Yes, and just think, next year, there will be little footprints in the snow."

Bianca laughed. "Unless your child learns to walk at an alarmingly young age, I should think not."

Poppy giggled, and now Calder understood why Darlington had handled her with such care.

Again, he felt a pang of envy. "Congratulations."

"Thank you," Poppy said. "I know you aren't aware, and why should you be, but I'd believed I couldn't have children. Gabriel and I have been married nearly three years and... Well, we are very happy."

A warm sensation sprouted in Calder's chest, then spread outward. Happiness—not for him, but for his sister, who was the kindest soul he'd ever known. If anyone deserved the joy of a child, it was her. "I'm glad for you," he said quietly.

Poppy turned her head and wiped a finger over her eye. "I wish Papa was here to share in our happiness."

And just like that, the faint flame inside Calder sputtered and died. "I don't." The words fell from his mouth unbidden, and he immediately wished he could take them back.

Of course, Bianca asked, "Why didn't you like him? He was so distraught that you never came to visit, especially at the end."

Calder couldn't tell them. They ought to go their entire lives without knowing how cruel he'd been.

He focused on Buckleigh, who'd returned with the axe. He and Darlington were discussing how to take down the tree. The footman stood nearby, ready to offer assistance. Calder would help too. He'd rip the damn thing from the ground in order to avoid this conversation with his sisters.

But before he could walk away, Bianca said, "Do you remember the Yule log that nearly set the house on fire?"

Poppy's eyes widened. "Yes! That was almost a disaster." She looked over at Calder. "Were you there that year?"

Calder had missed a few Christmases due to accepting invitations from friends at school. He didn't recall the fire. "I don't think so."

"My favorite part of finding the Yule log was Papa singing," Bianca said, smiling. "He had such a nice voice— which you inherited," she said to Poppy. "I could carry that tree better than I could a tune."

They both laughed, and suddenly, Calder couldn't stand listening to their fond memories of "Papa" a moment longer. Something inside him splintered and blew apart, like artillery that had jammed instead of firing cleanly as it was intended to. Calder was supposed to suffer his father in silence. But then that was what the man had wanted, wasn't it? Shouldn't Calder want to do the opposite, as he'd done with everything else?

He stared at them. "Here's a memory that neither of you likely remember. In fact, I believe Bianca was just a baby. Yes, that's right, because the year after Mama died was the very worst. And Poppy, you too would have been at home with the nurse."

Both his sisters looked at him, their gazes a combination of wariness and keen interest.

"We went on the Yule log hunt as always, except it wasn't the same without Mama. She's the one who sang, and she brought biscuits and a jug of wassail. I'd finally been allowed to drink it the last year she came with us." He couldn't help but look at Bianca, who'd never known the beautiful, vibrant woman who'd been their mother. When he thought of all the pain he'd endured, he knew hers was probably far greater. And yet, he wondered if it was better to have not known her at all than to miss what you could never have again. He'd thought the same thing about Felicity—that he would have been better off if he'd never known her.

"I don't really remember her," Poppy said softly. "I recall her smell—honeysuckle. But everything else, I knew from you." She looked at Calder. "I don't think I ever thanked you for keeping her memory alive for me."

Calder was nearly undone. Because he hadn't done it for her. He'd done it for himself. He was as selfish as one could be, just as his father had said.

"Calder, you were going to tell us about a Yule log hunt," Bianca prompted.

He would have abandoned it after what Poppy had said. But Bianca would press... And the story wanted to be told after all this time. "I chose a tree, but he said it wasn't right. It was too... I don't even remember." Calder stared past them into the distance, that day as clear in his mind as the landscape before him. "I really wanted that tree. It reminded me of the one Mama had chosen the year before. I just knew it was the one she would have wanted. But he wouldn't allow it, and because I argued, he left me there."

"Where?" Poppy whispered, her eyes wide with alarm.

Calder shrugged. "Far from the house. It took me hours to find my way home. And it had started snowing. I was near freezing, and when I got there, all he could do was tell me not to drip on the carpet."

"Oh my God," Bianca breathed, moving close to his side while Poppy came up on the other.

"Did he do other things like that?" Poppy asked, her voice barely more than a croak.

"All the time." Calder couldn't look at them. "He treated

me very differently than he treated you. And he was always careful to never to let you see." Now he glanced down at Bianca, who stared at him, her eyes sad. "I expected you—especially—to say it couldn't be true."

"I want to, if only because I don't want to think of him treating you like that, but I can see that he did."

She did? Yes, he heard the anguish in her voice.

"Oh, Calder, I wish you'd told us." Poppy slipped her arm around his back and laid her head on his arm. It was an attempt at a hug, but he was frozen, locked in the past.

"I didn't want you to know."

"Your pride is ridiculous," Bianca said gently, clasping his hand.

He pulled away from both of them. "It wasn't my pride! It was *him*. You loved him. He loved you both. He gave you the best of himself. I lost the only parent who cared for me, and when he lost her, I bore the brunt of his emotions. Nothing I did was ever good enough. He couldn't even let me have the woman I loved." Maybe now they would understand why he chose not to feel. Nothing good came of it.

Poppy moved first, taking a step toward him. "I'm so sorry."

Everything blurred. He didn't want their pity. He didn't want anything.

Turning, he stalked from the copse. Isis followed him, looking up in curiosity as he mounted his horse. "Stay," Calder said, knowing the others would take her back to the house with them. Right now, he wasn't sure where he was going. Or, frankly, if he was coming back.

⁓

*T*hankfully, the snow hadn't been too thick upon the ground, or Felicity would not have been able to travel to her old family cottage. She hadn't returned to see it in its entirety, and she wanted to do so before the beds were taken away today.

She arrived early, just as footmen and grooms from Hartwood arrived. She helped direct them, and wondered why Calder wasn't there. They'd told her that he was on a Yule log hunt with his family.

Now, as they loaded up the last of the beds, she was still smiling. It seemed Calder had truly come a long way. Maybe he was finally ready to let the past go and look to a brighter future.

One of the footmen came to speak with her in the entry hall. "We're ready to go to Hartwell House. Thank you for your assistance, Mrs. Garland."

"It was my pleasure. Happy Christmas to you."

"And to you. Will we see you on St. Stephen's Day?"

"I expect so. I wouldn't miss it."

He inclined his head with a smile, then left. Gathering her shawl around her shoulders, Felicity closed the door behind him before going upstairs to douse the small fire she'd built in the sitting room. While the footmen and grooms had moved furniture, she'd taken her ease in a chair that she hoped Calder would allow her to take home. She'd ask him later, maybe on St. Stephen's Day, since that was likely the next time she'd see him.

A creak in the floorboard drew her to turn from the doorway to the sitting room. Calder stood at the top of the stairs.

He wore no hat or gloves, and he was in the process of removing his greatcoat, which he dropped to the floor. He ran his hand through his dark hair, standing the thick strands on end. His gray eyes, usually so cold and aloof, were ablaze, like liquid silver. Something was very wrong.

She went to him and took his hands in hers. He wasn't as cold as she'd expected him to be, but he was still chilled. "You need a fire. There's one burning in the hearth in the sitting room."

He shook his head. "I just need you."

Oh. A current of desire rushed through her. The sensation was like nothing she'd ever experienced, and yet she recognized it immediately.

She slid her hands up his front and curled them around the lapels of his coat. Her shawl fell to the floor behind her. "Tell me how."

"Any way you'll let me."

She didn't know what had happened on their Yule log hunt to send him here in a desperate frenzy, and she wasn't sure it mattered. She was just glad she'd been here to meet him. At last, something had worked in their favor, bringing them together instead of pushing them apart.

"I'm here. I'm yours."

He clasped his arms around her and kissed her, his mouth crashing into hers. This wasn't the curious, eager kisses of their youth, nor was it the somewhat cautious kisses from the other day. This was fire and ice, the absolute extreme of kisses. Felicity felt she might wither and die if it didn't continue, if they weren't allowed to see this through to whatever end they both wanted.

Only, she didn't want an end. She wanted forever.

His lips and tongue moved with hers as if the last decade had never come between them, as if they'd been made for each other. She'd certainly thought that was true ten years ago. She fervently hoped it was true now.

His hands moved up her back and plucked at the pins in her hair, sending them cascading to the floor. Then his fingers were sifting through her curls, massaging her scalp and palming her head as he devoured her mouth.

She pulled away with a gasp, then took his hand and pulled him to the sitting room where she'd learned to stitch and write and so many other things. He allowed her to lead him to the fireplace, then he tugged her against him and kissed her once more, leaving no doubt as to what he intended. Good, because if he tried to walk away from her now, she might bring down the house around them to make him stay.

He loosened the ties at the back of her dress, and in response, she tugged his cravat until the knot came undone. They spent the next several minutes alternately kissing and removing their clothing until she stood before him in her stays and chemise and he in his shirt and breeches.

"It's cold," she said, wondering if that was why he hesitated to finish undressing.

"I'm not cold. I don't think that's possible when I'm with you. I'm just...savoring this moment. I've waited so long to touch you like this, to see you... I've dreamed of it a thousand times."

His words broke her heart yet also somehow repaired the cracks and holes that she'd learned to live with. She pulled at the laces on her stays—glad that these were in the front—her gaze locked with his. "You don't have to wait anymore. And this isn't a dream."

Loose, the stays sagged around her rib cage. She pushed them over her hips and down her legs until they hit the floor. Then she gently kicked them to the side.

Reaching for the hem of her chemise, she clasped the cotton firmly before tugging it over her head. She stood before him completely bare, something she'd never done with her husband. Their intimacy had always happened in the darkness, and she'd always worn her night rail. Just standing here exposed to him was the most erotic thing she'd ever done.

If it were anyone else, she might have been shy, but this was Calder. Her heart. Her soul. And he looked at her as if she were a goddess—*his* goddess. She'd never seen anything more alluring than the possession and hunger heating his gaze.

"You're even more beautiful than I imagined," he whispered, moving closer to her. He stroked the side of her face, his fingers gliding over her flesh, down her throat, gently caressing her collarbone. Then lower still until his hand moved over her breast. The contact of his skin against hers coaxed a moan from her throat. She felt utterly brazen as she pushed herself toward him, seeking more of his touch.

He seemed to know what she wanted, for he cupped her, softly at first, and then more firmly, his fingers closing over her nipple and giving it a gentle tug. He did the same with her other breast, both of his hands moving over her, arousing her, driving a sweet and desperate desire straight to her sex.

He pulled on her nipples in concert, and she gasped. Then he dipped his head and took one of them in his mouth, sucking on her. The sensation made her knees buckle as another wave of hunger shot through her.

He wrapped his arm around her and led her to the settee, which was only a foot away and situated in front of the fire. Guiding her down, he laid her back, then knelt on the floor beside her.

She looked at him in question, wondering why he was on the floor and not climbing on top of her. "What are you doing?"

"Worshipping you," he said simply before dropping his head to her breast once more. He cupped her, holding her flesh captive to his questing lips and tongue. And teeth—he nipped at her and she bucked up in surprise and pleasure.

As his hand trailed down her abdomen, she was aware of a throbbing need between her legs. She'd felt a similar sensation before, but nothing like this ache that begged to be satisfied. She squirmed, eager for something that she knew had always been just beyond her reach.

She cried out as his fingers skimmed across her sex.

"Part your legs, Felicity," he urged softly.

She followed his command, ready for whatever he would do and hoping this time would be different. It had to be—this was Calder. He stroked a spot at the top of her sex, and her body twitched with pleasure.

She closed her eyes and lost herself in his touch. "Oh yes. Oh yes. Oh yes." She couldn't seem to stop herself from saying that over and over.

He slipped one of his fingers into her and thrust deep, filling her. She whimpered and moved her hips, wanting more. He gave it to her, sliding in and out while his thumb continued to work that glorious spot.

His other hand cupped the back of her neck and turned her head to face him. "Open your eyes, love," he whispered. "I want you to look at me when I bring you to orgasm."

She did as he bade, his hand supporting her head as she looked into his silvery eyes. When he came into her next, there was more—two fingers, perhaps—and she cried out. Her eyes tried to close, but his fingers dug into her neck. "Look at me, Felicity."

He drove into her again and again, filling her, bringing her to a dizzying height. "God, you're beautiful. I can't—" He broke eye contact and moved his head down her body. Then his mouth was on her there, licking and sucking at her flesh as his fingers continued their wild, delicious penetration.

She couldn't keep her eyes open as she was overcome by a pleasure so great that it seemed as if she were flung into a dark night sky studded with brilliant stars. She floated there in absolute ecstasy. Until she fell. A glorious, spectacular fall that made her body shudder and her heart sing.

When she at last opened her eyes, she saw Calder sitting back on his feet, his breathing loud and fast, his eyes dilated as he gazed at her body. "I want to see you," she said, turning and sliding from the settee.

She knelt before him and found the hem of his shirt. He said nothing, just stared at her, his face tense, his body taut. She saw just how taut as she pulled the garment over his head. The muscles of his shoulders and chest were clearly defined, showing him to be an athletic man. She caressed his collarbones and drew her hands down his front, skimming her palms over his warm flesh so she could memorize every dip and plane.

As her hands moved lower, he sucked in a breath, holding it. "Is something wrong?" she asked softly, her hands pausing.

"No. Don't stop."

She trailed her fingers down to the waistband of his breeches. "How am I to undress you with you sitting like that?"

In a flash, he stood and divested himself of his remaining garments. As he knelt back down, she stared at his sex. She'd never looked at her husband's—never mind, she didn't want to think of anything but Calder.

Curious, she reached for him, then hesitated. "May I?" she asked shyly.

"Please." He took her hand and curled it around his shaft. "My cock would like nothing better than for you to touch it."

Cock. That word was both crude and incredibly arousing. She decided she would like nothing better than to touch it. "Show me," she said.

He kept his hand on hers and moved hers down to the base. "Stroke me. Not too hard. Not too soft." He looked at her intently, his hand guiding hers.

She did as he described, clasping his flesh with a firm grip and gliding her palm up and down. She found moisture at the tip, and, curious, she ran her thumb over it.

He groaned. "Felicity, get on the settee."

She started to rise, and he helped her, all but lifting her and laying her on her back. "I'm sorry there aren't any beds," she said, smiling.

"I wouldn't even need a settee." He covered her with his body and kissed her deeply, his tongue driving deep into her mouth as his hand found her sex once more.

She opened her legs, and he settled between them—as best as the settee would allow them—his cock pushing at her entrance. Desire pulsed from her sex and outward. She wanted that...orgasm again. Could she have it again? It certainly felt as if she could.

He slid into her, kissing her neck, as she stretched to accommodate him, her body welcoming him as if he'd come home at last. And she supposed he had.

He moved slowly, filling her, then retreating, then gradually filling her again. It felt divine and yet it was nowhere near enough. She clasped his backside, urging him to move faster. "Please, Calder."

Then he let go. His mouth claimed hers briefly as he drove into her. She groaned, digging her fingers into his flesh, desperate for the rapture spiraling through her. She moved with him, their bodies finding a rhythm that pushed her to the edge once more. She looked out over the inky sky with this carpet of stars and dove headfirst into sweet oblivion. Her body crashed and exploded beneath his, then she felt him stiffen. He called out her name, then shouted over and over as he thrust deep inside her.

A lethargy so complete and so wondrous fell over her. He turned with her, holding her close so she was pinned between him and the back of the settee. Smiling, she nestled against him, happier than she could ever remember being.

Gradually, their breathing evened, and his became steady and deep. She opened her eyes the barest amount and surmised that he'd dozed off. Content, she kissed his jaw and whispered, "I love you."

Then she joined him in slumber.

hy was it so bloody cold?

His skin felt like ice, as if he'd never be warm again. Mist swirled around him, prompting him to wonder how it was already night and how he'd gotten outside.

The mist faded. He wasn't outside. Before him was a cozy sitting room filled with people he didn't recognize. No, that wasn't quite true. The woman standing near the hearth was utterly familiar—her green eyes alight with joy as she took the hand of the man who came to join her.

His hair was gray and hers was white. The others were younger, and one woman was clearly their daughter. A child clutched at her skirt, and the woman swept her into her arms then carried her to the green-eyed woman—Felicity.

She smiled at the girl. "Happy Christmas, my sweet."

"Grandmama!" The child reached for her, and Felicity welcomed her into her arms. "Grandpapa!" She grinned at the man beside Felicity.

He chuckled softly, his eyes so full of love and pride, it tore at Calder's chest. What sorcery was this? Felicity's hair was blonde.

Her husband was dead. She wasn't a mother, let alone a grandmother.

And what was the pine tree, candles flickering on its limbs, standing in the corner, some sort of Yule log abomination? "That's going to catch the house on fire!" Calder called out.

No one seemed to hear him. He moved forward and waved his hand in front of Felicity's face. Her attention didn't waver from her granddaughter.

Granddaughter… They all looked so happy. And where was he? Why wasn't he there?

The mist returned, as did the icy cold. When the air next cleared, he remained outside. The sky above was gray, and around him, headstones rose from the dormant grass.

The drone of a voice carried on the wind. Calder walked between the stones, his heart pounding. A small gathering stood over a hole in the ground. The vicar finished speaking, then looked to those standing around the perimeter. Just four people—his sisters and their husbands.

Like Felicity, they looked older. Their hair was gray, and lines around their eyes showed their age.

He moved to the hole and looked down at the simple wood coffin. "Who died?" he asked.

As with Felicity and her family, none of them reacted to his presence. They neither saw nor heard him.

"I hope he's at peace now," Poppy said, looking sadly down into the hole. She turned her head toward Bianca. "I can't believe there's no heir anywhere. After all these generations, there will be no Staffords at Hartwood. What will even become of Hartwood?" Poppy looked at her husband.

The marquess shrugged. "The queen will decide."

Queen? There was a queen? What bloody year was this?

"It's such a mess anyway," Bianca said, frowning. "I can't believe how badly Calder let it decline before he died."

It was him *in the hole. Calder began to shake. He hadn't thought he could feel colder, but he did.*

"It's not as if he kept a reasonable number of retainers," Bianca's husband said. "Those he did have never stayed long, and can you blame them?"

Poppy shook her head. "No, he was absolutely horrid."

"Terrifying, actually." Bianca shuddered. "Last time I saw him —over a year ago—what was left of his gray hair reached to the middle of his back. He could barely focus his eyes, and his hands were like claws."

"Well, he always was a beast," Darlington murmured. "Sorry," he added, placing his hand on Poppy's back and offering her a sympathetic smile.

"He had only himself to blame, that's true," Poppy said with a sigh.

"He died alone just as he chose to live his life." Bianca shook her head with pity.

Poppy looked toward the young vicar. "Please say an extra prayer for our brother tonight."

"I will, my lady."

After a final look into the hole, Bianca turned away. Poppy's mouth pitched down before she pivoted and put her arm through her sister's. They walked from the grave together, their husbands trailing behind.

The vicar gestured toward the gravediggers. The two men came forward with their shovels and began to fill in the hole.

As the dirt hit the wood, the outside world around Calder disappeared. Now there was nothing but blackness and a stifling smell of cut wood and dank. A steady tap-tap sounded above him. It was like rain, but not. He reached out, and his hands struck wood right in front of him.

He was in the coffin.

He pounded on the wood, screaming, his hands becoming

battered and bruised. He couldn't be dead. Not now, not after what he'd just found…

The wood beneath him gave way, and he inexplicably fell. Into an abyss…

"Calder, wake up!"

He pushed forward again, expecting to find a barrier. There was nothing. He opened his eyes in panic to see where he'd fallen.

"Calder!"

A voice he knew. Her voice. He blinked and saw Felicity's youthful, unlined face and her golden-blonde hair. Lifting his head, he looked around in confusion, then recognized the sitting room in her family's cottage.

She was naked, as was he. Then he remembered. They'd been on the settee. "Did I fall asleep?" he asked.

"Yes, we dozed for a while. You started screaming, and then you fell to the floor."

He'd fallen to the *floor*.

He dropped his head back onto the rug and stared up at the ceiling as he gulped deep breaths to calm his racing pulse. It had been a dream. He'd been dead and his family hadn't seemed to care, though he supposed it was enough that they'd come to his grave. Even if they hadn't shed a tear? They'd sounded relieved. And disappointed—he'd let them and the dukedom down.

Then there was Felicity. Happy with her large family, including her husband, who obviously adored her. Calder squeezed his eyes closed to banish the image from his mind, but feared it was emblazoned in his memory forever.

"We should get dressed," Felicity said.

He opened his eyes to see her rising. She went about collecting their clothing and set the garments on the settee. Calder dressed quickly, which Felicity couldn't possibly do.

He itched to leave, to flee, but he forced himself to stay, to help her.

After he had her dress laced, he looked toward the door. "I need to go."

"Yes, I must get home to my mother." She sat down on the settee to don her boots. "Where do you need to be?"

Anywhere but here. He walked toward the door.

"Calder, did you hear me?"

He paused at the threshold. "Felicity, you must forget about me. You deserve a long and happy life." The one he'd seen for her. The one he obviously couldn't give her.

She stood, her brow furrowing with deep creases as she frowned. "I could never forget about you. Not if a thousand years passed."

Her words flayed him. There was nothing he could do to change who he was, who he was destined to be. That dream had been the future, and their paths separated most severely. It was as it should be.

He gave her his most frigid stare. "I am not the man you think I am."

"You're the man I love," she said simply, walking toward him.

Her declaration nearly drove him to his knees. Love was not an emotion he knew or understood outside of the context of loss. He'd loved his mother. He'd loved Felicity. He'd tried to love his sisters but, because of his father, had never felt they were his to love.

"I shouldn't be, Felicity, and it's time you understood that."

She rushed forward and clasped his hand. "I love the man whose best friend is a dog, who helps a little girl in her time of need, who would hire an expensive architecture firm to repair an old, drafty manor house so it can become a school for impoverished children."

Aside from Isis, none of that was really him. It was *her* influence. He pulled his hand from hers and drew himself up with forced contempt. "Ten years ago, I lost the only thing that mattered to me, then I spent the next few years losing everything else. When I couldn't sink any lower, my father kicked me—he took away his support and told me to sort myself out. I was broke and alone. I took the only thing of value I had left—my mother's jewels—and I sold them. From that, I have built everything that I am today. My father wasn't good with money. If not for me, there actually wouldn't be funds to support Hartwell House at all. There would barely be enough to pay Bianca's settlement." He'd never said those things to anyone, and now they flew from his mouth like caged birds free for the first time.

She gaped at him, her jaw open and her eyes round. "Calder, those days are behind you now. Your father isn't here. He doesn't matter."

"He will always matter! We are the Dukes of Hartwell! Beholden to our legacy of stern leadership and rigid duty." He'd never felt more encumbered. The boards of the coffin closed in around him.

Unable to bear the light of her presence another moment, Calder turned and stalked from the sitting room, pausing only to retrieve his greatcoat from the top of the stairs.

Outside, he paused, wondering how Felicity had gotten there and how she would return home. Though it wasn't yet midafternoon, it was still bitterly cold, particularly with the wind. Then he saw the stable with its telltale curl of smoke coming from the chimney and her vehicle outside. The coachman and horse had to be inside, which meant Calder didn't have to worry about her.

Not that he wouldn't.

He would care about her, want her, *love* her for the rest of his days. Until he was cold in the ground in that unforgiving wooden box.

~

*F*elicity rushed downstairs and watched Calder hesitate outside. Had he changed his mind?

She ran to the door just as he strode to his horse. He mounted, and she called out his name. Either he didn't hear her, or he was pretending not to, for he raced away.

Distraught, she turned and went back into the house. She trudged back upstairs to douse the fire in the sitting room, which she'd intended to do hours ago. Oh dear, what must the coachman think? She'd quite lost track of…everything the moment Calder had taken her into his arms.

Then they'd slept, their bodies entwined. She wasn't sure she'd ever known such joy, such peace. When he'd awakened her screaming, the sound had driven terror deep into her heart.

His eyes had been wild, his heart beating frantically. She suspected he'd had a nightmare—what else could explain his behavior when she'd roused him from sleep?

And what had he dreamed that had scared him so terribly? That had driven him not just from the house, but from her, seemingly forever? He'd told her to forget about him. As she'd responded, she wouldn't do that. She *couldn't*.

She wasn't going to let him get away.

After taking care of the fire, she went to gather her cloak, hat, and gloves. Once she was bundled up, she went to the stable and notified the coachman she was ready to depart.

"I'll just be a few minutes, ma'am," he said.

"We aren't going home. We're going to Hartwood."

He inclined his head. "Aye, Mrs. Garland."

When they arrived at Hartwood, Felicity had a bad feeling

he wasn't there. She rapped on the door as nervous energy coursed through her.

The butler, Truro, answered, his eyes warming when he saw her. "What a pleasure to see you again, Mrs. Garland. Happy Christmas."

"Happy Christmas to you too. I'm here to see His Grace."

A small pucker gathered between Truro's sherry-colored eyes. "I'm afraid he isn't at home. Would you care to see Lady Darlington or Lady Buckleigh?"

"Yes, please," Felicity answered with far too much zeal.

Truro showed her to the drawing room, then took her cloak, hat, and gloves. She went to the fireplace to warm herself, but she was so anxious, she ended up pacing in front of the hearth.

"Felicity?" Bianca came into the drawing room with Poppy following behind her.

Felicity stopped and faced them. "I'm sorry to intrude on Christmas Eve, but I'm concerned about Calder."

"So are we," Bianca said, frowning.

That only increased Felicity's alarm. "What happened?"

"We were on the Yule log hunt," Poppy said, her features creased with worry. "He shared some"—she glanced at her sister—"things."

Felicity had been shocked he'd gone with them, but she was even more surprised that he'd shared anything with them. "What things?" She couldn't help but wonder if they were related to his nightmare. Or the state in which he'd arrived at the house. He'd been disoriented, adrift, as if he were looking for something—or someone—to hang on to.

"About our father," Poppy said. She moved closer to Bianca and took her hand. "He was quite awful to Calder. We never knew."

Felicity could understand how they felt. When she'd learned her father had taken money from Calder's father, she'd wondered if she'd ever known him at all. "He paid my father to take us and leave Hartwell so that Calder and I wouldn't wed. He told Calder I'd greedily taken the money and gladly avoided marriage to him. Then he sent me a forged letter from Calder telling me we would never suit, that I wasn't worthy of becoming his duchess."

Both sisters' eyes widened, and their clasped hands fell apart. Poppy lifted her hand to her mouth, while Bianca clenched her jaw.

"That's why you left," Bianca said with enough disdain to fill a moat. "If not for our father, you and Calder would have been married these past ten years."

"Oh, Felicity, that's just—" Poppy's voice caught. She blinked several times before she could continue. "I'm so sorry."

"Thank you, but it's in the past, and we can't change what happened. All we can do is help Calder be the man he wants to be, the man he is deep down, the man I fell in love with." She looked at them both intently. "The man I still love."

Bianca grinned. "I'm so glad to hear that. Also, I knew it." She slid Poppy a triumphant glance.

Poppy looked as though she wanted to hug Felicity, but then her smile faded. "Why are you concerned about him?"

"He was with me—after your Yule log hunt, I would surmise."

"He left rather abruptly," Bianca said. "He seemed over-whelmed."

"And not in a good way." Poppy's tone was dark. "How was he with you?"

"Upset, but then…better." She tried to find a word that would accurately describe his mood without giving away too much. They didn't need to know the specifics. "When he left, he was upset again—more so than when he'd arrived. He told me to forget about him." It hurt to remember him saying it, but it was even more painful to repeat the words aloud to his sisters.

"Clearly, that's not going to happen," Bianca said briskly. "Where do we think he went?"

Felicity shook her head. "I can't begin to imagine." She would have thought the very house where they'd been, since she'd found him there the other day. Beyond that, she had no inkling where he might go. She considered the meadow where they'd had their picnic—yes, she'd look there.

"What about Papa's folly?" Poppy asked, looking to Bianca. Then she flinched. "I can't help feeling betrayed every time I think of him now," she said with soft anguish.

Bianca nodded, her mouth tight. "When I consider all the time I nursed him when he was ill, all the things he said in disappointment about Calder, not one word of praise or love. I never stopped to ask why. I just accepted that Calder was cold and unfeeling. It didn't occur to me to determine *why* he was that way." Bianca's voice broke. She pressed a finger to the corner of her eye. A tear fell anyway, and she wiped it away.

"None of us did, at least not enough to actually help him." Poppy's tone weighed heavy with regret. "We are as much to blame as our father."

"So is Calder," Felicity said. "He chooses to be this way because it's easy and familiar. Even now he's trying to please the man he could never satisfy. He says he does the things he does to make his father angry—and at some level, I'm sure he does. However, he's still waiting for the approval that will never come."

"That all makes such sense." Poppy wrapped her arms around herself. "What can we do?"

Felicity looked from one sister to the other. "We have to find him."

"You don't think he'll come back of his own accord?" Bianca asked.

"I don't know. He was extremely troubled." Felicity glanced out the window and saw the flutter of snowflakes drifting every now and again. "Unfortunately, I must return home to see to my mother." Agatha was with her now, but it was Christmas Eve, and she needed to get home to her family.

"You should fetch her and come back," Poppy said. "Gabriel will go with you and help you with whatever you need."

"Are you sure it won't be an inconvenience if we come?" Felicity wasn't sure how she was going to describe all this to her mother. She hadn't discussed Calder with her at all. A part of Felicity was still hurt because of the role her mother had played in keeping the truth from Felicity the past decade.

Bianca waved her hand. "Of course it's not an inconvenience. This is where you belong, especially on Christmas. You're family." She smiled. "Or you will be as soon as you and Calder wed."

Felicity wasn't sure that would come to pass, not after what he'd said. But after everything else that had transpired since she'd returned, she'd never wanted anything more. "I'll be back as soon as I can."

"We'll start the search immediately." Bianca moved toward her and took her hand. "We'll find him."

Poppy came and clasped Felicity's other hand. "We aren't going to lose him now, not when we've finally found him. He needs us, and we won't let him down."

Yes, he needed them, and Felicity would move heaven and earth to get to him.

CHAPTER 10

*F*elicity returned to Hartwood with her mother in a remarkably short amount of time. Retainers had already begun to look for Calder around the estate, and Ash and Bianca had gone to the folly that the former duke had built.

After settling her mother in with Poppy, whom Gabriel insisted remain at the house given her condition and the fact that it was now fully snowing, Felicity prepared to ride out with Gabriel. Isis whined from her spot in front of the hearth in the drawing room.

"Why isn't she out looking?" Felicity asked, thinking that if anyone would find him, it would be his beloved dog.

"I'm not sure, but she can come with us."

"She needs her coat." Felicity went in search of Truro, who helped her prepare Isis for their excursion.

As they walked toward the stable, Felicity shared her only idea as to his location. "I want to look in a meadow. It's northeast of here." The ride was probably a mile and a half, just past that edge of the estate's property.

"Lead the way," Gabriel said.

They rode swiftly, with Isis easily keeping pace, and thankfully, the snow let up until they'd nearly reached the meadow. The grass was white, and it was coldly beautiful—so very different from the day she'd spent here with Calder.

Bringing his horse to a stop next to Felicity, Gabriel looked about. "I don't see anyone."

"Look." Felicity pointed to Isis, who had paused with them and was now trotting toward a stand of trees. The trot became a run as she drew closer.

Felicity kicked her horse after the dog and heard Gabriel follow behind her. Calder's horse stood grazing nearby, on a patch of grass beneath the trees that hadn't been coated with snow.

Felicity searched for Isis and saw the greyhound's tail sticking from behind a tree. Sliding down from her horse, Felicity ran to the dog. Propped against the tree was Calder, his eyes closed, his lips a terrifying gray.

"Calder, wake up!" Felicity knelt beside him and drew off her glove to touch his face. His cheek was like ice. "Calder!"

Isis nudged him and then climbed onto his lap. She laid her head against his chest.

"She's trying to warm him up," Gabriel said. "We need to get him home."

Felicity turned her head to look up at the marquess. "How do we do that?"

"We'll get him onto my horse. I can ride back with him."

Stroking Isis's head, Felicity whispered, "We'll take care of him." She stood and faced Gabriel. "Let's move quickly."

He nodded, then went to fetch the horses. "Can you lead his horse?" he asked Felicity.

"Yes." She tried not to let fear paralyze her. Calder had never needed her more.

It took a great deal of effort, but they got him on Gabriel's horse, and Gabriel climbed on behind him. It was awkward, which made the return trip much slower than Felicity would have liked.

When they arrived at the house, Truro rushed outside to help Gabriel carry Calder inside. A groom came to care for the horses, and Felicity and Isis followed the men into the house.

Poppy stood inside the entry hall. "Where did you find him?"

"A meadow where we once had a picnic," Felicity said. "I'm afraid he's nearly frozen."

"Should we send for Dr. Fisk?" Poppy asked.

"I hate to trouble him on Christmas Eve. I'm sure we can handle things." Felicity sounded calmer than she felt. If Calder took ill, she wasn't sure what she would do. No, she wasn't sure what she would do if she lost him.

She hurried up the stairs and found her way to Calder's bedchamber, where Truro and Gabriel had deposited him on the bed. Calder's valet began undressing him under the watchful eyes of Isis, who sat beside her master. Her gaze held all the love and worry Felicity too possessed.

They got him tucked into the bed, and a pair of maids brought warming pans. A short time later, when Felicity felt his head, her worst fears were confirmed. He was no longer cold but burning hot with fever.

She exchanged a look with Isis. "We aren't going to lose him. I promise."

Isis ducked her head, laying it on Calder's arm. If Calder died, it wouldn't be because no one loved him.

She brushed his hair back from his forehead. "You have so much to fight for," she whispered. "Stay with us. *Please.*"

Then she prayed for a Christmas miracle.

～

*H*e was so cold. His finger and toes were ice. He huddled into himself, but there was simply no heat. Was this how he was going to meet his end? He'd expected to be much older, based on his vision of the future.

But maybe he was. Maybe he'd spent years in a trance, his life nothing but a dark void he couldn't remember. And maybe that was for the best.

Calder opened his eyes and gasped, his body jerking. He blinked, trying to bring the area around him into focus.

There was light and softness and…warmth. There was also movement against his side. That seemed to be the source of the warmth. He reached out and felt the familiar comforting silk of a dog's fur.

"Calder?"

He knew that voice. He blinked several more times until his vision finally became clear. Felicity stood beside his bed, her face splitting into the most relieved smile he'd ever seen.

"What are you doing here?" His voice sounded scratchy, and indeed, his throat felt as if it hadn't been used. Furthermore, his entire body ached. What had happened to him?

Isis nudged the hand he'd placed on her head. Calder looked over and stroked her several times, murmuring, "Good girl."

Felicity smoothed her hand over his forehead and exhaled before smiling even wider. "Your fever has broken."

He'd had a fever? "I was cold."

"I should think so. Isis found you in the meadow unconscious against a tree." Felicity glanced toward the dog in open admiration. "You were nearly frozen. You took a chill, obviously, and you've had a fever since."

He saw the purple streaks beneath her eyes, the rumpled state of her gown, and the wisps of hair that had escaped her chignon. It was clear she'd been nursing him. "Why are you here taking care of me?"

"Who else should do it? And don't say your valet or a maid or Truro. Of course I would be the one to care for you."

Of course. Only it didn't seem that obvious to him. After the way he'd behaved, she should have run far away—he'd told her to.

Felicity poured water into a glass. "Drink this for your parched throat."

He struggled to sit up, and the room tilted sideways. He closed his eyes briefly while she helped to get him situated against the headboard.

"Ready?" she asked, handing him the glass. He nodded and took a tentative sip, followed by a longer drink.

"You gave us quite a scare." She brushed his hair back from his forehead. "I was with Gabriel. Everyone had spread out to look for you on the estate. I thought you might be in our meadow."

"Isis was with you, apparently." He handed Felicity back the glass, and she set it on the bedside table next to the pitcher. "She is the best friend I've ever had." He stroked the dog's head again and looked at her with love. Yes, love. He knew what that emotion felt like after all. Then he returned his gaze to Felicity. "Next to you."

"How can I possibly be your best friend?" she asked, appearing bemused.

"No one has ever been so persistently dedicated in their desire to warm my heart. I should say that more than qualifies you."

Felicity laughed softly. "Indeed it does." She perched on the edge of the bed beside him, her thigh next to his. "Why did you run away from me?"

"I was overcome…with emotion." He didn't want to say too much.

"So I understand from your sisters. They told me about the Yule log story you shared with them. About your father." She put her hand on his arm, which was still beneath the covers. "I'd determined some time ago that your father had been particularly cruel to you. One need only look at what he did to us to realize he wasn't kind to you."

"But he was to my sisters. They loved him. They miss him."

"I'm not sure that's the case anymore. They feel terrible that you endured so much without them even realizing."

"I'm six years older than Poppy and eight years older than Bianca. Why would they have realized anything?" Defending them came naturally all of a sudden. He'd seen them as almost enemies since they'd been aligned with the person who was at the core of his misery, but how were they to know how their father had treated him? "I wish I hadn't told them. They deserve to remember him with affection." The way he recalled their mother, whom they couldn't remember at all.

"They are glad to know the truth. They want to help you however they can. *If* they can. They want to be a family." She looked at him sternly. "Before you ran off, you seemed to have had some sort of nightmare. I was terrified for you, and when we couldn't find you... You're a very selfish man, Calder," she said crossly.

He pulled his hand from beneath the covers and laid it over hers. "I am. But I don't want to be. In recent days, I've seen a past I desperately want to reclaim, a present I despise, and a future that terrifies me to my soul."

"Nightmares?" she asked, her beautiful face creasing with concern.

"Sometimes. The past and the present were real. I saw us together, planning to wed. Then my father said that would never happen." There was so much he needed to tell her. But he was so afraid of her reaction. "When you understand how I've lived, the kind of man I became when I thought you rejected me…You'll want to leave."

She put her other hand on top of his, curling her fingers around him. "Never."

"The future I saw—you were there. You were married to someone else. You had children and grandchildren. You were so happy."

"Did my husband look like you?"

He honestly couldn't recall the man's face. "I don't know. But I was dead. My sisters and their husbands—and no one else save a vicar I didn't recognize—came to my burial. I died alone."

"That is not the future, then," she said firmly. "Because I plan to marry only you, and if we're especially blessed, we will have children and grandchildren." She leaned toward him. "And I plan to be so very happy." Her eyes glowed, and he almost believed it.

"When my father said you'd left me, I went to London, where I behaved reprehensibly. I squandered everything— my money, my friendships, my reputation. None of it mattered to me without you. When I learned you'd wed, it only got worse." His voice cracked, and she squeezed his hand between hers. Isis pressed closer against his side. "Then my father cut me off. I awoke one day in a filthy alley outside a gaming hell. I hadn't been able to pay an IOU. Several men thrashed me. That wasn't who I wanted to be. From that moment on, I built myself back up—the money, anyway. And my reputation improved, somewhat." His mouth twisted into a sad smile. "I wasn't known as a wastrel anymore, but an arrogant miser with no interest in joy."

"You quite perfected that," she said with a heavy dash of irony.

"Yes." Miraculously, he chuckled, but it was short-lived.

"I've been awful to you. And to my sisters. And to the people of Hartwood and Hartwell."

"You remade yourself once before, I'm confident you can do it again. But this time, you shall be the joyful duke." She fell silent a moment, and he sensed there was a battle being waged behind her eyes. "If you want that."

"Yes, I want that. I'm just not sure I can *be* that."

"I just told you that you could. Do you doubt me?"

"No." He stifled a smile. She was managing him. He rather liked it.

"Do you promise not to run off ever again?"

He looked into her eyes. "I promise."

"Good, because we are in this together. We've lost too much time."

Isis stretched beside him. He turned his head to see her watching him with complete adoration. "I love you too," he murmured to his dog. Then he looked back to Felicity. "But I love you more." Wincing, he glanced back at Isis. "Sorry."

Isis laid her head on his hand. Apparently, she didn't mind.

Felicity cupped his face and stared at him, unblinking. "Did you just say you love me?"

He opened his mouth to repeat himself, but she kissed him. Then she pulled away, laughing. "I thought it would take months, maybe years, for you to say it. I love you so much, Calder."

"I've no idea why."

She arched a brow at him. "It's very telling when a dog loves someone as much as Isis loves you." She reached over and patted Isis on the head. "And Isis is a very smart dog."

"That she is." He frowned suddenly. "I'm afraid I have no idea what day it is. Did I miss Christmas altogether?"

She nodded. "I'm afraid so. It's St. Stephen's Day."

"It is?" He sat up from the headboard, straightening his spine. "I want to go to the party. Why aren't you there?"

She cocked her head to the side, laughing. "Because I was taking care of you, silly. I don't think you should get out of bed today."

"Sorry, love, but life is too short for me to miss this celebration. The dukes of Hartwell *never* miss it. I'm afraid I'm going, whether you like it or not."

She stood from the bed, her lips set into a deep, disapproving frown. "Fine, but only for a short while, agreed?"

He slipped his legs from the bed and held on to the post as he stood. "I'll agree if you consent to marry me."

"If that was a proposal, it wasn't a very good one. But it doesn't matter. Your sisters and I have already planned the wedding. It's to be at St. Cuthbert's the day after Epiphany."

Yes, she was definitely managing him, and he was absolutely fine with that. "Excellent. I agree. I would be delighted to be your husband."

Laughter, loud and joyous, spilled from her lips. He joined in, then took her in his arms. She kissed him again, far too briefly. He clasped her more tightly. "Perhaps we could take a few more minutes?"

She stepped back and shook her finger at him. "You're lucky I'm letting you go outside."

Indeed he was. "I'm lucky in every way a man can be," he said quietly, letting her go. "I am yours—happily—to command."

"Let's get you dressed." She gave him a brilliant smile, then walked with him to his dressing chamber.

"I could get used to having you as a valet," he said. Was this really happening? Was she really here with him? He clasped her hand, stopping just as they stepped over the threshold to the dressing room. "Tell me this isn't a dream."

She squeezed his fingers. "It *is*, my love. It's a dream come true."

~

The weather had thankfully warmed on Christmas Day, and the celebration happening on the grounds of Hartwood was a wonder to behold. Large tents housed tables laden with food, barrels of wine and ale, and seating areas for people, especially the old and infirm, to sit and converse. And laugh. Laughter was by far the music of the day.

Pine boughs decorated the tents, as did mistletoe. One of the tents was entirely dedicated to games such as snap-dragon. Children spilled from that tent running to and fro, engaging in other games such as Puss in the Corner and Hunt the Fox.

"I want to go speak with Mrs. Armstrong," Calder said. She stood laughing between Poppy and Gabriel near one of the games being played.

"Certainly." Felicity had insisted he hold on to her arm the entire time they were outside. He was weak from being abed with fever the past day and a half. Had it only been a day and a half? It had felt like the longest period of her life. She'd been so worried she would lose him. After all the time they'd spent apart and everything he'd been through, it just wouldn't have been fair.

Poppy's eyes lit when she saw Calder and Felicity coming toward them. When they arrived, Calder looked to Felicity and started to take his arm from her. Felicity understood what he was about and nodded that it was all right.

Turning to Poppy, Calder hugged her fiercely. "I'm sorry," he said softly, but Felicity could hear him.

"I'm so glad you're all right." Poppy pulled back in his embrace and smiled up at him. "You shouldn't be out here."

"I'm the duke. I most definitely should be out here." He kissed her cheek, then turned to Gabriel, offering his hand. "Darlington."

"Probably time you called me Gabriel. If you'd like."

"I would, but only if you'll stop calling me Chill. I never cared for that name."

"Fair enough," Gabriel said.

"I'm glad to see you're feeling better, Your Grace," Mrs. Armstrong said with a curtsey. "They said you were ill."

"I wouldn't miss the St. Stephen's Day party." He flinched. "I suppose I did try, but I've come to my senses now." He smiled at Felicity and took her arm once more. "Thanks to Mrs. Garland, who will soon be Her Grace, the Duchess of Hartwell."

Mrs. Armstrong clapped her hands together. "How wonderful!"

"I wanted to be sure to tell you that I'll be bringing several dogs—and more cats—to Hartwell House. The children need pets."

A small pleat gathered between Mrs. Armstrong's brows. "I have a cat, and there are goats."

"Goats do not make great pets," he said wryly. "You need dogs. And more cats."

"What a marvelous idea!" Poppy said.

"What's that?" Bianca and Ash joined them. She looked to Calder. "You're looking better, brother, but should you really be outside?"

"Felicity is managing me well enough," he said, lifting his free hand in supplication. "Though it sounds as if you and Poppy are helping. I understand you've planned our nuptials."

"It had to be done," Bianca said with a shrug before grinning widely. "That means you said yes?"

"*She* said yes." Calder laughed as he looked from Bianca to Poppy to Felicity. "I fear my life will never be the same." His gaze didn't waver from hers when he softly added, "And for that, I'm eternally grateful."

"What's the idea I missed?" Bianca asked.

Before anyone could answer, Alice, the girl from Hartwell House whom Calder had helped, ran to him and threw her arms around his waist. "They said you were ill."

"I was," he said, taking his arm from Felicity to hug Alice. "But I wouldn't miss the celebration. Are you having fun?" He squatted down to talk to her.

She nodded, her mouth splitting into a wide smile. "I've already beaten Freddie at snapdragon twice." She held up her fingers, which were bright red from pulling raisins from a flaming bowl of brandy.

"Splendid. You'll be delighted to know that Mrs. Armstrong has agreed to let me bring some dogs and cats to Hartwell House next week." He smiled at her. "You shall have the pick of the puppies."

Alice's eyes widened, and she launched herself at him so hard that he lost his balance and fell backward onto the ground. Horrified, Alice leapt up, her jaw dropping. "I'm so sorry, Your Grace!"

Calder lifted his head. "I'm fine."

Felicity rushed to help him, but Ash and Gabriel took charge of restoring him to his feet.

"All right, then?" Ash asked.

Calder clasped his hand in gratitude. "I am, thank you."

"I think you should go back inside," Felicity said, worried that he'd fallen, even if it was only because the girl had jumped at him. "You can sit in the drawing room and watch the festivities from the window."

"I have to make my speech first. The duke always makes a speech."

Felicity was going to argue that his sisters could do it, but Bianca spoke first. "He's right. I'll get everyone's attention."

Calder gave Felicity a look that seemed to imply it was out of his hands, to which Felicity rolled her eyes. She escorted him to the small dais, where Bianca blew a horn.

It took a minute, but conversation died down, and everyone paused in their activities or filed from the tents to look toward the dais.

Calder wiped a hand beneath his eye, but Felicity couldn't see if there had been a tear. She held on to his hand and squeezed him tight, giving him all the strength and love she had.

"Good St. Stephen's Day!" he called out loudly, surprising Felicity with the volume of his voice considering he'd been ill.

"Welcome to Hartwood. It is my pleasure—our pleasure" —he gestured to the rest of his family on the dais—"to have you here. I would like to start by saying we will have another celebration soon, for I am to wed the lovely woman at my side. May I present the future Duchess of Hartwell." He bowed to Felicity, and she blushed beneath the applause and cheering.

When the congratulations faded, Calder continued. "I want to thank my sisters, Lady Darlington and Lady Buckleigh, for their hard work and dedication to making this celebration happen, and for all they do for Hartwell House and our village."

This was met with more cheering. Poppy and Bianca curtsied on the dais.

After several moments, Calder was able to go on. "I also want to thank Lord Darlington and Lord Buckleigh for their help today and every day. I should also thank Lord Thornaby for his assistance and his willingness to host the party when I was… When I was an idiot."

Gasps and nods spread through the crowd.

"I have no excuse for my behavior since becoming the duke, but I shall promise you here today that the people of Hartwood and Hartwell are my primary concern. I look forward to refurbishing Hartwell House and assisting with the reconstruction of Shield's End. And I want each of you to know that I am here to support you and ensure your welfare."

The cheering and applause started anew and continued apace until Calder held up his hand. "Forgive me, but I need to rest before I collapse—it's true that I am ill. If I don't go inside, I fear my betrothed will drag me." He sent her a loving look. She shook her head at a round of guffaws.

"Before I go," he said, "I want to announce that we will add two new celebrations to the calendar. We will have a May Day Celebration and a Harvest Festival. Now go and enjoy your day!"

The applause and cheers rose to a crescendo, and Calder spent the next half hour shaking people's hands and even giving a few hugs. By the time Felicity wrestled him back inside, she could tell he was quite fatigued.

"Never mind what I said about watching from the drawing room. You're going back to bed."

"Thank God," he said.

"May I help?" Truro asked. The butler had apparently followed them inside. "It appeared as though His Grace could use some assistance."

Calder looked to Truro. "You should be outside celebrating. This is your day," he said.

"I will, but first I want to see you comfortable."

"I don't deserve you, Truro." Calder gazed at him

earnestly. "Truly. You've endured a great deal from me these past several months."

"I didn't think it would last, Your Grace. Besides, I put up with your father for far longer, and I'm still here." He winked at Calder. "You'll be fine. And I'm here to help. Come, let's get you upstairs."

Calder allowed them both to help him to his bedchamber, and a short while later, he was resituated in bed. Truro had insisted on having someone brew a pot of tea and promised it would be up shortly.

"Thank you, Truro," Calder called as the butler left. He turned his attention to Felicity. "I really don't deserve him. But I don't deserve you either."

"Please promise me you won't keep saying that."

"Every day for the rest of our lives. I'm afraid you must get used to it."

Isis jumped onto the bed and sat on his feet. She'd accompanied them outside, but had ended up playing with some of the children from Hartwell House. Now, however, she looked quite content to doze on her master's feet and keep him warm.

The tea arrived along with some toast, which Calder hungrily devoured. Then he yawned, and Felicity insisted he should sleep.

"But I've been sleeping for over a day." He yawned again and sank down into the bed, despite his protests.

Felicity tucked him in and kissed his temple.

"Aren't you getting in here with me?" he asked. "You look tired too. I know you can't have slept much."

"That's true." She glanced toward the door. "It's not really proper, though, is it?"

"A betrothal is as good as marriage, and I just announced our betrothal to everyone. Besides, I'm well past following the rules of propriety as far as we're concerned. I'm not spending another moment without you."

After stripping down to her chemise, she climbed into his bed and snuggled up beside him. His breaths were deep and even, and she was fairly certain he was already asleep.

Then he startled her by speaking. His eyes remained closed. "Thank you for rescuing me."

"It wasn't just me."

"Not in the meadow." Now he opened his eyes and turned his head toward her. "From the darkness."

She smiled softly and touched his cheek. "You rescued yourself—you just needed a little help."

"Thankfully I had an angel to help me." He kissed her forehead, then closed his eyes once more.

Now, she was certain he'd fallen asleep. She murmured, "I think we had angels helping both of us."

EPILOGUE

Christmas Eve 1812

"Is it going to fit?" Bianca asked, cocking her head to the side as Calder hefted the massive Yule log into the hearth with the aid of Gabriel and Ash.

"Maybe?" Felicity said as she stroked her round belly. Calder was practically obsessed with the fact that he was going to be a father. He couldn't stop staring at her.

"Calder, this is very heavy," Gabriel said, drawing his attention back to the matter at hand.

With a grunt, Calder wedged his side into the fireplace. "Set it down."

Gabriel stood on the opposite end and, heaving his side into the fireplace as well, let the log drop onto the coals from last year's log. They'd spread them that morning, taken from the box in which they'd been stored since the day after Epiphany.

The day he and Felicity had wed. What Felicity didn't

know was that he'd saved enough coal from that log so they would be able to use a piece for every Christmas. He smiled at the thought, his gaze drifting once more to his beloved.

She stood between Poppy, who held her four-month old son Thaddeus, and Bianca, who was also with child, but not yet obviously so. She and Ash would welcome their babe in the early summer, while his and Felicity's would be here in just a matter of weeks.

He could scarcely believe how drastically his life had changed—and how utterly grateful he was that the future he'd glimpsed was not to be. Or part of it, anyway. If he was the man standing beside Felicity surrounded by their children and grandchildren, he would count himself fortunate.

"It fits," Ash said, stepping back to put his arm around Bianca. "Barely."

"That should have no problem lasting through Twelfth Night," Bianca said, pressing against her husband's side.

Calder set to lighting the massive log, which was no small feat. After some time, it began to burn. Everyone cheered, including Felicity's and Ash's mothers, who were also present, and brandy was poured all around.

"To family," Calder said, raising his glass.

Everyone lifted their glasses with a resounding chorus of "Hear, hear!"

Calder assisted Felicity to a settee and sat down beside her. The mothers found chairs, and his sisters gathered on other settees with their husbands.

"My mother says the packing is going well at Hartwell House," Felicity said, glancing toward Alicia Templeton. "I'm sorry I haven't been able to help." She'd been rather tired the past week, and Calder had insisted she not overtax herself. While he wasn't as petrified of pregnancy and childbirth as Gabriel had been, he saw no reason to take unnecessary risks.

"We've had plenty of hands," Poppy said, juggling her son and her brandy glass. "Which is not the case for me right now." She laughed and handed her glass to Gabriel so she could better situate Thaddeus. "We still have a few weeks before Shield's End will be ready to be inhabited."

Indeed, there were many things still to be done, and that was with the hired firm conducting work along with assistance from Calder, Gabriel, Ash, and many other people from Hartwell. It had been a massive community effort, which was the only way the reconstruction could have happened so quickly.

Bianca leaned back against her settee and into her husband. "It can't happen too soon. The school will be taking its first pupils at the beginning of February."

Hartwell House would soon be known as the Hartwell School. They'd intended it to be a day school only, but the interest for boarding had been so great that they'd opened it up to a small number of applicants from County Durham. The spots had filled quickly, and already there was discussion as to how to enlarge the school so they could accept more.

Though young, Dinah Kitson had proved herself an excellent manager for the school. Actually, she hadn't been as young as they'd all assumed. She was, in fact, nearly Poppy's age.

The repairs on Hartwell House had been completed last spring.

"Pardon me for a moment," Poppy said, handing Thaddeus off to his father.

Bianca rose. "Oh yes, me too."

Calder watched in bemusement as they went to the corner to a small desk. A strong kick from the child in Felicity's womb drew his attention. She looked up at him, her eyes glowing. "He's very active this evening."

"*She* is usually active in the evenings. I fear she will keep us up at night."

"Perhaps." Felicity took his hand and set it on her belly. Another kick landed against his palm.

"Calder, we have something for you," Bianca announced. She and Poppy now stood before him, a box in Poppy's hands.

He blinked at them in confusion. "But we exchanged gifts on St. Nicholas Day. Poppy, you gave me a lovely embroidered waistcoat, and Bianca, you gave me a book."

"Yes, well, this gift wasn't quite finished," Poppy glanced toward her husband, then gave the box to Calder. "It took a long time to find the last piece, and it only just arrived yesterday."

Calder took the box and set it in his lap. He turned his head to look at Felicity. "Do you know anything about this?"

She shook her head. "I do not. But I'm quite interested to see what it is. Do hurry and open it."

The box was a foot long and half as wide. Its height was smaller, perhaps three inches. He would have guessed it was a box for jewelry, but why would they give him such a thing?

The lid was hinged with a small clasp that held it shut. Flipping the clasp open, he lifted the lid. The contents completely stole his breath.

Lying on a bed of brown velvet were his mother's jewels: the emerald necklace, earrings, and ring. He couldn't believe what he was seeing.

He had to blink back the tears blurring his vision as he looked up at his sisters. "Are these real?" he whispered.

They both nodded.

"Ash and Gabriel spent a great deal of time looking for them last Season," Bianca said. "I believe the ring ended up in a rather unsavory place."

Poppy elbowed her, murmuring, "Don't make him feel bad."

"How could I feel bad?" Calder touched the fine jewels, seeing his mother wearing them on Christmas when he was a boy. "This is the greatest gift I've ever received." He looked at Felicity, his heart so full, he feared it would burst. "Except for you and the babe."

She reached over and put her hand over his atop the jewelry. "I know what you meant." She smiled up at her sisters-in-law. "This is truly lovely."

"Well, I can't wear them, obviously," Calder said, angling his body toward Felicity. "And I'd always wanted my wife to have them. When I lost you, I couldn't imagine anyone else wearing them. While I hated to part with the set, I convinced myself that I didn't need it. Not without you."

She lifted her hand and cupped his cheek. "Oh, Calder."

He looked to his sisters. "Do you mind if I give them to Felicity?"

"Of course not," Poppy said, beaming. "We expected you would, and we're delighted for her to have them."

Calder wouldn't have blamed them if they'd wanted to keep the items for themselves. But then they didn't remember their mother, while he did. "Thank you."

He took the necklace from the box and held it up toward Felicity. She pivoted so he could fasten the piece around her neck. When she turned back, tears filled his eyes again.

She wiped her finger across his cheek to catch a teardrop, smiling. "Happy tears, I hope."

"The happiest. Thank you." He turned to his sisters. "Thank you." Then he looked to his brothers-in-law. "Thank you." He wiped at his eyes and glanced toward Felicity's and Ash's mothers, saying, "Thank you too!"

Everyone chuckled. Bianca grinned. "Happy Christmas, Calder."

He put his arm around Felicity and drew her close, pressing a kiss against her temple. "Happy Christmas, everyone."

Thank you so much for reading Joy to the Duke! It's the final book in my Regency holiday series, Love is All Around. I hope you enjoyed the trilogy; I had such fun writing it! If you think some of the secondary characters might need a story and an happy ever after, drop me a note!

Would you like to know when my next book is available and to hear about sales and deals? Sign up for my VIP newsletter at https://www.darcyburke.com/readergroup, follow me on social media:
Facebook: https://facebook.com/DarcyBurkeFans
Twitter at @darcyburke
Instagram at darcyburkeauthor
Pinterest at darcyburkewrite

And follow me on Bookbub to receive updates on pre-orders, new releases, and deals!

Need more Regency romance? Check out my other historical series:

The Phoenix Club
Society's most exclusive invitation...

Welcome to the Phoenix Club, where London's most audacious, disreputable, and intriguing ladies and gentlemen find scandal, redemption, and second chances.

The Untouchables
Swoon over twelve of Society's most eligible and elusive
bachelor peers and the bluestockings, wallflowers, and
outcasts who bring them to their knees!

The Untouchables: The Spitfire Society
Meet the smart, independent women who've decided they
don't need Society's rules, their families' expectations, or,
most importantly, a husband. But just because they don't
need a man doesn't mean they might not *want* one…

The Untouchables: The Pretenders
Set in the captivating world of The Untouchables, follow the
saga of a trio of siblings who excel at being something they're
not. Can a dauntless Bow Street Runner, a devastated
viscount, and a disillusioned Society miss unravel their
secrets?

Wicked Dukes Club
Six books written by me and my BFF, NYT Bestselling
Author Erica Ridley. Meet the unforgettable men of
London's most notorious tavern, The Wicked Duke.
Seductively handsome, with charm and wit to spare, one
night with these rakes and rogues will never be enough…

Secrets and Scandals
Everyone has secrets and some of them are a scandal … six
sexy, damaged heroes lose their hearts to strong, intelligent
women in the glittering ballrooms and lush countryside of
Regency England.

Legendary Rogues
Intrepid heroines and adventurous heroes embark on
exciting quests across Regency England and Wales!

If you like contemporary romance, I hope you'll check out my Ribbon Ridge series and the continuation of Ribbon Ridge in So Hot.

I hope you'll consider leaving a review at your favorite online vendor or networking site!

I appreciate my readers so much. Thank you, thank you, *thank you.*

AUTHOR NOTE

One day , I thought it would be fun to write a Christmas trilogy and base the stories on classic holiday tales. I knew right away I wanted to write The Duke of Scrooge, except Joy to the Duke seemed like a much better title. In fact, I think that title popping into my head was actually the seed that grew into Love is All Around.

The task of writing a rather nasty character who would need to transform into a swoon-worthy hero is actually something I relish. I love, love to read about redemption, and boy is Calder's arc a doozy. In writing a series about siblings, I wanted to explore how their experiences and perspectives can be very different and how we all have our own path to take. Hopefully you enjoyed Calder's and Felicity's.

The Institution for Impoverished Women is something entirely of my own creation. It's based on workhouses of the time, but I didn't want a "real" workhouse which separated men and women (and children—they didn't see their parents often) and was typically more like a prison.

Thanks and love to Rachel Grant for the super helpful writing sprints and always fabulous friendship.

I hope you enjoyed this inspired story! And Merry Christmas. :)

ALSO BY DARCY BURKE

Historical Romance

Love is All Around
(A Regency Holiday Trilogy)
The Red Hot Earl
The Gift of the Marquess
Joy to the Duke

The Phoenix Club
Improper
Impassioned
Intolerable
Indecent
Impossible

The Untouchables
The Bachelor Earl
The Forbidden Duke
The Duke of Daring
The Duke of Deception
The Duke of Desire
The Duke of Defiance
The Duke of Danger
The Duke of Ice
The Duke of Ruin
The Duke of Lies

The Duke of Seduction

The Duke of Kisses

The Duke of Distraction

The Untouchables: The Spitfire Society

Never Have I Ever with a Duke

A Duke is Never Enough

A Duke Will Never Do

The Untouchables: The Pretenders

A Secret Surrender

A Scandalous Bargain

A Rogue to Ruin

Wicked Dukes Club

One Night for Seduction by Erica Ridley

One Night of Surrender by Darcy Burke

One Night of Passion by Erica Ridley

One Night of Scandal by Darcy Burke

One Night to Remember by Erica Ridley

One Night of Temptation by Darcy Burke

Legendary Rogues

Lady of Desire

Romancing the Earl

Lord of Fortune

Captivating the Scoundrel

Secrets and Scandals

Her Wicked Ways

His Wicked Heart

To Seduce a Scoundrel

To Love a Thief (a novella)

Never Love a Scoundrel

Scoundrel Ever After

Contemporary Romance

Ribbon Ridge

Where the Heart Is (a prequel novella)

Only in My Dreams

Yours to Hold

When Love Happens

The Idea of You

When We Kiss

You're Still the One

Ribbon Ridge: So Hot

So Good

So Right

So Wrong

Boxed Sets

The Untouchables Books 1-3

The Untouchables Books 4-6

The Untouchables Books 7-9

The Untouchables Books 10-12

The Spitfire Society

The Pretenders

Secrets and Scandals Volume One: Books 1-3
Secrets and Scandals Volume Two: Books 4-6

Legendary Rogues Volume One: Books 1-2
Legendary Rogues Volume Two: Books 3-4

So Hot

ABOUT THE AUTHOR

Darcy Burke is the USA Today Bestselling Author of sexy, emotional historical and contemporary romance. Darcy wrote her first book at age 11, a happily ever after about a swan addicted to magic and the female swan who loved him, with exceedingly poor illustrations. Join her Reader Club newsletter at https://www.darcyburke.com/readerclub.

A native Oregonian, Darcy lives on the edge of wine country with her guitar-strumming husband, artist daughter, and imaginative son who will almost certainly out-write her one day (that may be tomorrow). They're a crazy cat family with two Bengal cats, a small, fame-seeking cat named after a fruit, an older rescue Maine Coon with attitude to spare, an adorable former stray who wandered onto their deck and into their hearts, and two bonded boys who used to belong to (separate) neighbors but chose them instead. You can find Darcy at a winery, in her comfy writing chair balancing her laptop and a cat or three, folding laundry (which she loves), or binge-watching TV with the family. Her happy places are Disneyland, Labor Day weekend at the Gorge, Denmark, and anywhere in the UK—so long as her family is there too. Visit Darcy online at https://www.darcyburke.com and follow her on social media.

facebook.com/DarcyBurkeFans

twitter.com/darcyburke

instagram.com/darcyburkeauthor

pinterest.com/darcyburkewrites

goodreads.com/darcyburke

bookbub.com/authors/darcy-burke

www.ingramcontent.com/pod-product-compliance
Lightning Source LLC
Chambersburg PA
CBHW020521110726
47899CB00004B/1194